PRAISE

NORA ROBERTS LAND
Selected as one of the Best Books of 2013 alongside Nora
Roberts' DARK WITCH and Julia Quinn's SUM OF ALL
KISSES. USA Today Contributor, Becky Lower, Happily Ever
After

"Ava's story is witty and charming." Barbara Freethy #1 NYT
bestselling author

FRENCH ROAST
"An entertaining ride...{and) a full-bodied romance." Readers'
Favorite

THE GRAND OPENING
"Ava Miles is fast becoming one of my favorite light
contemporary romance writers." Tome Tender

THE HOLIDAY SERENADE
"This story is all romance, steam, and humor with a touch of
the holiday spirit..." The Book Nympho

THE TOWN SQUARE
"Ms. Miles' words melted into each page until the world
receded around me..." Tome Tender

COUNTRY HEAVEN
"If ever there was a contemporary romance that rated a 10 on
a scale of 1 to 5 for me, this one is it!" The Romance Reviews

THE PARK OF SUNSET DREAMS
"Ava has done it again. I love the whole community of Dare
Valley..." Travel Through The Pages Blog

THE CHOCOLATE GARDEN
"On par with Nicholas Sparks' love stories." Jennifer's Corner
Blog

Dare Valley Meets Paris Billionaire: Billionaire:

The Complete Mini-Series

by

Ava Miles

ISBN-13: 978-1-940565-42-2
www.avamiles.com
Ava Miles

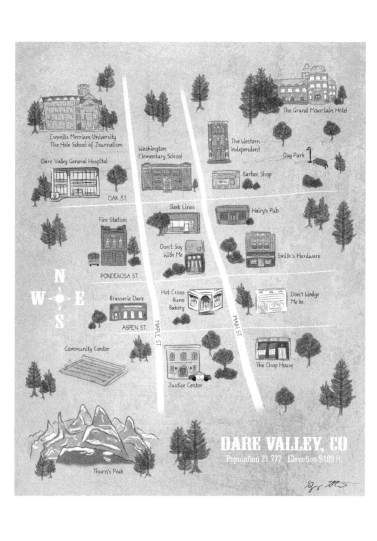

THE
BILLIONAIRE'S
GAMBLE

To all the women who baked bread and handed down their recipes.

And to my divine helpers, who helped me remember the power of love in bread.

Author's Note:

When I started writing this mini-series, Paris' famous poker venue, Aviation Club de France, was still open. Unfortunately, a few months ago, it closed. Because of its lavish history, I decided not to change this venue to another one.

CHAPTER 1

Paris, France

Evan Michaels was considering the biggest gamble of his life in the famous Aviation Club de France poker room.

Rising poker star Jane Wilcox had just thrown out an enticing and unconventional side bet. He didn't have enough poker chips to stay in the game, but if he accepted Jane's terms, he'd have a chance to play his ridiculous hand of trip kings and win the day. Still, while side bets were often brutal, this one was in a category of its own. Her words still hung in the air— "You have to lose your billionaire ways for a month and live in our small town, Dare Valley, Colorado, like a normal person."

Was this the sign he'd been waiting for? For two years, Evan had been unable to invent anything new. His company's growth had stagnated, and his business partner was concerned, to say the least. On a recent yachting trip to Greece, Evan had watched the sun rise over the Mediterranean and shouted out across the water that he wanted to invent again, that he wanted his creative fire returned to him. He'd seen a statue of the Greek goddess Artemis on an excursion into town the day before, and it had sparked something inside him.

Evan recognized the problem—his hubris had drained him of the very things that had made him special. He would do anything to regain what he'd lost, but this side bet? While he'd never been a "normal" person, he knew what it was to be poor.

And it totally sucked.

Rhett Butler Blaylock, Jane's former boss and the only other player still in the game, was trying not to smirk at her suggestion. Evan had played against the World Series of Poker champion in Paris before. And won a few times. Being a billionaire at twenty-nine meant he had brains *and* luck.

Neither of those characteristics had ever impressed these two when their paths had crossed in the past. Point of fact, Evan had hit on Jane years ago, back when she was posing as Rhett's poker babe, the mysterious Raven. What could he say? She'd been smoking hot in a poker babe kind of way. So when she had blinked at him flirtatiously one day at a casino bar, it had seemed only natural to slide his hand around her waist and suggest they go somewhere quiet to play a game of strip poker. She'd turned him down flat after telling him in an all-too-embarrassing fashion that she hadn't been batting her eyelashes at him at all. There was something in her eye.

"*And* you have to be celibate while you're in our town," Rhett added, confirming he knew about Evan's misunderstanding with Jane. It probably didn't hurt that Evan had a reputation as an international playboy—even if that reputation was an exaggeration. One incredible thing about being a young, handsome billionaire was how many gorgeous women liked to be seen with him. Still, most of what the tabloids reported about him was total codswallop.

"Celibate, huh?" he croaked, his poker face starting to slip. Just because he wasn't a womanizer didn't mean he didn't like women. Even discussing a bet like this made him feel like he was giving away his man card.

He eyed the beautiful Parisian model who'd accompanied him to the tournament. She matched his height of six-three in her killer stilettos and was currently looking at him with a stunned expression on her face. Paris' bad-boy billionaire, Evan Michaels, going celibate for a month? The lights might as well blink out systematically across Paris. She didn't know his reputation was as fake as her blond hair.

Before amassing his fortune, he'd been a nerdy scientist with pimply skin, a lanky frame, and horrible curly hair. Celibacy had been par for the course. Of course, that secret would go to his grave. He'd been a recluse then, working for endless hours on school and the inventions that would make him his fortune.

"Celibate," Jane drolled as if tasting the sweetness of the word on her tongue. "Rhett, I like where you're going with this."

"If boy wonder wants a side bet because he can't pony up the half a million dollars to make the raise," the not-so-gentlemanly Southerner said, "it's going to have to be a humdinger."

They both knew he could cut them a check for that kind of money in a flash without blinking. But that's what Evan loved about poker. No one cared that he had a fortune in reserves in one of Paris' finest banks, BNP Paribas. Everyone played the cards they were dealt with the chips they had in front of them. But the Aviation Club, which had been founded in 1907 by Europe's daring aviators of the day, was a place where rules were meant to be bent.

The poker room Evan had secured for their private use dripped with antique crystal chandeliers, carried the scent of cigars smoked in times past, and conveyed the vulgar flash of old money. Even better, it kept the paparazzi and other bystanders away. Evan focused better without people staring at him. Right now, the only people watching were the four players who had already busted out of the poker game and all the players' significant others for the night.

These onlookers seemed thrown for a loop. Jane's fiancé was giving Evan a puzzled glance, and even Rhett's sweet-as-honey wife was openly staring at him. He could tell they were trying to figure out the subtext behind the side bet. He gave them a toothy smile—the one his money had turned from average to spectacular— as a show of pure bravado.

"Define normal," he said to Jane, buying time. "Because, no offense, but Rhett's not exactly what I would call a *normal* person." The Southerner was larger than life, topping out at six foot six, and there were enough down-home colloquialisms in his playbook to send even the most cunning linguist running for a dictionary.

Jane traced her lower lip thoughtfully. "I define normal as you living on the first salary you ever drew... Oh, and you can't spend your time idly—you'll have to get a job."

His first salary? He cringed, which only made the corner of Jane's mouth tip up. His first job had been as a research assistant at Massachusetts Institute of Technology for the grand total of two thousand and three hundred dollars per month. This was so going to suck if he lost. But what if this was the price he needed to pay to regain his genius?

"For me, it means you'll need to dress like everyone else," Rhett said, gesturing to his gunmetal gray tailored suit from Dolce & Gabbana. "And go without your expensive aftershave and all the crap you put in your hair. I caught a whiff of you earlier, Evan, and while you smell as nice as a widow angling for another husband at

Sunday church, you smell like money."

If any man other than Rhett had said that, it might have made him uncomfortable.

"That's Tom Ford's Private Blend 'Noir de Noir,' you aftershave sniffer, you. Now stop. All your compliments might go to my head."

Evan could ditch the aftershave, sure, but his hair products? They'd changed everything. His hair would resemble a tangled ball of yarn in a heartbeat if their small town had even an ounce of humidity, and while he could handle a lot of setbacks, this was one he'd rather avoid. *Hubris*, he heard echo distantly in his mind.

Right.

"Like your head isn't already as big as a blimp," Rhett bandied back. "Too bad your pockets aren't as flush tonight. So what it's going to be, Evan?"

"You don't have to do it, *cherie,*" Chloe entreated, flicking her long blond hair over the shoulder of her strapless black gown. "Why would you want to be poor and celibate for a month? It's so *bourgeois*. And where is this small town in Colorado anyway? It could not even begin to compare with Paris."

No one needed to remind him of how priceless Paris was. He'd lost his virginity in the City of Lights at twenty-one. He'd decided to make it his home after that. If the gorgeous women weren't enough of a selling point, there was the food and the art scene. Evan had traveled the world over on his private jet, and few cities could top Paris' magic.

"Dare Valley has Paris beat hands-down in lots of categories, sugar," Rhett said to Chloe with an exaggerated drawl. "But we don't need to debate its merits. What we need to know is whether Evan has the chops to follow through on this little side bet. Personally, I don't think he does. What do you think, Jane?"

The former poker babe played with the fringe on her

red flapper-style dress. Dressed like that, she looked like she'd been plucked out of the 1920s, when the Aviation Club had risen to prominence. She fit in perfectly with the old-world décor of wood paneling, brass, and warm lighting.

"Personally I think he's bored." She fingered her chip protector, an old Roman coin with Diana, goddess of the hunt, stamped on the ancient metal.

Goosebumps rose along his skin. Wasn't Diana Artemis in Greek mythology? Was that another sign?

"I think he's learning one of life's greatest truths," Jane continued. "Money can't buy happiness."

Evan felt his poker face slip yet again. Money hadn't been able to restore his inspiration. And truth be told, he *was* bored, not to mention tired of people using him for his money. Of course, he wasn't one to talk. In the beginning, he'd used his money to get what he'd never had: possessions, women, respect.

He'd grown up as an impoverished genius surrounded by people who didn't understand him—an odd duck. His father had left when he was seven, and after that, his mother cleaned houses to make ends meet. They moved into a one-bedroom apartment in a bad neighborhood on the south side of Chicago. At school, he was so far ahead of the rest of the students that he kept getting bumped into classes with kids who were years older than him. But MIT scouted him, and he entered the elite school at the tender age of fifteen to pursue a degree in quantum mechanics. By twenty, he graduated with a doctorate and had three patents to his name. In all that time, he'd never had a girlfriend.

Suffice it to say, he'd made up for lost time after losing his virginity in Paris while on a much-needed vacation. But even the beautiful women who offered themselves to him didn't excite him any more.

"I thought *everyone* knew money didn't buy happiness," Rhett drawled, kicking back in his chair.

"Even people without a pot to piss in know that."

Evan stared them down. To bow out of the side bet now would be like reverting to the weakling he'd been. There was no way he was going to do that. And if this was the answer he'd asked for, well, even in Greek mythology, the twists and turns were what made the quest interesting, right?

What was he thinking? He was acting like he was going to lose. Focusing his mind on the positive for a moment, he returned to a state of calm. He'd asked for the side bet because he knew his odds of being beaten were almost zilch. He didn't need to take a second glance at the cards in his hands or the ones laid out in the Texas Hold'em spread to tell him that.

The dealer was waiting, his bushy eyebrow raised in eagerness. Evan was sure the man had heard some interesting side bets in his time.

"I accept your conditions for the side bet," he said and threw out his hand to signal the dealer to lay down the next card on the board: the much-feared River card. The ace of spades that surfaced on the River changed his fate in an instant; there were a couple of hands that could beat him now.

He cast a glance to see Jane and Rhett's reactions, but their poker faces gave nothing away. Not that he was surprised. This was why they played professionally, and he only dabbled.

When it came time for everyone to lay down their cards, Evan felt a spurt of something hot and juicy in his belly. It wasn't lust, and it took him a moment to identify the sensation. It was excitement—something he hadn't felt in way too long.

Jane laid her cards down first, the engraved visage of Artemis winking at him from her chip protector.

She'd beaten him with trip aces. He barely glanced at Rhett's hand. There was no way the man could beat Jane's hand. No one could.

Not even him.

Evan laid his cards down, his fingers trembling slightly. There it was again, that unexpected excitement. This was the answer he'd asked for on that lonely morning on the Med. He knew it down to his bones.

"Guess I'm going to Dare Valley."

CHAPTER 2

Small towns had never held much of a pull on Evan, not since visiting his grandparents' farm outside of Champagne, Illinois, when he was three. A goat had bitten him in the behind, and he'd cried the whole way back to Chicago. That was the breadth of his experience with the rural life.

Dare Valley wasn't a farming community, but it might as well have been. The population topped out at twenty thousand people. Sure, it wasn't totally dead—there was a highly ranked liberal arts university and Mac Maven's sleek boutique poker hotel called The Grand Mountain. Not that he was going to be playing poker there on his measly twenty-three hundred dollars a month. He was back to living on a budget.

There was no better proof of that than the Rent-A-Wreck 1988 tan Dodge Aries he was driving. He'd picked it up at a car dealer in Denver after a wickedly uncomfortable ride in coach class—his attempt to get back into the spirit of being normal. The plane ride had reminded him why he preferred first class. He hadn't slept a wink with his long legs folded uncomfortably into the cramped space. But it would all be worth it if this crazy gamble worked.

He pulled into the driveway of the massive Victorian home that had a room for rent. The local newspaper had a wealth of real estate ads, but this place was his top choice. The owner, Margie Lancaster, had sent a prompt and welcoming reply to his query. He was about to be interviewed for the room, and since he liked the look of the pictures and it fit nicely into his budget at five hundred dollars a month—utilities included—he hoped it would work out.

The door to his car creaked audibly when he opened it, and he had to slam it shut to get it to close properly. The tan beauty was a stick shift with one hundred and eleven thousand miles on it. In Paris, he had four cars at his disposal: a Rolls-Royce Phantom, a Lamborghini Veneno Roadster, a Koenigsegg Agera S, and a Ferrari F12berlinetta. Sometimes he drove, but he wasn't above letting his chauffeur ferry him around. Parking in Paris could be a nightmare—notwithstanding the insane traffic.

The two-story Victorian had a circular eating nook off the front porch and a fabulous tower atop it. As he rang the bell to the house, he felt a spurt of adrenaline surge through his blood again, the kind he usually experienced when pushing one of his race cars to one hundred and twenty miles per hour. He'd gambled away a month of his life in a poker game, which most people would regard as a bad thing. But even though he was wearing off-the-rack clothes and his business partner thought he'd gone cuckoo, *he was on an adventure*. He hoped to reclaim his creative fire and make something new—an invention surpassing everything he'd done before.

No one in Dare Valley, save Jane and Rhett and their better halves, knew who he was, and he planned to keep it that way. As poker players said, he was *all* in. He'd made Jane and Rhett and their partners swear not to give him away. The cover story was that Evan was an artist they'd met in Paris. He was between jobs, so they'd talked him into visiting Dare Valley for a month.

People in small towns were notoriously curious about newcomers and would undoubtedly ask for his story. It would make his life easier to say he knew people in town, so the decision to include Jane and Rhett in his cover story made sense. Still, Evan was a little wary about trusting Rhett not to spill the beans. While he didn't know the man well, he knew him enough not to consider him sleuth material.

The door of the Victorian opened then, and shock held Evan in place for a moment. He'd expected a sweet elderly lady—after all, weren't they normally the sort to own sprawling old homes?—but the woman who stood in front of him could have been the inspiration for Alexandros of Antioch's rendition of the Venus de Milo, one of Evan's favorite sculptures in the Louvre.

Her sable-colored hair was cut to the chin, and her emerald eyes matched her dress. The tango music that was playing softly in the background suited her. He could easily see her in a red dress doing a simple salida step with a man worthy of leading her. His nostrils filled with cinnamon, and for a fleeting moment, before he realized she was baking something, he thought the scent was hers. Surely this woman was all spice and sex.

When his gaze scanned the rest of her, he couldn't help but appreciate her curves. His mouth dried up instantly, thinking about what it would feel like to run his hands down the perfect figure-eight shape of her body.

Then he remembered he was supposed to be celibate for a month, and his Ferris wheel of excitement screeched to a halt.

"Hi," he said, extending his hand, trying to be more professional now that he was done gawking. "I'm Evan Murray. Thanks for agreeing to show me the room."

His tongue didn't trip over the alias, which he'd practiced saying in the rearview mirror all the way from Denver. Since everyone was Googleable these days, he'd decided to use an alias in Dare Valley.

"Margie Lancaster," she said, giving him a thorough once-over of her own. "You're prompt. I appreciate that."

The assessing look in her eyes told him what she was seeing. He'd grown what he thought was a sexy beard to further disguise himself—not that he worried he would be recognized in this small town, but one could never be too careful. His jeans still had crease marks from the packaging since he hated to iron. He hadn't dealt with cleaning and pressing his own clothes for years. Fortunately his T-shirt had fared better. And since Colorado wasn't too humid, thank God, his sandy blond hair wasn't unruly yet.

"I hate to keep...anyone waiting." Thank God, he'd stopped himself from saying *I hate to keep a beautiful lady waiting*. He stuffed his hands in his pockets and reminded himself not to flirt with her—something he did without even realizing it these days.

She smiled, and boy was it a winner. "I was glad to hear from you," she said. "Any acquaintance of Rhett and Jane's is most welcome. And honestly, since it's July and most of Emmits Merriam's students are out for the summer, it's a little slow on the rental end. I only have one other renter right now. Martin's finishing his master's degree in molecular biology. He's going to summer school and teaching a class, so he's barely around. Hopefully you'll be a good fit. Rhett and Jane had great things to say about you."

He'd mentioned his association with them to put her at ease.

"They're nice people." The words weren't as hard to voice as he'd anticipated. They *were* nice people. Sure, they'd decided to play with him, but he wasn't sorry to be here.

"Please come inside."

The Victorian's entryway belonged in another era. The wood floors were a gleaming walnut, if he had an eye—and he did—and the stained glass Tiffany-like panel over their heads was designed with intertwining yellow and green flowers. The custom molding was four inches thick with the kind of curly Q pattern that made Evan think of a string of commas. But the real showstopper was the staircase. It spiraled against the wall like a woman reclining on a divan after a tiring day of social engagements. The newel posts were hand-carved in the shape of crowns. A hint of lemon tickled his nose beneath the warm aroma of cinnamon, hinting that the house had been cleaned prior to his arrival.

"It's a pretty impulsive move, coming here for a month," Margie said, leading him into the front foyer.

"Rhett and Jane are quite persuasive," he replied neutrally. "I had to check Dare Valley out."

Her rosy-red lips twitched. "I'm afraid you may find the scene here a little less...cosmopolitan than in Paris. There's only one coffee shop, Don't Soy With Me. I'm the manager, though not for much longer, so I guess I'm partial. We have a French brasserie too, and I can personally attest to it being scrumptious."

"I read about those places online when I researched the town," he said. "They sound great. What are you planning to do next career-wise?"

"I just bought Kemstead's Bakery, which is a local institution. The business has been in the family for a few generations, but the current owner's children don't want to take it over." She grinned. "I think I won them over with my promise to continue to serve their famous cinnamon rolls if they taught me how."

He sniffed appreciatively. "So, *that's* what I smell. Feel free to use me as a taste tester. I have a real passion for anything that's bread after living in Paris."

She nodded. "Few people can make bread better than Parisians, which is why I'm heading there in six weeks to study with a master baker. Brian McConnell, my boss' husband, owns Brasserie Dare, and he's the one who managed to set up the apprenticeship for me. I'm going to be supplying his bread from now on. That's the other reason I was so excited about your arrival. I hope I can ask you all about the city. I haven't been in years." She paused to look at him, and he could feel her regard. It was like a punch to his solar plexus.

"I'd be happy to tell you what I can," he said easily, liking this better and better. She was easy on the eyes, had a fire for business, and would be visiting his hometown after he returned from his month-long stint in Dare Valley. And he wouldn't be celibate then...

"Let me grab you a cup of coffee and a cinnamon roll," she said. "Then you can tell me more about what you do in Paris."

He followed her into the modest kitchen. While it wasn't large and the appliances were old, the wood cabinets were stunning. Some were hand-carved while others were set with glass to show off finer dinnerware and glassware. His gaze shot to the steaming hot cinnamon rolls on the counter, which were oozing a caramel cinnamon sauce an inch thick.

"I think I've died and gone to heaven," he said, watching her as she tore off a roll and slid it onto a bright blue plate.

"Go ahead and eat it while it's hot," she said with a twinkle in her eyes. "I'll make you a coffee. What's your pleasure? I'm a trained barista, so I can pretty much make anything."

"Five hundred dollars for a room with utilities included," he said, lifting the cinnamon roll off his plate, not bothering to sit down. The dough seemed to cradle his fingers, and the caramel-cinnamon sauce called to him like a baking siren. "Please tell me cinnamon rolls and gourmet coffee are included too. I'll even pay six hundred."

He realized what he'd said and wanted to shove the words back into his mouth. Billionaire Evan Michaels could throw around his money. Evan Murray couldn't. He needed to remember that. "I was only teasing." He cast her a discreet glance to gauge her expression.

Her shoulders shook. "I know you were. I like your enthusiasm. Now what can I make you?"

"How about a latte? The coffee on the plane could hardly be called a beverage. It was horrible." And they still served it in Styrofoam cups, which had the double misfortune of being bad for the environment and making the coffee taste like shit.

"I'll remember not to order coffee when I fly," she said easily, walking over to a gorgeous espresso machine, probably the most expensive item in the place. The woman clearly had her priorities straight.

"So you were telling me about what you do?" she prompted him as she made his latte.

"In a sec. I'm about to have a date with this beauty." He bit into the cinnamon roll. The caramel coated his tongue. The cinnamon fired up his blood. But it was the sponginess of the bread layered with cinnamon, butter, and cream that had him groaning. "Holy mother of God. You're going to make a fortune selling these."

Her hands worked the coffee machine like a pro. "I hope so. The Kemstead family did fairly well. And with the changes I'm making, I hope to do even better. Dare Valley has changed a lot since they first opened back in the day. I'm planning to give it a new name and look."

"What are you going to call it?" he asked between bites.

"Hot Cross Buns." She waggled her brows.

"Cute." And it was—just like its new owner.

"I thought so. Jill—who owns Don't Soy With Me— started the cute trend when she named her coffee shop.

We also have a cheese shop called Don't Wedge Me In, and an exercise studio called Sleek Lines. The rest of the business owners try to live up to her standard."

"And Jill is Brian's wife? The Brian who got you the baking apprenticeship?" He was trying to follow the Dare Valley six-degrees-of-separation game.

"Good memory."

If only she knew. It was one of the downsides of being a genius.

She slid his latte across the gold Formica counter. It was in a red pottery mug, and the foam on top was decorated with a little coffee heart. The artistic splash suited her.

"Okay, now you," she said, making a cup of coffee for herself.

Well, there was no putting it off. "I'm an artist...of sorts. Writing. Painting." It *was* true. He did write—or he used to—for technical journals. And he had dabbled with painting after making the move to Paris, hoping he might be an undiscovered Degas. He wasn't.

"That's so cool. I love artists. They have such a fabulous way of seeing the world. Not like other people."

On that they could agree, even though it sometimes felt isolating. "Rhett and Jane assured me this place would inspire me. Maybe I'll write about a man who learns how to make the best cup of coffee, like you clearly know how to do. Or maybe he'll invent the world's best coffeemaker—one to rival any on the market."

He could see it now. People would rave about his invention, calling it the singular most impressive addition to the home since the woodburning stove.

"The Italians already invented the best coffee machine," she said. "I don't think it can be improved. Don't tell your French friends."

Every machine could be improved, but he wasn't going to argue the point. Instead, he made a cutting motion at his throat. "I wouldn't dare. They might lop off my head."

Those gorgeous lips twitched again, and he could feel it settle in his gut. Not only was she downright sexy, but she was likeable. He was attracted to her. Terribly so.

"So Rhett also told me you're going through a celibate phase right now and that you'd mostly keep to yourself."

It took effort not to let his jaw go slack. No wonder this had been so easy. Leave it to Rhett to tell a beautiful woman he was celibate. Not that he'd planned on breaking his promise, but he hadn't exactly wanted to go public with it.

"Yes, I am," he said, taking a sip of his latte, trying to think up a rational excuse for why any man would *ever* contemplate celibacy, least of all admit to it. "Ah...it's a spiritual thing. I thought it might help me focus on the more important things in life for a while. Help my creative fire return." Okay, that part wasn't a joke.

She traced the edge of her green cotton dress, making him reconsider his priorities in an instant. With legs like that, she could make him believe sex was the *only* thing worth pursuing.

"It's wise of you to take a break," she said, lifting her blue pottery mug and taking a drink of her coffee. "I did it a few years ago. It was one of the best things I've ever done."

He choked on the cinnamon roll he'd bitten into. "How long did you take a break?"

Her brows shot up as if the question surprised her. "Over a year. I waited until I was sure I could have sex for the right reasons."

There were wrong reasons? Now he was really interested. "And what would those be?"

The pause she took made him wonder if she was offended. Then she said, "Until I was sure I wanted to have sex with the man I was seeing. Now, I think that's enough chitchat. How about I show you the two rooms that are available? You can choose your favorite. I've already decided I'm going to rent you one. I appreciate Rhett and Jane's input, of course, but I had to make sure we'd be a good fit."

His knees turned weak at the phrase "good fit," so he stuffed his mouth with another bite of cinnamon roll. He followed her to the stairs and watched her hand trail along the wood in a way he found incredibly arousing. Her nails were painted a cherry red that suited her.

"How did you come to own this house?" he asked after he finished chewing. After all, she couldn't be much older than he was, and managing a local coffee shop wouldn't translate to wealth. Even though it was old, a house like this would command a special price. "It's absolutely gorgeous. Was it in your family?"

"I bought it when it foreclosed," she told him when they reached the second floor. "An old boyfriend helped me restore it. When we split, it was like having the best of him."

"It must have been pretty serious between the two of you for him to have put his blood, sweat, and tears into this house."

An old mirror stood at the top of the stairs, and for a moment, he caught a trace of nostalgia on her face.

"It was," she simply said and walked down the hall, leaving him to follow her with more questions swirling in his mind.

The sway of her behind made him think Hot Cross Buns was the perfect name for her bakery. Thirty days of living with her and being celibate wasn't going to be easy. Not that she was the type who'd just jump into bed with him. Far from it, based on what she'd said. Unlike most of the women he knew, who threw themselves at him for the clothes, dinners, vacations, and jewelry he could give them, she was exactly who she portrayed herself to be. He could tell she was going to be a breath of fresh air. And maybe, just maybe, flirting would be enough.

"That's Martin's room," she said when they passed a closed door. "He's such a pig. I make him keep the door shut even though the room could use a good airing out."

"Maybe Martin is growing things in there for his molecular biology degree," he told her.

"Haha. I don't think so. He has full access to the biology lab at Emmits Merriam." She stopped in front of the next open doorway. "This bedroom may be too feminine for you, but I still wanted you to see it."

The room was painted a rich gold that reminded him of sandstone under the full noon sun in Provence. A white bedspread covered what looked to be a queen bed. Free of any carvings, the headboard was simple and elegant, and it matched the dresser in the corner of the room. The curtains were also white.

"This room has a window unit in case the heat bothers you," she told him. "We don't have a lot of ACs in Dare Valley since it cools off at night. The mountains, you know. My ex hated any kind of heat, which is why there's one in here."

So, she'd changed rooms after their split. Curiouser and curiouser. This time he held his tongue and didn't press her for more information.

"The bathroom is on the other side of this room. You and Martin will share it, since you're the two males in the house."

"If Martin really is a pig, that sounds like a raw deal."

She laughed. "He knows better than to treat the bathroom like that. However, if you ever have a concern, let me know. I hire a cleaning service that comes once a month. The charge is included in the rent. Like the utilities. Some people balk and promise to take turns cleaning and such, but few follow through."

Personally, he was pleased. He hadn't cleaned his own place in years, despite how much it upset his mother, who thought it was the only thing she'd ever taught him. He was about to say as much, but he decided not to mention his mom. It felt too personal, and they'd only just met.

"Smart of you to find a solution," he said, giving the room a final glance. "Let's see the other room."

The room she showed him across the hall was much more masculine. It was tan, which bored him to tears after all the bright colors in Paris, and the bedspread was navy. The furniture matched the set in the other room. She must have bought them wholesale.

"I like the gold room better," he said.

Her head angled back. *"Really?* You'd be the first of my male tenants to pick it."

"What can I say? I like color, and I'm not ashamed to admit it."

While one in twelve men were colorblind, he wasn't one of them. His Paris apartment was painted with many of the colors popular during the Belle Époque: cream, plum, gold, emerald, and indigo. Growing up, his mother had never been able to afford to buy paint, and MIT students weren't allowed to paint their dorm rooms. He'd been starved for color by the time he moved into a place of his own.

They journeyed to the bathroom, which was clean, as she'd promised. There was an old white claw-foot tub that doubled as a shower if the green plastic curtain was any indication.

"Do you ever take a bath in that tub?" he asked, tracing the inviting curves of the porcelain-lined cast iron. He had a similar tub in his penthouse, but he expected his had cost ten times more than this model.

"I have my own bathroom," she explained. "But no. No one ever takes a bath in here. I'm trying to imagine Martin doing it." Her laugh was as inviting as a champagne cork that had just popped.

"Martin is pretty manly then?" Evan asked, interested in the third member of their household.

"Manly? Ah...I'll let you decide on that." She walked into the hallway. "Now that you've chosen your room, do you have any other questions?"

"Talk to me about the communal kitchen," he said, his eyes straying down the hall to the two closed doors at the end. Apparently Martin wasn't the only one who kept his sanctuary to himself. Evan suspected Margie liked her privacy, and who could blame her? She shared her home with other people.

"Good question. Everyone has a shelf. As a rule, we don't share things unless we agree. Martin and I share milk, for example, since he only uses a little in his coffee in the morning, and I use a ton of it to practice making cinnamon rolls."

"I think you have the cinnamon rolls down," he told her.

"Thanks," she said. "I do too. But I still want a few more people to try them. Ones who have been eating the Kemstead kind for generations. I'm having a special cinnamon roll tasting next Friday."

"Please tell me I can come," he said with a half-cocked grin. "Smelling all those rolls without eating any might kill me. I'd even pay to attend." There, he'd done it again.

"How about this? You're invited if you promise to help me set up and clean up," she said, sticking her hand out to him.

"Done."

They shook on it. He didn't let himself hold her hand any longer than was perfunctory.

"Can I pay you for the month now?" he asked.

She nodded. "That would be great. I don't expect you to skip out, but I've made it a policy."

He dug into his pocket to pull out his simple money

clip. All the cash he'd allotted himself for the month was in that clip. As he handed her the five hundred dollar bills, he calculated his remaining largess. After the car, clothes, accessories, and rent, he was down to seven hundred dollars. And it was only the first day of his adventure. Since the town was small he could walk to cut down on gas, but he would have to manage his remaining funds carefully. God, he hoped he didn't have to go back to eating ramen noodles three times a week.

"It's a good policy. You have to make a living too. You rent the rooms out to bring in extra income, right?" he asked.

"Yes," she replied, leading him down the stairs again and through a dining room decorated with a simple farm table and benches instead of chairs. "Even with Howie's help, I had to take out a loan to renovate the house. Once I paid that off, I realized the rent money would pad my savings account so I could make my big dream come true. Hot Cross Buns is finally becoming a reality."

When he reached the edge of the kitchen, he turned and gave her his complete attention. He recognized the excitement in her voice—it was how he felt about his own new adventure.

***

Margie nearly shivered when Evan looked at her that way. While it wasn't surprising Rhett hadn't thought to warn her that Evan was a hottie, she rather wished Jane had said something. When she'd opened the door to find him standing on her threshold, her insides had turned to liquid. It wasn't how he was dressed. It wasn't even the sexy rakish-looking beard, the curly blond hair, or the lakewater blue eyes.

No, Evan Michaels was downright sexy in a way that had everything to do with his absolute focus on her as she talked. Add in the appealing awkwardness he'd exhibited about the whole celibacy and sharing-a-bathroom thing, and she was already feeling a strong pull toward him.

His smile was going to get her into trouble.

Good thing he was on a celibacy kick because she didn't allow hooking up or dating amongst her renters—herself included.

From the way his eyes were always on her—so intense it sent shivers down her spine—it wasn't hard to see that he was attracted to her too. She fought a deep sigh and reached for a cinnamon roll. A good cinnamon roll was a perfect substitute for chocolate when lust came a calling.

"How long have you wanted to open a bakery?" he asked, resting his hip against the kitchen island.

"Since I started working at Don't Soy With Me. We serve some baked goods there, including French pastries from Brasserie Dare. Everyone in town still goes to Kemstead's for cinnamon rolls though. Jill finally started letting people bring them into our shop since we have better coffee. It's how this community works. When I tasted their cinnamon rolls for the first time, something happened to me."

A snowstorm had blown through on a freeze-your-ass-off Wednesday. She'd just moved to Dare Valley and was on her way to Don't Soy With Me for the late shift. Someone came out of Kemstead's bakery, and she caught a whiff of cinnamon and baking bread. She decided to treat herself to a cinnamon roll for braving the horrible weather when all she wanted was to call in sick and snuggle up on the couch in her fleece PJs and watch chick flicks.

Time stood still when she took that first bite. Her eyes fluttered shut. Her nose was saturated with the smells of cinnamon and caramel and a part of her soul cried out, *Yes, this is what you've been looking for.*

Her mother had never cooked. They'd hired a string of high-priced private chefs, and while the food had always been excellent, something had been missing.... In that one cinnamon roll, she'd found it. The mingled flavors of comfort, love, and the sweetness of life were rolled up in the bread's very layers. Her heart burst open. She got teary-eyed—not her usual—and she fell in love. With the taste as much as the sensation.

From that moment onward, she'd been eager to share that wonderful feeling with others. As a barista and now manager at Don't Soy With Me, she poured it into her coffee and everything she did at the shop. And she saved and saved and saved, knowing the time would come for her to have her own business in Dare Valley— one that would give people the same sensation as Kemstead's cinnamon rolls.

Then fate had delivered her dream to her. When word spread that the current owners were selling Kemstead's, she pounced. Grandma Kemstead, nearing seventy, cried when she shared her story and promised to continue their legacy of feeding Dare Valley with love, one cinnamon roll at a time.

"Sounds like quite a revelation," Evan said, returning her to the present moment. "As an adopted Parisian, no one knows the power of food better than me. Trust me, you have a winner here."

She grinned. "Thanks. I think so too, but it never hurts to have other opinions."

"I have a feeling you're going to wow the town with your baking," he said, leaning a little bit more on the island like he was suddenly tired.

"You must be jet-lagged," she realized. "Why don't I help you carry your things inside?"

He took out his keys. "I can get everything. I'll be right back."

She found herself admiring his excellent tush before she realized she'd forgotten to ask him how he'd be spending his days in Dare Valley.

"Evan," she said, and the word felt as delicious on her tongue as the cinnamon roll's caramel sauce. He turned around and gave her that same look—the one that told her he was really paying attention. "What are you going to be doing all month? I mean, will you be around the house most of the time?" Normally, she respected people's privacy, but no one had ever worked from the house full-time, and she rather liked coming home to find it empty sometimes.

"I need to get a job," he said, rolling his eyes. "Otherwise I'll go crazy. Got any ideas? I can work for free since I know most people wouldn't want to hire someone just for a month."

Hmm...her mind started to spin with an idea.

"You mentioned painting," she said. "How would you feel about painting Kemstead's for me? I know it's not quite art, but I have quite a lot to paint, and it will go faster if I have help." Maybe she could even delegate it to him completely if he was more than merely competent. "I can pay you fifteen dollars an hour," she added, calculating her outlay costs in her mind.

"You just found yourself a painter," he said and gave a sexy shrug. "Just don't expect Degas, okay?"

Her laughter bubbled out of her. "What? No Degas? I'm crushed. I was so looking forward to a ballerina mural."

CHAPTER 3

The next day Evan wasn't painting willowy ballerinas all Impressionist-like. No, he was measuring out and laying blue paint tape in preparation for the painting, which was about as far from glamorous as a person could get. He'd watched a few how-to videos on YouTube, and it hadn't looked too hard.

No one had told him how much time it would take to do all the prep work. His eyes were starting to cross as he ripped off a measure of tape and tried to lay it exactly against the baseboards. The problem was that each time he laid down tape and stepped away, it looked crooked. At first he figured it was ineptitude on his part, but after repeating the process a few too many times, he finally grabbed one of the tape measurers in Margie's toolbox— a girly pink number that made him cringe every time he needed something from it. After taking the measurements and then grabbing a level, he finally realized what was wrong. Nothing in the entire bakery was level due to the building's age.

This job was so going to suck. But he was going to grin and bear it. She was trusting him with her dream, and after seeing her eyes light up like stars as she walked him through her vision, he was determined not to let her down. He'd had a dream once, one he'd made into reality with his business partner and current chief financial officer, Chase Parker. He rather liked the idea of helping someone achieve her dream.

The bakery hadn't been remodeled in decades, and according to Margie, the décor had been old-school diner, with red leather booths and a long counter lined with red bar stools, before her contractor had ripped them out. The old coffee-and-donut crowd wasn't going to like some of her changes, but she couldn't cater to everyone.

Margie was planning on bringing in a new kind of community focus while preserving some of the old-time favorites like peanut butter pie, jelly-filled donuts, and—of course—the famous cinnamon rolls. She also hoped to draw in a younger crowd since Dare Valley was well populated with students and young families. Based on the crowd passing by the front windows, with people peeking in occasionally to see what he was doing, Evan knew she'd have plenty of foot traffic.

She'd left him alone two hours ago to run over to Don't Soy With Me, where she was training the new manager, Rebecca Merriweather. He hoped to be further along by the time she returned.

When he heard a metal sound near the front door, he swiveled on his haunches to watch her unlock the front glass door. So much for that. The bell chimed as she opened the door, and she looked upward as she shut and locked the door behind her.

"I am so going to have to get rid of that bell," she said, briskly coming inside and setting her zebra-print purse on the plastic he'd lined the floor with in anticipation of painting. "Hot Cross Buns is going to play the kind of soulful music you'd hear at Don't Soy With Me. Anything from Coltrane—one of my favorites—to John Legend. I might have to play some

ABBA when Jill shows up. She's a rabid fan."

"I love Coltrane," he responded, standing up. He was slightly embarrassed to hear his knees crack like an older man. People who painted for a living deserved a heck of a lot more respect than he'd ever realized. "And Miles Davis."

"Oh, Miles." Her green eyes sparkled as she patted a hand to her heart. "If anyone's voice could be compared to a cinnamon roll, it's his."

He felt his mouth twitch. "A cinnamon roll, huh? He'd be singing the goo instead of singing the blues."

She laughed. "Oh, that's terrible. Don't quit your day job. And my cinnamon rolls are *not* filled with goo, Mr. Murray. That's a rich caramel sauce, thank you very much." She stomped her foot indignantly.

He held up his hand like a white flag. "Don't shoot. I surrender. No goo."

"You definitely won't be writing my menu," she said, putting her hands on her curvy hips.

For a moment, all he could imagine was covering her hands with his and pulling her to him. "I wouldn't presume. Now, you might be wondering why I've only laid painter's tape across this one wall. It might be a revelation to you, but nothing in this place is level."

Her head shook in confirmation, making her sable hair sway around her face. "Yes, I know. My contractor had to forbid his wife from bringing their young children to visit when he was over here since he was dropping the f-bomb so much."

He opened his mouth in feigned shock. "You mean I can actually drop the f-bomb around here? I thought people who did that were kicked out of Pleasantville."

She gave him a playful shove, one he found altogether too arousing. "That's Paradise, you idiot. We have normal people in Dare Valley who swear and everything."

"Color me surprised," he mocked, wishing she'd

shove him again.

For a Pocket Venus, she was stronger than she looked. Most of the models he dated barely ate anything, giving a whole new meaning to "couldn't lift a finger to help." He'd given up on trying to tell them that it was okay to eat.

"I see you already poured the paint out," she said, pointing to the flat tray on the floor.

"I was feeling pretty positive when I started." He'd covered the tray with plastic thirty minutes later, after his non-level tape-laying nightmare had turned that dream to ashes. "I'm glad you're not upset."

She cocked her head and looked at him. "Why would I be?"

Her trust in him moved something powerful in his chest. For a moment, it was hard to breathe. Most of the rich people he knew didn't have patience for excuses when things weren't done correctly. For years, he'd watched the people around him cuss out everyone from car valets to hotel maids for taking their sweet time or making a negligible error.

This attitude of entitlement had always bothered Evan, even more so when he found himself acting the same way. One time, a supermodel he was seeing complained about a valet, saying he'd scratched the door of her Porsche. The young man was insistent the scratch had already been there, but Evan took his companion's side. In the middle of dressing the guy down, he had realized what he was doing...and the fact that the valet seemed to be shrinking before his eyes. It was the way he had felt years and years ago when his dad would yell at him for some imagined offense.

He immediately stopped, told the supermodel he'd pay for the scratch, and tipped the man a couple hundred euros as an apology. He'd never done it again.

"I don't know," he finally said, not meeting Margie's eyes. "I didn't want you to think I was making this take longer because I needed the money. Or that I was incompetent."

"I would never think that." A soft hand settled on his shoulder, making him jump. "And if you need me to pay you more than fifteen dollars an hour, Evan, tell me. I could probably make it eighteen if you made sure to clean the rollers and brushes really well so I don't have to buy more."

His ears burned. She thought he needed the money? Even if his deal with Jane had required him to live in Dare Valley for two months on a single month's salary, he still wouldn't have accepted her generous raise. "I would never take money away from your dream. Fifteen dollars is fine. I want you to succeed, Margie."

For a moment, her mouth pursed like she was fighting strong emotion, and with her hand still resting on his shoulder, he felt a new connection grow between them. This one was beyond their undeniable attraction for each other. This one was about them becoming something like friends and supporting each other. He hadn't experienced this strong of an instant connection with someone since meeting the man who now ran his company.

Chase Parker had been raised on a ranch outside of Laramie, Wyoming, before attending Harvard on a scholarship. After wrapping up his M.B.A., he'd started a venture capital firm, the one Evan had approached with his first invention. After securing the financing, Evan had managed to lure Chase away so he could spend all his time in research and development. Besides being excellent at his job, Chase was everything Evan had always wanted to be—handsome, dashing, a ladies' man without trying too hard, and comfortable in his own skin.

Thank God, he'd taken Evan under his wing and helped him throw aside his cloak of nerdiness. It had been embarrassing to ask for that kind of help from a man who was a decade his elder, but Chase hadn't so much as blinked. The makeover program Chase had created for him had involved copious amounts of gym workouts, which had given him muscles and the six-pack the paparazzi loved to photograph when he dove off The Spell Caster, his yacht, into the Mediterranean. And of course, an excellent team of stylists, tailors, and makeover artists had tamed his wild hair and cleared up his skin.

Still, money couldn't buy an inside fix. Sometimes he still felt like the geeky kid who could name the full value of pi to 10,000 digits.

Right now, he felt like a fraud for a completely different reason. A sable-haired woman with a heart of pure gold was willing to put a dent in her bank account because she thought he needed the money.

"Margie," he said, and the simple act of saying her name made the octaves of his voice deeper, slower.

Their eyes met, and he could see her pupils dilate from the shared awareness between them.

She shivered and snatched her hand away. "I need to get back to the coffee shop. Text me if you need anything. What's your number, by the way?"

The distance she was putting between them was probably for the best, but he found he missed the warmth of her hand. "Ah...I still have a Paris number. Since I'm only planning to stay for a month, I figured I could get by. I don't want you to have to incur extra charges to text me. Don't Soy With Me is only a block away. I'll find you if I need anything."

One side of her mouth lifted first, and then the other, like smiling took effort. "I'll leave you to it then."

He watched her walk away, desperate to call her back to him, to tell her how much her trust and generosity meant to him.

Instead all he was able to say was, "Margie. You're doing something special here."

After she finished unlocking the door, she turned and leaned against it, her green eyes all soft. "Thanks, Evan. I'll see you around."

***

Margie was off balance for the rest of the day. The connection she felt with Evan was more powerful than the spark she'd felt with Howie, the only man she'd ever loved. Her former boyfriend had been finishing up his Masters in Creative Writing at Emmits Merriam when they met at Polar Fest. His creativity was instantly compelling to a woman who'd been raised around corporate business types like her father.

Howie could write heart-stopping poetry and work with his hands. His capacity for knowledge was as great as hers even though she'd dropped out of Dartmouth— which had been one of the final straws for her parents after years of her rebellious behavior. Unlike them, he'd listened to her dreams—really listened. And when she told him about the Victorian house and how she wished she could buy it and restore it to its former glory, he'd promised they would do it together.

They'd done that and everything else together, and only in retrospect did she realize the extent to which she'd isolated herself. At the time, she hadn't seen the need to make friends other than the ones she worked with at Don't Soy With Me. My, how wrong she'd been.

Howie had been passionate, but sometimes wildly moody. She'd figured it was part of being artistic until she discovered the oxycodone in his dresser drawer. Since he didn't have any reason that she knew of to take a prescription pain killer, she asked him about it. He got defensive and told her it enhanced his creativity. When he wouldn't tell her how long he'd been using it, they had a huge fight.

In the end, his refusal to address the drug problem

was what had broken them apart. She'd grieved him and promised herself to never ever again date a man with secrets or let one man become her everything again. But while she'd dated off and on over the last couple of years, none of the men she'd met had tugged at her heart and soul in the same way. Even though she'd only known him for a couple of days, she could tell that Evan was different.

The door to Don't Soy With Me opened, and Rhett sauntered over to the counter wearing a T-Shirt that read, "I'm A Good Ol' Boy—Sometimes." She found it hard to contain her smile.

"Howdy, darlin'," he said in his signature drawl.

"Hi, Rhett," she said, walking over to the cash register to ring him up herself. "What can I get you?"

"How about a banana cream iced latte? I have to hide treats like this from Abbie these days. I'm giving up alcohol while she's pregnant since she can't have a glass of wine, but I can't give up coffee."

"How is she?" she asked, nodding to her barista to go ahead and start Rhett's drink.

"Doing great. She's finally starting to show, and she's so beautiful I almost tear up every time I see her. I still pinch myself sometimes. Me! A papa. I mean we have Dustin, and he's like my son in every way, but this one... Well, it's like I planted him myself."

She elected not to point out the basics of biology to Rhett by telling him that he had...ahem...planted the seed. "You're going to be a great dad."

He ran his hand through his hair. "Man, I hope so. I've been reading every book I can find about how to be a good father. Mine sucked the big one. But that's another tale, and not a happy one. So...I heard Evan is painting your bakery for you."

There was something strange in his tone, but she couldn't put her finger on it. "Yes. I'm so glad you shared your thoughts about him with me when I asked.

I rented him the room yesterday, and when he asked if I knew anyone in need of work, I offered him the chance to paint Hot Cross Buns."

"That's mighty nice of you," he said, but his voice lacked its usual sing-song cadence.

"He has some experience, being an artist and all, and I need the help. I figured I wouldn't need to pay him what a regular painter would run." Which was out of her budget. She'd gotten quotes. But she was still feeling a little guilty about only paying Evan fifteen dollars an hour, which was why she'd offered him more. And what he'd said to her when he refused...

"I'm glad he can help you," Rhett said, shuffling his feet. "Just...well..."

"What?" she asked, eyeing the line of customers snaking behind him. Her other barista was on a break, so she was in this alone for the moment. "Spit it out."

"Keep your head on your shoulders, is all." Rhett scrubbed his face. "Some women think he's pretty...hot. And I cannot believe I am having this conversation."

Was he worried about her? His concern was too sweet for words. Growing up, no one had looked out for her. "I guess it's getting you ready for fatherhood in case you have a daughter."

He gulped. "A girl? Maybe Abbie and I had better find out the baby's sex, after all."

"Go on now and get your drink," she said with a laugh. "There are people behind you."

Swiveling, he winced and held out his hands. "Sorry, folks. I was shooting the breeze and lost track. Margie. Just remember what I said."

"I will," she responded and signaled to the next person in line to approach.

She dealt with the new customers, and when the other barista returned, she detoured to the office to check on Rebecca's progress in learning the software they used to track inventory. The woman was doing great, and Margie had no doubt she would do a terrific job for Jill. She'd worked in a coffee shop in Aspen before deciding she wanted a change of scenery.

When Margie was finally able to pull herself away from Don't Soy With Me, she headed down the block to Hot Cross Buns. The very thought of visiting her new bakery—her dream shop—gave her a thrill. And with a fresh coat of paint, it would look much closer to how she envisioned it.

She had trouble hiding her shock when she opened the door. Four hours had passed since she'd left the shop, but Evan hadn't started painting. Instead, he was sitting cross-legged in the middle of the floor, muttering over a roll of painter's tape and what looked like an old adding machine with a paper rollout.

"Ah...Evan?" she asked, coming forward.

He didn't even look up.

"What are you doing?" Since he still hadn't noticed her, she crouched down and touched his shoulder. "Evan?"

His face tilted up, and his eyes popped open as he finally noticed her. Then he smiled what Rhett would have called a shit-eating grin. "Hey! So, you're probably wondering why nothing has changed since you left."

She nodded. "I was. Yes."

"Something amazing happened." He held up a level, and the yellow fluid swayed in the air. "I got to thinking about the whole level thing. I don't know why someone hasn't thought of it before. What we need is a machine to measure the wall and dispense the tape as the angle changes. That way we can make it *look* level."

Huh?

Her face must have conveyed her confusion since he immediately added, "I went to the hardware store to find some things I could cobble together into a prototype. The guy at Smith's Hardware Store—Wayne—didn't have everything I needed, but he dug out his dad's old adding machine, and that's when my idea snapped into focus. If I program the adding machine to dispense the painter's tape and then add a level, we're in business. Now, I'm trying to reprogram a microchip I bought at the electronics store to communicate from the level to the adding machine so it knows when to roll out. Isn't that terrific?"

She didn't understand much of what he was saying, but what did come through was his excitement. "Evan, I told you before. It doesn't have to be perfect."

"Sure it does! It's your dream, Margie. There shouldn't be a crooked line in this whole place."

A sigh was building in her chest. "I really appreciate your earnestness, but I had hoped you would have at least started painting by now."

The way his whole face fell made her feel like she'd kicked a puppy.

"Oh," he said, looking down in his lap, his makeshift invention resting on a muscular thigh she couldn't help but notice. "I don't expect you to pay me for all this time. I...know this isn't the conventional way to paint, but...trust me, this is going to make *everything* easier. And just think. Anytime you ever need to paint anything again, this machine is going to cut the prep work in half. I promise."

Howie used to have big ideas too. He'd tried to convince her they should lead ghost tours of the Victorian and tell tourists the ghosts of small-time mobster Aaron the Kid and the card dealer from a local hotel who'd killed him—and vice versa—in a shoot-out inhabited their basement. And then there was his notion about making holiday candles and selling them at art shows around Colorado. Big ideas were all well and good...when they didn't put a halt to progress.

As gently as she could, she said, "Why don't you take a break? Did you have lunch? I can start taping, and depending on where I end up, you can take over tomorrow."

His brow furrowed. "You hate my idea, don't you?"

She put a hand on his forearm, and the defined musculature bunched at her touch. She almost yanked her hand away, feeling the electricity spark between them from even that simple contact. "No, I don't hate it. I'm only suggesting you step back for a bit while I take over." At this rate, she was going to be taping until midnight to make up for lost time.

"You don't believe this will work, do you?" he asked, staring straight into her eyes.

She'd been wrong to think his eyes looked like lake water. Right now, they were a much clearer blue—the kind only seen at sunrise, a color so transparent, it was almost fathomless.

She made herself smile. "I'm no genius, Evan. I'm only a small business owner who wants to get my place painted in a reasonable timeframe so I'll have enough time for installation and to decorate it before the opening when I get back from Paris."

"It *will* work," he said, his voice hard. "You'll see. Give me...thirty minutes."

Since his stubborn side had decided to make an appearance, she allowed herself to heave a sigh. "I'm going to start now."

"Thirty minutes."

He was tempting her to lose her temper. "I said I'm starting now."

"Fine," he said, grabbing his laptop. "But you're going to want to undo any tape you lay once you see what a straight line I can make with my machine."

What was this? The World's Fair? "I didn't know you could make things."

"There's a lot you don't know about me," he snapped. "Now, don't talk to me. If you're only going to give me thirty minutes, I need to concentrate."

He needed to concentrate? Well, fine. Suddenly her

new renter and contract painter seemed more like a pain in the butt than the charming artist who'd made her insides go beep-beep.

The sun was setting in the west, cascading soft golden rays through the front windows, when she went to work. Evan muttered in the background, cursing a few times. Thank God she'd bought two rolls of painter's tape. The way Evan was acting, he'd likely bite off her hand if she asked him for the one he was jimmying through the adding machine between typing things into his laptop.

Halfway down just one wall, Margie wanted to curse herself. There *was* no way to make a straight line. It was a mystery to her why her contractor had not simply up and quit on her. She'd barely started, and she was ready to throw aside the painter's tape and simply paint. What did it matter if she got a little paint on the baseboards or ceiling? If any of the customers wanted to make an issue of it, they could take their business elsewhere.

"Aha!" she heard Evan cry out. "I've got you, you sweet little bitch."

"Don't talk about me like that," she said in a dry tone, knowing he was referring to the object in his hands.

His head popped up, and he blinked. "I didn't mean..."

"I'm just kidding," she said, trying not to laugh at the expression on his face. From now on, she'd have to remember he was sensitive—more so than she would have expected. Perhaps it suited his artistic temperament.

"Step aside," he said, jumping up from where he sat and running over to her. "Now, watch and be amazed."

She felt like a circus barker was trying to lure her into a tent of curiosities.

Evan laid his contraption against the wall. She watched as the yellow liquid in the center of the level grew even, and then all of the sudden, the adding machine tape started to crank out tape. Evan ran it along the baseboards, readjusting as needed to make it level, but sure enough, he'd soon lined the whole baseboard with painter's tape. And it *was* straight—a veritable miracle.

"Did I say it would cut prep time in half?" he asked when he stood, puffing his chest out. "I'd say three-quarters more like. This machine could revolutionize the painting industry. Not just for professional painters, but for your home-improvement types."

Had she said big ideas? "Yes, I can see the modified adding machine at Lowe's now. I'm glad it worked, and I'm sorry I doubted you. How about you use that thing to get us prepped?"

She cast a glance toward the front windows. The sun was setting, which meant it was nearing nine o'clock. They might get lucky and paint a couple walls before they had to throw in the towel.

"This thing has a name—or rather I just gave her one. I'm calling her the Paint Prep Mistress."

She scratched her head. Why were men always referring to objects as females? "Mistress, huh? Sounds like someone has a wild imagination."

When he didn't respond, she looked over at him. He was staring at her with an electric intensity she found deeply arousing.

"Imagination is the spice of life, and it's something I've had to do without for a while." He held his machine against his chest, almost the way a woman would hold a bouquet of flowers from a lover. "Don't steal this moment from me."

Her chest grew tight. "I'm sorry."

He nodded. "Go on home. I'll make up for the time I spent today on the Paint Prep Mistress. You look tuckered out."

Did she? Well, no wonder. Closing down her

position at Don't Soy With Me while preparing to launch Hot Cross Buns meant she was burning the candle at both ends. "I can stay."

"I'm a night owl," he said, turning back to the wall and resuming his prep. "If I know anything about bakers, you're one of those early riser types."

Baking would require her to be up early—well before dawn. "Yes, I am, but this is my place."

He swiveled on his haunches. "Do you not trust me after today?"

She glared at him. "No, I just think you're more of a perfectionist than I am, and I'm going to stay."

"You don't have to. I have this."

They were arguing like an old married couple, and they'd only known each other for less than forty-eight hours. "I'm staying."

"Fine. Don't touch my paint tray."

She eyed the one he'd covered with plastic wrap. "I wouldn't dream of it."

They worked in silence after that. Sure enough, Evan had the whole restaurant prepped in no time. Margie took care of stirring the paint—a luscious periwinkle blue for the walls that would contrast beautifully with the teal she'd chosen for the baseboards. She poured it into *her* paint tray. He could keep his.

Why was she always attracted to temperamental artistic types?

***

Evan was trying to preserve the euphoria he'd been feeling most of the day after the Paint Prep Mistress' prototype had formed in his mind. Sure, he'd had to make do with less-than-high-tech equipment, but he'd made it work. When he'd told Margie not to steal this moment from him, he'd meant it.

The signs that had led him to Dare Valley had

delivered. A spark of his creative fire had returned.

The part of him that had always been innately curious about life, about how things ticked, about how things *could* tick if he invented something, was back. Before he'd lost himself through his hubris, it had been his whole purpose for living. He'd craved the euphoria—the highs and lows of the invention process. Today had been an abbreviated version of the excitement, the frustration, and finally the victory. He now understood that this ability to create and discover was worth more than his billions.

He couldn't wait to tell Chase about his progress.

Margie was using a roller on the walls to cover them in a sharp periwinkle. The color was at once bold and welcoming—a perfect representation of Margie.

"I meant to tell you that I like the color," he commented, setting his prize invention down on the counter so no one would accidentally step on it.

"I'm glad," she responded, looking cute in the white paint smock she'd donned.

Since Evan wasn't planning on keeping his off-the-rack clothes once he returned to Paris, he didn't care if he got paint on them.

He carefully unwrapped the paint tray he'd prepared earlier. After giving the paint a stir, he moved his roller through it until it was evenly covered. Then he followed her lead and started to paint. "You know. The experts say we're missing a few steps."

He caught her eye roll when she looked over at him. "Really?"

"Really. First we're supposed to use primer on the walls. Then paint with the color. Both times, we're supposed to paint about a two to four inch barrier above the baseboard and below the ceiling before moving on to the rest." Of course, some modern paint brands already contained primer, but he expected she couldn't afford the higher-end product.

"That sounds excessive to me. First, we only need to do an extra coat of the paint to cover the wall. And second, the paint tape is supposed to keep us from getting anything on the baseboards or ceiling." She rolled toward the ceiling as if to prove him wrong.

He could see it coming a mile away, but he forced himself to bite back a warning. She was going too fast. Sure enough, the roller nudged the ceiling and made a stain.

She turned and glared at him. "Don't. Say. A. Word."

He made a motion of zipping his lips. The perfectionist part of him wanted to paint the place the expert way, but he figured she'd only growl at him if he tried. So, she was a woman who liked to cut corners—totally the opposite of him. Then he noticed how pale her face was from fatigue. He well remembered how exhausted he'd been when he was starting out. Maybe she was cutting corners because she was tired. He opened his mouth to say something again and then closed it. She'd been very clear on her plans to stay, and he wouldn't challenge her twice.

They painted until midnight, and he finally made a show of yawning like a sleepy lion sunning himself on the Serengeti. He darn well knew she'd stay as long as he did. The woman had pride, and he admired her for it.

"You're probably still jet-lagged," she said, setting her roller into the paint tray and stretching her back.

Her breasts thrust out with the motion, and even though he felt like a total pig, he couldn't take his eyes off the beautiful line of her body. His mouth went dry, his palms grew damp, and all he wanted to do was throw aside his paint roller, cross the room to her, and kiss her. Wildly. Passionately. Ardently.

"Okay," she said, straightening. "Let's clean up and head back to the house."

He cleared his thick throat, and she looked over. Her whole body stilled, and he made himself look away. He had twenty-nine more days of celibacy since he'd based it on a thirty-one day month like an idiot. Lusting after her now would do neither one of them any good, especially if he let her know how he felt.

"I'll clean the rollers if you want to pour the paint back into the cans," he said, picking them up and heading to the industrial kitchen.

When he returned, she was turning his invention from side to side like she was trying to decipher how her artist tenant had turned into MacGyver. The comparison was more apt than she knew, which made Evan pretty proud given that it was one of his favorite shows of all time.

"You're pretty handy," she commented, staring at him now. "Why do I have a feeling you're more than an artist?"

He forced a poker face. It hadn't dawned on him that he might give himself away by inventing something so simple. All she had to do was Google "Evan the inventor," and he'd show up in the results.

"Even da Vinci had to create inventions to make his artistic work come alive," he told her. "I like to create things."

"Da Vinci, huh?" she said, setting his new pride and joy aside. "That's a pretty big comparison."

For Evan Murray, it was. For Evan Michaels, well...he didn't like to brag, but he thought Maestro would be impressed with some of his inventions if they ever met in a parallel universe.

Evan made himself shrug casually. "You know what they say. 'That which you admire in another is already inside of you.'"

It was exactly what Chase had said to him after he'd finally confessed how much he admired the other man's ease of being...well, a man's man.

"I've never heard that saying," Margie said, picking up her purse and walking to the door. "I'll have to remember it."

He turned off his laptop and stuffed it into the backpack he'd bought. Then, he delicately tucked his new mistress into the bag. It was going to sleep beside him tonight. He didn't care if that made him weird.

"You're taking that with you?" she asked, her gaze flicking from the backpack to him.

"Ah…" He felt his ears flush. "I want to see if there are any other improvements I can make. When I was in your kitchen cleaning the rollers, I realized that space could use a good coat of paint too. You should add it to the list."

"Already done. It's going to be painted a sunny yellow since I'll have start baking at three a.m., well before the sun rises."

"The mere thought of that schedule makes me want to throw up," he answered honestly. When he was in Paris, he was usually still partying at three a.m. or strolling on the streets in the quiet. Paris was beautiful at night, and when he was lonely, he liked to walk amongst the statues and imagine that they were alive and keeping him company.

"Don't judge my new routine. If I don't get up then, I'll be depriving Dare Valley of their morning pastries. I'm sure you've enjoyed Paris' baked goods. And their bakers begin at two a.m., not the wimpy three a.m. I can get away with in Dare Valley. Did you think the fairies left the bread in a nice straw basket by the baker's doorstep at sunrise?"

Paris was so magical, he could halfway believe such a story. He lifted the backpack over his shoulder after zipping it closed. "I do like a croissant with my café crème. And don't even get me started talking about my love affair with la baguette."

"I can't wait to learn how to make both of those from the experts," she said, letting him out and then locking the door.

"Who are you apprenticing with?" he asked, not that he would likely know.

"Andre Moutard of Boulangerie Ma Belle. His place is in St. Germain."

"I live in St. Germain," he said. Or Evan Michaels did. In a fancy penthouse. "It's one of the best parts of the city. I love how the window displays are always changing. It's like they're inventing something new each time." Which is why he lived there. It had fed his imagination at first. And then nothing had. Until now.

He paused, wanting to say he would show her around when she came to Paris, but it was too soon for that.

"I've never thought about a shop window as an invention. I might have to look at my own storefront in a new way once I open."

He almost wished he'd be there to see it. "Just put cinnamon roll after cinnamon roll in the shop window. That will speak for itself."

She laughed. "When I'm not so tired, you'll have to tell me where I need to go when I'm not working."

"That I can do." Of course, the places he went would be out of her price range. He would have to do some research.

"Where are you parked?" she asked as they walked down Main Street.

"I walked here," he said, tipping his head up to take in the starry sky.

In Paris, he rarely saw a sky so filled with stars. The city's famous lights obscured the galaxies beyond Earth almost as if Paris were a woman who could not stand the competition to her beauty.

"Come on," she said. "I'll take you home."

It was odd for a woman to say that to him without intending it as an invitation into her bed, but everything in Dare Valley was different from his usual.

She bid him goodnight almost immediately when

they entered the quiet Victorian, which was likely for the best. Neither of them needed any awkwardness. He grabbed himself a glass of water in the kitchen before heading upstairs to his room.

Inside, he dug out his cell phone and called Chase. His friend lived outside Washington D.C., only two hours ahead of his current time in Dare Valley—not that he couldn't call Chase at any time of the day. He had carte blanche.

"How's normal life so far?" Chase asked the minute he picked up.

"I invented something!" he immediately said, not bothering to keep the old nerdy glee out of his voice.

"You did? That's terrific. I knew you could get back in the game." He laughed that loud, gusty laugh of his. "Evan, I'm going to freeze all of your accounts from now on so you'll be poor for the rest of your life. Tell me what you cooked up."

Evan described his makeshift prototype in grand detail, and goosebumps broke out across his arms. When he was finished, he was nearly breathless with excitement. "It's terrific, right?"

There was a long pause. "I don't think the Painter's Prep Mistress is going to make us millions, Evan. There's no money in retail."

Since he had to shake something, and it couldn't be Chase's neck, he shook his cell. When he put it back to his ear, he said, "Don't you dare steal my thunder. You know I haven't had a real idea in two years." And the ones before that had fizzled like day-old champagne.

"Your company, Evan, the one I run for you, is a defense contractor. We—i.e. you—invent top-secret thingamabobs that we sell to increase a nation's national security. Your Paint Prep Mistress isn't going to keep the bad guys away."

"Stop talking about my mistress like that!"

"Evan!"

"Dammit, Chase. I know what we do, or what I *used* to do. Today, I found the spark again, the one that used to mean everything to me. I thought you'd understand." He hung up and put his head in his hands, losing that heady feeling he'd experienced all day.

The phone immediately rang.

Since it would have been sulky not to pick up, he answered. "Yes?"

"I'm sorry," Chase began. "I got all excited when you said you'd invented something, and then when you told me what it was... You're not the only one who can feel disappointment, Evan. I'm really glad you found the spark again. But we need some new products. There are only so many new government contracts I can win with old technology unless you want me to start selling INV-333 to non-NATO countries."

After the successful testing of his invisibility cloak a la Harry Potter, which he called INV-333, he'd told Chase they could only sell to countries that were strong allies of the United States and France. Evan watched the news. There were plenty of governments who would pay top dollar for INV-333, and while he couldn't be completely sure how any governments would ultimately use his defense equipment, he was at least going to make sure they didn't use it against his country of birth or residence.

"I still don't want to sell to non-NATO countries," he said, rubbing the heel of his hand against his forehead. "Something is happening here, Chase. Like I hoped it would. I can feel it."

"I told you, all you needed to do to light that spark again was cut down on the partying. I might have to send Jane Wilcox and Rhett Butler Blaylock a thank-you card."

That would be the day. "I'm still going to tinker with my Paint Prep Mistress. Maybe we should create a retail arm of Quid-Atch Incorporated."

All Evan's early inventions had been inspired by *Harry Potter*. Mrs. Alice, a kind librarian at his middle school, had given him the first book the year his father had left to take a job in Texas. His dad had promised to send for them, but in the end he'd only sent divorce papers. With few options and fewer resources, Evan's mom had started cleaning houses and office buildings at night to keep money in the bank, and after that, he'd rarely seen her.

His identification with the boy wizard was immediate—like Harry, he had no real adult caretakers and kids his age misunderstood him. But that didn't mean it always had to be that way. The books helped him appreciate his gifts, his knack for taking things apart, putting them back together, and inventing something new. They lit his inner fire.

Years later, when Chase had asked him what he wanted to name his company, the answer had been obvious. He named it after the game he loved from the famous book series that had unlocked his imagination.

He'd tried reading the books again last year, hoping they would spark something new in him, but nothing. Zilch.

"Evan, I know you don't want to run the company, but trust me when I say if you want to start a retail arm of Quid-Atch Incorporated, you're going to have to do it yourself. I have my hands full on the defense side."

Chase traveled back and forth from their headquarters in Virginia's high-tech corridor, Tyson's Corner, to the major NATO-country capitals. "I've told you to hire more people."

"I have, but there are some things I have to do myself. The heads of defense departments don't like to be wined and dined by vice presidents." There was a long sigh. "Evan, our clients have been raising concern over your...non-business activities for a while now. People are starting to think you've lost your edge. This paint invention isn't going to change that perception."

And perception was everything. For the last two years, he'd been making frequent trips to Tyson's Corner to keep his employees motivated. If the people at Quid-Atch learned their magician had lost his magic, it would create massive panic. Not just in terms of their employees and clients, but their stock price. And it wasn't like he hadn't been doing anything. He'd tweaked their inventions, putting out new and improved models all the while hinting at a big design in the works. Of course, there was no big design. Heck, there wasn't even a big idea.

Desperation had brought him here. But after the spark today with his first invention in two years, however practical and non-defense like, he *did* believe something bigger than him was at work. Now all he had to do was follow his gut.

"Tell them I'm in seclusion. Working."

"Now you sound like a monk." Chase laughed. "Oh, right. I forgot. You rather are right now, aren't you?"

Evan kicked off his hiking boots—his only other pair of shoes besides flip-flops and tennis shoes—and laid back on the bed. "I should never have told you about that part of the side bet." Chase had laughed so hard he'd snorted on the phone, something Evan had never heard him do.

"And yet you did. I'm going to get back to sleep now since I have to get up in the morning and run your company."

"You always say that. Quid-Atch is as much yours as it is mine. I'm only the brains, and right now, we both know I'm not contributing much in that department."

"You'll get it back. I have faith in you. I always have."

His chest squeezed. Chase had never wavered in his loyalty. "Thanks."

"Good night, *Brother* Evan."

He was laughing at the monk joke when Chase hung up the phone. Pulling his paint mistress close, Evan rolled onto his side with a smile on his face and gave in to the jet lag that had been dogging him all afternoon. And he dreamed about a magical paint.

CHAPTER 4

The next morning Evan awoke to the sound of water running in the house. The simple red letters of the alarm clock read five, so he expected it was his sexy landlord who was up and about and not the still-mysterious Martin. He was tempted to fall back asleep, but he couldn't stop thinking about Margie in the shower. Soon he was awake for reasons other than the start of the new day.

Finally, he rose to open the blinds. The mountains surrounding Dare Valley filled him with awe. Ribbons of sunrise spilled over the rocks and pines, turning everything to liquid gold. Say what you would about this town being small, but it sure had box seats to nature's glory.

Since physical fitness had turned him from a nerdy scientist into what some tabloids called a towering Adonis, he dressed in a T-shirt and running shorts, laced up his cheap running shoes, and headed out for a long run.

Margie was in the kitchen when he came down the stairs, her hair wet and her face all rosy from her shower. She was already measuring out ingredients for some recipe. Even unadorned, she pulled at him unlike any woman he'd ever seen.

"Are you putting chocolate chips in your banana bread?" he asked, noticing the chocolate neatly measured out in a cup near the bowl of over-ripe bananas she was mixing with a fork.

"Uh-huh," she said, pushing her hair behind her ears. "Are you up this early because of jet lag?"

"Yeah. I thought I'd get a run in before I start painting. Can you recommend a trail?"

Her eyelashes lifted playfully as her gaze met his. "How much of a challenge are you looking for?"

He wanted to tell her he could do the toughest one out there to impress her with his manhood, but that would be stupid. The altitude would kick his butt. "Let's go with a medium one today."

She explained where he could find the park soon to be named The Park of Sunset Dreams, and he headed out. It was as beautiful as it sounded, and he was delighted to see other runners out for a morning jog. Paris never felt as crammed to him as New York City, but Dare Valley was almost scarce in its people-to-places ratio. The altitude did make his lungs burn, but it would only make him stronger.

His visit to the local produce market was outright depressing. On the rare occasion he shopped for his own food in Paris, he never looked at prices. But since Evan Murray was on a budget, he needed to keep track of each penny. When had eggs gotten so expensive? And grapefruit? He splurged on the grapefruit to accompany his yogurt and granola, thinking it had better be the best damn grapefruit he'd ever eaten. To offset his splurge, he picked up ramen noodles for dinner. He was already missing the three-course meals he'd enjoyed without a thought in Paris.

When he returned to the house, he was greeted with the delicious smell of baking bread, chocolate, and bananas. His stomach growled. He put his groceries in the refrigerator as Margie puttered around the kitchen in a yellow cotton dress, her sable hair dry now.

"Something smells delicious." Even he could hear the begging in his voice. He blamed it on the grocery store experience and the dinner of ramen awaiting him.

Her eyes twinkled. "I might give you a taste when the bread is cool enough to slice. If you cut it when it's too warm, the chocolate streaks."

"We wouldn't want that," he said. Apparently he wasn't above flirting with her, after all.

"No, we wouldn't." She ran her eyes over him, and while she wasn't obvious about it, he could tell she liked what she saw.

He might have puffed out his chest a bit. "I'll just go grab a shower."

Leaving the kitchen, he realized he was aroused, and it was mortifying when he met Martin on the stairs. The guy was only a little taller than Margie and had wire-rimmed glasses that made Evan want to take him under his wing. Thank God his own vision had always been twenty-twenty.

"Ah, hi," he said, sticking out his hand. "I'm Evan."

"Martin," the man responded. His clasp was bony and lacked confidence. "Margie says you're only staying a month."

"That's right."

"I'm not here a lot, but if you need anything, let me know. Although Margie knows everything."

"She seems very capable." And sexy. Don't forget sexy, he told himself.

"That woman could run a small country," Martin said. "I'm off to the lab."

"Enjoy."

He watched Martin sail out of the front door. In a way, he reminded Evan of himself, and it took him a moment to shake off the old memories.

Margie was in the kitchen when Evan came down from his shower. He poured himself a cup of coffee from the pot she'd made and added granola to a strawberry yogurt before cutting open his grapefruit ever so slowly so no juice would escape. With the sugar she gave him, he feasted on the grapefruit, but its flavor didn't quite make up for its price.

Sure enough, when he was finished, she gave him a piece of her chocolate banana bread. After one bite, he knew this would become his substitute for pain au chocolat while he was in Dare Valley.

"This is incredible, Margie," he said, savoring the warm chocolate and the playful hints of banana. The bread was moist and had a hint of crunch from the nuts she used—walnuts, he guessed from the slightly bitter taste. "I think I'm in love."

She made a humming sound. "I'm glad you like it. I'm thinking about having a few breads with chocolate in them."

"There's no way you're going to apprentice at a boulangerie in Paris without learning how to make pain au chocolat."

She smiled. "I will be, yes. I've splurged on buying one of the machines you need to make croissants. There's no way I'm going to make them by hand."

He didn't know anything about baking, but even he could imagine all those buttery layers would be a bitch to make.

"You're a smart woman. It will be a good investment." He finished the last bite of his breakfast and put his dishes in the dishwasher, making sure he hadn't left a crumb on the counter. "Well, I'm off to paint your castle."

Her lips twitched, and he noticed a speck of chocolate in the corner of her rosy-red mouth. She had clearly enjoyed her newest concoction. For a moment, he was overwhelmed by the thought of kissing that chocolate away and sucking on her lip.

"I made you a key to Hot Cross Buns yesterday," she said, walking across the kitchen to her purse. "I forgot to mention it last night."

"Thank you," he said, taking it from her. The grooves were so fresh, there were metal shavings clinging to the edges.

"I'm heading out soon if you need me to give you a lift." She made a fluffing motion to her hair. "I...ah...still need to put on my makeup and finish up my hair."

Even though he was used to women who would rather be caught dead, literally, than be seen without cosmetics and perfectly coiffed hair, she looked terrific to him. He wanted to tell her as much, but he bit his tongue.

"It's a nice day out." The temperature was likely seventy already, but the air was clear and crisp. "I'm going to walk."

"I'll see you later, then," she said. "Just holler if you need anything."

"I will."

That day, he found pride in finishing the painting of the main part of the bakery. When Margie came by later in the afternoon, she twirled around the shop with her arms outstretched after seeing it all come together like it had in her dreams. It was so hard not to kiss her senseless—she was so full of light. Not the cold glamour of models coated in diamond jewelry, but a genuine, warm exuberance that made it seem like her very body glowed with it.

She must have felt the pull between them too because she didn't stay to help him. His dinner that night was a sandwich he bought at Don't Soy With Me since he couldn't work up the courage to eat the ramen. Margie was nowhere to be seen when he looked around the coffee shop, and he didn't ask to see her as he paid for his meal.

When he got back to the house, he inhaled the smell of hazelnuts and apricots. So, that's why he hadn't seen her. She'd already gone home. He headed into the kitchen and smiled when he saw Margie sitting on the counter, her head bowed over a legal pad covered in scribbles.

"Did you eat?" she asked.

"I grabbed a sandwich at Don't Soy With Me."

He knew he was splurging, but he'd found that while he could live without his fancy cars, surviving on plain, no-frills food was another matter entirely.

"What did you think of the shop?" she asked with a fond smile.

"It's a nice place. I liked seeing the art on the walls from local painters."

"I want to do something like that at Hot Cross Buns, but different."

He thought for a moment. "What about showcasing local foods like honeys and jams?" Then he wondered how pricy those might be. Surely not too terrible.

When she blinked and then gave an enchanting grin, he knew she liked his idea. "Great idea! I'll have to look into that. Feel free to grab a slice of my newest bread."

A slice was already waiting for him, and when he sampled it, sure enough, he tasted the sweet and tangy apricots and the crunch of hazelnuts.

"I'm a sucker for hazelnuts," he said, staggering back playfully.

"Me too." Then she put her nose back in her legal pad.

"One of my favorite restaurants in Paris makes the best hazelnut soufflé," he told her. "It's unlike anything you'll ever taste."

She made a humming sound. "Sounds delicious. We'll have to sit down and talk about Paris at some point so I can soak in all of your suggestions. Right now, I need to focus on my menu."

"Sure thing." He poured himself some water. "I'll leave you to it."

He ate the rest of his slice on the front porch step as the sun went down.

She opened the door some time later, as twilight was descending. "I'm going to turn in. I've been getting up earlier and earlier, trying to ease my way into baker's hours. Will you lock the front door when you come in?"

He nodded, wishing she'd sit a moment with him. Still, if she did, he knew he'd be tempted to reach for her hand and point out the constellations that were just making themselves known in the sky. "Good night, Margie."

"Good night, Evan."

As Cassiopeia drew his gaze, he calmed his mind and let design ideas pour forth like a herd of wild horses.

In the quiet, he found a new contentment.

* * *

The next day, another challenge on the painting front prompted a new design idea. After learning what a pain in the butt painting baseboards could be, his brain had started designing a wheel-based roller that could paint the suckers by sensing the top of the baseboard and the bottom of the floor. So far, the only designs he'd envisioned while in Dare Valley were his paint mistress and another painting improvement tool yet to be named. But it was a start. He was giddy with excitement.

When Margie swung by around five o'clock, he walked her through his progress.

"I hate baseboards," he finally confessed. "I'd be happy if I never saw one again."

She cringed. "I know. I didn't envy you. Too bad your paint mistress whatnot couldn't help you."

Little did she know he was three steps ahead of her.

"How about I order some pizza and help you use your mistress on the kitchen?" she asked, donning the paint smock she'd laid on one of the cardboard boxes that held the cans of paint.

"Unfortunately, there's only one paint mistress," he said. "Why don't you head home and rest for a bit? Don't take this the wrong way, but you look tuckered out." He rather admired the circles under her eyes.

She gave a yawn. "I am tired, but it's a good tired, you know? This is my dream, and I just want to work on it every hour of the day. Right now, I feel trapped between two worlds. I'm trying to create the easiest possible transition for Rebecca at the coffee shop. She's begun to shadow me, so at least we're progressing. Pretty soon, she'll take over."

"That other chapter in your life will be over soon enough," he said, striding across the room to her and helping her out of the smock she'd just wrapped around herself.

"It's been a special chapter," she said, "one of the happiest of my life. I'm going to miss it, but I keep reminding myself the bakery's only a block away."

The nape of her neck drew his gaze, and he fought the urge to trace that delicate skin. She smelled of baked bread and coffee—delectable. "But you know it won't be the same."

She turned her head. Their eyes met, and he couldn't look away from her. For a moment, he couldn't see anything but the green of her eyes. The sensation was like falling backwards.

"No, it won't," she said softly. "Sometimes things happen, and our lives never feel the same way again."

He had a feeling she wasn't only talking about her new career change—there was something happening between them, something that both alarmed and delighted him. But he forced himself to take a step back.

She shook herself and headed to the door. "Oops. I forgot my purse." As she walked over to it, he noticed her cheeks were a little pink. "Thanks for...suggesting I take some time. Don't work past seven, okay? I don't want anyone to think I'm a slave driver. You don't want to chase off my future staff, do you?"

"I wouldn't dream of it."

When she left, he sat on the floor in the quiet for a moment. She was so enchanting and filled with light he found it impossible to stop staring at her when she was in the room. But he wasn't who she thought he was, and besides, he was going back to Paris. Their real lives were as different as could be. He needed to remember that.

That night, he went to an Irish pub in town called Hairy's and had a beer, staying out until he thought she would be asleep.

But moments after he unlocked the door of the old Victorian, she crept into the hall. "Where were you? I went by the shop when you didn't come back after seven. I've been worried."

Something sharp and warm moved through his chest. "I went for a beer at the pub. I...thought you could use some time alone."

The slope of her throat moved when she swallowed. "I know you don't have a phone you can use here, and maybe I'm being a mother hen, but...can you call me next time or use someone's phone to text me?"

He wanted to ask her if she'd ever asked Martin to provide her with his whereabouts, but he already knew the answer.

"People here are nice," she rushed on, "and they'd be happy to let you make a call."

He wanted to smooth the frown line between her brows. So, the little time they'd spent away from each other hadn't changed anything. He still felt an incredible pull to her, and clearly, so did she.

"I will next time. I'm sorry I worried you."

She clutched her hands. "It's just that you're new in town, and... Well, I'm going to turn in now that I know you're safe and sound."

He bid her goodnight, and let himself outside again, more than a little off balance. Other than Chase, no one ever worried about him. His mother meant well. She'd just never understood him, so he'd given up trying to explain himself to her a long time ago. And his father had never contacted them again after the divorce.

How long was a month? he asked himself as he sat on the front porch again with his friends—the constellations, his thoughts, and his design ideas.

A long time.

For the rest of the week, he painted, savoring the quiet focus it gave his mind. Sometimes Margie would swing by to help him after her other job was over. Other times, she would go back to the house to do more test baking.

He didn't stay out again without telling her, and she didn't say anything about worrying about him again.

The next week, he continued to paint her bakery, bringing her vision to life.

Coming home to the smell of fresh-baked bread each night made his stomach growl pretty much constantly, but he would usually make a quick dinner, sometimes of the dreaded ramen, and then get out of her way unless she was chatty. So far she hadn't been as chatty, and he knew it wasn't only because her mind was on her new bakery.

She'd pulled back a little as well.

He and Martin ran into each other a few times, but they didn't speak much since the graduate student didn't hang out in the common rooms when he was home, which was rare. And that was just fine. He wasn't here to make friends, even though in truth, he didn't have many real friends except for Chase. Sure, he partied with a lot of people. Heck, he could command the most sought-after invitations in Europe, but he wouldn't call any of those people if he needed to express this thoughts.

By Thursday, Evan had perfected his Paint Prep Mistress and sent his high-tech design and mock prototype to his head of research and development. Chase was blustering about his use of company manpower, but Evan was managing it. He'd hired Chase for his business sense, after all, and they'd always agreed business and R&D were like oil and water when it came to innovation. Evan had to run with the inventions coming to him because he knew they were leading him somewhere. He just wasn't sure of the destination yet.

The only parts of Hot Cross Buns he had left were the bathrooms and the kitchen. He was going to paint the bathrooms first. The kitchen would probably take him a few days since Margie wanted him to paint the concrete floor as well. She was pleased he was so meticulous, but he knew she wished he would work a bit faster. To him, it was more important to do it right.

Once he finished the kitchen, he was going to head out front to give her exterior a new look. She'd chosen to go with a black and violet paint combination that would match the bakery's new sign, which was currently sitting in the middle of the main floor, waiting to be hung.

On Friday as he was leaving for work, she slid him a slice of the freshest rye bread he'd eaten since Berlin and asked if he thought he could handle hanging her sign once he finished painting. Of course, he agreed. He helped her set up a few things in the dining room for the cinnamon roll tasting later that night, and then they were off.

When she dropped him at the bakery that morning, he headed to the local hardware store. Wayne Smith was quickly becoming his handyman chum. For every question he asked, Wayne had an answer, so when Evan asked what kind of screws he'd need to hang Margie's sign, Wayne led him to the screw section in the bowels of the hardware store.

When he returned to the bakery to begin painting the kitchen, he'd barely stepped inside before he heard a knock on the front door. While curious spectators had stopped and peered into the shop before, no one had ever rapped on the glass door before. He swiveled on his heels. Rhett Butler Blaylock and Jane Wilcox were outside. He jumped to his feet and walked over to the door to open it.

"I'm afraid the bakery isn't open yet," he said dryly. In truth, he was surprised they hadn't come to see him sooner.

Jane gave him a look and handed him a long white paper bread bag. "Funny. We thought we'd drop by and give you one of Brasserie Dare's baguettes in case you were homesick."

Now he really knew they had something on their minds. "Thanks," he said, taking the bag. "Good to see you."

"How about you let us in for a spell, Evan?" Rhett said amiably.

"Sure." He stepped back, giving them room to enter, and then closed the door behind them. Nerves were tickling at his belly all of a sudden.

"How's it going?" Rhett asked, hooking his thumbs in the pockets of his cargo shorts.

"Good," he answered easily, setting the bread on his backpack. "Margie's been great, and I've found a new calling in painting."

No one laughed.

"Dare Valley is a wonderful town," he continued, trying to sense their mood. "It's been good...to find a new routine over the last couple of weeks. Don't get me wrong, I hate to lose at poker, but I'm really glad I ended up coming here."

Jane studied him as intently as when she'd sat across from him at that fateful poker table. "We're happy to hear that, Evan. According to Margie, you hang the moon."

He could hear the question a mile away. "Something on your mind?"

Rhett kicked at the plastic on the floor. "We don't think you've gotten fresh with her."

Evan rolled his eyes because the man's voice didn't ring with certainty. "I haven't. I made you a promise, and I'm keeping it. If Margie says I hang the moon, it's because the feeling is mutual. We've become...well...friends in our own way. It won't go any further than that while I'm here."

Of course, he wasn't about to tell them that Margie had become the main feature of his daydreams, alongside a cast of inventions working its way through his subconscious—mostly about painting. Oh, and rainbows made out of paint.

"But you like her," Jane said baldly.

He went for the truth. "What's not to like? She's smart, funny, kind, and beautiful. Let me say again, I'm not coming on to her. Okay?" Crap, they made him feel like a high school kid getting called before the principal. Not that *that* had ever happened to him.

"Okay," Rhett said, nodding in that slow Southern way of his. "We just wanted to make sure."

His gut burned a moment. "Margie trusts me. Why won't you?"

"She doesn't know you, Evan," Jane said, worrying her lip. "When we made this side bet, neither Rhett nor I envisioned you—"

"Living and working with someone you know?" he finished.

"Exactly," she said. "It doesn't sit well, keeping things from her."

He wasn't ready for Margie to know about him,

wasn't ready to see if it would change her reaction to him. "We agreed I would live like a normal person here for a month. I'm doing it, and doing it well, I think. Let's not mess with that. This was your idea..."

"But Margie is going to Paris..." Jane said, casting a glance at Rhett.

"What Jane wants to know is if you're planning to see her there?"

He'd thought of it about a hundred times, of holding her hand as they walked along the Seine at sunset, of kissing her slowly in his favorite park off Pont Neuf Bridge. "Look, I don't know. We haven't talked about it. She did ask me to give her some suggestions about what to do in Paris, not that she'll have a lot of time with her apprenticeship. Did you know she'll have to be at the bakery at two a.m.?" The thought still horrified him. "If she wants to hang out, that's great. As I said, even though we haven't known each other for long, we're friends. Now, will you two stop worrying and let me start painting? I have a job to do." He didn't feel inclined to share any of his feelings with these two.

Jane released a long breath. "Margie says you're being meticulous."

He laughed to ease the tension inside him as much as the tension in the room. "That's code for slow, but this is her dream, so I'm doing the best job I can."

Rhett came over and clapped him on the back. "And we appreciate it. We just...wanted to make sure you understood how special she is."

He did. More than they realized. "I hope I've allayed your concerns."

Jane fidgeted with her hands. "Are you planning to tell her who you are if you see each other in Paris?"

It had been hard to keep quiet about the truth, especially since he kept daydreaming about them being together in his hometown. But part of him enjoyed his current anonymity. Would she change how she reacted toward him when she discovered he was a billionaire? Worse, would he change once he returned back to his life in Paris? He didn't have the answers.

"Like I said, it hasn't come up," he said, walking over to the gallon of paint he'd use on the kitchen. "Now, I really do need to get back to work."

Rhett and Jane shared a look again.

"All right," Rhett said. "We're glad to see you fulfilling your end of the deal. It takes a real man to honor his word, and you did that by coming here."

"But if you want to wrap up the painting you're doing for Margie and go home to Paris, that's okay with us too," Jane said in a soft tone. "In hindsight, this really was a crazy side bet, and you've already lasted two weeks. I didn't expect you to agree to the deal."

He couldn't contain a half smile. "I'm seeing this gamble through to the end," he said, picking up the paint can. "Jane, you were right when you said I was bored and...searching for a purpose. Things have started to become clearer for me here. That alone has made this trip worthwhile."

She smiled, and now he saw the kind woman behind the poker face. "I'm glad, Evan. I...came from money. No one knows better than I do that money can't buy happiness."

Since he was starting to feel like he was caught in some 1960s sitcom, he simply shook his head and reached down to grab one of the remaining paint trays. "Thanks for stopping by and checking on things. Trust me. Everything is in good hands."

They still didn't look completely convinced.

"We'll let you get back to painting," Rhett said. "When you finish working for Margie, Abbie and I could use your help painting the nursery. That is, if you don't have any other jobs lined up."

"I don't," he said, touched the man would extend the offer.

"And Matt and I finally have agreed on paint colors in a few of the rooms in our house now that we've moved in together," Jane added.

"Great." Maybe if he spent more time painting, he would finally achieve the breakthrough he was on the verge of making. "I'll let you know when she's run out of things for me to do."

They said their goodbyes and walked out the door. He closed it behind them and paused for a moment.

It was weird being checked up on and looked after.

Funny thing was that while part of him was annoyed, another part of him kind of liked it.

***

Margie hated how nervous she was about the cinnamon roll tasting. Jill had given her a half day off so she could bake rolls that would be warm from the oven when her guests arrived. She'd already prepared a pan of rolls that would be served room temperature alongside Grandma Kemstead's rolls.

Earlier that morning, Margie's sexy tenant had helped her set out the dishes she wanted to use. Her nerves must have been evident judging from the sweet way Evan had handled her.

Evan was good at handling things, she had discovered. Anything from a paint roller to a lively conversation about science fiction with Martin, who usually couldn't be coerced into saying two words.

She forced her gaze back to the ingredients she'd arranged on the counter. The microwave dinged, signaling the milk was ready. She used the tip of her finger to test the temperature, and finding it warm, took out the bowl and added the melted butter. Once it was well mixed, she whipped in the egg yolks, which would give the bread its beautiful buttery color. The yeast was proofing nicely nearby, bubbling and frothing in a small bowl.

Grandma Kemstead used industrial mixers at the bakery, but she'd told Margie she used a simple hand mixer at home. While Margie had tried that once, she'd settled on using her bread machine. Easier all around.

One of Grandma Kemstead's secrets was to let the dough rise twice. Not all bakers bothered with it, but the older woman had made a zealous defense. Margie had tried it both ways and concluded she was right. It *did* make a difference.

After adding the flour, a dash of salt, and the sugar to the bread machine's Teflon pan, Margie poured the milk mixture and yeast over the dry ingredients. The machine beeped when she activated the dough cycle, then erupted with a few loud swoops as it began to mix. Unfortunately, her bread machine was of the loud variety. She waited to see if she needed to add more flour, and once she was satisfied with the consistency, she closed the lid.

With that done, Margie put together the ingredients that would turn into the gooey caramel sauce. It was a simple mixture of cream, sugar, cinnamon, and corn syrup. Grandma Kemstead said the cinnamon rolls turned out better when she poured the mixture on the risen rolls when the sauce was room temperature.

The pungent and alluring scent of cinnamon hit her nose, and she closed her eyes for a moment. Cinnamon now smelled like success to her. Her success. She dabbed some behind her ears for luck.

Tonight she would find out how close she was to achieving one of her major goals for the bakery. Her guests would each bring something special to the tasting. First, there was Control Group A: the Dare Valley born locals. All of them had been eating the famous Kemstead cinnamon rolls for their entire lives, and Arthur Hale alone had nearly seventy years of experience. Jill would also bring her background in the food and hotel industry in Dare Valley to the table, so to speak, and her husband Brian was an accomplished, traditionally trained chef who could offer a more technical perspective on her pièce de résistance, as the French said.

Then there was Control Group B: Dare Valley newcomers. This group included Chef Terrance Waters from The Grand Mountain Hotel, whom Jill had put her up to asking. She'd also invited his fiancé, Elizabeth Saunders—the teacher of the Latin dance class she loved taking but hadn't found time for lately. Then there was Evan, the late addition. This way there would be an even number in both groups.

A little breathless from thinking about it, she glanced up when the bread machine finished its first kneading cycle and opened the lid. Sure enough, there was a gorgeous ball tucked into the bottom, anchored by the kneading ring. She touched the yellow dough to confirm it was spongy, closed the lid again, and left the kitchen to prepare the dining room for the tasting. Evan had promised to help her clean up after everyone left, to which she'd easily agreed. Being in his company sometimes felt just as magical as baking that first loaf of bread in the morning.

When the bread machine turned on sixty minutes later and started the second knead cycle, Margie already had the table set. She'd chosen to use small dessert plates in a green and gold pattern she'd found at a consignment shop. Chunky blue candles were fitted into crystal candle holders. The silverware sparkled under the light. The water glasses didn't have a single errant drop on their exteriors. The room was warm and inviting, and after she finished checking on the bread—rising for the second time—she took a moment to stretch and think through her plan for the evening. She planned to serve room-temperature cinnamon rolls as well as ones straight out of the oven.

Grandma Kemstead had stopped by a few hours ago to drop off the rolls Margie would serve with her own room-temperature batch for the taste test, but she'd declined to stay for the tasting. With her hands on Margie's shoulders, the older woman said the mantle was now on her. She got a little teary eyed every time she thought about it.

Then she opened a bottle of red wine, inhaling deeply before she poured herself a glass. Out loud, she said, "Here's to me and all my cinnamony awesomeness for following my dreams."

"I'll drink to that," a familiar voice said, causing her to jump and the wine to slosh around in her glass like ocean water in a powerful storm.

"Evan! You startled me." She pressed a hand to her chest. "Now I'm embarrassed. You heard my toast."

His mouth tipped up in that killer smile of his. "Cinnamony awesomeness? That has to be the best toast I have ever heard." He had one hand tucked around his back like he was hiding something, and then he swung around a huge bouquet of flowers and presented them to her with a courtly bow.

"You got me flowers?" she asked, taking the mixed bouquet of pink roses and lime-green hydrangeas from him. No one had gotten her flowers since Howie.

"It's a big day for you," he said simply.

She rose on her toes and kissed his cheek. "Thank you. That's...you're going to make me cry." The heat in her cheeks felt like she'd stuck her face in the oven. "Care to join me for a glass of wine?"

"I'd love to. You deserve to be celebrated."

She set the flowers aside as the flush rose again, but this time, it lodged between her breasts. Suddenly she could imagine him *celebrating* her and how good he would be at it. To veil her gaze, which only wanted to take in the strong lines of his muscular shoulders and chest, she reached into the cabinet for another wine glass and poured him some of the spicy ruby liquid.

When they lifted their glasses in the air, he said, "To Margie's cinnamony awesomeness and all the success she's going to have with Hot Cross Buns."

Hearing his deep voice say the words made her chest tight. In a good way. "Thanks, Evan. I'm really grateful you're here."

He nodded, and they drank in silence for a long moment. The bread machine dinged, signaling the conclusion of the second rising. She opened the lid and liked what she saw. There were small bubbles around the top and sides, and the dough bounced when she touched it.

"One of the things I love about bread is how alive it is."

Evan peered over her shoulder, and she fought a shiver as his subtle scent washed over her. There was pine from his soap with a touch of turpentine from cleaning the rollers and brushes. The fragrance was all man to her nose. Having grown up around wealthy men who wore expensive cologne as a nod to their masculine power, she preferred ones who smelled like they worked for a living. She'd loved the smell of sawdust on Howie, but she had to admit there was something tantalizing about turpentine.

"Of course, it's alive. I think it's cool that yeast is a single-celled organism, and yet its cellular organization is similar to ours."

"I didn't know that." She loved all the little unexpected things he knew. Part of her wanted to step back until his arms were around her. She'd bet he knew how to hold a woman close—but with gentleness. "I think it's cool that with bread, what you want is the carbon dioxide, whereas when you use yeast for wine, you want the alcohol."

"The best substances in nature give off more than one bio product."

Leave it to him to say something like that. "I'm glad you don't think I'm weird."

"Moi? Am I not the inventor of the Paint Prep Mistress?" His chuckle was as dark and gooey as the caramel sauce she stirred with the spoon resting nearby. "We'll overlook the fact that you thought I was weird at the time."

He was still standing close enough to touch her, following her progress. She could step away, but that was the last thing she wanted to do. "You're a bigger man than I am for forgetting that."

"I think Mother Nature would agree," he said, gesturing to his tall frame. "Not that you aren't perfect the way you are. You're a pocket Venus."

Her mouth parted. "Wow! No one has *ever* called me that. It might be the best compliment I've ever had. I love that statue—"

"In the Louvre," he finished.

It was weird, how they read each other's minds. Now that she was one hundred percent sure he found her attractive, her skin buzzed with sensation.

"What about your cinnamony awesomeness?" he quipped. "That's a pretty cool compliment."

But she'd made that one up herself. "True. Okay. You got me there."

She washed her hands and dried them off so she could handle the dough, needing space so she could avoid breaking her own rules and his current celibacy vow. Gently setting it on the floured surface she'd prepared to roll it out, she eyed the clock on the stove. Her guests would arrive in ninety minutes. The timing was perfect.

"Can I watch you assemble them? I have an idea in my head, but..." He gestured to the dough. "I like seeing how things are put together."

"I got that about you," she answered, oddly touched. "Of course you can."

The dough was already calling to her, so she grabbed the rolling pan and dusted it with flour. Working gently, she exerted a downward pressure until the dough started to thin out into the shape of a large rectangle. Her passes over the dough grew more sweeping, and she paused from time to time to dust the rolling pin and the countertop to make sure the dough didn't stick. When she was satisfied that the dough was an even half an inch thick, she stepped away to pop the butter in the microwave.

"Ah, butter," he said with a cute smile on his face. "Anything worth eating must by definition have at least one stick of butter in it. I love the French for how much they worship butter."

The microwave chimed when the cycle came to an end, and she stirred the butter with the tip of her finger. She wanted it melted, but not too hot. "I know. They even have different butter than we do in the States."

"Yeah," he said, squatting down until he was eye level with her rolled out dough. "There's a higher butter-solids-to-water ratio in France."

Again, she had to marvel at his mind. He was a man with a genuine curiosity for life, and it was so downright sexy, she felt like the dough: all laid out before him. She swallowed thickly.

"Where do you learn all this stuff?" she asked.

"I read a lot," he said, but his frame went from relaxed to stiff. "Or I used to. I need to start doing more of it again. Are you basting the bread with all that butter? No wonder it's so delicious."

He clearly didn't want her to ask him any more questions along that line, so she nodded. "Yes, I'm using all of it. Grandma Kemstead doesn't baste. She dumps." Tipping the bowl, she let the butter spill over the dough like a giant yellow flood. "She uses her fingers to spread the butter." It was rather sensual, but Margie couldn't say that to him, not when the atmosphere around them already crackled with electricity.

Once the butter was spread, she picked up the bowl of sugar she'd measured and poured it evenly over the dough. Then she grabbed the industrial-size cinnamon, not caring that her hands were tacky, and shook a healthy stream on top. The sugar was already being absorbed by the butter, and the cinnamon soon turned from rust to dark brown as the butter enveloped it as well.

"That's a masterpiece," Evan said, staring at her doughy canvas. "I can see why you love this so much. It's a layered process filled with what the French would call *la sensualité.*"

Sensuality. So he felt it too. The word hovered between them. His eyes locked with hers, pinning her in place.

"The French are all about *la sensualité*," he said, but this time his voice was deeper, darker.

Places below the countertop turned liquid, and she fought for breath. "And *joie de vivre,*" she burst out. "Don't forget that."

His gaze dropped, releasing her back to herself. She was finally able to inhale.

"I could never forget the joy of life," he said, stepping away to give her room. "What's next?"

Wishing she could shake her body free of the goosebumps shivering up her arms, she took the ends of the dough between her fingers. "Now, you simply roll the dough. Almost like you're making hay bales."

He laughed, and even to her ears, her description sounded lame. She kept going, letting the familiar motions ground her. When she finished rolling all the dough into one long...tunnel—okay she really needed a new metaphor—she pinched the ends and reached for a large knife.

"Now you cut them into rolls," she said and did, slicing the first one about two-and-a-half inches thick.

The buttery mixture oozed out, streaked with the brown flecks of cinnamon. "Then you lay them down on a greased pan so the rolled layers face up."

"Awesome," he said, and her breath caught again at the trace of awe in his voice. He was acting like he was watching her create a masterpiece, and since that's how she felt making bread and other yummy delights, the urge to reach for his hand to strengthen their connection was too strong to ignore.

He stilled when her fingers touched the back of his palm, which was resting on the counter. His blue eyes locked with hers again, and she met them dead on. In them was the same desire she was feeling, along with a touch of surprise. He hadn't expected her touch, and because he hadn't, it only made her want to touch him more.

"Evan...I...thank you for sharing this with me," she said. "Other than Grandma Kemstead, I haven't baked with anyone. It's..."

"Nice to share our passions," he finished for her. "I know. I have a friend who shares mine sort of, but not too many other people get it. Creating can be a lonely process sometimes."

She saw it then, with her eyes on his, unflinching. There was a deep well of loneliness inside him. That's what had led him to Dare Valley. She allowed herself to give him a spontaneous hug and then jumped back, not trusting herself. He still lived in her house, and...and... Things just hadn't worked out with Howie. He'd been an artistic type and loner too.

She knew she was making excuses.

He cleared his throat and picked up his wine glass, then took a healthy sip as he watched her finish cutting the rolls and laying them in the pan. Unable to meet his eyes now, she grabbed a towel and covered them.

"Now, we let the yeast do its job," she said, placing the rolls in a sunny spot in the kitchen so they could expand and rise.

"Thanks for showing me," he said in a deeper voice than usual. "It's an honor to watch a master at work. I'm...ah...going to take a shower before your guests arrive."

"Okay," she said, and she dared a glance at him again.

His eyes met hers one last time before he stepped out of the kitchen. She sipped her wine, thinking about the water trickling down the hard lines of his body. Deep in her belly, she wanted to join him, but she breathed through the longing until it subsided. She hoped he would come back down and keep her company after his shower, but the water shut off. A few minutes passed, and he still didn't come.

The rolls rose under the towel as the wall clock ticked off the time. When they were ready, she warmed the oven to three hundred seventy-five, struggling with herself and all the new emotions Evan had awoken in her. Finally, she walked to the base of the stairs, gripping the railing.

"Evan?" she called out.

His door opened, and he came to the top of the stairs. "Hey."

"Hey," she said like they hadn't just gotten all hot and bothered in the kitchen. "I'm about ready to finish the rolls and pop them into the oven. Do you want to see the final step?"

As he came down the stairs, she saw his hair was still damp from his shower and curlier than when it was dry. It was rather sexy, and so was the pine scent of his soap that flooded her senses as he approached her.

"Sure thing."

She fought a huge smile. "Great. Follow me."

Back in the kitchen, she bumped the bowl she reached for, spilling a little cream on the counter. "This is the sauce," she said, reaching for a paper towel to swipe up the mess. She stirred the mixture until the cream was fully blended with the corn syrup and cinnamon.

"Sometimes, Grandma Kemstead adds some melted butter to this if she has any left over," she told him as she poured the uncooked mixture evenly over the top of the rolls.

The mixture started to seep into the layers of bread, collecting at the edges. She walked over to the preheated oven and slid the pan inside. After setting the timer, she turned to him. "Now, you just let the heat do its thing. In about twenty-five to thirty minutes, we'll have fresh cinnamon rolls right out of the oven."

"Incredible. Everyone is going to love them." He wasn't meeting her eyes now either, she noticed. Had he realized they were walking a dangerous line?

The clock showed her guests were due to arrive in fifteen minutes. "Would you like to have some more wine?"

He tugged on his Rebel T-shirt, which he'd laundered with the rest of his clothes last night. "Margie. I...if I wasn't living here and...on this celibate kick, I'd..."

When he didn't finish the sentence, she gulped and said, "I know. It's probably best for us to talk about it. It's been building between us since you first arrived. And you're going to be here for a few more weeks. We need to be...restrained." At least until she was in Paris when they weren't living together. Okay, she'd already decided she was going to see him in Paris. With no constraints between them.

Something dark came and went in his eyes. "It was the Paint Prep Mistress, right? That's what made you want me."

Her chest was almost too tight to laugh, but she did anyway. It seemed the only safe emotion in the moment. "Actually, it was seeing you rig up that old adding machine like MacGyver. He was kinda hot back in the day."

"He was, at that," Evan agreed, walking to the corner of the kitchen. He paused in the doorway. "I'd like to say it was your cinnamon rolls, but I can't. From the moment I opened the door and saw you standing there like a sexy pocket Venus fallen from Mount Olympus, I've wanted you. But over the past couple of weeks, I've seen so much kindness and bravery from you, it's made me a complete goner."

"I'm coming to Paris," she found herself saying out loud.

The intensity in his gaze was magnetic. "I know."

"I don't usually..." she found herself saying, picking up the towel she'd covered the bread with so her hands could hold something.

"I know you don't." His voice was growing more mesmerizing with each word.

"And I won't be staying long," she said in a quiet voice. "I don't want either of us to get hurt."

His mouth tipped up. "Then it's good I'm celibate now, and you don't date your tenants. We both have time to think about it."

She nodded her head because she couldn't bring herself to tell him that she agreed.

"Do you need any help setting things up last minute?" he asked.

"No, I have everything covered."

"Great," he said. "Call me when they arrive."

He took a few steps to the door before spinning around and striding toward her. Purpose filled his movements, and she found her mouth going dry at the thought—the hope—that he was going to throw caution to the wind and kiss her senseless like they both wanted.

But he only laid his hand on her bare arm and stared into her soul. "I'm really grateful I'm here with you too," he said, echoing her earlier words after their toast.

Then, he retraced his steps and left the kitchen.

With the scent of cinnamon and bread baking around her, all she could do was lean against the counter with her hand on her heart, wondering what would happen in Paris—and eager to find out.

CHAPTER 5

Evan had been to the finest wine tastings the world over, but he was more excited about Margie's cinnamon roll tasting than he'd been about any of them. He'd changed into Evan Murray's best clothes after their last exchange—jeans and a black T-shirt. As he came down the stairs, he realized why he'd done it. He wanted to look his best for her. Tonight was going to be special.

It was a good thing he'd called out their mutual attraction in the kitchen. He wasn't sure he could have continued to ignore the growing intensity between them, and after overhearing her sweet toast and sharing it with her, he'd seen the vulnerability lying underneath the surface of her confidence and determination. He remembered those feelings all too well—they were inescapable when you risked everything for your dreams.

His first big invention was the INV-333. He'd known down to his bones that it would change the defense landscape. Still, he'd feared sharing it with the world because it was his baby, his own special creation, and he was afraid someone might not appreciate how special it was. It had happened many times before, after all. Few people saw the world the way he did. In the beginning, it had made him a nerd. With Chase's backing and friendship, he'd come to believe the way he saw the world made him unique.

And though the successes he'd experienced over the past years had been staggering, he still felt that same vulnerability, particularly in the months prior to this trip to Dare Valley. With success came the fear of future failure.

When he reached the doorway of the kitchen, he halted and allowed Margie's beauty to steal over him. She was folding the napkins so precisely his chest hurt from watching it. She wanted this so badly. The approval. The confirmation that she'd gotten Kemstead's age-old recipe right and could make a go of it as a small business owner.

She'd changed out of her casual baking clothes and now wore a simple sleeveless cotton black dress that hugged her curves like the warm caramel sauce hugged the cinnamon rolls cooling on wax paper on the counter. Her sable hair was tied back in a simple ponytail, and somewhere in the midst of prepping, she'd paused to put on some red lipstick and a touch of mascara with some smoky shadow or liner in the corners to make her eyes pop.

"You look wonderful," he said, both because it was true and because she needed to hear it.

"Oh," she said, dropping one of the half-creased napkins on the counter. "I didn't see you. How long have you been standing there?"

"Not long," he said, stepping into the kitchen and holding out his arms. "I...ah decided to change. I didn't know what one wore to a cinnamon roll tasting."

She laughed, long and loud and with such gusto, she threw her head back.

His heart exploded at the sight.

"I'm laughing because I was actually wondering the

same thing. I...ran upstairs after you...ah...I put the rolls in the oven to look more presentable."

Could she be any more adorable in all her nerves?

Then she ran her gaze over him, leaving lust in her path. "I think you look great."

He pointed to his black T-shirt. "Apparently, you and I got the same memo." And suddenly it felt intimate that they were both wearing black—as if their minds were so in tune they'd reached for the same frequency. Black: the color that absorbed all the wavelengths of light and transformed it into heat.

Like the heat exploding between them.

"Seems like we did," she said as the doorbell rang. "Come on. Let's see who's here."

When she opened the door, he rocked on his heels as the most adorable twin girls ran inside. Well, ran was an exaggeration. They wobbled with incredible speed and balance, somehow defying gravity.

"Whee!" one of the girls cried and plowed straight into Margie's leg, making her laugh.

The other toddler headed straight toward him, and for a moment, he wasn't sure what to do. He'd never spent much time around kids. The people in his circle who had children always left them with their nannies.

Her hair was bright red with small soft curls, and she latched on to his leg and looked up at him with a drooling smile. *"Hi."*

He found himself grinning. "Hi."

A tall redhead snatched her away, making the little girl fuss. "Sorry, we usually introduce ourselves before we start mauling someone and drowning them in drool. I'm Jill Hale McConnell, but I mostly go by Jill Hale since that's how everyone around here knows me. You must be Evan." Her eyes twinkled. "I've been hearing a lot about you. Sounds like you're pretty handy."

Evan liked her immediately. Especially the saucy innuendo she was firing out like microwaves—the form of electronic radiation, not the appliance. "That's right. I've heard a lot about you from Margie. Sounds like *you* have skills with coffee beans."

She planted the toddler on her hip, striking a pose. "Among other things."

A dark-haired man approached and extended his hand. "I'm Brian McConnell. Please ignore my wife. She flirts with everyone, and by everyone, I'm including Old Man Beviens who's nearing a hundred and has ear hair."

Jill socked Brian in the arm. "Oh, yuck. I have higher standards than that."

The guy leaned in and gave his wife a gentle kiss. "Red, I hope you'll still want me when I sprout ear hair."

"*Please*. I'll shave it off so I won't barf. Just like I do with Grandpa's."

"What's this?" an older man said, tapping his cane on the hardwood floor as Margie led him inside, one of the twins still attached to her leg. "Don't be talking about the perils of getting old. You don't know shit from Shinola."

"Grandpa! The girls."

"That phrase is as old as dirt. Just like me. They'll live." The man thrust out his hand. "Arthur Hale. Good to meet you."

"Evan," he answered. After introducing himself to a few people around town, he'd decided only to use his alias when he had no choice. He felt much less guilty that way.

The older man peered closer. "Evan what? You look a little familiar to me."

He hoped not. From his research on the town, he knew Arthur Hale was a celebrated journalist, and the last thing he needed was for the older man to discover who he was. Not when Margie didn't know yet.

"Murray. I'm not from these parts, so I'm sure we've never met."

His eyes narrowed as he pushed his rimless glasses

up his nose. "No, we haven't met. It will come to me. It always does."

Evan fought the urge to gulp. Then he *did* gulp when Rhett Butler Blaylock's other former poker babe, Elizabeth Saunders, walked in the room on the arm of the famous celebrity Chef T. He'd known Elizabeth lived in Dare Valley. He just hadn't realized she was coming to Margie's cinnamon roll tasting. She'd recognize him for sure, but if she and Jane were still as close as they'd once been, maybe she already knew about the side bet.

His breath arrested in his lungs when their eyes met. He didn't break Elizabeth's gaze as Margie led the couple over to meet him. Like Jane, she'd forsaken her former poker babe clothes and duties, but she was still Rhett's publicist and scout. He waited for her to out him.

"Evan, I'd like you to meet Chef T and Elizabeth Saunders," Margie said.

He shook Chef T's hand and then turned to Elizabeth, his gut quivering.

"Evan," Elizabeth said, shaking his hand hard enough to crack a knuckle. "It's good to meet you."

So she knew and disapproved, but she wasn't going to spill the beans. He exhaled the trapped air in his chest.

"Elizabeth," he forced himself to say. "Would you be willing to help me pour some wine for folks while Margie helps everyone settle into the tasting room?"

"Sure," she said way too brightly.

"You're an angel," Margie said, squeezing his bicep, and if he hadn't been quaking in his boots—figuratively—he would have enjoyed the ping down his arm.

When he and Elizabeth reached the kitchen, he turned to her. "I'm here because Jane and Rhett—"

"I know. When I told them about the cinnamon roll tasting, they felt they had to tell me why you were here so I wouldn't spill the beans the minute I saw you." She crossed her arms, all business.

"I appreciate that."

Shaking her head, she went over and started pouring out glasses of wine. Margie had decided to go with a light white wine for the guests because it wouldn't compete with the cinnamon roll.

"I don't like this, Evan. Not one bit. It doesn't feel honest." She picked up three glasses. "Grab the rest."

"I don't like it either," he said, "but Rhett and Jane are the ones who set the terms. I'm holding up my end of the bargain."

She blew out a breath. "Are you, Mr. Celibate?"

"Never, never, never call me Mr. Celibate again." His ears grew hot.

Walking to the doorway, she turned. "If you hurt Margie, I'll make sure celibacy is no longer a choice for you. It'll be your *only* option."

Fighting the urge to put his hands over the front of his jeans, he took a deep breath and then picked up the remaining glasses and joined everyone in the dining room.

The Hale family was sitting on the right side of the table. Elizabeth sat beside Chef T on the left once she finished passing out the drinks. Margie told him to sit at the head of the table across from her. Jill and Brian held the twins on their laps, and he was pretty impressed by their ability to drink the wine without spilling it when the girls reached for the glasses.

Suddenly, one of the girls broke out and said, "Whee!" She had impressive pipes for one so little.

"Oh yeah, Violet!" Jill said, patting her back. "We can show everyone the new song."

These girls had a special talent? Evan sat on the edge of his seat, eager to listen to their performance.

Brian nestled the other girl against this chest. "Ready, Mia?"

Jill gave an impressive, *Mmmm,* to signal the start of the overture. Evan waited to be blown away.

"Whee!" Violet squealed out for all she was worth.

Brian picked up a spoon and pointed it at Mia. "Go on, honey."

She patty-caked her hands together. "Burp!"

Jill pointed to Violet. "Okay, now you."

The girl gave another, "Whee!"

Followed by her sister yelling, "Burp!"

Jill made figure eights in the air like a conductor. "All together now."

He met Margie's gaze, and both of them fought the urge to laugh.

"Whee!"

"Burp!"

"Whee!"

"Burp!"

The Whee-Burp chorus continued. Evan finally gave in to a chuckle since everyone else had started laughing. So, he wasn't going to be treated to a baby rendition of "Madame Butterfly." But it was cute.

And so it went, the adults grinning and laughing, and the girls giving their drooling version of a song Evan expected would never be recorded to fame and glory.

When it finished, Arthur Hale had a soft smile on his face. "Well, at least their pitch is perfect. Can't say much about their lyrics though."

Jill turned and made a face at him since he was sitting on her right side. "They're not even two years old, Grandpa. I think they're doing great."

"They are pretty sweet," Arthur said. "Margie, honey, let's try your rolls. I almost up and died when I walked into your house because it smelled so good."

Margie stood and stooped to kiss his cheek. "No up and dying on my watch. I'll grab the room-temperature rolls first, which will be compared to the originals, made by Grandma Kemstead herself. The other rolls might still be too hot. That caramel sauce can burn the roof of your mouth when they come straight out of the oven."

"I can't wait to try them," Chef T said, putting his arm around Elizabeth.

Margie brought out two plates of cinnamon rolls, and the scent alone was enough to make Evan salivate. When he received his plate with two tasting samples, he took a moment to clear his head before taking the first bite. The caramel sauce coating the pastry hit his tongue like a freight train, but the soft bread cushioned the impact. He moaned as cinnamon and butter danced on his taste buds in pure abandon.

"The right one has a touch more cinnamon than the left." Chef T chewed each sample thoughtfully as everyone watched and listened. "But honestly, Margie, both of them are delicious. I don't think it matters who baked which one. And no one but a highly trained chef could detect the extra cinnamon."

"Well, I'm not a highly trained chef," Arthur said, holding up the remaining bite of one of his tasting samples, "but this one is Kemstead's."

Margie sat at the end of the table and tucked her hands out of sight. "What does everyone else think?" There was a Mona Lisa smile on her face as she asked the question.

Elizabeth shrugged playfully. "I can't tell the difference. Honestly, Margie. They're both incredible."

"Brian?" she asked.

"I feel like the one on the right has a touch more butter, but it's so slight a difference, I would be hard-pressed to say that it changes the taste for me. I couldn't guess which one's which, but my guess would be that the Kemstead's one has a touch more butter. Either way, they're fantastic, Margie. I'm so happy you're continuing the tradition."

"Jill?" Margie asked the woman, who was feeding

thimble-size bites to the two girls as they bounced up and down in glee.

"I can't tell which one's which," Jill said with a laugh. "Honestly. I just want more."

"What about you, Evan?" she asked softly, so softly that Elizabeth paused in taking another bite of her sample and gave him a pointed glance.

He didn't care. At the moment, he only had eyes for one person. "I'm no expert on cinnamon rolls, but I live in a country where people revere bread. You could open up your shop in Paris and sell these, and you'd be the hottest bakery in town."

"Hear, hear!" Brian said, rapping on the table. "Margie, after tasting these, I'm convinced you were meant to do this. I can't wait for you to come back from your apprenticeship in Paris. Hot Cross Buns is going to be awesome, and my restaurant is going to be supplied with the best baguettes and croissants in town."

"Me too!" Jill said, pulling Violet back when she lurched for the plate of cinnamon rolls like a pirate swinging onto a ship to capture its booty. "Don't Soy With Me is going to love selling your croissants. Brian can have the baguettes. It's not our thing. But you know we'll use your bread for our sandwiches."

What a coup it was for her to have supply arrangements with two successful Dare Valley businesses before she even opened. Evan was so happy for her, and he hoped Chef T would consider buying her bread for his restaurant at the hotel.

A sheen of tears appeared in Margie's eyes. "Thanks, Jill. Brian. Just...thanks."

Jill sniffed. "No, don't look at me like that. I'm going to start bawling. I am so freaking proud of you, girl. I mean...crap. Bri, can you take Violet for a sec? I really need to hug Margie."

She jogged over to Margie, who rose to her feet. The two women embraced, and because Margie was facing him, he watched a tear slide down her cheek before Jill started jumping up and down like the DJ in a club had just changed the music to a party classic.

"You're living your dream," Jill cried, and her exuberance made Evan smile.

After they separated, Margie left to prepare the warm cinnamon rolls on a plate.

"I realize this isn't the perfect control group," she said when she returned and laid the plate in the center of the table, "but I couldn't ask Grandma Kemstead to make a second batch of rolls that would be hot out of the oven right before you arrived. She's already done so much for me. These rolls are mine. I'll be serving hot ones in the morning to the early birds."

Jill grabbed a whole roll and stuffed a good portion in her mouth, chewing and moaning in a way that could only be described as endearing. After spending so much time around models who watched every ounce they ate, it was refreshing to see someone go to town on bread.

"Oh. My. Gosh." Jill swallowed and let her eyes roll back in her head.

"They're good, right?" Margie asked, and it gave Evan a pinch in his chest to see that vulnerability again.

"They're ridiculous!" Jill cried. "Bri, take a bite of these and tell Margie."

The poor guy barely had time to blink before Jill shoved the roll into his mouth. "Oh, yes," he said after taking a bite. "Margie, Jill's right. They're incredible. I might have to become one of your early birds."

Everyone else ate the rolls and gave her the praise she so needed to hear.

Margie finally pressed her hands to her cheeks. "It's really going to be okay, isn't it?"

Evan's heart melted, and if Jill hadn't pushed back from her chair again and pulled Margie into another bear hug, he would have. Everyone savored the remaining warm rolls with the twins demanding more bites from their mom and dad.

"Okay," Arthur said when he finished his roll. "Now, tell me I'm right. That one on the right was Kemstead's, wasn't it?"

Evan knew the answer before Margie responded. Her soft smile had been clue enough.

"I'm sorry, Mr. Hale, but that one was mine." She clapped her hands in delight, and the little girls mirrored her.

"Fooled you, old man," Jill said with a laugh. "And that so rarely happens, I feel the need to dance to 'Dancing Queen.' Elizabeth, let's show these guys what we've got. Margie, get the music on."

Chef T groaned suddenly. "I know what moves you have, Jill," the chef said. "And I seriously don't need to be reminded. Especially not at a cinnamon roll tasting."

"You can't stop the music." Jill put her arm around Margie. "Let's get this party started. Elizabeth. Grab your man."

Chef T groaned again as the pretty blond pulled him out of his seat.

"I'm going to head home," Arthur said, rising from his chair. "ABBA was too modern for me in the '70s, and I don't expect that's changed much. Evan, why don't you walk me out?"

His heart stopped beating in his chest, but somehow he managed to rise from his chair. "Of course."

Everyone clustered around Arthur to bid him farewell. It was clear how much everyone esteemed the older man. Even Elizabeth and Chef T seemed amused by his crusty charm. The little girls were the last to say goodbye, giving him sloppy kisses.

When Evan escorted him outside, he made sure to close the front door. They walked down the sidewalk. A sickle moon hung in a mostly clear sky. The quiet reminded him for a moment of Paris streets after midnight when most Parisians had gone home after enjoying a fine meal and a bottle of wine.

"Where is your car, sir?" Evan asked when they reached the curb.

"In good time, son," Arthur said, facing him under the lamp light. "Or should I call you Evan Michaels?"

He wanted to curse. "You are way too canny, Mr. Hale."

"Arthur, please," he said. "Do you want to tell me why you're renting out a room from Margie under an assumed name and painting her new store for peanuts?"

At least he could go with the truth. Elizabeth—and presumably—Chef T already knew who he was. Arthur Hale might as well know too. "I lost a side bet to Jane Wilcox in a poker game in Paris with Rhett Butler Blaylock." He told him an abbreviated version of the events. "Our agreement was that no one was supposed to know."

"Even our sweet Margie?" Arthur asked, rubbing his chin.

"Especially her," Evan replied and felt the guilt twine tighter around his heart.

"I see the way she looks at you. You're known as quite the playboy, if I recall."

"As a journalist, it won't surprise you to learn much of that is hyperbole." He stuffed his hands in his pockets. "But if it makes you sleep better, Rhett stipulated that I have to be celibate the whole time I'm here."

The man barked out a laugh, and then another, until he was actually wheezing from laughing. "Celibate! That's a good one. Rhett has one devious mind."

"He does indeed," Evan agreed. "Now, are you pacified for the moment?"

Arthur tapped his cane on the sidewalk. "Evan, I'm a family man first, and a newspaper man second. If there's an infamous billionaire secretly living in Dare Valley in some real-life adaption of *The Prince and the*

Pauper, I sure as hell want to know more. At least tell me what you invented that earned you all these billions. No one has ever been able to find out anything more than that you make highly sensitive defense equipment for NATO governments."

"Exactly. That equipment falls under the category of 'that which cannot be named.'"

The Lord Voldemort joke was an old one between him and Chase.

"Sorry, Arthur, you know I can't give away top-secret information."

The older man shrugged. "I had to try. In the meantime, you watch your Ps and Qs with Margie. She's like family to Jill, which means she's family to me."

He wondered how a man nearing eighty would follow through on that threat, but he refrained from asking. "She's a special woman who's been...kind to me." Yes, that was right, but it didn't touch on all the other things she'd made him feel again. Self-worth. Trust. Fun.

"I'm glad you can see that about her," Arthur said. "Makes me think your head isn't as far up your butt as most people seem to think."

"I like that you don't pull any punches, Arthur."

"When you get to be my age, son, you couldn't pull a punch if you bothered. I'll head out now. And I can find my car just fine. My request was only a ruse to get you out here."

"I know," Evan said, extending his hand to the man. "If we don't meet again before I leave, it was good to meet you, sir."

Arthur's clasp was strong—ageless. "You too, son. I hope you find whatever it is you're looking for...because my guess is that you must have been looking pretty hard to have accepted a side bet like this one."

When Evan went inside after watching Arthur drive away, his eyes immediately found Margie. She was dancing with a grinning, drooling Violet in her arms. He distantly noticed that the others were dancing too, and that Jill was really shaking her stuff with Mia, but his focus was entirely on his Pocket Venus.

Seeing Evan, Margie handed the baby to Brian and bounded over to him in one long bounce, like her shoes had springs on the soles. She was glowing from all the praise that had stoked her inner fire.

His tongue grew thick in his mouth when she reached him. "You're..." he said, unable to get out the words inside him.

She held out her hands. "Come dance with me."

He clasped those strong hands he'd seen make a masterpiece earlier out of live organisms, flour, sugar, and cinnamon, and let her lead him into the center of the party.

CHAPTER 6

Margie followed the blurry taillights of Evan's car through Denver's rainy streets. Her heart was swollen with the knowledge that he was leaving for Paris in only a few hours. These last two weeks with him had been so precious to her. After he'd finished helping her with her main tasks at Hot Cross Buns, he'd spent his days painting for people in her circle. First with Rhett, and then with Jane, and finally with Arthur at the newspaper.

And they'd spent almost every night together, either enjoying a night in with dinner and a movie, or hiking in the waning light in the mountains surrounding Dare Valley.

But the last time they'd really touched was their dance the night of her cinnamon roll tasting.

Everything inside her wanted him. She was like a wave waiting to crest onto the beach.

Paris would be the beach. She already knew she would give herself to him. Even though their lives were in two faraway places. Even though she knew that if she was already feeling bereft, she would be inconsolable when she had to leave him for good.

Evan pulled into the car rental place, and she turned after him. After opening his car door, he jogged over to her, rain pelting his face. She rolled her window down, feeling the mist against her skin.

"I'll turn the car in and be right back. Why don't you park over there and wait for me?"

She was smiling as he dashed off through the rain to the front door. Pretty soon, he was jogging back, and when he opened the passenger door and slid in smelling of rain and pine and earth, she wanted to press herself against him and take his mouth in all the heated kisses she'd imagined these last weeks.

But she respected his celibacy thing, even though they hadn't talked about it any more. Hopefully it would be over when she came to Paris. She *prayed* it would be over when she came to Paris.

He brushed the rain back from his hair. "Just so you know. I'm picking you up at Charles de Gaulle when you land in Paris. No arguments."

Her lips curved. "So we *are* going to see each other in Paris."

Her heart beat in rapid bursts of joy. They hadn't talked about that either. For some reason, seeing each other again had been implied even though they hadn't worked out any details. It was almost like he'd been letting her make up her mind about them. Sure, he'd told her about some of his favorite places to visit and how to order a carafe of water like the locals instead of paying for bottled natural or eau de gas—sparkling water—but little else.

He cleared his throat. "I can just pick you up at the airport if that's what you want. It's a haul from CDG, and I don't want you to have to figure out how to take public transportation into the city when you're jet-lagged."

She smiled as the windshield wipers swished back and forth. "Is that the only reason you're picking me up?"

"Do you really want to get into this now?" he asked with a sigh.

She turned onto I-70 and increased her speed, the rain pinging on the car's roof more audibly now. "We've been letting it hover between us these last weeks. I want to see you again, Evan."

He reached for her slowly. She could see his hand coming out of the corner of her eye. Then it rested on her thigh, close to her knee. His hand was warm and slightly damp, and it felt *right*. She wanted to take it and place it on her breast, but it wasn't the time. Besides, she was driving.

"I want to see you too," he said, but there was something in his voice, and she knew he was holding himself back when he removed his hand.

She decided to put it out there. Sometimes their connection had felt so strong it was like a tangible living force. But at those moments he would always step away and look off in the distance. She could sense him struggling with himself, though she wasn't sure why.

"What's the matter? All of a sudden you're somewhere else." Then a horrifying thought struck her. "Is there someone else in Paris?"

"No," he immediately said and touched her thigh again, but briefly this time, like he still didn't feel he had permission to touch her.

"Then why are you holding back?" she asked, and turned her head briefly away from the interstate to look at him.

There was a pinch between his brows and a tightness around his mouth.

"Evan," she said softly. "Talk to me."

***

Like the rain washing away all the grime outside,

Evan felt like Margie's words were stripping him bare. Every day of their time together since the cinnamon roll tasting had been magical. His ability to invent had returned to him, and even though he'd only come up with painting tools while living in Dare Valley, they were leading him to something more. He could feel it.

Then there was Margie. She glowed like a nebula in the Milky Way, filled with radiant color and starlight. And even though he'd barely touched her, he'd fallen for her. And his feelings were so deep and rich and exciting.

But she didn't know who he was.

Except she did. She knew who he was *inside*, and she liked him. Still, the lies he'd told stood between them, and for two weeks, he'd been terrified of how she'd react to the truth.

Last night had been a long sleepless stretch of time, and all he'd done was brood. He'd decided to tell her who he was in Paris if she wanted to see him again. But now he wasn't sure he should wait.

The exit sign for Denver International Airport loomed, and he could feel the clock ticking. He *had* to tell her before he left. She deserved the truth.

"Margie," he said, wishing he could take her hand. "This past month has been one of the happiest of my life."

Her hand slid from the steering wheel to his thigh this time, and everything in him surged with joy at her touch. God, he wanted her, craved her.

"Mine too." She put her blinker on and took the exit lane.

Since the roads were slick, he placed her hand back on the steering wheel. "Not that you're not a good driver…"

The signs for departures appeared, and he felt the tightness in his chest amplify. "I'm on Air France."

God, he just had to say the words, but the crushing fear was back. What if she changed her mind?

"Okay," she said and became engrossed in following the labyrinth of lanes leading to the main terminal.

When she navigated the car to the second innermost lane to find an empty space amidst the sea of parked cars, he knew his time was up. He turned in his seat.

"Margie," he said, taking her hand. "There's something—"

A car horn beeped loudly, making her look to the left. Evan watched as a white Lotus Elise cut her off and raced into the spot she'd been angling into. Margie had to slam on her brakes not to hit him.

"Asshole!" she cried out and honked her own horn. "Oh, I *hate* rich people. They think they're entitled to everything."

The vehemence in her voice rooted him in his seat. Evan felt the words he'd been about to speak shrivel in his mouth. She hated rich people?

As if he were watching a bad movie, Evan watched the Lotus' car door open. A slick-looking young guy rose out of the low seat in an Armani suit, popping open a black umbrella before he got out of the car. He walked around to the passenger side and helped out a gorgeous blonde dripping with diamonds and Donna Karan. On another day, in another place, Evan *had been* that guy.

As Margie angled her car by the Lotus, she gave the couple the middle finger.

"Not all rich people are bad," he made himself say, but he could hear the rasp in his voice through the buzzing in his ears.

"All the ones I ever knew were," she said, radiating with anger. "I grew up with them."

She had? His belly twisted. He hadn't known that, but then again, they hadn't talked much about their pasts. He hadn't wanted her to ask too many questions he couldn't answer.

Her breath gusted out as she crawled through the line of cars until another vacant spot opened for her to park.

"Well, that sucked," she said. "It reminded me of all the jerks I knew when I was a kid. The ones with the flashy cars who steamrolled over everyone around them to get what they wanted. Okay, I'm shaking it off."

"You grew up wealthy?" he asked as she parked the car.

Her eyes were a bit wild when she turned her head to face him. "Yes. Another life. One I am so glad is over. I never want to be a part of that shallow crowd ever again."

His heart and all his good intentions turned to ash in his chest. She'd never accept him as a billionaire. He knew it like he'd known his first invention would make him rich and famous.

"Maybe we shouldn't meet while you're in Paris," he made himself say. "You're going to have crazy hours. I don't want to distract you."

She studied him for a moment, then undid her seatbelt and turned sideways in her seat. "You're a good distraction, and you're not backing out of your offer to pick me up at the airport now."

He could send a car and have it take her wherever she needed to go. He wouldn't have to see her or tell her the truth. He could have the driver say it was a gift from a friend of his.

Her hands on his beard brought him back to the present moment. When he looked into her green eyes, everything else fell away. His heart rose from the ashes like a phoenix, resurrected by the power of his feelings for her.

"Don't back away from me now," she whispered. "Not after everything."

He reached up and laid his hands over hers. "Okay. I'll be there."

The corner of her mouth tipped up. "Good. And will you be past the whole celibacy thing by the time I arrive?"

"That was only in Dare Valley," he responded, touching the backs of her hands, familiarizing himself with the strength that she used to create bread everyday with such passion—a passion he wanted her hands to release in him.

"We're not in Dare Valley right now," she said, the delicate line of her right eyebrow arching.

Lust poured into his system. "We aren't, are we?"

"Why don't you kiss me goodbye?" she asked, her voice lush with desire and invitation.

Even though he knew kissing her would only make him fall harder, he turned his head so he could touch his lips to her warm palm. "Why don't I?"

She moved toward him like a sensuous wave of water, and he let her cover him. Her lips were cool, almost as though kissed by rain, but her mouth was hot once she opened it to him. After so many weeks, there was no pretense between them. Perhaps he could kiss her softly and sweetly in Paris, on one of the magical bridges, but not now.

His tongue plunged into her mouth. She half crawled into his lap, her hands still on his face, almost as if she couldn't bear to let him go.

A hard rapping sound on the window jerked them apart. When he looked over, a man from airport security was leaning against the window, eye level with them.

"Get moving," he shouted through the rain.

Margie slid off his thighs and let her hands trail away from his face slowly. "Leave it to the airport police to ruin a romantic moment."

He grabbed her hand and kissed it again. "We'll have more romantic moments in Paris. I promise."

She smiled, a mysterious smile that made him think of his nickname for her. Oh, how he would miss his Pocket Venus. "I'm holding you to that."

Her car door opened, and he followed her out to the

trunk to heft out his suitcase. When he set it on the ground, he turned to face her in the rain.

"Margie," he said, taking both her hands. "Be sure. About us. When you come to Paris... If you change your mind—"

"I won't," she said, rising on her tiptoes to give him a kiss on the cheek. "Now, you'd better go. That airport guy is giving me dagger looks for parking this long."

He grabbed his suitcase. "Margie—"

"I'll see you in two weeks," she said, interrupting what he might have said. "I'll be counting down the time until we're together again."

She waved and ran back to the car, her sable hair a darker black now that it was wet.

He waved as she drove off and then stood standing in the rain.

He should have told her the truth.

But now that he knew how she felt about rich people, the die had been cast.

He was going to have to keep his billionaire status secret for a little while longer.

THE BILLIONAIRE'S SECRET

To Hem and Fitzie and all my writing spirits.

And to my divine helpers for opening up the magic of Paris to me all over again.

CHAPTER 1

Paris, France

Few cities had captured Margie Lancaster's imagination like Paris had.

The weeks she would spend in the City of Love stretched before her like a gift waiting to be opened. She had finished most of the preparations for her new bakery in Dare Valley, so there was nothing to impede her enjoyment of her ten-day baking apprenticeship. While she was away, her contractor would install the new glass display cases she'd ordered, and her manager would oversee the shipments of the new tables and chairs. Hot Cross Buns would be ready to open shortly after she returned. This was her time to forget about home for a while.

And soon she would see Evan Murray again. Her heart skittered with anticipation. Back in Dare Valley, Evan had been her tenant and her painter/handyman, but now that he'd returned to his apartment in Paris and she was here for her apprenticeship, nothing stood in the way of them being together. Romantically.

Evan had come to Dare Valley for inspiration, to

reset his buttons, and to decide what his next chapter would be. Though she hadn't expected it or asked for it, meeting him had changed her life too. It wasn't easy for her to let people in, but with him, it had felt natural from the beginning.

She rushed into one of the ladies' bathrooms at Charles de Gaulle Airport to tidy up her hair and makeup after the twelve-hour journey. While she wasn't vain per se, Evan was picking her up, and she hadn't seen him in two weeks.

After applying a few dabs of fresh powder and a touch of lipstick, she navigated the twists and turns of the airport—Customs, baggage claim, and then finally the exit.

She spotted Evan the moment she walked through the doors. Her rapidly beating heart seemed to burst at the sight of him. His sandy blond hair was less curly than she remembered it, but his lakewater blue eyes were familiar and warm. He gave her a rakish smile, the effect enhanced by his sexy beard. He wore a simple outfit of jeans and a white T-shirt, but his clothes seemed different somehow, more tailored. Perhaps it was just the romance of Paris. In his hands, he held a bouquet of red-tipped pink roses. When she arrived in front of him with her wheeled suitcase, she felt like she'd melt into a puddle at his feet.

"Hi," he said in that deep sexy voice she'd missed so much since they'd said goodbye.

"Hi," she returned with a grin and then leaned in to kiss his cheek.

His free hand curved around her waist, and she breathed in deep. He was wearing some wickedly spicy cologne, and she allowed herself to rest her head against his muscular chest for a moment.

"I know it was only fourteen days, but I missed you," she whispered. And she had, in little ways that kept surprising her. Every time she pulled something out of the oven, she remembered how he'd smile and hum to himself while sampling her creations, and when she turned on the TV at night to relax, she'd remember all the cooking shows they used to watch together. Most of all, she found herself missing the way he'd explain his oddball ideas to her—and how his face would light up with the happiness of sharing himself.

Against her cheek, she could feel his heartbeat, its beat as rapid fire as her own.

"I missed you too," he said softly.

Then any need for talking disappeared. The connection between them had been immediate, and it had twined them closer and closer over the course of his four weeks in Dare Valley. Now those delicate ribbons were weaving them together all over again.

Part of her had wondered if their connection would follow them to Paris, but her heart had known the truth. It wasn't just Dare Valley that bound them together, and while she was scared she was going to leave Paris with an aching heart, she wasn't going to pass up the chance to be with him like she wanted. He'd come into her life unexpectedly and given her something precious—a reminder of how joyful passion and friendship could be. Before coming to Dare Valley, he'd pledged to stay celibate on his journey of self-discovery, but now that they were in Paris together, she planned to soak him up like a sponge.

He kissed the top of her head since he was so much taller. "I can still smell your cinnamon rolls in your hair," he said, finally breaking the silence.

"I brought you some rolls as a present." She had purposefully not washed her sable hair after preparing his present, knowing how much he enjoyed the scent of her baking. A few people on the plane had commented on the heavenly smell, making her smile in secret.

He edged back, but kept one hand on her. "You did? That was nice of you."

She looked up at him through her lashes, the full force of her flirtation coming out now. "I've been known to be nice."

He gulped. "You're always nice. And these are for you. Obviously." The roses smelled like sunshine and earth and magic.

"Thank you. I couldn't have asked for a better welcome."

"Did you have a good flight?" he asked.

"I didn't sleep much," she admitted, "but I didn't care. All I could do was imagine how things would be here."

"You're going to love it," he said. "Let me take your bag while you hold your flowers."

They made the switch, which was awkward and fun, and had her laughing.

"And give me your carry-on," he said, holding out his hand. "But I draw the line at taking your purse."

"I wouldn't dream of letting you carry my purse," she said. And she gave him what she hoped was a saucy wink as she handed him the bag.

"Shall we?" he asked.

She nodded, and together they followed the signs to the parking area. When he opened the door to a shiny red Fiat, she put her nose into her roses again to inhale their sweet scent.

"The car suits you," she said.

He looked over at her sharply, pausing with her suitcase suspended over the trunk. "You think so?"

"Yes. Sexy and understated. Maybe even a little practical."

He rolled his eyes and arranged her suitcase and carry-on in the tight space. "Practical? I'm almost offended."

"Are you not the man who invented the Paint Prep Mistress? I'd call that practical."

He opened the door for her, which made her smile.

But when was he going to kiss her? She'd spent half the flight imagining his hungry mouth devouring hers again like it had in that moment of pure passion they'd shared when she'd dropped him off at the Denver airport for his return flight to Paris.

"That was efficient," he said, waiting for her to sit and tuck her legs inside. "Practical sounds boring."

"It's not," she said when he folded himself into the driver's seat. "Practical is getting up at two every morning and baking bread because you love it. Someone has to bake it."

He winced as he turned on the car. "I have a whole new respect when I eat my morning croissant, let me tell you."

"It's going to be wonderful. Everything is going to be wonderful."

She'd spoken with her boss briefly on the phone before leaving. Brian had said Chef Andre was a pretty easy-going guy whose passion for bread matched her own. He'd assured her they would get along great, and she wasn't worried. Well, only a little bit.

When Evan reached down to put the car in gear, she placed her hand on his to stop him. Deciding to ask for what she wanted, she simply said, "Are you going to kiss me?"

His eyes darkened. "I had hoped to, yes, if you still wanted me to. But not at the airport. Your first kiss in Paris should be somewhere special."

The roses fell onto her lap as his sweet regard rolled through her. "Are you planning to take me there soon?"

His brow lifted. "You must be tired after that long flight. I thought I would drop you off at your apartment so you could grab a shower and then nap. When you wake up, I'll take you to dinner, and we'll make sure your first kiss in Paris is as romantic as in any Hollywood movie."

That sounded like too long to wait to her, but the

romantic side of him appealed to her. And he was right. Her first kiss in Paris *did* deserve to be special.

"It's sweet of you to have thought about it," she said, removing her hand so he could put the car in gear.

"I thought of little else while we were apart," he said with an edge to his voice. He paused. "That sounded—"

"I felt the same way," she interrupted. "Evan, we knew things were going to be different between us here."

"I just want you to be sure," he said, navigating them out of the airport and accelerating onto the highway. "There's still so much we don't know about each other."

His brow knit like he was struggling again. She could tell he was worried about something, worried about her, and it was sweet, really.

Her friend, Rhett Butler Blaylock, had gone all big brother on her before she left town, warning her again to be smart about Evan. Rhett was one of the people who'd convinced Evan to take his siesta in Dare Valley in the first place, so he clearly liked him. She'd assured him—again—she'd be fine. She knew how to handle artistic types. From the tension in Rhett's face, she could tell she hadn't convinced him. But she was a big girl. And she trusted Evan. Even if he didn't trust himself.

"So, we'll get to know each other while I'm here."

"And what about when you have to leave?" he asked.

"We live in the moment," she told him. "I know we live in two different places, Evan. Let's just—enjoy being together in this magical city."

He shifted to second gear as traffic suddenly slowed to a crawl. "I don't want to hurt you."

She put her hand on his knee for a moment until he met her eyes. "No one can hurt me unless I allow it."

The corner of his mouth tipped up. "You really are Venus incarnate, aren't you? Talking big like that."

"It's the truth," she said, settling back in her seat

and removing her hand. His nickname for her—Pocket Venus—was just another thing she'd missed. "Now, I want to know what you've been up to since you've been back. Texting doesn't give enough details."

He was silent for a long minute, and she wondered what he was thinking. Then he reached for some reflective shades on the dashboard and put them on, covering his gorgeous lakewater blue eyes.

"Well, I..."

***

Evan was feeling the weight of his secret. He'd had two weeks to think it through from every angle imaginable, but it boiled down to two simple facts.

Margie hated—no, loathed—rich people because of her upbringing, one he still didn't know much about.

It was undeniable that he was a rich person—a billionaire—and had sometimes lived the shallow lifestyle she'd eschewed.

Since they were only going to be together for her time in Paris, it wasn't like she needed to know everything about him. After all, there were plenty of things he didn't know about her. Perhaps if she told him about her past, he would change his mind.

Besides, he loved the fact that she liked him for himself, not his success or money. People hadn't liked him when he was a nerdy scientist with bad skin and untamable curly hair. And he'd finally admitted to himself that the wealthy jet setters he palled around with weren't exactly friends. Margie was a breath of fresh air.

Being around her had relit the creative fire inside him, and since he'd gotten back, he'd continued to work on the simple inventions he'd started in Dare Valley.

His secret would remain a secret. For now at least.

But there were some truths he could tell. "Well, I've

been working on the prototypes that came to me while I was painting your bakery. You should see them now."

Her brow arched. "So you really *are* an inventor and an artist?"

The traffic was slowing down the closer they came to the city, and he forced himself to divide his attention between her and the road. If he hadn't been hiding the truth, he would have picked her up in the Rolls Royce and let his chauffeur handle Paris traffic. He'd bought the Fiat to perpetuate the ruse that he was the normal person he'd pretended to be in Dare Valley.

He lifted a shoulder. "Yes." The answer contained a grain of the truth, but it was an unforgivable understatement. After all, his inventions, which supported the defense departments of the major democratic countries in the world, had made him rich and famous. "I've also been painting since I've been back." Granted, he was just painting a few rooms in his penthouse—ones no one but him would see.

"I would have thought you'd want a break from painting after Hot Cross Buns," she said.

"No," he answered. "There's something about it. I can't explain it, but it's helping me...I don't know, find my way back to something I'd lost." Painting cleared his mind, and he was certain it had put him on the cusp of a huge discovery, something that would revolutionize his company. He just wasn't sure what it was yet.

"Your creative fire," she said, and it wasn't a question.

This was why they were so good together. She knew him. Really knew him.

"Yes." He steered them to the exit that would take them through downtown to her rented flat in St. Germain. "I've been without that spark for a long time."

"I'm so glad you've found it again," she said. "I remember what it feels like to live without it. It's a...dark place to be."

Her tone had changed to one of loneliness, and he reached for her hand and gave it a squeeze. "You'll have to tell me about that time. How you came to Dare Valley." About why you came to loathe rich people so much, he thought.

"Maybe I'll tell you," she said in a small voice. "But maybe not. I just want to be happy here. There's so much to be grateful for. The past is past."

Her openness to life awed him, and since he wanted to give her back some of the awe she had given him, he angled the car to drive along the Seine—even though it would take them a little out of the way.

When she started to ooh and ahh next to him, his chest expanded with the same effervescent feeling he had while working on a new invention. How wonderful it was to share this with her, as she had shared her home with him. He pointed out the landmarks as they traveled down the Quai de la Tournelle, Margie was glued to her window. Notre Dame, in all her magnificence, never failed to make an impression, but it was too bold and touristy for him.

"Even though it's an incredible church architecturally," he said, "it's not my favorite."

"I remember going there in high school when I visited with...a group from boarding school."

He nodded because he could almost sense her feeling him out after revealing this new piece of information. "That doesn't sound like a fun way to see Paris," he said casually.

"It wasn't." She looked over her shoulder at him, shadows in her green eyes. "Besides, I wasn't too interested in churches then. I was in my rebellious stage."

"You? Rebellious?" He couldn't imagine it. But she was nothing if not independent, so it made sense she would rebel against a life she hated. In his own way, he'd done the same.

"Like I said, it's in the past." When she looked away, he didn't press for more details. Apparently he wasn't the only one who needed time to feel out what—and how much—to say.

They passed the stream of tourists wandering along the Quai, stopping to browse at the Bouquinistes of Paris, or "green boxes," for antique books and artwork.

"If you're interested in picking up a print or book, I'll take you to some of my favorite dealers. Did you know there are nine hundred of those green boxes along the Seine on both the Right and Left Banks?"

"Wow! Nine hundred? How do you know that?" she asked, but didn't take her eyes off the scene.

Who could blame her? The sky was blue, and the Seine sparkled like diamonds in the sun.

"When I moved here, I read everything I could about Paris." In truth, he'd never really felt at home anywhere else—until he was with Margie in Dare Valley. To him, it had only seemed logical to learn everything he could about the place where he'd decided to plant his roots.

She settled back into her seat with a gusty sigh. "I still can't believe I'm here. And with you."

"I'm glad you're here, Margie." His voice was gruff. "Paris was waiting for you." He wanted to say, *I* was waiting for you, but it was too much, too soon.

He continued on the Quai de Conti and pointed out Pont Neuf Bridge, where he planned to take her later. When he came to Rue de Saints Peres, he turned left and headed to her flat.

"Your street is one of the finest in Paris, but it's not the quietest." Which worried him. She needed to get her rest if she was going to get up at two every morning for her apprenticeship. He'd wanted to find her the prettiest and quietest flat available with the best views of Paris. The flowers and the small gift he'd made her would have to suffice as welcome gifts.

"I'll be fine," she said. "I know I'm not going to sleep much between the jet lag and my apprenticeship."

"But you're already exhausted from finishing up your job at Don't Soy With Me and starting Hot Cross Buns."

"Evan," she said softly as he maneuvered the Fiat down a side street to her flat, which sat on Boulevard St. Germain. "I can take care of myself. I've been doing it a long time."

But he didn't want her to have to be so stalwart in her independence. "I know you can, but sometimes it's nice to let other people worry about you and have your back. Promise me you'll tell me if I can make anything better or easier for you while you're here."

Her smile made him think of rainbows. "I will. You're an angel."

That was stretching things. Big time.

Since there were no open spaces on the street, he double parked his car in front of her apartment building and put the hazards on. None of the other drivers would like it, but if he got a ticket, he'd simply pay it. After popping open the trunk, he took out her luggage and grabbed the gift he'd made her. Her building was a drab gray stone, three stories tall, with a nondescript black door.

"I'm really happy you're staying close to the bakery," he said. "How'd you find it?"

"Brian and Andre asked a couple of their chef friends if they knew of an available place close by. Lucky for me, one of the chefs was going on vacation and offered me his flat. St. Germain is such a great area. How far is your place from here?"

"It's only a five-minute walk," he said and felt the internal tug of war inside his belly. Could he show her where he lived? She wouldn't know he was a billionaire, but it would be obvious that he had money. Penthouses in Paris didn't come cheap. *Play it by ear,* he told himself for the hundredth time.

"Let me get the code to the building out," she said, rummaging in her purse.

When she found it, she keyed the numbers into the call box. The downstairs light turned on as soon as she opened the door, but it didn't illuminate the first floor much. When he squinted, he could make out a sagging staircase to the back. Like older Paris ladies, this building was old, but she'd retained her beauty well.

"It doesn't look like there's an elevator," she said, stepping onto the cracked tile floor. "Let me have my carry-on."

"Don't insult my manliness. I can get both. But you can take this package." He handed her the present he'd boxed up, and her eyes narrowed in curiosity for a moment.

"Evan, it's three flights of stairs." She put her hand on her hip, and even though he didn't want to argue with her, he had to admit he'd missed her stubbornness.

"It's Paris," he said, moving past her with the luggage and starting up the steps. "Most of the old buildings don't have elevators."

"Does yours?" she asked.

"No," he answered honestly. "We have an old dumbwaiter that carries up the heavier items." It was one of the features that had convinced him to buy the place.

"Let me guess," she said, her footsteps scraping the concrete steps as she followed him up. "You fixed it."

He stopped on the stairs and turned back to look at her. "How did you know that?"

Her wink was beyond sexy. "I could hear it in your voice. You sounded like that when you were trying to tell me how you'd made your paint mistress."

He resumed the climb. "That's the Paint Prep Mistress to you, Ms. Lancaster."

She laughed. "Well, excuse me. I didn't mean to

offend her."

The impulse to drop her luggage and kiss her senseless on the stairs was so strong he increased his speed, needing to distance himself from his own temptation and the cinnamon fragrance in her hair.

He climbed to the third floor, and at the top noticed there was only one other door. Even though it was daytime, the light here was miniscule. "I'll find you a flashlight. You're going to be leaving in the pitch dark to get to work."

"I'll manage," she said and edged around him in the small corridor. "Does it say 3A?"

Again, he had to squint to see the markings. Apparently the building was old enough for the ink to have faded. "I believe so."

She leaned down, giving him a fabulous view of her backside. "Jacques said he'd put the key under the mat. Aha! Wow, this is a really old key."

It looked like a skeleton key to Evan. He was practically holding his breath in anticipation. What if the place was a dump? She inserted it and had to wiggle it around in the lock before the tumblers caught.

"I'll fix that," he said. "I don't want you getting locked out."

She opened the door and felt for the light switch. "I'll be fine. Oh, wow. Look at this place."

He hauled her bag into the tiny kitchen. To the right was a bedroom. The doorway at the end of the galley kitchen sported a small eating and sitting area. And that was it.

"It's wonderful!" she exclaimed and then did a little jig in place.

He didn't see much to dance over. "It's not very big," he said, his eyes scanning the old wooden beams above their heads and the cracked plaster lines streaking across the ceiling. Was it safe? So many places in Paris wouldn't pass a home inspection. "I'll have to check—"

"No, you won't," she said, giving him a playful shove. "No checking. If Jacques can live here, so can I."

"Where is he, anyway?" he asked.

"In Malta for a long holiday," she said, tracing the sagging wooden cutting board anchored in the middle of the kitchen counter. "Just imagine how many people have used this surface to cook."

All Evan could imagine was how many types of kitchen bacteria were living in that ancient wood. "Maybe I should—"

"No," she said again, this time more firmly.

He held out his hands. "You don't even know what I was going to say."

She gave him a saucy look. "I don't have to. It involved fixing something. Everything in here is perfect."

Turning on the water to make sure it worked, he bit his tongue. Okay, at least she had water. She sailed past him through the small door leading to the bedroom. Should he follow her?

"Oh, come see!" she called out.

He ducked his head under the doorway. The bedroom had a small full bed—likely two twin beds pushed together if he knew Paris—and a twenty-foot-tall ceiling again covered with age-old beams and cracked plaster. He had a horrible vision of the whole thing caving in on her while she slept.

"Margie—"

"Oh, look at this bathroom door!" she cried out.

"It's a hobbit door," he said dryly, eying the four-foot-tall door cut off at the top in a diagonal line. "One thing is for sure. You can't run to the bathroom without knocking yourself out."

She peeked in, ducking her head like an explorer going into a tomb in the Valley of the Kings. "It even has a bidet."

"Yeah!" he called out sarcastically.

She stuck her head out through the hobbit door and glared at him. "Don't make fun of me or my bidet."

His mouth twitched. "I know I've been calling you Pocket Venus, but now I think you might have found your home in the Shire."

"Why am I not surprised you like *Lord of the Rings?*"

"I pretty much like all things Tolkien." So sue him. He liked fantasy and magic. Life needed more of it, if you asked him.

"I like those movies too," she confessed. "Maybe we can watch the first one while I'm here."

"You're suggesting we watch TV in Paris?" He clutched his heart. "Hundreds of hardworking artisans just rolled over in their graves. This is not a city to watch TV in, Margie."

"Don't you?" she asked, looking so cute in the short doorway, her sable hair curving around her jawline.

"It's different for me," he said. "I live here."

She disappeared from view again and closed the door on him. He gave her some privacy and meandered through the small kitchen, opening cabinets. At least this room was up to snuff, but since this Jacques guy was a chef, he wouldn't have expected anything less. As for the dining and sitting room, it was obvious the guy barely lived here. Paris was like New York City that way. Most people spent more time outside their apartments than in them, working and eating and socializing in the streets of the city.

"I know it's small," she said from behind him, "but I love it. And it's free. What could possibly be better than that?"

He was glad to hear Jacques wasn't charging her to use his flat. He knew money had to be tight for her since she was starting her own business. It would be so easy for him to cut her a check for millions and erase any worries she had about money. He wanted to do it, but she'd hate him for it. She was a woman who needed to stand on her own. That much he knew and respected.

"What could possibly make this place better? How about a full-sized bathroom door?" he asked.

"Enough! Now, I am going to get settled in and take a nap like you suggested. I bought a data pack, so we can text while I'm here. When I'm ready, I'll text you, and then you can take me to this special place to kiss me."

Fire erupted in his belly. "I was planning to take you to dinner first."

She shook her head. "Too long. I want my first-ever Paris kiss before dinner. Aren't most Parisian dinners like two hours long anyway?"

He cleared his throat, remembering how it had felt to kiss her, imagining how it would feel this time. The kitchen was suddenly three times too small. "The good ones are."

"Then I'm the one being practical this time."

She lowered her eyes for a moment and then peered at him through her lashes—a look he found incredibly sexy. She hadn't looked at him that way in Dare Valley.

"Evan, I can't wait that long."

He lost his ability to breathe. It was like the fire inside him had sucked all the gas from his lungs. "I can't either."

"Then go," she said softly. "And thanks for picking me up and making it so easy to begin my time here."

He grabbed the package she'd set on the kitchen counter. "This is another gift to make your time here easier."

She gave him a half frown mixed with a smile. "You shouldn't have."

Inside the plain box was a lavishly wrapped gift in gold paper with a red ribbon. "It's so pretty, I don't want to open it."

But she did, carefully peeling away the ribbon and

paper and setting it aside with reverence. Then her brows knit together as she turned the machine from side to side.

"Okay," she said, "you're going to have to tell me what this is."

"It's a sound machine," he told her, "specially designed to mask both real and white noise."

She blinked at him.

"So you can sleep when all of Paris is outside your windows."

"Oh!" She hit the red button on the top, her mouth gaping when it turned on. "Can you hear me?" she asked, saying the words slowly.

"Smart ass," he told her.

"Thank you, Evan. This was really sweet." Then she took off into the bedroom and returned with a box of her own.

"It's not wrapped pretty like yours," she told him, handing it over. "I had to put the rolls into something solid so they wouldn't get squished in my carry-on."

When he opened the box, he inhaled the cinnamon and bread fragrance he'd dreamed about since leaving Dare Valley. There were four large rolls inside, oozing with the caramel sauce for which they were famous.

"These look incredible," he said. "Thank you for bringing them to me. I've missed them." *I've missed you. I've missed everything about you.*

His mornings seemed colder now that he wasn't greeted with her beautiful smile and the tantalizing scent of her baking every time he came into the kitchen. In idle moments, he'd found himself daydreaming about the time he'd caught her dancing to the tango music she liked to play, her red skirt flying through the air with the power of her movements. But perhaps most of all, he missed the way their fingers would brush as they walked together in the park she liked, both of them wishing they could hold hands.

Crossing to her, he didn't think twice about grabbing her hand now and raising it to his lips. He kissed the back of it gently, looking directly into her emerald green eyes. "I'm really happy you're here, Margie."

"Me too," she said and led him to the door.

Before he could leave, she laid her head on his chest. He wrapped his arms around her, and she traced something in the middle of his ribcage before he pulled away.

After closing the door, he realized she'd traced a heart.

CHAPTER 2

Margie had planned to save her sexy dark green silk dress for a special dinner with Evan. While she hadn't expected to wear it on her first night in Paris, it seemed like the perfect choice.

He'd planned their kiss.

No one had ever done that before—or thought to buy her a sound machine so she could sleep better. She sighed as she arranged her roses in small kitchen glasses since Jacques didn't have a vase anywhere in the cabinets.

She finally allowed herself to admit she'd fallen for Evan big time. While she'd known their connection was strong in Dare Valley, it now seemed to be woven with steel threads. And while she still felt he was struggling with something, he was the same sweet, curious, sexy, and sometimes stubborn man she'd come to care about. She'd texted him earlier to say she was ready whenever he was.

Her stomach felt a little queasy from the lack of sleep and jet lag, but her blood thrummed through her system in excitement.

She was in Paris! With Evan!

She did another impromptu jig in the kitchen and laughed. There was a knock on the door. When she opened it, she pressed her hand to her heart.

"You brought me groceries!" She leapt at him and hugged him, not caring that a sprig of parsley was sticking her in the eye.

"The market will be closed by the time we finish with dinner, and you need to have food before you go to work."

She had to report to work at nine a.m. tomorrow. Andre had given her the night to settle in. He said it would be easier to give her a tour of the bakery when it wasn't super busy beyond customers coming into the shop to buy their morning croissants and baguettes. Of course, Andre also sold baguettes to a number of French restaurants. She couldn't wait to learn everything he had to teach her.

"It looks like you brought me a feast," she said, taking one of the bags from his hands and putting it on the counter.

He set his own bag down. "Let me look at you," he said in a husky voice.

When he held out his hands to her, she took them and simply gazed into his eyes. He'd worn a simple navy suit with a white shirt underneath. The combination was so sexy and so Paris.

"You have the fashion here down to a T," she told him.

He chuckled. "I had lots of help, trust me. If you'd seen me before..."

"Oh, do tell!" She wanted to know everything about him, everything from his past experiences to how he'd become the man he was today.

"In a sec." His gaze ran down her body, and she felt the heat in his eyes curl around her. "First, I need to tell you how ravishing you look."

"Ravishing? That seems a little thick."

"Don't analyze my compliment."

He raised her hand to his lips again. Man, she could get used to that. Why had kissing a woman's hand *ever* gone out of style? Someone needed to bring it back into fashion.

"And you look ravishing too," she said as he let her hand go. "Like you always do." Her smile was as coy as she could make it.

"I don't think guys can be ravishing," he said, taking out the vegetables, eggs, and cheese from the bag and putting them in the refrigerator. The baguette he set on the counter.

She followed suit, squealing with delight when she saw the purple raspberries in her bag. "These are so awesome!"

His smile was a mile long. "I thought you might like those. I'll draw you a map so you can visit the best market to buy produce. It's a bit more expensive than the Monoprix, but you can find special items there no one else carries."

"Like purple raspberries," she said, clutching them to her heart. Then she dashed to the sink to wash them. "I have to try these."

"You're going to ruin your dinner," he chided, leaning against the kitchen counter after closing the refrigerator door.

"I'm only going to have one," she said and then popped it in her mouth. There was a lushness to the fruit and a floral taste that regular raspberries didn't possess. "Okay, maybe not one. Thank you for getting these. For all of this. You'll have to let me pay you."

His jaw locked. "No way. You're in my town now. Anywhere we go together, I'll pay. It's not negotiable."

She set the raspberries aside, his stubbornness stealing some of her joy. "Don't be silly. You're—"

"I'm not poor, Margie," he said and kicked at the tile floor with his incredibly fashionable brown loafers. "I—I needed to get in touch with another part of myself in Dare Valley, and it suited me to spend my time there a little more...simply than usual."

"Kinda like the celibacy thing?" she asked.

His lips twitched. "Leave it to you to remind me. Yes, it was kinda like that."

"So...you were essentially living like a monk in a communal home, working for barely an hourly wage."

This time his laugh was loud and deep, from his belly, and she found herself joining in.

"My friend Chase called me Brother Evan."

His lakewater blue eyes were alight with warmth, and it gratified her to hear about his friend. In Dare Valley, he'd seemed so lonely. It was good to know there was someone looking out for him, someone in whom he could confide.

"I hope Brother Evan is gone now," she said in a husky voice.

"Completely." His stare curled her toes.

"Then let's put away these groceries so you can sweep me off for my first-ever kiss in Paris." She grabbed the fabric of her dress and made a swishing motion like she imagined the belle of a ball would.

"I thought we'd walk tonight," he said, taking the rest of the groceries from her and putting them in the refrigerator. "Paris is the most beautiful city in the world to walk in."

She could feel the romance already. "I'd love that."

"And I plan to kiss you near the Pont Neuf," he added in a husky tone. "It's my favorite bridge in all of Paris."

"I'd love that even more," she said, and when he offered his arm to her, she took it with a smile of pure anticipation.

***

Evan navigated Margie along Boulevard Saint-Germain, letting go of her hand a half dozen times so she could sprint to a shop window and ooh and ahh over the display. Right now, she was exclaiming over the Ralph Lauren window display. The female mannequin was wearing a gorgeous gold dress, and he had to fight the urge to usher her inside, find her size, and have her try it on so he could buy it for her.

"You weren't kidding about the people here making art out of their show windows," she said. "I still remember you telling me that. I've been seriously thinking about what I want to do with mine. I have some ideas."

"I'm glad it sparked your creativity," he said. She had done that for him.

Once she was finished marveling at the display, they continued to stroll along the busy streets. People were already out in the cafes having a coffee or pre-dinner drink.

"I'll have to bring you back to this place," he said, nodding his head to the green café in front of Brasserie Lipp. "Ernest Hemingway and F. Scott Fitzgerald used to come here."

"They did?" she asked, stopping to peer into the restaurant. "I'd love that."

He angled them across the square past the Cathédrale Saint-Volodymyr-le-Grand so she could enjoy the art displayed on the Rue de Saints-Peres leading to Quai Malaquais.

When they reached the Pont de Arts Bridge, she just had to go up and read a few of the locks that lovers around the world had signed and left to represent their feelings for each other.

"It's so beautiful," she exclaimed with stars in her eyes, touching one of the many locks cascading down the metal railing. "There's so much love here. Can you feel it?"

For the first time, he could. He'd always found the display kind of corny, but the look on her face made him want to find the closest peddler to buy a lock for them. Reaching out a hand to touch her face, he said, "I do now."

Her face seemed to glow.

"Come on. Pont Neuf is the next bridge."

Her breathing shattered, and she looked away, as if searching for the spot. When she met his eyes again, she said, "Don't let me dilly dally anymore. Not until later." So she was thinking about the kiss too.

His throat grew thick. "Okay, I won't."

When he finally led her down the back stairs off Pont Neuf, her hand tightened around his as if she too could feel the tension, the passion gathering between them. Some people missed the stairs leading to the little inlet in the middle of the Seine, but it was one of his favorite places. The park benches lining the slender field of grass were already filled with other couples and families enjoying the day. He led her down the sidewalk right along the edge of the water.

When he reached the willow trees whose branches were dancing in the wind, almost like they were beckoning them closer, he turned to her and placed his hands on her shoulders. He'd never anticipated a kiss like this before, and it seemed as if everything in him was rising with a force greater than himself. He felt like Edison must have when the lightbulb had first worked. When Henry Ford had cranked that first car.

"Margie," he said softly because he had to say her name just now.

And then he lowered his lips to hers as she rose on her toes to meet him.

Something electric sparked and fanned out between them, and he couldn't hold back. He wrapped his arms around her waist and crushed her to him. She gave a breathy sigh, and he moaned into her mouth, wanting more. She opened to him like a Paris rose, beautiful and delicious, and he savored every slick slide of her tongue on his. He supped at her lips like she was his last glorious feast, like she was the key to paradise itself.

She was his paradise now, and there was no end to the feast. Not even when they finally separated.

Her green eyes glowed, and inside them, he could see everything she was and would ever be. A piece of eternity seemed to hang in the air between them, and he traced her face.

He brought her hand to his chest. Let her feel his heart beat as they watched each other. It was the most passionate kiss he'd ever experienced. He saw her swallow thickly and knew she felt as lost as he did.

"Oh, Margie," he finally whispered and buried his head in the curve of her neck, inhaling cinnamon and feeling the branches of the willow trees twirl around them almost as if in delight.

She traced another heart against his chest, and this time he understood what it meant. It was her way of giving her heart to him.

"That was the most beautiful kiss any woman could ever hope for," she whispered.

He realized she didn't say "first" or "Paris." This kiss had defied time and place.

"It was the most amazing kiss anyone could ever hope for," he said in a husky voice.

She looked up at him, and the willows seemed to cradle them in a lover's embrace.

"How about we stay here for a little while?" he asked.

"I'd love that."

And so they remained in an embrace as the wind wrapped the willows around them and the Seine rushed by, as powerful and special as this growing force between them.

***

Margie felt like her entire body was filled with the unctuous ribbons of river water flowing through the city. She'd never had a more magical kiss, and she didn't think it was Paris. It was Evan.

Her head rested on his arm as they left the tiny inlet and strolled along the Seine toward Notre Dame. In the waning light, the spires of the famous cathedral looked more ominous, and coupled with the gargoyles, she found herself wondering if others before her had felt intimidated in its presence. Evan was telling her about the Île de la Cité, one of two natural islands on the Seine. It was where the original medieval city was founded and where the cathedral now towered over everything around it.

"Do you want me to take a picture of you?" he asked her when they stood in front of the cathedral.

She was tired, but the good kind of tired that came from being happy. "How about one of you and me?"

Something flashed in his eyes, and then he smiled. "I like that idea." He fished out his smart phone and positioned them with the cathedral in the background.

"Say cinnamon rolls," he suggested with a grin.

He caught them both laughing, and after he pocketed the phone, she threw her arms around him. "Evan, I'm so happy."

His arms tightened around her. "I am too." He kissed the top of her head. "Let's go to dinner. You're practically asleep on your feet."

"No, I'm not," she protested, rubbing the back of her neck when he drew away from her. "But I could eat."

"You're going to love where I'm taking you," he said, reaching for her hand again.

"I have a feeling I'm going to love everywhere you take me."

He looked down at her, and for a moment, she could

feel the swell of passion between them.

"So, as I was saying about Notre Dame..." he continued, clearing his throat.

As they walked, he told her more about the history of the cathedral and the land where it was built, recounting even the pre-Christian times when the temple of the Egyptian goddess, Isis, had sat on the island. His command of history and facts astounded her. So she asked all of the questions that popped into her mind. About how deep the Seine was, and how many bridges there were throughout the city. He had answers for every one.

When they reached a quaint street off the Quai de Montebello, he stopped in front of Le Reminet, a lovely bistro with a purple storefront. What struck her first was the profusion of candlelight she could see through the windows. When he opened the door for her, she wanted to sigh. Every table had its own candles and cut flowers. Coupled with the white tablecloths, the setting was cozy and intimate all at the same time.

"I love it," she whispered as the maitre d' approached them.

"I knew you would," he said. "You struck me as a sucker for candlelight."

"What's not to like about candlelight?" she asked. In fact, she wished there was a way to incorporate it into her bakery, but there was the whole fire code thing to consider...and the fact that she was only open during the day.

Evan spoke French to the maitre d', and it was the first time she'd heard him speak the language. He seemed sexier now, all of a sudden, as if the exotic words had changed him into a magician.

She'd studied French in boarding school. To piss off her parents in their never-ending war to package her into a perfect upper-crust daughter, she'd purposely tanked most of her exams at school. But she'd secretly loved French. While her language skills were rusty, she hoped to polish them up a bit now that she was in Paris.

"Your accent sounds marvelous," she said after they were seated.

Their waiter appeared and spoke to them in French. She caught a few of the words, but was too tired to focus her brain on translating. Maybe tomorrow, once she was rested.

"What would you like to drink?" Evan asked her. "Champagne to start? Or wine?"

"Champagne sounds decadent."

He rolled his eyes playfully and grinned. "Pink or white?"

She leaned forward. "Pink, seriously?"

"Everywhere you go, people will give you the choice of pink or white."

"Then pink," she said and smiled at their waiter, who gave her a flirtatious grin.

Evan ordered and then arranged his napkin in his lap. "I see how this is going to go. All the men in Paris are going to fall in love with you."

And what about you? she almost asked. Their kiss had told her plenty about how much he wanted her. But love? Don't get ahead of yourself, she reminded herself. You're only here for ten days.

"So long as everyone's nice to me, we won't have a problem," she told him, setting her napkin in her lap and reaching for the menu.

When she saw the prices, she almost winced. She'd known things in Paris were going to be pricey, but this...

"Do I need to remove your menu and tell you what's available so you won't see the prices?" Evan asked in an aggrieved tone.

He was staring at her when she lowered her menu. "Evan—"

"I told you I'm totally fine on the money side, Margie," he said.

He *had* told her that, and she couldn't help but wonder what it meant. Unless he'd found a new job in the past two weeks, he was unemployed. Perhaps he'd saved enough that he didn't feel the pressure to have a constant job. She knew some artists did that—they would work long enough to save up some money in the bank and then take time off to create until they needed to replenish their reserves.

"Evan, that's really nice of you, but I still want to contribute my share," she said.

He frowned. "Please let me spoil you a little while you're here. I don't...have company much. It would mean a lot to me if we could end this struggle right now so we can enjoy all Paris has to offer."

Again, she caught a hint of loneliness in his voice. She found herself wondering, not for the first time, what had brought him to Paris and where his family was. Where his friend, Chase, lived. Like where his money came from, his whole background was a mystery to her.

Then she reminded herself of what she did know. He supported her dreams, and while his perfectionism had sometimes frustrated her, she appreciated the effort he'd poured into painting her bakery in tune with her vision. He was sweet and thoughtful and so smart she wondered how all his knowledge fit into his beautiful head. He invented weird things out of adding machines and could program a computer chip. And then there was the way he looked at her—like she was the only thing worth gazing at in the whole world. She wasn't sure anyone else had ever looked at her that way.

"Okay," she said as the waiter filled two crystal glasses with pink champagne. "I won't fight you if you allow me to make you bread while I'm here. That will be my gift to you."

"You already brought me cinnamon rolls all the way from Dare Valley. That was an incredible gift. I might have had one while you were napping."

"I want...no, I *need* to give you something in return, Evan." She reached for his hand. "It's important to me."

How could she explain that her upbringing had left her feeling like a parasite?

"You asked me earlier to tell you about...that dark time in my life. Well..."

Oh, this was going to be hard. She rarely shared her background with anyone—in part because it was in the past, like she'd told him, but also because she feared people would treat her differently if they knew she'd come from money. Or that her own parents had disowned her. But she found herself wanting to tell him, so he would know the whole of her—just like she wanted to know the whole of him. And maybe, just maybe, he would open up and share with her in return.

"My...ah...parents...It's weird to refer to them that way now. They're really wealthy. Old family money. They...never gave anything back in any meaningful way—not to me or to anyone in their circle. They threw money around to advertise their power and status."

His mouth tightened. "Go on."

"They wanted me to be just like them. To dress a certain way. To talk a certain way. To think a certain way. Do things rich people are supposed to do. Go to art gallery openings and ride horses and crap like that. They sent me to boarding school when I was seven because I cramped their lifestyle." She took a breath. "I tried to please them in the beginning, but they didn't even notice. So I rebelled. Hard. That didn't work either. The calls from the school after I was caught drinking, sneaking out, or whatever were just a bother to them. One day I finally woke up and realized I was only hurting myself."

There was a line between his brows as he listened to her. She fiddled with her napkin and made herself continue.

"I sought help in books and found a good counselor,

one my parents hadn't chosen." There had been childhood shrinks from early on, but they'd always made her feel like she was in the wrong, like she was a bad girl like her parents called her. "A new world unfolded for me, one filled with love and generosity."

The book that had changed everything was one she'd seen on *The Oprah Show*: Marianne Williamson's *A Return to Love*. "I started college, but I was still struggling with what I wanted to do with my life. Then I ran into some people one night while volunteering at a local homeless shelter. They'd just come back from teaching English as a second language to children in a border town in Mexico, run by some nuns."

His quiet intensity was making her nervous. What was he thinking? Her and nuns? It must sound crazy. He was so hard to read as he picked up his champagne glass and took what looked to be a fortifying sip.

"Something in me wanted to go down there. They talked about how giving back to this community had changed their lives. I'd never been part of a community before, and well...they made it sound so great. When I told my parents, we had the row of a lifetime. They made threats, everything from taking away my car to cutting me off. And I snapped. I told them to cut me off. That I hated them and everything they stood for and never wanted to see them again." The ugliness wasn't as sticky as it used to be. Now it felt like dust she could brush off with a gentle pass of her fingers over her skin.

"Oh, Margie," he said finally, setting aside his glass and grabbing her hand.

"It's really not as awful as it sounds," she said, releasing the huge pocket of air in her lungs. "We were never much of a family. My mother was a party girl who married my father for his fortune. He's twenty years older than her, and he's spent his entire life living off a trust fund. She got pregnant with me right away to dig her claws into him. She'd run away from her own family in North Dakota to become a model or an actress, you see, but she was too lazy to pursue anything serious."

The judgment coming through her made her seem hard, so she pressed her free hand to her chest to re-center herself. "I finally realized my mother was completely unprepared for life in the big city. She did what seemed most logical to her."

"Does your father know that's why she married him?" he asked, his voice taut with tension.

"Yes, but he's a vain man. He likes having a beautiful, younger woman for a trophy wife. They have an agreement..." The time she'd found her mother in bed with one of the waiters at a party at their house was forever ingrained in her mind.

"They didn't deserve you," he said in a hard tone.

She shrugged. "They never had any more kids. I was only a safety net for her and a nuisance to them both. After they disowned me, I sold what I had at a pawn shop, bought a cheap car, and left Dartmouth to teach English as a second language. The people I'd met at the homeless shelter helped set it up for me."

"And have you spoken to your parents since then?" Evan asked, caressing the back of her hand with his thumb in comfort.

The candlelight flickered on the table, and she focused on the steady flame as the old sadness rolled through her. "No. They said if I quit school to teach, it was the final straw." She'd left without a backward glance, knowing that if she stayed on their terms, she'd be cutting off that unique part of herself that made her Margie...and she would never be able to reclaim it.

"I'm so sorry, Margie," Evan said, his blue eyes gazing at her and not looking away, like he wanted to see all of her.

She was happy for the comfort. Her throat was raw from the retelling. "Don't be. I realized something after it happened. If they hadn't pushed me so hard to be like them, I would never have found the courage to rebel and break free. Maybe I would have ended up just like them." Sure, it had been scary to lose her financial security, but she would have preferred to work at a fast food place for minimum wage than to be on a tether made of money. "Teaching in that small border town saved my life."

"How long did you teach there?" he asked.

"Two years," she said. "Then the diocese closed the mission since it wasn't bringing in enough money and combined it with another parish. The nuns were forced to leave, and so were all of the volunteers."

"That must have been hard," he said quietly.

"It was." She'd bled inside, feeling like she was losing her home, her haven. "Evan, the parents of the children I taught had so little, but they would give me anything from their last chicken to a plate of their special tortillas as a way of saying thanks. They taught me how important it is to give as a way of saying thank you. That's why I need you to let me give back to you while I'm here."

The murmur of the other diners' conversations was a pleasant buzz in her ears, but her focus was on Evan. Like his was for her. The tightness of his features made her stomach queasy.

"Did I share too much?" she asked softly.

He leaned forward and shook his head. "No. I...no. I'm honored you told me."

His pause had her tapping her foot on the floor in nervousness.

"So how did you end up in Dare Valley?"

A soft smile touched her face, softening her inner tension. "That's an interesting story. When I left El Milagro—the town where I'd been teaching—I didn't have any plans. I decided to go somewhere cooler. That summer had been especially intense with temperatures up to one hundred and twenty degrees. I lived in a small room in the mission, which wasn't air-conditioned. It was brutal. So I decided to drive to Calgary. I'd fallen in love with the place when I was a kid watching the Olympics. After passing through Denver, I decided to take the scenic route through the Rocky Mountains."

Like most pivotal moments, that day was as clear as crystal in her mind. She'd been in awe of the mountains rising up in the sky after living in the flat desert for so long. "I stopped in Dare Valley for gas and felt the pull to stay there. I can't explain it, but when I saw the town sign that said, "Welcome," I knew it was where I belonged." She shrugged. "That probably sounds weird."

"No, it's not," he said, raising a brow. "That's how I felt when I came to Paris for the first time. I knew I had to live here."

Again she wondered what had led him to Paris. "So you get it," she said, almost releasing his hand because her palm was clammy with nervous sweat. "It was like the town had been waiting for me, and from there, everything fell into place. I found a group house I could afford. Got a job waiting tables at The Chop House. I even enrolled in a few classes at Emmits Merriam until I realized I didn't care about getting a degree. Pretty soon I made some friends. Jill Hale was one of them. When she decided to open her coffee shop, she asked if I could help. I had some experience with food service, but none as a barista. I taught her what I knew, and the rest we learned together. My entire life changed again...for the better."

"And you met Howie," he said, his lakewater blue eyes even more intent now.

"Yes," she said, finally removing her hand to wipe it on her napkin. Bringing up Howie right now didn't feel right. "And I got the house and now the bakery... My life is so wonderful now, Evan. I mean look at me. I'm in Paris! Tomorrow I'm going to study with a master baker. And I'm here with you."

"I'm here with you too," he said, taking another drink of his champagne.

"So now do you understand why I need to balance the scales?" she asked. "I realize that was a long-winded story."

"I wanted to know." He tugged on his ear like he was weighing her request. "All right," he finally agreed. "You can bake me bread while you're here. But only at work. Not in your spare time. Is it a deal?"

"Yes," she said, reaching for her champagne and taking a healthy sip. Her throat still felt dry and scratchy.

As if sensing their intense conversation was over, their waiter reappeared. She ordered a meal of duck confit—since Paris was known for its duck—and a simple watercress salad for a starter. Evan ordered them red wine, and the Cote de Rhone was full and ruby-rich when it arrived. Between the jet lag, the explosive kiss, and the champagne, she already had a delightful buzz going.

For the rest of the meal, she asked him about his favorite places in Paris to keep the conversation light. The waiter kept her glass filled, and she didn't stop herself from enjoying the wine's mystery and spice.

"I'm getting tipsy," she finally confessed after Evan had talked her into sharing a dessert of fresh berries and Chantilly cream.

"You're exhausted," he said, holding out his spoon so she could take a bite of the dessert. "Don't worry. We can catch a cab when we're finished." He signaled to the waiter for the check, and when it came, she had to bite her lip.

"Just say thank you, Margie," he said as he signed the slip the waiter gave him after punching the credit card information into a cute little handheld machine.

"Thank you, Margie," she quipped. Laughing, she swiped the last of the Chantilly cream with her finger and stuck it in her mouth.

Evan stood and came around to help her out of her chair. Did he think she was that far gone?

"Come on. Let's get you home."

"I'm okay," she told him, feeling not too steady on her feet.

"Humor me and take my arm." He gave it to her, and she took it. "Makes me feel more manly."

"I can't imagine you feeling unmanly," she declared as they left the quiet candlelight behind and walked into the soft lamps illuminating Paris' streets. His arm felt strong under her fingers.

"I don't tell many people this, but I didn't exactly have my man card until Chase came along." He led her to the Quai. "You've seen how much I geek out over inventing things, and well, I used to look the part. I *was* a geek. And...promise you won't laugh."

He looked so vulnerable, her heart shot up into her throat. Unable to speak, she shook her head.

"I pretty much lived and breathed all things fantasy and sci-fi growing up. *Harry Potter* saved my life in some ways when I was a kid, and those books sparked my imagination so powerfully that I...created my first invention."

"So you do like to invent."

He paused for so long she didn't think he was going to continue. All of the sudden he was fidgeting, shifting from foot to foot. "Yes. It's made my life very comfortable."

Well, that answered some of her questions about his job situation and how he'd gotten his money.

"And then you met Chase," she said to encourage him, watching the cars pass as they waited for an available taxi. "Who is he, and can I meet him?"

He signaled to a cab, which pulled over to the side of the road. Evan helped her inside and then climbed in after her and gave the driver directions in his smooth-as-silk French. The sound sent a little thrill through her.

"Chase is my business partner of sorts," he finally answered, "but he doesn't live here. He...ah...sells my inventions."

"Oh, I see," she said. "What else have you invented? Anything I'd know?"

He cleared his throat. "No. Nothing you'd know."

She put her head on his shoulder as the sights flashed by through her window. The lights of Paris were breathtakingly beautiful, and she couldn't wait to stroll through the city at night with Evan holding her hand.

"You really care about Chase, don't you?" she asked.

"He kinda...helped me become what I'd always wanted to be."

He dropped a kiss on the top of her head as he said it. The simple touch was beyond endearing. Self-sufficiency had become so important to her that she'd stopped expecting comfort from others, least of all taking it.

"And what was that?" she asked.

His sigh was so strong it made her shiver. "Someone special. Someone worthy of pride. Someone who...could command...ah, shit, I've never said this out loud to anyone."

She turned in her seat. "You can trust me, Evan."

He scrunched up his face like he was about to do something unpleasant. "I wanted to be the cool guy everyone liked and admired. Not the geeky guy scared of his own shadow who...didn't know how to man up."

Because he needed it, she traced his face, letting the tips of her fingers caress the edges of his beard. "I think you've become a man anyone could admire."

He looked out the window. "I thought so too for a while, but then I got lost somehow. Margie...I found a part of myself in Dare Valley. With you."

She turned his face back to her and stared into his eyes in the darkness of the cab. There was wonder there and that reluctant vulnerability that touched her heart every time. "I'm glad. I think I found a part of myself too."

When they arrived at her apartment, Evan paid the driver as she exited the car. She keyed in the code to the apartment, but when she went to open it, Evan grabbed her hand.

"I'm going to say goodnight here," he told her. "You need to sleep. You have a big day tomorrow."

"I was going to invite you up." They were the only two people on the street, and an air of intimacy surrounded them.

"I know you were," he said, moving toward her and blocking out the light of the streetlamp. "And I want to come up. That's why I'm saying goodnight here. You're exhausted."

"I'm not here for very long, Evan." She gripped his hand. "I want to make the most of our time together."

He raised her hand to his lips, holding her gaze. "We will. You said being with someone is big for you, and I want to honor that. For you. *And* for me."

She let her mouth curl. "The celibacy thing helped you see sex in a new light, didn't it?"

A reluctant smile touched his lips. "Yes, but don't tell anyone that either. Besides, I have to find a more romantic place to make love to you."

Now that surprised her. "Why?"

"If you think I'm going to knock myself out on your hobbit door trying to carry you to the shower after we make love, you're kidding yourself. I want...I want it to be everything you've ever dreamed about. You've...made me dream again, Margie."

In that moment, she almost heard the clock ticking down their time together, and it sent a sharp pang through her. She already knew leaving him was going to tear her to pieces. "I don't want you to go," she said, wrapping her arms around him.

His heart beat in rapid bursts in his chest, echoing the thundering passion in her body.

"I have to," he said, disengaging her arms and kissing her softly on the mouth. "Everything needs to be perfect. So you'll remember."

She faced him on the street. "I'll always remember you."

He pushed a lock of hair back from her brows. "Text me when you finish up tomorrow. I won't say good luck because you don't need it. The bakery is going to be so damn happy to have you there, Margie. Good night."

His footsteps echoed in the quiet street as he walked off.

"Good night, Evan."

She let herself inside and found her bed, promising herself it was okay to give her whole heart to Evan while she was in Paris.

It had to be. She didn't know how to hold herself back.

CHAPTER 3

Boulangerie Ma Belle had a red storefront with sparkling glass windows showcasing the bakery's amazing breads. Margie paused in front and peered through the glass. She saw the curved style of croissants, made mostly in France. From the research she'd done on French baking, she knew this signaled the use of faux fats instead of butter, which was used in the traditionally round croissant shape. To her amazement, there were laws—actual laws—that governed the shape of specific types of bread. And some baguette designs even had their own patents.

When she opened the door, a discreet bell rang. A beautiful blond woman wearing a fabulous white dress looked up from behind the counter. "Bonjour."

"Bonjour," she replied, doing her best to deliver the words in an appealing French accent. "I'm Margie Lancaster, Andre's new baking apprentice."

The woman came around the counter. "Oh, the American! How lovely. We have been waiting for your arrival. You came in yesterday, oui?"

"Oui," she replied. "I was grateful Andre gave me a little time to settle in."

She threw her long hair over her shoulder. "Not enough time if you ask me. That man is a slave driver. I know. I'm married to him."

"Oh," she cried out. "How lovely."

"I'm Belle," the woman said, kissing her on both cheeks Parisian style.

"He named the store after you," she said. "That's very romantic."

Belle gave a mischievous smile. "If I didn't work here, I would never see him. This way we are not parted too long. Bakers' hours are horrible, no? You will see. Andre told me you are opening your own bakery in the United States."

"Yes," she said and then added, "Oui," like an idiot.

"What is the name of your shop?" Belle asked.

"Hot Cross Buns."

Belle laughed. "You have a wicked sense of humor. I like it. We are going to be friends." She walked over to the door behind the counter and opened it a crack. "Cherie, your new apprentice is here."

Margie took a moment to enjoy the sight of all the bread around her. There was an entire wall of the most gorgeous round loaves with the letters BMB cut into the top for decoration. Many bakeries carved their initials into their bread. Margie loved the idea and planned to do it for Hot Cross Buns.

"That is our rustic farm loaf," Belle said. "The recipe is from Andre's great-great grandmother. And these are our sourdough loaves, which we also bake as baguette."

The sourdough loaves she indicated were round, but decorated with different inscriptions. One had a rose while another showcased a tree. They were so artistic Margie almost teared up at the sight of them.

"They're beautiful," she said, wishing she could trace the patterns.

"Wait until you try one. They are pretty, yes, but they also taste divine. Our sourdough is nothing like the kind from your San Francisco, though, and Andre will tell you why."

"Giving away all my secrets, Belle?" a man asked from behind them.

Margie wrested her gaze away from the bread to look at him. Andre appeared to be in his early forties, and was completely bald in that sexy way Michael Jordan and Patrick Stewart were. His body had the muscular build of a man who kneaded dough for a living. And his smile was pure gold with a dimple winking out mischievously in his right cheek.

"Andre! It's so good to finally meet you," she said.

He crossed the room and kissed her on both cheeks with an enthusiasm that made her laugh.

"You say that now." His wink had Belle rolling her eyes. "Let us hope you feel the same way at the end of your apprenticeship."

"Let me know if I need to tell him to...how do you say it in English?" Belle said. "Reverse back?"

It took a moment for her to understand. "Throttle back."

"I only want to share everything I know with her," Andre said, throwing his arms out with gusto.

"It's only ten days, Andre," Belle reminded him. "He is as eager as a child."

"We will make the most of our time, Margie," Andre said. "Brian tells me I must have you teach me how you make your cinnamons rolls while you're here. He said I would revolutionize Paris with the recipe."

"Brian is sweet to say so." She eyed the man's white apron, which was streaked with flour and dried dough. Soon she would look like that every day too. "I would be happy to show you, Andre. The recipe is from the owner of the bakery I am buying. It's been in her family for generations."

"As have my recipes," he said, gesturing grandly to the wall. "Our bread is like a living, breathing family tree of our ancestors. In the quiet hours of the night, I can feel their spirits gather around me as I help them live on through my work. You will see."

She shivered. "That actually gave me chills."

Belle patted her arm. "Don't worry about our baking spirits. They mean no harm."

Her chills weren't due to fear, but rather the realization that these people *understood* her. On a primal level, Margie understood people had baked bread for millennia. Bread had nourished humankind since after the first hearth fires were lit. And when bread was unavailable, people starved.

"Bread is life," she echoed. "I believe that."

"Good," Andre said, laying a hand on her shoulder and peering into her eyes. "You have an old soul. I can see that. You make good bread because of it."

She flushed. "An old soul?"

"You see things. In people. In life. Bread is your way of giving back to the world, no?"

Something powerful rose in her chest, an emotion she could not name. She thought of what she'd told Evan last night over dinner. "I...yes...bread taught me so much, and now I want to give back through my bakery."

Andre pulled Belle in close with his other hand, and the three of them formed a circle. "I knew you would feel the ancient power of the yeast, of the leavening, of the baking. You must in order to become a master. We are going to do great things together while you are in Paris, Margie."

"I'm...my heart is about ready to burst with gratitude," she said to them, and they both hugged her. "You speak my language. I know that sounds weird since English is my first language, and French is yours. But making bread and baking it—"

"Is a language all its own. It's magical, no?" Andre asked. "We are going to make some beautiful magic together, ma petite, Margie, from Dare Valley."

Though her parents and the people in the circle she'd been born into had never understood her—or cared to—since leaving them, she'd slowly found other people who fed her soul, so to speak. These people were going to feed her soul. She just knew it.

"You must try one of our punitions," Belle said, breaking the circle and dashing over to the display in the corner.

When she darted back, Margie took the special French shortbread cookie from her. "Thank you."

"I mix the ingredients and form the shapes," Andre said, slapping his chest. "Belle adds her magic by sprinkling them with fairy dust, and the ancestors stoke the fire for our creations so they will be baked to perfection."

The punition simply melted in Margie's mouth. "Oh! Oh my!" she said when she could finally speak.

Andre gave a dirty little laugh. "That's what Belle says when we are home, and the children are asleep."

"Oh, Andre," Belle said, slapping him playfully on the arm. "You are a scoundrel. A rogue."

He waggled his brows. "And you love it, ma petite."

His wife's beaming smile was answer enough. "Ignore us. He is...how do you say it in English? Friskier than usual? He has been waiting for your arrival with much anticipation. No one likes to teach like Andre does."

"I am eager to learn all you wish to show me," she answered as he grabbed her hand and led her to the door that could only lead to the bakery.

"We must have a tour, ma cherie," he said to his wife. "We will return when the ancestors are satisfied."

"That might be a while." Belle laughed. "I will remain here to sell our bread."

Andre led Margie behind the door, and the second she stepped inside, she was engulfed by the familiar scents of bread: sour, sweet, yeast, and baking.

"We have two levels where we work," Andre said, gesturing to the stainless steel counters. "Here we have the preparation area for the croissants and pain au chocolat. You see the machine in the corner. Do you know how to use it?"

She shook her head, eying the massive press that rolled the croissant dough into its famously thin layers. "Not yet. I wanted the kitchen to be ready before mine arrived."

"No problem, ma cherie. I will teach you how to use it. It is easy. You simply have to make love to the bread." His brown eyes twinkled. "You know how to make love to the bread, right?"

Margie didn't embarrass easily, but she could feel her cheeks heating. "Ah...I think so."

Andre made a kneading motion with his hands. "You stroke it and stroke it until it surrenders with a sigh."

She couldn't help but laugh. "I'll...try and remember that."

His brow knit in puzzlement. "It is perhaps different for a woman. Belle!"

His wife poked her head through the swinging door. "Oui?"

"How do women bakers make love to the bread? I am trying to tell Margie, but I think it is different."

Belle gave him a seductive smile and winked at Margie. "You work it hard when it needs it, and you gently caress it when it wants to resist. And you do it all with love so it always rises to your touch."

Andre grabbed Belle to him and gave her a soft kiss. "That is why I love this woman."

Instead of feeling like a voyeur, Margie felt like she was seeing the highest version of a relationship. Here Andre and Belle were, working together in the bakery they shared, loving each other, and supporting each other's dreams. It was so lovely to behold.

"How many children do you have?" she asked when

Belle gave Andre a playful shove so he'd let her go.

"Three," she said with a wide smile. "This one here wants five, but he has moments of insanity. I blame it on all the yeast he inhales."

"I'll have to remember to use that excuse the next time I'm having a moment," she said.

"Yeast is better than PMS," Belle said with a glance at Andre. "I hate that line."

"Me too," she easily agreed. Howie had blamed her moods on PMS, and it had angered her to no end. In truth, his secret drug problem had not been the only fissure in their relationship. *Evan would never say something so simplistic or unkind*, she thought, surprised to realize she was comparing them.

The bell rang, and Andre pulled Belle in for another fast kiss. "We installed the bell so she can sneak back here and steal kisses from me when customers aren't around."

"Ingenious, no?" Belle asked Margie before disappearing through the door.

"Now," Andre said, taking her hand. "Let me show you where we make the real magic."

The stairs leading down to what was essentially a basement were steep, and like when she was using her hobbit bathroom door, she had to duck down to avoid hitting her head.

The heat in the room they entered poured over her body like a wave of molten fire. The ovens in the back were lit and baking row after row of golden brown baguettes. The thick smell of yeast hung in the air, and she inhaled deeply. Detecting a hint of something fruity and sour, she looked at the flour-dusted stainless steel counters for the source, but didn't see it.

"This is Fabian and Ronan, my two assistants. Meet Margie from America."

"Enchante," they both said.

"Enchantee," she replied.

"They don't speak English," Andre said. "You told me you have some French."

She winced. "It's really rusty, but I hope to practice while I'm here if you can stand to hear me bungle the words."

"Speak away," Andre said. "We will help you find the right words. But we will use English for instruction, I think, so you miss nothing."

She nodded.

"Now, this is where we make the bread. We have a few signature breads everyone who visits us expects to see. But every once in a while, especially around a holiday or if I'm feeling inspired, we will make something special. I don't use any starters like some bakers do. My people were farmers, and our recipes are done differently. Our farm loaf uses potato water from the yellow potatoes Belle buys in the market and boils before she closes the bakery for the night. The red bucket in the corner is for the water we drain from the cooked potatoes once they cool."

He gestured to the wall opposite the wall of ovens. Sure enough, a couple of massive buckets stood on the stainless steel counter next to the huge industrial bread mixers.

"It is empty now," he said, picking up the bucket and shaking it before setting it aside. "This bucket however—the green one—is almost always full. Our sourdough bread is made from the water of the apples and pears we cut up into quarters and leave for three days. The natural yeast forms on the top in white bubbles, and when it is ready, we discard the fruit and use the water to mix with the ingredients. The water we use is warm, not like the cold water used to make your San Francisco sourdough. Pretty simple, no? Our process here is not difficult. And while yours is very dense, ours is light and airy with a floral essence all its own."

"I can't wait to try it," she said, intrigued. "I've researched bread starters, and honestly, I find them rather intimidating. I like the idea of using potato water or fruit water to give a bread flavor and leavening."

"Here, try some."

He grabbed a baguette resting in one of the many trays in a bakery rack that stood six feet tall. Breaking off a chunk, he handed the end to her. The other two bakers stopped cleaning the empty baking pans to watch her. She took her first bite and sighed. While she loved San Francisco sourdough, the texture and taste resembled play dough. This was...something uniquely different, and she knew in that moment, she was going to bring this recipe back to Dare Valley and bake it at Hot Cross Buns.

"This is incredible, Andre," she said. "I don't think I've ever enjoyed sourdough more."

He slapped his chest. "You stick with me, Margie. I will show you all my magic, and you will show me yours."

Fabian and Ronan laughed and said something in French about the whole bakery being filled with magic, but that was all she caught of their interplay.

"I don't think I have as much magic as you do, Andre," she said, tearing off another piece of bread and savoring it. Bread like this made butter seem superfluous, and she knew most French people ate their bread plain.

"You have more magic inside you than you realize, ma petite," he said, looking into her eyes. "I will help you remember this."

Unable to look away, she only nodded, chewing slowly.

"Now, as you can see, we have five industrial mixers. Four are for a specific type of bread unless I'm making a special. I labeled them to help you while you're here." He pointed to the handwritten labels taped to the bottoms of the mixers. "Two are used for traditional baguette since we supply some of Paris' finest restaurants. Then one is for baguette sourdough and our farm bread with the potato water. The last I use for treats like the punitions. Remember?"

"Yes," she answered, recalling the buttery shortbread. "I've got it."

He moved on to the stainless steel counters and picked up a baker's blade—a wicked-looking curved razor blade, which looked to be glued to the end of a pen. Evan would get a kick out of the invention, she thought, and couldn't wait to tell him about it.

"This is the baker's weapon," Andre said, making slashing motions with it like he was wielding a small dagger. "It is how you differentiate yourself as a baker and put your stamp on the bread you sell. In Paris, this is very important."

"This has to do with the patented bread types, right?" she asked.

"In some cases," he said, reaching behind him on another line of stacked trays and pulling off a beautiful ball of dough. "Feel this."

"I haven't washed my hands," she said, looking around for a sink.

"Did you not put a hunk of bread in your mouth?" He rolled his eyes. "The ovens will burn off any germs, ma petite. Do not be so nervous. Touch it."

He almost made it sound like an invitation to sin. She poked the dough with her finger. It gave to her touch unlike any other dough she'd ever felt. Bubbles formed where she'd made contact.

"Tell me you have not felt anything softer."

"I haven't. Truly."

"My bread lives and breathes like a human being," he said. From anyone else it would have sounded crazy, but he meant it. On some level, she felt the same way about her own baking, although she would have described it differently.

"This is love," he said and kissed the dough. "Now, let me show you how I wield my weapon." He abruptly laughed and looked toward the ceiling. "Belle would call me...how do you say? On the carpet? For talking like that to a lady. But we bakers are a pretty dirty lot. Our bread dough reminds us of breasts, and it is our life's work to craft a recipe that makes the perfect breast so we can play with it in the dark hours of the night. No wonder the priests used to make the bakers go to confession once a week."

"I hadn't heard that before." Confession for bread making? She tried and failed to disguise her chuckle. "I'll have to find another...ah...goal to inspire me."

"Yeah, it does not work the same for a woman," he said, putting the dough in the center of the floured surface of a well-used pastry cloth. "It's said the first great male bakers in France were monks. I always thought it was one of the few good outcomes of a vow of celibacy, n'est-ce pas?"

"I agree," she said, laughing fully now. Confession, sin, and now monks. France had a long, colorful history. "I'll have to share your view with a friend of mine."

Evan would find the story amusing after his recent celibacy kick. Goosebumps suddenly rolled across her skin as she thought about them coming together as lovers. Would it be tonight? She hoped it would be tonight. Already, her insides felt like over-risen bread loaves, ready to explode, needing heat for completion.

"You are not here, ma petite," Andre said. "Come rejoin me. You must be present to make magic."

"I'm sorry." She shook herself. "Please continue."

"Brian must have shown you how he learned to make bread, but everyone makes it differently, even when they use the same recipe."

She nodded. "I know. Even though I'm using Grandma Kemstead's cinnamon roll recipe, mine still turn out differently. It's slight, but I can tell."

He rubbed her shoulder. "You understand me then. So, I will show you my way, and you will find your own."

"Actually, Brian didn't teach me how to make baguettes. He didn't want to give me any bad habits," she said, touching a finger to the flour on the cloth, itching to get her hands dirty. "He wanted me to learn from the master."

"Just so," Andre said, nodding his head in approval. "First, you must make the proper baguette shape." He used the heel of his hand to roll the ball of dough into a circle. "Now you tuck one side into the middle and pinch the seams. Then, you do the same thing on the other side. Then there's the third tuck. You take one side and connect it all the way to the other side."

His hands moved slowly so she wouldn't miss any of the steps, and he glanced at her every few moments to make sure she was still with him.

"The last part is easy. You use both hands to roll it into the shape of the slender arm of a beautiful woman. A dancer's arm. See?"

And she *could* see it. He left one end of the baguette a little thicker than the other so it looked like a woman's arm from elbow to wrist.

He reached for a baker's blade. "This little tool is your paintbrush. You are going to slash it across the bread to make the cuts everyone has come to expect from a proper baguette." He made the diagonal slashes with the precision of a master. "Slash. Don't saw. She will open to you better if you treat her with swiftness and gentleness."

When he set the baguette aside and reached for another ball of dough, she watched in fascination as he worked ten times faster than he had during his first demonstration to shape it into another baguette. This was a true professional at work, and she wondered how many baguettes he could shape and slash in a minute.

She decided to ask him.

"I've never counted. The bread sets the pace. You find your rhythm with the dough."

Margie felt that way with her cinnamon rolls. Sometimes it felt like the dough wanted her to go slower. She mostly listened—unless she was in a rush.

"Once you master the proper baguette," Andre said, "you can allow your imagination to come forth. That's where the true magic comes." He grabbed another ball of dough and shaped it. His slashes this time were more like the lines that divided a highway. "You can do anything with the blade, ma petite. Don't be afraid of putting your mark on the dough. It's like putting your mark on a lover, no?" He bumped her playfully. "Do you know what I mean?"

She thought of the fingernail marks or soft nips she'd made on past lovers, and the delicate bites she'd received in kind. Then she thought of Evan and wondered what kind of marks they would leave on each other.

"You are ripe, ma petite," Andre said, studying her. "It is not just the sensuality of the bread. There's a man. You are flushed."

She raised a hand to her chest, embarrassed the heat her skin was releasing was visible to the naked eye. "Yes, there's a man."

"When it's good between a man and a woman, the bread rises higher, but when it's sour, the dough seems to struggle, and the taste is flatter." He patted her on the back. "Just a word of wisdom. I became insanely successful when I met Belle. There were no accidents in that regard, ma petite."

The notion of becoming more successful because of love appealed to her romantic side. "I appreciate your wisdom, Andre. I hope you will always share it with me."

"As long as you are here, Margie," he said. "Now,

you will show me what you can do with the bread. First, you will form a traditional baguette. Until you have made it perfectly, I will not be satisfied."

When he inclined his head toward the tray filled with rising balls of dough, she reached for her first one. It felt like the softest pillow in her hands. In that moment, she decided that was the way she'd envision them—as pillows. Breasts would never work for her. She laid the dough on the pastry cloth and reached her hand out to the nearby container of flour to add some more to the cloth.

"Do not use too much flour," he said, shaking her hand free until she was only holding a pinch. "The downfall of many bakers is their over-use of flour."

"Grandma Kemstead said the same thing about the cinnamon rolls," she told him.

"She knows then," Andre said. "Now, roll it into a circle."

She used the heel of her hand like he did. The dough was so alive, she could feel the bubbles burst at her touch. "You make it look so easy. Getting the thickness even as you roll it out is a challenge. Do you never use a rolling pin?" That's what she used for the cinnamon rolls.

"Never for bread." He gave a wicked wink. "A rolling pin for bread is like a kinky sex toy. You only bring it out when all else fails."

Margie disagreed, but she declined to comment. Somehow, bantering with Andre about the sensuality of bread felt dangerous, and she wanted to get to know him better before she threw back a comment so incendiary. Instead, she rolled the bread until she felt it was even and then tucked it together three times like he'd shown her. Rolling it into a baguette that resembled a woman's arm proved more challenging.

"Mine looks more like a rabbit's leg."

He put his arm around her shoulders and jostled her

good-naturedly. "You practice. I made an entire tray of bread dough for you today. But to inspire your imagination as you learn the basics, let me show you something else."

He grabbed another ball of dough and rolled it into a perfectly formed baguette. Then he used some kitchen shears to cut the top of the bread every few inches.

"You see? It is a completely new presentation." Then he leaned in with a cocky grin. "But there's still more I can do." He connected the ends of the bread and made a wreath. "Sometimes we make it this way, and then serve it with fresh berries and cream in the middle. People love it. And it's so simple. All it takes is a little imagination."

"Wow!" she said, touching the cut ends of the bread. "You're incredible."

"Wait until I teach you how to braid baguettes together." He leaned back against the stainless steel counter. "You won't believe how beautiful that can be. But that's an advanced lesson. For now, you practice making baguette. Then I will show you how we bake the bread."

She glanced over at the ovens and saw Fabian and Ronan working in tandem, taking out an enormous batch of piping hot golden bread loaves.

"You will have your own baguette to take home, ma petite," Andre said. "Be sure to savor it. There is nothing like sampling the first baguette of your hands. It is like a first kiss."

Margie immediately thought of her first kiss along the Seine—how the willows had wrapped her even closer to Evan, how his mouth had felt as it moved in urgent, heated passes over her own.

"And share it with your man," Andre said with a knowing smile. "But know you will be sharing a part of your soul with him."

She trembled a bit, hearing that. She'd already

shared parts of her soul with him by divulging her dreams and her past with her parents, but somehow she knew sharing this bread with Evan would be huge and intimate. It would leave her feeling even more vulnerable than she already did.

"Do not overthink love, ma petite," Andre told her and handed her another ball of dough like it was a queen's crown. "It is like bread. Keep it simple and do not over-mix or over-knead it. Now, practice. I am going upstairs for a while." He spoke in smooth French to Fabian and Ronan. The men smiled and nodded at her. "They will keep you company. You do not need to speak French to speak the language of bread. They will advise you if you have questions."

She looked over at the men and gave them a kind of bow, like she would at the end of a yoga class. Somehow it seemed appropriate.

When he reached the stairs, Andre turned to look at her with that wicked smile of his. "And have fun with the bread, Margie. Always have fun."

After that, time fell away. She made baguette after baguette. Her early ones took longer to form and showed the marks of a beginner. She was still feeling out the best way to roll the dough into a circle with the heel of her hand. She had the three tucking steps down. The hardest part remained rolling out the dough to look like a woman's arm. A few of hers looked like a crooked water pipe while another resembled a dog's leg.

When Andre returned, he hovered near her and eyed her progress. "You are improving, ma petite."

"I hope you aren't selling the baguettes I am making," she said honestly. "I will give your bakery a bad name."

"No worries, ma petite," he said, wrapping his arm around her shoulders. "We will put your loaves in a special basket that says apprentice bread and discount it. If it doesn't sell, we will give the rest to the neighborhood church. We rarely have bread left at the end of the day, but when we do, either Belle or I walk to the church to give them to Father Charles. He hands the loaves out to the poor who visit their door every night. I cannot abide bread being thrown away. If I could make it for free and still live well, I would. It is not about the money."

She nodded. "I feel the same way." She knew how hollow the happiness bought by money felt.

"But money makes the world go around, as they say, and so we play our role," Andre said. "Now, show me what you have done."

He critiqued each loaf, noting the unevenness of some of them and a few lazy pinches that would come apart as the bread started to rise. "Remember, ma petite. You must give the bread its structure because once it starts rising again, it will break free of any loose shaping."

She nodded, and he moved down the row of her baguettes, which Fabian had helped her lay out on baking trays that would eventually go into the oven.

"Your slashing technique is improving as well," he said. "I would say it's your best feature so far."

Picking up the baker's blade, she made a slashing motion. "I've kind of fallen in love with this tool. It's rather fun." When she could concentrate on her cinnamon rolls again, she wanted to consider other options besides simply rolling them out and placing them in a pan. What might her imagination inspire her to create?

She and Andre continued to work side by side as she practiced and practiced. When he finally called out for her to stop, satisfied with her progress, she'd made fifty baguettes to her count. Not too shabby.

"Now for the easy part," he said. "The baking. Come closer to the ovens."

She stood as close as she felt comfortable. Andre was

about a foot closer to them than she was.

"The heat is impressive, no?" he asked. "I use a Winkler oven to bake my beauties. As you can see, it's a gas oven. I'm old fashioned this way. I like having the hint of fire bake my bread. What kind did you buy?"

"I have a Bodgette I inherited from the former owner. It still works beautifully. I used it to bake cinnamon rolls with the former owner before she handed the keys over to me."

"It is a good brand, I think," Andre said, "and how nice that you did not have to pay for it yourself, although I'm sure the equipment was included in the price of the bakery."

"It was," she said, thinking back to what a dance she'd had to do to make it all work. She and Grandma Kemstead had itemized all the equipment in the store, and Margie had chosen what she wanted to keep. "The bread slicer I inherited goes back to the 40s, and it's still in top shape. There's a man in town who's been sharpening the blades for forty years." And now he would sharpen the blades for her.

Whenever she thought about continuing the special legacy begun by Grandma Kemstead, she got teary-eyed. After walking away from the legacy her parents had tried to force on her, she'd never expected it would make her this happy to find a connection to something that spanned the generations.

"Good equipment can last forever with the proper care," Andre said. "So, after all the shaping, it's pretty simple to bake the bread. We just pop the trays inside. At this point, they don't need to rise much. The dough has already reached its apex, so to speak. The heat takes it home. Would you like to do the honors? They're your baguettes."

"I'd love to," she said and picked the first of the three heavy trays she'd filled with her baguettes.

"You are stronger than you look," Andre commented

as he opened the oven door for her.

"I added extra weights to my routine when I decided to buy the bakery." Not that she'd been doing much working out lately. She hadn't the time.

The heat was intense on her face as she slid in the first tray and then followed suit with the next two. Andre shut the door and gave her an impromptu hug. Fabian and Ronan clapped, interrupting the cleanup they were doing near a small sink next to the stairs.

"You have made your first magic in Paris, Margie," Andre said. "I feel like a proud papa. Oh, I will teach you so many things. Now, we will let the bread bake. Come upstairs with me. We have some champagne in the refrigerator. Belle insists on keeping it. We must celebrate."

"Ah...maybe we should wait to taste my baguettes before we celebrate," she said.

"Nonsense," Andre said, leading her to the stairs. "You are using my dough. They will be perfect. Now, when you make your own dough..."

She saw where he was going with this. "It's going to take practice," she said and almost winced, wondering how much. But it was exciting too. She was learning how to make baguettes in Paris with a master baker. She needed to kick her perfectionism to the curb and enjoy this.

"You will get it right, with practice and my fine instruction," he said with a laugh. "After all, you will be using *my* recipe. And it's perfect, no? The angels weep when they eat my bread. Jesus himself might have—"

"I get it," she said, climbing the steep stairs. "You're a regular saintly baker."

"There is already a Saint Andre," he teased when they reached the top. "But I will figure something out to ensure I leave a legacy."

"I have no doubt."

Andre called out to Fabian and Ronan, and they

climbed the stairs as well. In the small back room of the bakery's first floor, Andre produced a bottle of champagne. His wife came through the swinging door with a huge smile.

"Success!" she said and hugged Margie. "There is no better feeling."

"No, there truly isn't," Margie answered, accepting a glass of champagne.

Once everyone had a glass, Andre raised his to her. "To Margie from America. May she learn to bake bread like a Frenchman."

"French woman, ma cherie," Belle said, nudging him in the ribs.

"As you wish," he said with a laugh. "To making the bread of life."

The words held a spiritual significance she'd never fully understood before. Bread was life. She'd known that for some time. Now she understood the deeper nuances of that statement. Bread *did* give life. It had given her life. And now she wanted to share that life with others—like she had with Evan. Her new knowledge humbled her mightily.

"To making the bread of life," she said and connected their glasses in the toast.

CHAPTER 4

Evan was counting the minutes until Margie texted him to tell him she was free. He had no idea how long her master baker would keep her today. He hadn't been able to resist looking Andre Moutard up on Google. The guy seemed legit, but who knew if he was a good boss?

The events of last night had shaken his foundation, everything from their kiss to her revelations about her painful past. As he glanced around his luxurious penthouse apartment filled with every modern convenience—and not a hobbit door in sight—he felt a familiar fear rise up in him.

She wasn't going to like him when she learned he was obscenely rich—billionaire rich—and had been entrenched in the same shallow circles as her parents until recently. He just knew it would ruin everything between them.

The ruse would have to continue…at least until he knew she cared about him as much as he did about her. Since she wanted to make love with him, he knew she cared. A lot. And it both humbled him and excited him.

He decided to call L'Hotel again to make sure everything was ready for them should she still want to be with him tonight. His body tightened with lust as he imagined slowly undressing her and kissing every inch of her glorious body. But they wouldn't have the entire night together. She'd have to leave for the bakery before two a.m. Normally he didn't stay with women afterward. He rather liked his space and solitude, but he wondered what it would be like to wake up with her all warm and tousled from sleep. And he found himself wanting something he'd never before thought to want.

The phone rang, and he snatched it up, seeing it was Chase. "Did you see the new prototype for the Paint Prep Mistress? It's looking great, isn't it?"

"Evan. I told you we can't do this." His friend paused. "I know you're happy about the invention, but we need something else. Something that will complement the rest of what we do."

This was an argument they'd carried on every day for a week—ever since Evan had diverted a few key staff in their Research and Development Department to work with him on improving the design.

"Chase, I know you don't see this going anywhere, but it will. I can't explain it, but there's a defense application here somewhere. I can feel it. I just don't know what it is yet."

"You keep saying that," Chase said in an aggrieved tone. "And I keep trying to believe it. But most of our clients in the countries we currently serve don't need help painting their buildings. Or their planes or their ships..."

Didn't he know that? *But there's something there.* He kicked the desk, feeling the frustration well in his gut. The key that would unlock this whole thing was hidden from him. But he couldn't find it. Right now it was like he was trying to walk the famous labyrinth at Chartres Cathedral outside Paris in the dark. He couldn't find the center.

"I'll use my personal funds on this, Chase," Evan

said in a hard tone. "I know I'm blowing your perfect corporate budget right now." Some of the materials he'd ordered to modernize the invention and make it sleek and lightweight were astronomically expensive.

"Did you really need the specially insulated titanium?" Chase asked. "That seems kinda excessive for a painting tool."

It probably was, but he hated working with inferior metals. And besides, the voice that kept telling him this was more than a painting tool wouldn't be silenced—not by him, not by Chase.

"I'll send you a check today." They'd never done it this way, but if Howard Hughes could finance his own projects, so could he.

"Dammit, Evan, this is about more than money, and you know it." Chase let out a tortured breath. "You're taking our best R&D people away from their current projects. We have contracts, Evan, with strict deliverables. If you keep having them work on this project, we're going to end up defaulting, and that's a whole other ballpark of hell. One we cannot dig ourselves out of. Right now, all I can do is deliver your old designs. If we lose that, with nothing new to sell plus the defaults, we *will* lose this company, Evan. It won't be quick, but it will happen."

He crossed the room to the French doors leading to the balcony. In the distance, the Eiffel Tower speared the sky. After the inventor, a civil engineer named Gustave Eiffel, created it for the 1889 World's Fair, he came under significant criticism for its design. People had said he was crazy. But he stuck to his guns like every other famous inventor, and look how things had turned out. No one could imagine Paris without his invention. Gustave had combined art and aerodynamics and a whole stream of other theories into an awe-inspiring collage of metal. Evan wished he could buy the man a beer for reminding him to press on.

"So money isn't going to fix it," he said, realizing he was seeing way too much evidence of this lesson in his life right now. "What will? I need my staff, Chase. And they are *my* staff."

"Did you just hear what I said?" Chase asked. "If you keep diverting staff and funds in one of the most critical departments in this company, we're going to hit rocky shores, Evan. I love this company as much as you do. Do you want this ship to go down?"

"Of course not," he said, gripping the curved metal rails of his balcony as he thought through a solution. In some ways, it had been so much easier to invent things when his future had been the only one at stake. "How about this? We need more staff to accommodate this new project and our existing orders. How about you start hiring, and in the meantime, I'll ask who wants to work overtime on my special projects?" He hadn't unleashed his next idea on them yet. He was still fussing with the drawings in his head.

"There's more?" Chase asked. He sounded downright appalled. "How much painting did you do in Dare Valley anyway?"

"A lot, and I liked it. Chase, every unnatural surface is painted." He saw it now, everywhere he looked. Paint was a common thread throughout all modern life. "There's something here."

"You keep saying that!" Chase said, losing his usual cool. "Are you sure the fumes didn't go to your head?"

It was enough to make him think of the chemical composition of paint. There was something about the polymers. They were trying to tell him something. He'd been playing with the equations, trying to decipher the secret.

"Chase. I want this to happen, so I'm telling you. Make it happen. I gave you a solution. If you don't like it, find another one and run it by me."

"You don't usually play hardball with me, Evan,"

Chase said.

"Do you call this hardball?" Evan asked. "If so, you need to take up poker."

"I don't share your appetite for risk," Chase said, "which is why I manage the company and you invent. You know that, Evan. It's why you hired me. But I'll see what I can do about implementing your solution."

"I'll finance the employees' overtime myself so it doesn't cut into your budget," Evan said. "As my way of not playing hardball with you." His gut burned a bit. "I don't like fighting with you, Chase."

"I don't either," his friend admitted. "Usually we're on the same page."

But not this time. And damn if that didn't make him feel alone. If not for Margie...

"Chase," he said quietly, feeling the geeky boy he'd been emerge through the ether. "Do you trust me?"

The man blew out a breath. "Mostly. Evan, you know how much...oh hell...you know what I'm saying. I *do* trust you. It's only that you haven't been yourself these last couple of years."

Truer words were never spoken. "I know. But I've found a lost piece of myself. Only this time it's better."

The long pause made Evan shuffle his feet. He could feel Chase gathering himself to say something unpleasant.

"I know Margie Lancaster is in Paris, Evan," Chase said. "And I know you care for her. If you're falling for her... Don't mistake love for creative inspiration."

Chase was wrong. What he felt for Margie had opened up his creative inspiration, but the two things were still separate, like hydrogen and oxygen. Both interacted to become water under the right circumstances, but they still retained their separate properties. And when added to other elements, each could become something else, something new.

"You're still jaded after your divorce, so I won't try

to explain this to you." Chase's wife had taken him for all he was worth in the divorce. His friend's private wealth had suffered, but it was his spirit Evan was still worried about.

"All I can say is prenup," Chase said in a harsh tone. "If the paint fumes have you thinking that far ahead."

Evan was surprised to find the thought of marriage didn't freak him out...not like it did when it was mentioned by one of the gorgeous gold-diggers who had hoped to snag him so they could have access to his billions. Margie would never be like that.

In fact, she would rather hate his money.

For a moment, he let himself imagine what it would be like to be married to her. As he gazed across Paris' rooftops, he could see them strolling along the Seine hand in hand. Every morning she would greet him with that sweet smile of hers when she woke. Of course, he would have to wake up well before dawn for that to happen, but this was his fantasy, so there was no need to account for her unusual hours.

Her kisses would anchor him in a whole new level of happiness. And she would bake her cinnamon rolls, which she could sell to a bakery in Paris, while he worked on his inventions. And after they both finished doing the work they loved, he would sweep her off her feet and make love to her until neither one of them wanted to move. Yeah, he liked that.

"Evan," Chase urgently said. "You're scaring me with all this silence."

"How did you know Margie was here?" he asked even though he suspected he knew.

"You know I have a few people keeping an eye on you due to corporate espionage," Chase said. "I get a call every time a new person comes into your circle. Especially in Paris, your hometown."

He understood Chase's paranoia. His wife had taken some important corporate documents from him and used them as leverage in the divorce proceedings. Chase had feared one of Evan's shallower girlfriends might do the same even though Evan had promised to keep everything confidential in his private R&D room in the penthouse or the special security box he'd designed for travel. Unlike some inventors, Evan still liked to hand draw until he was ready to start designing his work in AutoCAD. Of course, they were supposed to abide by these protocols anyway due to their security clearances, but things happened.

"So your guys did their job, and now you know she's not a threat to me. You can stop following her or whatever it is they're doing. If you knew her, Chase, you'd laugh at the ludicrousness of the thought." He didn't think Margie would laugh though. She'd be insulted, and rightly so. It was another secret he'd definitely be keeping.

"Are you sure about her, Evan? She grew up super rich, so she's used to the lifestyle, but her parents disowned her years ago. She currently has just over twelve hundred dollars in her personal banking account. If she landed you—"

"Shut the fuck up, Chase. Right now."

There was a shocked silence on the other end. Evan's heart rate lurched from normal to anaerobic in seconds. He'd never said anything like that to Chase before. But hearing him say those things about Margie...

"You do love her," the man finally said with a groan. "I'll excuse what you just said. But I'll tell you this once, Evan. No one talks to me like that. Not even you."

The younger boy in him, the one Chase had cultivated and helped grow into a man, wanted to kowtow, but he planted his feet on the balcony and stared off into the horizon. "Then promise me that you'll never say one more bad word about Margie—to me or anyone else—ever again."

"I apologize," Chase said easily. "I was out of line.

I'm only trying to protect you, Evan."

"You're not my father, Chase," he said. But as he said it, he realized something—for a long time, he had looked to Chase to be his friend, brother, and dad all in one. "At least I don't need you to be anymore. How about we just agree to look after each other as friends?"

There was another pause. "That sounds okay. Do I need to come to Paris to meet her?"

Evan had never introduced Chase to any of the other women he'd dated. "I don't know." When he thought of it, he did want Chase to meet her. "It's complicated right now."

"Right. She still doesn't know who you are. I think you should keep it that way until she tells you she loves you. It's the only way you can know with one hundred percent certainty that she's not just after your billions."

Hearing Chase give that advice helped alleviate the guilt he'd been feeling all day. He knew he shouldn't make love to Margie without telling her the full truth, and yet...

"I agree. For now."

"Good," Chase said. "Now, I'm going to let you go so we can both get back to work."

"Go to bed," Evan said even though he knew it would make no difference. "It's almost ten o'clock there."

"It's early," Chase said with a chuckle. "I'll talk to you later, Evan."

"Bye, Chase," he responded and hung up.

He pocketed his phone and leaned against the rails. They'd never gone at each other quite like that before, and while it scared him a bit, how much he'd asserted himself with Chase, he also felt powerful. Like he'd just slayed a dragon from his past. After all these years, he was finally man enough to speak his mind and not run from conflict.

Everything seemed to be changing.

***

When Andre finally called an end to her first day of instruction, Margie was in possession of his secret baguette recipe and a new wealth of knowledge about the different types of flour. Rye flour softened wheat-based flour, and chestnut flour—a decadent pale yellow color—added sweetness and was gluten free. Of course, the latter was used sparingly, both because of its lofty price and its dense texture.

All but six of her apprentice loaves had been sold. Her heart glowed in her chest when she thought of the people who would be eating her bread with their evening meal. She'd fed people before, but they were her friends. These loaves had been her first sale as a professional baker, and she planned to celebrate.

"You will take your extra loaves home with you now, ma petite," Andre said, tucking them into a large cloth bread bag.

"We can't possibly eat them all," she said, laughing. "Can I take five of the loaves to Father Charles to give to the poor?"

His whole face softened, and he pulled her in for a warm hug. "You have the heart of a baker, Margie. In the smaller villages in France, bakers would always make an offering of the first loaves at their new shop to the church."

That cinched it. "Can you call him and tell him I'm coming? Does he speak English? My French..."

"I will call him and draw you a little map to the church." He immediately took his phone out and called Father Charles. She was catching more words in French, but he was speaking so fast. Her brain felt like it was ready to explode, especially after all she'd learned today.

"He said to ring the bell to his residence. It's a small gray stone house with a blue door, off to the right of the church. If you feel so called, ma petite, give him four of the loaves. Keep one for you and your man. And then take the remaining one and lay it at the feet of the Madonna in the courtyard behind the church. Even though St. Honore is the patron saint of bakers, our Lady loves those of us who make bread as well."

Margie had never grown up in organized religion, but she felt oddly moved. While in Mexico, she'd been surrounded by the rituals and faith of the people there. She'd never felt a part of it, being an outsider, but she'd respected the reverence people had for Mary and the saints.

"There's a patron saint of bakers?"

Andre laughed. "There's a patron saint for everything, and while I'm no regular church goer anymore, the roots of the old traditions still run through my veins like they run through all of Paris. If you know where to look, you will see this everywhere. The Green Man. Various gods and goddesses. Jesus. The saints. Angels. Paris has been around longer than the Catholic church."

She remembered Evan mentioning how an Egyptian goddess had been honored on the site where Notre Dame was now built. "I will have to pay more attention."

"Sometimes you don't have to pay attention, ma petite. What wants your attention will always find a way to capture it. This town has magic. I hope you will allow it to feed your soul."

Rare tears popped into her eyes. She was holding the loaves she'd made in her arms like they were her children. It was only the first day of her apprenticeship, and she already felt transformed by the experience.

"Andre...I don't have the words to thank you. This apprenticeship and you..."

"Come now, ma petite," he said thickly. "You will make me cry too. I share with you all I know because it was shared with me. And now you will share it with others. And we will feed the world from the love we have for the bread, as we are meant to do. Now go. All this emotion is making me long to head to the park with my family so Belle and I can watch our children play."

The others had left the shop after it closed at three, but Andre had insisted Margie spend just one more hour there so he could show her his grandmother's hand-written recipes. The cards had yellowed with age, and the ink was smeared in places from a stray drop of water here and there. She'd felt honored Andre would show her these prized treasures. Recipes were magical time capsules, and one day, Margie decided, she wanted to give her hand-written recipes to her children after teaching them how to make bread. It would be another part of this new legacy she was a part of.

After collecting her purse, she stepped outside with him and watched him lock the shop. People were walking on the street, chatting in French. Laughter reached her ears, and she turned to see a young girl skipping with a red balloon in her hand next to her mother. The charming sight brought a smile to her lips, and she nodded to them as they passed by.

Andre kissed her on both cheeks. "I will see you at three, ma petite. Enjoy your time with the Madonna. And your man."

"But you start at two!" she protested.

"You are still adjusting to baker's hours and the time change. The extra hour will allow me the time to get some things started so I can give you more of my attention. Don't frown, ma petite. I *want* to give you my attention. Ask Belle. I love to hear myself speak."

She laughed. "All right then. I will see you at three, not two."

"Now go left and follow the directions I gave you," he said. "This journey is yours to make on your own."

He headed off, and she looked down at the map he'd drawn. Finding the church wouldn't be difficult. She only had to go four blocks, turn right, and then walk two more. She thought about texting Evan to tell him she was finished with her apprenticeship for the day, but part of her wanted to wait. This way she could take her time and wouldn't feel rushed to meet him. She could savor each part of her day rather than rushing through it.

When she arrived at the gate to the modest neighborhood church of St. Francis, she immediately spied the small gray house with the blue door. She crossed the courtyard lined with red roses and knocked on the door. It opened, and before her stood an older man in black pants and a black shirt with a white collar.

"Father Charles?" she asked in English, her brain too full of new knowledge for her to attempt speaking French yet.

"Oui," he said. "You must be Margie. Thank you for bringing bread to us. People will not go hungry tonight due to your generosity."

She had to be jet-lagged or something, but more tears popped into her eyes. She reached into the bag and took out five loaves. How could she keep one for her and Evan when people might go hungry?

Father Charles smiled. "Andre said you would try to give me five loaves, and I was to remind you that you must keep one for yourself. You bless yourself when you eat the bread made from your hands. Even the baker must be nourished, for if you go hungry, who will make the bread?"

He gave her back the extra loaf, and she clutched it to her chest.

"The Madonna is right around the corner. She is going to like you. You have a kind heart, child." The grooves around his mouth transformed as his smile stretched even wider. "Enjoy your time in Paris, Margie. And come back here whenever you want. We will always welcome you."

She felt the urge to do a yoga bow and decided just

to give in and do it.

His smile grew wider. "Yes, the Madonna will really like you. Bonsoir."

"Bonsoir," she said as he closed the door.

The cobblestones on the path leading around his house to the back of the church were smooth with age. Everywhere she looked, red roses opened to the ribbons of sunlight streaming through the ancient trees towering above her. She spotted Mary easily in the middle of a circle lined with more roses. The statue was stone, but she looked alive. Her eyes seemed to stare at Margie as she placed the bread at her feet beside other offerings—a flickering candle, a blue rosary, a fading red rose, and a letter.

Stepping back, she placed her hand on her heart. They gazed at each other.

"Thank you," she whispered and then bowed to the lady and retraced her steps with her one remaining loaf to find Evan.

CHAPTER 5

When Evan met Margie on the street in front of L'Hotel, she ran to him and threw her arms around his neck. He only had a moment to process how gorgeous she looked in her bright yellow dress.

"I did it!" she cried. "I made my first baguettes in Paris!"

The glorious smell of baked bread saturated her hair, and he took a long inhale to drink it in. Like he wanted to drink her in. "I'm so proud of you."

"Andre is incredible, and so is his wife, Belle," she rushed on, pressing away so she could rearrange the bread bag hanging over her shoulder and reach for the one loaf inside. "This is my baguette."

The golden brown color was like afternoon sunlight on sandstone. The unmistakable slashes on the bread were a lighter shade. And the bread smelled as heavenly as she did.

"It's so perfect," he said, "I don't want to eat it."

She laughed. "Oh, we're going to eat it! It might be our main course tonight. I want to eat it and eat it and eat it with you until there's nothing left."

He was both touched and aroused to hear her say

that. "I can't wait to try it."

"Oh, Evan! I'm so happy."

Her arms wrapped around him again, and he clutched her to his chest. Seeing her like this reminded him of how he'd felt after landing their first major defense contract for INV-333. He'd man-hugged Chase and all his other scientists. Then Chase had poured out a thirty-year old whiskey from Ireland to celebrate, and they'd all gotten rip-roaring drunk.

"We have to celebrate," he told her.

He would take her to the most expensive restaurant in Paris. She deserved the best. He was glad he'd booked the grand suite at the hotel as well, even though it was sure to raise questions. It wasn't a mere hotel. It was one of the most luxurious and highly regarded hotels in Paris.

Wiggling out of his arms again, she leaned back, her green eyes twinkling. "Andre insisted I keep this loaf— just for me. For us."

Then something passed over her face. Her smile shifted from its mega-watt power to something else. Not unhappiness, he realized after studying her for a moment. No, it was peace. He wondered what she was thinking. Perhaps she had a secret too.

"That was nice of him," he said, keeping his hands on her waist, not wanting to let her go.

She looked away for a moment, and a flush covered her cheeks. "I gave the leftover loaves to a priest at one of the local churches."

He tipped her chin up so she'd meet his eyes. "That was very nice of you."

"Andre does it with the leftover bread from his shop." Then she blew out a massive breath from a buildup of oxygen. "And I...well, I want to tell you...even if you think it's weird. I left one of my baguettes at the foot of the Madonna behind the church like Andre suggested, and I...it touched me. Here." She pointed to her heart.

Something moved in his own chest, and he couldn't resist anymore. As he lowered his mouth to hers, she rose on her tiptoes to meet him. The corners of her lips were curved from her soft smile. He traced them with his tongue. Then she opened her mouth to his, and he was lost. It didn't cross his mind for a moment to step away. This was Paris. It's what was done.

He fell into the moment. The heated moisture of her mouth as he kissed her over and over again warmed him. Everywhere. Their tongues danced, and by the time they finally broke apart, they were both breathing hard. Her eyes were glassy, and the rose on her cheeks this time was from passion.

"Can we eat in our room?" she asked. "I...don't want to be around people tonight."

Every muscle tightened with lust. "I don't want to share you either." He took her hand. "I already checked in. Let's go inside."

When they entered the lobby, she gasped. Her neck arched as she stared at the multi-story circular rotunda ending with a skylight at the top.

"Oh my," she whispered, clutching the tan suit jacket he'd thrown on over his casual outfit of a white shirt and jeans. "I've never seen anything like it."

"I thought you'd like it. L'Hotel was built in 1828 and is one of the oldest hotels in Paris. Oscar Wilde lived here until his death, and for over a century, it's been the place to come for artists, writers, and entertainers. There are only twenty rooms."

Her eyes were enormous as she looked at him. "We're staying here?"

From the outside, it was hard to imagine the grandeur of the interior. "Yes," he said, ushering her to the elevators. "It's like I said. You deserve something special."

The doors shut without anyone else entering the lift.

Though he wanted nothing more than to be alone with her, he found himself wishing they had company. It was the only way he could stave off her questions. And the lies he was about to tell.

"There's no way you can afford this place," she said with a frown. "You told me not to worry, but I can't help it. I don't want you living beyond your means for me. When you said we'd go somewhere special, I never imagined a place like this. I'm sure your apartment would do just fine. Evan—"

"It's not that crazy actually," he said. "They have a special deal due to the exterior refurbishment they're doing, and when they didn't have one of their regular rooms, they upgraded us." The first was true. But the second...

When they reached their discreet door, he opened it with a flourish and nudged her inside.

He'd chosen the Belle Époque junior suite over the hotel's apartment because such a significant upgrade wouldn't have been believable. The interior was done in golds and maroons—the style he favored in his apartment—and boasted a massive sitting room with double doors leading to the bedroom.

"No freaking way," she said, setting her purse and her bread bag down along with a small overnight bag he'd failed to notice earlier in their mingled excitement. "Evan—"

"I don't want to hear anything else," he said, putting his hands on her hips. "We're here. We deserve to be here. Tonight is...too special to be anywhere else."

A line appeared between her brows. "Evan, I want you to swear to me right now the cost of this room isn't hurting you financially."

He made an X over his heart, the one knocking in hard beats against his chest. "I swear. Now, let me call for some champagne to celebrate." Better to change the subject as she wandered around their rooms with her mouth gaping. "Would you like some foie gras or pate to go with the baguette?"

She was standing at the white French doors, staring into the bedroom. The bed had already been turned down, and the white pillows were freshly fluffed. The navy cloth behind the headboard contrasted elegantly with the white and gold linens.

He made himself turn away as razor-sharp lust poured through his system. Seeing her so close to the bed where he hoped to make love to her was too much of a temptation. He picked up the phone and ordered room service as best he could since she hadn't responded to his question about what she wanted. Later, when she was over her shock, he could order anything else she wanted.

When he was finished, he looked over to see she was gone. Instead of following her, he decided to give her a minute and went to the window in the sitting room. He looked onto Rue de Beaux Arts, watching the scene unfold on the street. There was a woman in a purple dress below holding the hand of a girl wearing hot pink, and they almost looked like two moving flowers on the sidewalk.

He felt something on his back and turned.

Margie's eyes were now intensely green and dark. "This is more than I ever imagined."

"I told you I wanted our first time to be special," he said hoarsely. "I...please just let me do this. No more questions tonight."

His gut burned as she gazed at him for a long moment, her eyes intense, but a knock sounded and he strode off quickly to answer the door. When room service entered, he instructed them on where to set everything up. Since it was early, only shy of six o'clock, he hadn't ordered anything heavy. Only some duck foie gras with a blackberry sauce and an assortment of charcuterie, berries, and cheese. They could have dinner later. He tipped the staff after everything was prepared to his satisfaction. Alone with Margie again, he turned to see her tracing an undecipherable pattern on the sofa.

"Bring your baguette over here," he said, gesturing to their spread. "I can't wait to try it. I know it's going to be as good as your cinnamon rolls, even though that's hard to imagine."

She took her baguette out of the white bread bag, gave him a long look he couldn't decipher, and then walked toward the bedroom. At the door, she turned to face him.

"I want to eat my bread here," she said in a velvety tone and disappeared.

He followed her, telling himself to cool down. Perhaps she thought the view from the bedroom was nicer. Or the bed was more comfortable than the chairs.

When he entered, her yellow dress was pooled at her feet. She faced him in a lacy soft pink teddy that touched the tops of her thighs. The baguette was resting in the center of the bed.

His mouth went dry as he gazed at her. Her toes were painted red, and her legs were slender and sun-kissed. The flare of her waist seemed to be waiting for the imprint of his hands, and her breasts hung like ripe apples waiting for him to savor them. Her pulse beat rapidly in her neck, and he watched as her chest rose when she released a heavy breath.

"We don't have to rush," he made himself say.

Her lips curved, and suddenly he was seeing the full power of Venus herself. "I'm not rushing. You're slow."

The flirtation was welcome. While he'd fantasized about making love to her, he hadn't known exactly how it would be between them. "Slow, huh? Is that going to be a problem?"

She walked over to the bed and lay down in the center, holding the baguette in front of her. A painter from old would have begged to capture her like she was:

a goddess with a loaf of bread.

"It only is when you have more clothes on than I do." She inclined her head. "Like now."

He unbuttoned his jacket and slid it off, hanging it on a nearby chair. "Better?"

Her brow rose. "Still too many clothes."

Even though his body was growing more and more impatient, something made him slow down even more. They were dancing to a different tune now, and he planned to make all the right steps. He slowly raised his T-shirt over his head and took it off, leaving it in his right hand. Her gaze locked onto his chest.

"Keep going."

Heaven help him, he was going to come before he even touched her if she kept talking to him like that. He dropped the shirt to the ground and undid his jeans, sliding them down his legs after kicking off his loafers. Her eyes traveled up and down his body before resting on his black briefs.

"Good," she said, rising into a half-lounging, half-sitting position. "Now, come here."

As he approached the bed, a strange feeling overcame him, both exciting and scary. He knew neither of them were going to be the same after this.

***

Evan's body was all muscular ridges and bulging lines—a masterpiece of strength. Margie was beyond restless. Being here with him was about living in the moment and enjoying every second. He'd asked her to accept the situation, so she'd decided to do just that. After her initial shock over the suite, she'd studied the bed and seen a flash of her and Evan in it. He was poised over her, about to take her, and her head was thrown back in bliss.

This wasn't the time for drawing things out or

demanding more explanations.

She wanted to feed him her baguette.

And she wanted them to feed each other with their bodies.

He stretched out in front of her, the baguette resting between them. In his lakewater blue eyes, she could see him trying to figure out what she wanted, what she was thinking. She reached for the baguette and gently tore off the end.

"Lay back against the pillows," she instructed him. "I want you to taste what I made with my hands."

He settled onto his back with one knee raised. She wondered if it was to relieve the pressure of his desire. The long line of him made her mouth water. Edging closer until they were mere inches apart, she pressed the bread to his mouth.

"Take a bite," she whispered.

He did, his eyes never leaving hers, and when he was finished, she took one too, from the place he had. Somehow that made it more tantalizing. Chewing slowly, he groaned, and his eyes closed for a moment.

"It's incredible, Margie. A masterpiece."

She knew what he was feeling, for her own eyes had fluttered shut for a moment. The baguette was crusty on the outside and soft on the inside, but it was *more* than that. She was transported to the field that had made the wheat in the French countryside. The grain had grown from seeds and risen to meet the sky and sun like hands raised in celebration. The velvety texture of the loaf filled her mouth, and the sensation of eating her own bread and sharing it with Evan broke open her heart even more. Tears filled her eyes.

"I'm so glad I can share this with you," she whispered.

He'd finished chewing and was gazing at her with lust and sweetness, all wrapped into one. "Your bread is...unforgettable—like you. I've never tasted any like it, and I know I never will."

She'd left her mark. On the bread. On him. And they were about to leave an even greater imprint on each other by making love.

He took the hand that held the bread and brought it to his lips. Her heart squeezed as she fed him again—by his request. She took another bite too, savoring the lush feel and taste of the baguette. But soon, she had to share herself with him. She laid the baguette on his chest and leaned down to kiss him.

His mouth opened, and their tongues dueled and danced. She could taste the water and the yeast that had made all the ingredients rise together. The sensation of his hot mouth, of his slick tongue called to something wild in her. Pressing back, she tore off another hunk of the baguette and ran it across his muscular shoulders. He grabbed the baguette on his chest, broke off a piece, and set aside the remainder of the loaf. He slid the bread between her breasts. The touch was raw and edgy and made every nerve in her body tingle.

Then, he pressed her onto her back and rolled onto her until he was poised between her open legs. He traced the lacy edges of her teddy with the crust and then used it to raise the lingerie up her thighs, exposing more skin. Angling forward, he kissed the tops of her thighs, the swell of her belly, and the rise of her breasts.

Then he pressed the bread to her mouth. She opened for him and took another bite, humming at the taste as much as from the pleasure of his caress. Then he bit into the bread from the spot she'd touched and chewed, watching her with an intensity that made her legs shift under him.

She traced the edges of his muscles with the remaining bread in her hand, delighting in his groans. He in turn drew lines across her almost like he was mapping the secret places that gave her pleasure. Finally, she could stand it no longer. She rose to a siting position and tugged off her teddy.

Lying back, she took his hands, which were empty now, and drew them to her breasts. "Evan, I need your hands and mouth on me."

His eyes sparkled with intensity—a lake under the hot afternoon sun—and his hands settled on her breasts. He drew circles around her nipples, and soon she was straining into his touch. She rose up to kiss him, and they fell into a deep, urgent embrace before he rolled onto her again. Her hands settled on his back, stroking the strong muscles there. The kisses made her achy with need, and she gripped his waist when he broke away and set his mouth to her breasts. He licked and sucked and tugged and pulled until she was crying out.

"I need—"

"I know you do," he whispered back as his hand moved between her legs and gave her what she craved.

She came in a long series of cries and arches, and through it all, his touch only took her higher and higher. When she finally became aware of him again, she was flushed and exhausted and blissful and never wanted the feelings to end.

Then he kissed his way back up her body until he reached her lips. He tugged her bottom lip into his mouth, and while she knew he was corded with desire, she couldn't make herself reach for him yet.

"Give me a moment to come back," she whispered.

"There's no rush," he said, but even through the glowing, pulsing haze they'd created, she could hear the edge of raw need in his voice.

She struggled to resurface, to give him something of what he'd given her. After pushing him onto his back, she rose over him. She shook her hair back from her face, the sensation of the strands brushing her neck unbearably arousing.

"We didn't talk about birth control," she said, tracing the top of his briefs, which were strained with need.

"I have condoms," he said, his mouth a tight line.

"I'm on the Pill, but I'd still like—"

"No problem," he said as she tugged down the last barrier between them.

He was massive and perfect and so beautiful she couldn't help but place a kiss on the hard line of him.

"Oh, God," he breathed out.

She pulled his briefs down his legs. He was so far gone, he could barely help her.

"I'm sorry," he said, squeezing his eyes shut. "I don't usually tremble like this...before."

Her mouth curved. So he was feeling it too, this incredible power between them.

"Tremble all you want," she said and made him tremble even more as her mouth lowered to learn the taste of his skin.

He groaned and shifted and jerked under her hands, from her touch, and when he couldn't take anymore, she slid the condom on him and lowered herself over him.

His head arched back against the pillows. "Oh, God."

She understood what he meant and let her body bow to take him even deeper inside her. "Oh, Evan."

His hands gripped her waist as she started to rise and lower over him. "Margie."

The urgency fanned out in her belly, and she rocked over him, her moans mixed with his groans. When he pressed his fingers to the center of her back and pulled her hard onto him, she came again in a rush. Her hands pushed against his chest as sensation thundered through her.

She felt him shift her to her side, and then he rolled over on top of her and thrust into her body in deep, hard strokes that had her pleasure peaking again.

"Oh, God," he called out again as he came, bearing down on her with all his force.

She took him further into her, pulsing in glorious

waves. He lowered onto his elbows, his sweaty body melding with hers. His mouth found the side of her neck, and his rapid breath tickled her ears. She let out puffs of air, her eyes closed. Everything was golden sensation, as if she were one of her own baguettes baking in a warm oven.

Finally he turned them onto their sides, his hand curved around her waist. She dozed off somewhere between sleep and dreams, her body still caught in an ecstasy more powerful than any she'd previously known.

And when she finally opened her eyes, he was gazing at her with so much emotion her heart expanded like bread dough rising in a kitchen window.

Making love with him had forever changed her.

She loved him.

***

Evan was still trembling from the most emotional, erotic experience of his life. Since Margie's eyes had been closed for so long, he knew she was feeling it too. He'd tucked her close to his body and watched her sleep.

When she finally opened them to gaze back at him, he couldn't smile. His heart pulsed in deep beats of pleasure, but it felt larger than any other organ in his body, as if it had undergone some remarkable transformation.

And it had.

He still didn't want to put a name to it. He might as well have discovered a new element on the Periodic Table.

All he could do was lean forward to sup at her lips, explore their texture until she let out a quiet sigh. Snuggling closer, she put her hand on his chest, and they just lay that way.

Neither of them said a word. It was like both of them understood no words were needed after what had happened between them. That there *were* no words for what had happened.

Soon, she kissed him on the mouth and left the bed. He watched her pad naked across the bedroom to the French doors. Ballerinas would have envied the pure perfection of the muscles in her back from all her baking. He knew she wasn't going far, so he didn't call her back. He only ran a hand through his messy hair. She came back into the room with the plates of food he'd ordered earlier.

He settled back against the headboard, tucking a sheet around his waist. She sat beside him and grabbed the rest of the sheet, which she fitted around herself like Venus might have after an amorous rendezvous. He scooted closer until their bodies touched. She reached for the remaining part of the baguette he'd placed on the bedside stand.

Once again, she tore off a hunk of the bread she'd made and fed it to him. His chest grew tight again, tasting all the love, intention, and dreams she'd kneaded into the dough. Tasting it was no different than tasting Margie's skin, he realized, and he leaned over to kiss the top of her shoulder.

They ate in bed after he fetched the champagne, and then they made love again. This time, he slid over her, slid into her, and didn't stop until she cried out his name. Only then did he let his release pour forth.

He watched the alarm clock march on, ticking off the minutes until their time together ended, until she had to go to the bakery to make more bread. She would draw him back with kisses or a gentle caress, and he would fall back into the space where time didn't seem to exist.

Even when they weren't making love to each other, everything they did was a prelude to it. He learned every rise and curve of her body, the sweetness of the sweat on her skin, and the unbearably erotic scent of cinnamon between her legs. She, in turn, laid him bare with her slow, gentle caresses and her soft, slumberous green eyes as she traced the planes of his chest and thighs and the desire he felt for her.

When they could ignore the time no longer, he stood beside the bed and reached for her hand. She rose with a soft smile and then gasped as he swept her into his arms and carried her into the shower. As the water rained down on them, he slid down her body like the drops, inviting her to take more pleasure, as much as she was willing to receive. Then she slid herself around him, and together, they discovered even more ecstasy.

She dressed in the bakery-appropriate clothes she'd brought in her overnight bag: white cotton pants, a white shirt, and some black Crocs. Even now, she didn't speak, only raised her hands and shoulders in an adorable shrug as if to say, do you like my outfit?

He pulled on his earlier clothes, holding her gaze.

"You don't have to walk me to the bakery," she finally said.

"Try and stop me," he only responded.

Fortunately, she didn't fight him, only took his hand as he led her out of the quiet hotel and into the soft glow of St. Germain's streets. Due to the lateness of the hour, they encountered only two other people on their walk.

When they reached the bakery, he pulled her into his arms. His heart hurt suddenly, and it took him a moment to realize why.

"I'm missing you already," he whispered against her neck.

"Me too." She squeezed him tight. "I'll text you the minute I finish if you're free."

"I've rearranged my schedule so I'll be free whenever you are," he told her.

Her eyes were dark as she edged back, but he could still see the single beam of light emanating from them, almost like he was seeing into her soul.

"Tonight was one of the best nights of my life, Evan."

His throat grew thick with emotion. "Mine too."

She rose on her tiptoes and kissed him again. "See you soon," she said and turned to rap on the door.

He stepped back as a bald man's bulky shape appeared in the doorway, realizing he was about to meet her boss. He'd been too caught up in the throes of their evening to let reality intrude.

When the door opened, the soft light from the bakery's interior painted the man's face. "Bonjour, ma petite. Are you ready to make more magic?"

"Bonjour, Andre," Margie said brightly, reaching for Evan's hand. "Andre, I'd like you to meet Evan."

Stepping into the shadows wasn't an option, so Evan extended his hand in greeting. "Bonjour, Andre. It's good to meet you."

"You as well, Evan," the baker said.

"I will let you two get to work," he said, stepping back now. "Have a wonderful time, Margie."

When she went inside with Andre, he felt oddly bereft. For the past few hours, he'd felt a oneness with Margie he'd never experienced with another person—a oneness so powerful only touches and gazes were needed to know the other person's thoughts.

As a scientist, Evan had read studies about telepathy, and he believed it was possible under the right conditions. He'd experienced that with Margie just now. It fired up his imagination and his interest in the topics science still didn't fully understand. He wanted to call Chase, but knew this would be too woo-woo for his friend, especially after their earlier conversation.

Instead, he detoured to his penthouse apartment, eager to investigate telepathy more as he continued to work on his newest invention.

And as he walked down the street, he reached into his pocket for the last slice of Margie's baguette, the one he'd appropriated from the remains of their dinner. Taking a bite, he fell into the sensation of being fed by her all over again.

It was as though she was with him as he journeyed through the dark night.

CHAPTER 6

Margie was exhausted by the time Andre told her to go home. It was only eleven o'clock in the morning, and yet she had barely slept the night before.

Not that she wanted to sleep now.

Her time with Evan was too special to waste on sleep. She would go back to her apartment and take a shower and a short nap. She couldn't wait to be with him again.

Belle was reading a fashion magazine in between customers. Most of the baskets and shelves displaying their bread were empty, and Margie felt a spurt of pride as she thought about all the people her loaves would be feeding tonight.

Andre had taught her how to mix the ingredients for the bread they baked. Her baguette dough hadn't bubbled quite like Andre's, but he'd told her to have patience. It took some time to develop a proper relationship with the yeast. The farm bread had been the easiest for her, but it was the sourdough that fascinated her most. Andre had showed her the white ribbons of yeast floating on top of the water with the apples and pears.

After all the mixing, she'd kneaded and formed the

bread under Andre's watchful eyes, each loaf more precise than the last. Then she'd taken time to get to know the ovens, feeding the bread into their fiery bellies, watching them rise and turn golden brown from the heat.

"Your apprentice bread is selling very well, Margie," Belle said. "Tomorrow we will likely remove the sign and simply sell it with the rest of our offerings."

"Wonderful!" she said, stretching her stiff back. "I *want* to keep getting better."

"And you are," Belle said, setting her magazine aside and coming around the counter. "Andre told me to keep my nosiness to myself. Is that how you say it in English?"

"Close," she said, her brain fried. "What are you nosy about?"

She pressed her hands to her cheeks. "You did not mention that your man in Paris was Evan Michaels."

"Michaels?" she asked, her head darting back. "Andre must have misunderstood."

"No," Belle said, reaching for the fashion magazine and thumbing through it until she exclaimed, "Ah, here it is. Evan Michaels, no? Andre recognized him from all the magazines I leave around the house. He is quite the catch, ma petite. And very handsome."

Margie's head started to pound as Belle thrust the magazine at her. In the two-page spread, Evan was pictured with a gorgeous French model at a party. The article read: "Super Models at Play."

"You are very pale all of the sudden, ma petite," Belle said in an alarmed tone, rubbing her back.

Margie grabbed the magazine from Belle's hands and started to translate what she was reading in her head.

Paris' hottest fashion model, Chloe, was seen with billionaire inventor and Paris local, Evan Michaels, at Huntley Haverstock's three-day party on his yacht, The

Calypso, in the Mediterranean. The model, known for her pouty lips and dramatic cheekbones, was modeling outfits from Givenchy, Chanel, and Christian Dior. Since the billionaire always dresses with style, the two made a beautiful couple, we thought.

She fell back a few steps in shock as she examined the photo more closely. The man had on black designer shades and a white suit with a tan shirt. While he didn't have a beard, she knew instantly it was Evan.

Her stomach twisted, and she bent over as the hurt washed over her. He was a billionaire! And he hadn't told her. Her breath came out in hard pants, and she heard Belle distantly calling her name over the buzzing in her ears.

A billionaire!

Now the incredible suite at the hotel made sense. He could more than afford it. He could buy it outright. He'd referred to his income as comfortable. What an understatement!

Then she flashed to her memories of their time together in Dare Valley. She'd made fun of his inventions, but apparently he'd made billions on them. He'd told her his inventions had made him a good living, but she could never have imagined this.

Then shame filled her. She'd paid him fifteen dollars an hour to paint her bakery, and he hadn't said a word. He'd lived in a spare bedroom in her home and rented a crappy car.

Why would he do that? Why had he come to Dare Valley at all?

Then she remembered how weird Rhett had been about Evan, the way he'd warned her to be careful. Rhett must know about him being a billionaire. Did Jane know too?

Betrayal made her gasp. Why wouldn't they tell her?

"I can't believe this!" she whispered. "Oh, God!"

"You did not know who he was?" Belle put her arm

around her and led her to the chair behind the counter. "That scoundrel!"

Scoundrel was right.

He'd given her the most intimate and sensual experience of her life, but he hadn't told her who he was. And after she'd shared her whole life story with him...

She'd fallen in love with another man with secrets, and he'd broken her heart.

THE
BILLIONAIRE'S
COURTSHIP

To Paris—for welcoming me back into its magical arms—and to all the marvelous people I've encountered there while writing these pages.

And to my divine entourage, who continues to show me how magical adventures taken in faith can be life changing.

CHAPTER 1

Discovering Evan Murray wasn't the man she'd believed him to be had broken Margie's heart.

As she stared out the window of the Paris apartment where she was staying during her baking apprenticeship, she continued to turn the problem around in her mind, looking for answers. Ultimately, she had to admit there had been signs he was keeping something from her. She'd chalked it up to them getting to know each other better.

In her wildest dreams, she'd never imagined he was a jet-setting billionaire—more a member of the wealthy elite than her estranged parents were.

Or that his real name was Evan Michaels.

He'd finally admitted he had money, but this...this was something different.

The streets of Paris didn't look as welcoming to her now as she stared off into the distance, still numb from crying. Couples strolled hand in hand, and the sight of their happiness made her feel like her heart was being run over by the yellow cabs passing below.

Her phone buzzed again, and she knew it was Evan. She'd promised to call him after she got back from work, but hours had passed since she'd discovered his true identity in a fashion magazine at Boulangerie Ma Belle.

She still couldn't bring herself to talk to him. Belle had invited her to come home with her and Andre, but this was the kind of news that needed to be processed alone. Her boss, the master baker, was so enraged by the news of Evan's deception that he'd offered to beat him up for her. If she hadn't been so upset, it might have been sweet. Even though she'd only known the couple a few days, they already felt like old friends.

Less than twenty-four hours ago, Margie and Evan had been entwined in bed after making love for the first time. She'd gone to her apprenticeship feeling as if she could barely make it through the hours she'd committed to working without seeing his seductive smile, feeling the sweet touch of his hand to her cheek as he stared at her. Evan didn't stare at her so much as he stared *into* her.

Now confusion reigned inside her. She'd looked Evan up on the Internet after excusing herself from the bakery. Could this be the man she knew?

Her phone buzzed again, and she finally made herself leave the window. The phone was sitting on the small coffee table in front of the green sofa. She sank onto the cushions and tucked her legs under her before picking up the phone.

There were four texts from Evan. The first text had come an hour after her shift was supposed to have ended at the bakery.

Missing you like crazy. You must be baking more heavenly baguettes. I can't wait to see you and share your bread like we did last night. Text me when you're finished, and I'll run over.

She brushed away more tears as she remembered feeding him the baguette she'd made with her own hands. They'd eaten the bread in bed together, and the act of sharing it had fed the soul connection between them—the one she couldn't explain, the one she'd decided not to risk by asking lots of questions.

Like whom he worked for as an inventor. At least he hadn't lied about that part. He was a famous inventor, so famous he'd made billons on top-secret devices used by the defense arms of major democratic nations. And the friend he'd talked about, Chase Parker, ran his company so he could focus on inventing.

According to Evan, he'd found his lost creative fire in Dare Valley, but that couldn't be true if he was this successful, could it? When she thought of how she'd teased him about the painting tool he'd invented to increase the efficiency of the painting of her bakery in Dare Valley, for which she'd paid him a mere fifteen dollars an hour, her cheeks flamed. Little had she known that inventing wasn't just a hobby for him.

Now she did, and she felt like she was staring at two men on a Janus coin. One was the endearing geeky guy she'd fallen in love with, who shared her excitement over Hot Cross Buns and moaned while eating her cinnamon rolls. This new one, the billionaire, wore designer clothes, raced fast cars, and hung out with famous fashion models. This Evan partied with the crème de la crème of the jet set in places like Monte Carlo and Saint-Tropez.

She'd grown up around people like that, and she hadn't missed the lifestyle after leaving behind her parents' legacy of squandering money and living from one party to the next. It wasn't hard to imagine what Evan's normal life was like. Except he didn't seem like he would find the jet-setting high-society life fulfilling.

Something else confused her too. After reading about him online, it was hard to imagine why he would have chosen to be celibate for a month while in Dare Valley. There was photo after photo of him with some of Europe's most gorgeous models, women who redefined the words cheekbones and pouty lips. He'd said it was a spiritual thing, like taking a time out. Since she'd done something similar a few years before, she hadn't thought it odd.

And yet...

He wasn't the playboy the media portrayed him to be. He was too sensitive, sweet, and romantic. Playboys didn't confess to being geeks, and they certainly wouldn't admit to having received makeover help from a friend.

If there hadn't been so much evidence to the contrary, she would have said Evan Murray was the real man, and Evan Michaels the fake. There was more to the story. There had to be. What situation would inspire a billionaire to show up in Dare Valley, pretend to be a normal guy, rent a room from her, paint her bakery, and embark on a celibacy kick?

She knew her friends Rhett and Jane, the ones who'd supposedly convinced Evan to make the trip, probably knew the truth, and the fact that they'd kept it quiet cut her deep.

She forced herself to scan the final three messages from Evan. The last couple had arrived close together.

Hey! Since you're a stranger to Paris, I'm getting a little worried here. Are you lost? Did a pickpocket snag your phone? Are you napping? I know you didn't get any sleep last night. Please text me so I know you're okay.

His concern normally would have made her as warm and airy as rising bread on a warm stove. But not right now. She felt paralyzed.

What was she supposed to do about him? About them?

His next message had her taking some deep breaths.

Don't think I have stalker-like qualities. I'm worried, okay? I just checked, and the bakery is closed. Are you home? Are you sleeping? It's been four hours since you were supposed to have left.

She glanced at the clock. It was nearing seven at night, she realized. There was no way she wouldn't have contacted him by now if she hadn't learned this news. He would know it. In his shoes, she would have been worried sick. Hadn't she been concerned when he came home late one night in Dare Valley? She felt a pinch of guilt.

But how could he have made love to her without telling her this? The thought was enough to restore the edge to her anger.

His last text confirmed she had to respond—at least briefly—to assure him she was okay.

I'm sitting at the café around the corner from you. I didn't have the heart to ring the call box to your flat in case you fell asleep. I've decided to think you're okay, but if I don't hear from you by two a.m. when you have to be at the bakery...well...I'm going ape-shit crazy here.

She had to give him some points for not wanting to wake her. One thing she believed to be true was that Evan deeply cared about her. She just didn't understand why he was keeping secrets.

Then it hit her. She'd poured out her sob story about her rich parents, telling him how much she hated their lifestyle. Then there was her reaction to the rich guy in the sports car who'd cut her off at the Denver airport. Was Evan afraid she'd see him differently once she knew he was a billionaire? Did he fear she'd turn her back on him?

She didn't think she'd misread how deeply lonely and sensitive he was. Of course, she'd blamed that on him being an artist. But a lonely and sensitive guy *would* be afraid she'd reject him, and Evan had hinted at years of rejection before the makeover that had helped him become the man he'd always wanted to be.

What the hell was she going to do?

Buy time, she decided. She could use her jet lag, lack of sleep, and her new baking hours as an excuse until she had time to think things through. Too many emotions were running through her for her to make a sound decision now.

And she wanted to talk to Rhett and Jane to see what they knew. They owed her that much.

Bracing herself, she started to compose a reply. It would have to be something that wouldn't alarm him. After erasing three different replies, she bit her lip and finally sent one off.

Didn't mean to scare you. I did fall asleep and am still so tired, I can't move. I'm sorry to bail, but I think I need to catch up on my rest tonight so I won't be a zombie for Andre. I'll be refreshed tomorrow and will let you know when I'm free. Thanks for understanding.

The latter part sounded a little stilted, but she didn't feel up to second-guessing herself. Her phone immediately buzzed with his reply.

Whew! Thank God you're okay. I was hoping that was all it was. My mind has been spinning horrible stuff. Can I get you anything? Drop off a meal? I promise I won't stay. I know you need to sleep even though I want to be with you. I don't think I've ever missed anyone this much. Is that crazy?

The screen blurred as tears filled her eyes, and she pressed the phone to her aching chest. He *did* care about her. She had to trust that.

She wiped the tears away and tried to think of a suitable reply to his message.

I'm too tired to eat. I'll grab something before I head to the bakery. Get some rest too. I'll talk to you tomorrow.

His reply didn't come as quickly this time. In fact, she stared at her phone for a good seven minutes until it came through. She could almost hear his mind whirling, and since she now knew what an intricate mind it was, she expected he was trying to decipher her signals like he would a rough invention he'd created.

Okay, I'll stop pestering you and let you get back to

*sleep. Don't forget to set your alarm so you make it to
the bakery on time. And…I'll count the hours until we're
together again. Bonne nuit, cherie.*

Her tears rose up again like a flood. She loved the
practical man who'd reminded her to set her alarm. She
loved the shy man who was so endearing and sweet he'd
use a word like pester. And she loved the romantic man
who'd said he was counting off the hours until they
could be together.

When she was spent, she decided to call Jane rather
than Rhett. Surely one woman would understand
another woman's predicament. The cost of an
international call would be a small price to pay.

She explained why she was calling, and Jane
immediately said, "Evan hasn't told you yet? I was
worried something like this might happen. Rhett and I
wanted to tell you, but we'd made this bet…"

And so the whole story came out, leaving Margie
light-headed.

After hearing about the side bet Evan had lost to
Jane at poker—a bet requiring him to live in Dare Valley
anonymously for a month on a small stipend…and, oh,
stay celibate—she couldn't help but feel sorry for him.
What would make a man like him bored and
directionless enough to risk such a gamble?

She found herself admiring him for his resilience.
Leaving his billionaire lifestyle behind couldn't have
been easy, even if only for a month. No one in her
parents' circle would ever have done it.

And yet Evan had followed through on the gamble
and, in the process, captured her heart.

"I take it things have gotten pretty serious for you,"
Jane said when Margie failed to respond.

"Yes," she responded, her throat raw.

"I'm sorry for not telling you, Margie," she said.
"Evan said he was going to if you met up with him in
Paris."

"Maybe he just hasn't gotten around to it yet." That was easier to believe even though it still made her angry and sad. "I've only been here for three days. It was mere happenstance that I found out."

"I'm not making excuses for him," Jane said. "He should have told you."

"I agree, but I think he's afraid I won't like him anymore." Margie flashed back to the tense expression on his face as she shared her story about her parents.

"If he cares for you, he has to tell you." Jane clucked her tongue. "I had to tell Matt I'd been Rhett's poker babe. It wasn't easy, but it didn't stop him from caring about me."

"How long did you wait to tell him?" Margie asked.

"Ah...longer than I should have, in hindsight. I...wanted to make sure I could trust him first."

It was implied Jane had waited until she was sure of Matt's feelings. Perhaps Evan had similar motivations.

"Thanks for telling me, Jane," she said. "I need to go."

"Margie, again, I'm sorry about all this. I know Rhett will be too."

Rhett had given her more than one oblique warning about Evan before she left for Paris. At the time she'd written it off as overprotectiveness. "Tell him not to worry."

"Rhett will want to take Evan to the woodshed for hurting you."

Just like Andre. "Please tell Rhett I'm a big girl. I...want to handle this alone. And don't contact Evan about this, okay? We...need to work this out."

And they did. She just wasn't sure how. After all, she was only in Paris for ten days, so it wasn't like they were planning a future together. They both understood this thing between them would need to end. At least she thought they did. Her life was in Dare Valley, and his life was here. Now that she knew all his life here entailed, it was even clearer how far apart their lives were—geography aside.

"I'll tell Rhett," Jane said. "He won't be happy, but I'll make sure he understands."

"Thanks. Now, I'm going to sign off before I have to take out a loan to pay for this call."

"I'll let you go. Good luck."

After Jane hung up, Margie set her phone back on the coffee table and glanced at the clock. It was nearing eight now, and she had to be at the bakery at two. Maybe she should get some sleep after all, not that she was hopeful on that end. Her mind was racing like one of those fast cars Evan apparently liked to drive.

But still, as she stretched out on the couch, she remembered Evan's practical reminder to set the alarm. The thought brought a batch of fresh tears to her eyes as she did as he'd suggested.

*****

Evan was freaking out. There were no two ways about it.

As he sat at the outdoor table at the café near Margie's apartment, Evan wanted to believe everything was okay. But he couldn't.

All his insecurities were looming large, and he kept thinking about how the girl he'd liked at MIT had stopped liking him because he'd been too...hell, too open about his feelings. And he'd never given himself over to a woman like he had with Margie. Until last night, he realized, he'd never made love to a woman before. Being with Margie had stripped him bare and then filled him all up at the same time.

When he hadn't heard from her at first, he'd worried something was wrong. Had she lost her phone? His worry had only grown as the hours stretched by. She didn't know Paris, and while he'd always thought it to be a safe city, his mind started to imagine the worst. So he finally gave in to the urge to make sure she was safe at the bakery. The sight of its dark lights and "fermé" sign had felt like a punch in the gut, as had the revelation that came next.

He hadn't fully processed it the night before, but he loved her. He really loved her.

And now he felt raw and exposed, particularly since she didn't know the truth about who he was. But maybe, just maybe, she'd forgive him if she felt the same way. Perhaps her heart would soften the news.

But her text about being tired had burrowed under his skin like a worm, and he couldn't ignore the feeling she was blowing him off. What if she had decided to take a step back?

The thought killed him.

They had so little time left before she left Paris—seven days—and all he wanted to do was spend every moment with her. He didn't know what he was going to do when she left. She'd given him back his creative fire, and now that fire inside him burned for her.

He decided to head home and regroup. Maybe painting would clear his mind so he could figure out the best way forward with her. He'd been testing out his latest iteration of the Paint Prep Mistress on his own apartment. Desperate to unlock the secret possibilities he knew were locked within his new creation, within the act of painting, he had taken to painting his living room wall various shades over the past weeks.

Thirty minutes later, as he stroked the walls the same shade of periwinkle Margie had selected for her bakery, the one he'd painted for her, he realized their time was too precious for him not to seek her out and find out what she was feeling. And tell her what *he* was feeling, all the garbled up mass of it lodged in his chest.

When he realized it was just past one o'clock and Margie would be heading out to the bakery soon, he grabbed a shower and changed into fresh clothes. He headed out into the quiet streets and detoured close to some of the more popular cafés on Boulevard Saint Germain, hoping to find one of the vendors who sold single red roses there. Luckily he did, and while the man only had three wilted roses left, Evan felt like he'd discovered a special treasure. Margie deserved better flowers than this trio, but as a simple gesture, they would do.

When he turned onto the street where the bakery was located, he spotted Margie two blocks away. She was the only other person out. He would recognize that determined stride and hourglass figure anywhere. Since he was behind her, he didn't want to freak her out. She would probably think he was a certified stalker as it was.

"Margie," he called.

She looked over her shoulder, and he waved and picked up his pace to join her. It took him no time at all to reach her because she'd stopped walking completely. In the warm glow of the lamplight, he could see the shock on her face before her mouth twisted.

He hadn't misread the situation. She *had* stepped back from him. He felt his heart break like a machine dropped on the floor.

"I didn't mean to scare you. I just...wanted to make sure you were okay."

She said nothing.

"These are for you," he said, thrusting out the roses.

Her hands were shaking when she took them. A petal fell, but neither of them reached down to catch it.

"I'm pretty good at reading you," he made himself say as she clutched the roses in front of her stomach. "I know a brush-off when I feel it. Did you...what...oh hell...did I do something wrong last night? I thought...we...shit...I thought it was special to both of us. What happened? Did you change your mind? About me? About...this thing between us? Just be straight with me. I'd rather know the truth."

His heart was already broken. How much worse could it get?

Tears filled her eyes, which had his insides grinding like machine gears. He braced himself as she took a long breath and blew it out.

"Evan…"

Before he even realized what he was doing, he cupped her face softly and stared into her eyes. "Don't step back from me, Margie. Don't. Not after last night. What I feel when I'm with you…" He wrapped his arms around her. *"Please.* Don't give up on me. On us. Whatever scared you, we'll fix it." He was making a complete ass of himself, he realized, but he didn't care. Some things were worth the risk of lost dignity. "I'm good at fixing things, remember?"

She was rigid in his arms for only a moment, and then she softened into him like butter on warm bread.

"I've come alive with you," he whispered. "It's not just that you've given my creative fire back to me. You've given myself back to me."

Her head lay on his chest, and he felt her fingers begin to trace something on his back. It was the heart she'd traced on his body before. His own heart sped up in response.

She released a deep breath. "I believe you, Evan."

He pushed back so he could see her face. "Did you have doubts after you left me? Margie, I'm pretty much falling more in love with you every minute we're together…and…oh shit…I'm scared too."

She pressed her lips together like she was fending off tears. Then she said, "What are you afraid of?"

Of her going back to Dare Valley and leaving him here in the city he feared would no longer speak to him the same way. Of her learning he hadn't been too different from her parents and the people in their circle. Of her believing he hadn't changed.

And then the light bulb went on, and he knew what he needed to do. He needed to win her love. He needed to show her he was different. That he wasn't the Evan Michaels in the tabloids. Because it was true. One thing was clear now. He would never go back to that lifestyle—however things ended up between them.

"There are pieces of my past I'm not proud of, and I'm afraid you'll turn away from me when you find out about them," he decided to admit.

A lone car rumbled down the street, illuminating their shadows on the sidewalk. Even though he towered over her in the momentary street painting, he didn't feel that large. He felt small and human as he watched her rub her hand over her forehead like she had a punishing headache.

"You weren't happy when you came to Dare Valley, were you?" she asked softly.

He undid his suit jacket, suddenly feeling like it was squeezing him to death. "No, I wasn't."

She looked up, and her eyes were as mysterious as the watery depths of the Seine after midnight. "What are you afraid I'll find out, Evan? Tell me."

An arrow found its way straight into the center of his heart. Was it time to tell her everything? He'd hoped she would tell him she loved him first, but maybe he needed to take a risk and lay it all on the line. He couldn't keep any more secrets from her, not after what they'd shared.

"Margie, I've been playing it safe, but I'm done with that now." His hands cupped her face, and even the wind seemed to fall away on the quiet street. "I love you," he told her in a strong, steady voice. "I've loved you since my last weeks in Dare Valley, and being with you in Paris has only made my feelings stronger."

"*Oh, Evan,*" she said, placing her free hand over his. "I love you too."

He closed his eyes tightly for a moment. She loved him. She really loved him. He braced himself to tell her the rest. "There's something else you need to know. I...wasn't completely honest with you about my inventions and what I do for a living."

She gazed at him without a trace of fear in her eyes, which gave him the courage to continue.

"I planned to tell you the day you took me to the airport in Denver, but then you made that comment about rich people. And when you told me about your upbringing and your parents...well, I've been *afraid* to tell you. I thought I'd lose you once you knew. But tonight I feared I already had."

His diaphragm was so tight from the tension inside him, he felt like he'd explode. She seemed to know because she lowered her hand and traced a heart right in the middle of his chest with her index finger.

The breath he blew out was agonized. "I love it when you do that. Margie...I'm not just an inventor, although that's really my main function. I came up with some important stuff for the defense industry when I was at MIT, where I went to school, and then I formed a company with Chase's help. We've done well. Really well."

She nodded, her gaze unwavering.

It gave him the courage to say the words.

"Margie, I'm...a billionaire, and my real name is Evan Michaels."

***

Tears filled Margie's eyes. She couldn't help it. Evan had told her he loved her, and now he was telling her the secret he'd been so afraid to share.

"I lost a side bet to Jane when I played poker against her and Rhett here in Paris," he continued. "She...ah..."

She gave him a tentative smile to encourage him to tell her the rest. Once he was finished, he stared into her eyes and said, "I'm sorry for keeping this from you. I hope you'll forgive me because you're the *best* thing that's ever happened to me, and I love you. I needed to say that again."

She felt tears slip down her face at the fierce emotion in his voice. "I know who you are, Evan."

His heart darted back, and he dropped his hands from her face. "What do you mean you know? How could you know?" Then something dark flashed across his face. "Did Rhett and Jane tell you? Dammit! All this time I've been twisted up inside, and you knew?"

She grabbed his hand and laid it against her chest to keep them connected. "I only found out last night. There was a picture of you in one of Belle's fashion magazines."

His mouth parted. "That's why you stepped back.

"Yes."

He looked crestfallen. "I'm sorry I hurt you, Margie. I'm so sorry."

"Me too," she admitted. "We'd just made love, and it—"

"Hurt you to think I could keep something like that from you after we'd been so intimate," he finished for her.

She shook her head. "But then you chased after me tonight and poured your heart out. It made me realize I knew who you were—who you *really* were—all along."

The corners of his mouth tipped up. "Yeah, more than anyone besides Chase, you really do."

This time she leaned up and kissed him on the cheek because they both needed it.

"I'm so sorry, Margie. I was stupid and...when Chase and I got to talking about it, I thought it would be better to tell you once you said you loved me."

She arched a brow. "Why did I have to be the first one to say it?"

He shrugged. "Maybe because you have more

courage than I do."

"Not from where I'm standing," she said, laying her head against his chest. "I understand why it was so hard for you to tell me the truth."

"It wasn't just because of what you told me about your family. There are so many exaggerated media reports about me being a playboy. I didn't want you to think—"

"Evan, I know you're not a playboy." This time her mouth curved.

"What? How could you know that?"

She gave him a look. "Give me some credit. A playboy wouldn't try to win a girl over by talking about being a geeky inventor. He certainly wouldn't have bared his soul to me."

His wince was downright endearing. "No, probably not."

"I don't want a playboy, Evan," she said. "I just want you." And she did. Even though he was a billionaire, the thought of which still made her tremble with nerves.

He stared into her again and traced her brow gently. "And I just want you, Margie Lancaster, in all your cinnamony awesomeness."

She let her fingers trace the fullness of his bottom lip. "Then kiss me, Evan Michaels, because I'm not sure how much longer I can wait."

And he did. His mouth seemed to press her back a few inches with his urgency, but she was there to meet him. Her mouth opened under his, and it all began again. Just like the previous night, her body fell away until she was pure sensation. Her eyes fluttered shut, and she was aware of nothing but the feel of him—of his mouth on hers, of their bodies pressed together, of their joined light. Tonight, his seemed to be a warm orange, the kind of glow a campfire emitted after the first hot blast of wood and fire. Hers was a bubbly effervescent pink, and when he pulled her tighter to him, their life forces merged in a way she'd never experienced with another soul.

Off in the distance, the sound of a car intruded, and she came back into the present moment. She raised her hand to his chest, the one still holding the roses. Even though she wanted to stay this way forever, she pressed away ever so slowly.

"Evan, I'm so glad you told me. I don't want there to be any more secrets between us."

"I was so afraid you would turn away from me after you found out," he whispered.

"*Evan*," she said, her voice infused with all the love she had for him. "I know what's important. What's inside you. Just like you know with me."

"So I can shower you with presents now, right?" he asked eagerly, pulling back so they could look at each other. "I can have my chauffeur take you to and from work. You can move out of the hobbit flat—"

His words squeezed her heart. *This*, this she had feared. That he would want to lavish her with gifts and take her back to that life she'd left behind, the one that had smothered her.

"No, you can't do any of that," she said in as gentle a voice as she could muster. "I *love* strolling to the bakery on the quiet streets at night. And I love my place, hobbit door and all. And I love you." It felt important to add that last part.

He frowned, and she could practically see the wheels of his mind turning. "Okay. I heard everything you said. And I'm going to listen. Mostly. Just...don't stop me from giving to you. You told me on our first night together that you needed to give to me. Well, I need to do that too. I *need* to show you what you mean to me, Margie."

But could she trust him to find a balance? Or would he forget how to do normal people things with her? She couldn't bear that.

"All right," she agreed because she understood the need to give. "But in moderation."

"You're talking to a billionaire, Margie. Moderation is defined differently in my world."

Memories rose up like a black cloud. The pony her parents had bought her when she was eight before leaving for the Costa del Sol for three months. The single diamond necklace her dad had purchased her at Tiffany's before buying his current mistress something lavish, thinking Margie was too young to notice. No, Evan's world would not mix with the world she had built for herself. But she was only going to be in Paris for a short time, and while it cracked her heart in two to think about leaving, there was no need to worry about their future together when she knew there wouldn't be one.

"You only need to be you," she told him. "You know I like things simple. Lavish stuff is lost on me."

The study he made of her might have taken seconds, minutes.

"But there are so many fun things we could do. Like a helicopter ride over the city. It's impossible to arrange, but—"

"*Evan.*" She laughed, but this time it sounded more like cut glass than tinkling crystal. "I don't want you to go crazy. I'm only in Paris for another week."

"Then let me court you," he said, reaching for the hand holding the roses and pressing it to his chest. "Let me court you like you've never imagined anyone ever could. Let me share everything I love about Paris with you."

"I'll still have to leave at the end," she reiterated as sadness bubbled up inside her.

The grooves around his mouth deepened, almost as though he was feeling the pain of their separation like she had moments ago.

"I know. We'll have to make every second count."

Her other hand wrapped around his, and they stood that way, with their hands pressed against the beat of his heart.

"It's going to be hard to leave here," she said, biting her lip. "To leave you."

"It's going to be hard regardless."

She raised her free hand to his face and traced the hard line of his jaw. "I need to go to work. Andre will be worried I'm late."

"I'm sorry about that."

"I'm not." Andre would understand.

"Can I walk you the rest of the way?"

She shook her head. "No. I need to clear my mind before I get there so it won't affect the bread."

"And you think the Paint Prep Mistress is weird," he said, his tone teasing.

"But you can send me off to work with another kiss," she said softly.

Taking her face in his hands, he rubbed her cheekbones with his thumbs and lowered his mouth to hers. When Evan's lips touched her own, seeking and somehow also sustaining, all of the nerves still dancing from their confrontation on the empty street quieted in her body.

She poured everything she felt for him into that one kiss.

When they finally separated, they stared into each other. Suddenly his brow knit, and his hands gripped her arms.

"Please don't step back from me again while you're here," he whispered in a ragged voice. "I...don't think I could take it."

"I won't," she said, kissing him on the cheek. "I'll call you the minute I leave work."

A flash of vulnerability lit up his eyes.

"I promise, Evan."

He nodded. "Okay. Have a great day at work."

She jogged a little in place, as much to reconnect with the world outside the bubble she shared with Evan as to prepare to dash off. "See you later."

As she'd taken a couple steps away, Evan called her name. She looked over her shoulder. He was less tense than when she'd first seen him, but there was still a rigidity to his body.

"Thank you, Margie."

Even though she kind of knew what he meant, she still found herself asking, "For what, Evan?"

This time he was the one who released an agonized breath. "For not pushing me away after learning the truth about me. For not thinking I'm crazy for bringing you roses in the middle of the night. For everything."

Her heart bled a little for him, for the unhappy, lonely billionaire she now knew him to be. "Thank *you*, Evan. For the roses. For everything." Because she thought it would soothe him, she finally raised the trio of roses to her nose and inhaled their sweet, fading scent.

His mouth tipped up.

She walked off, picking up speed as she approached the bakery. Now that she knew he loved her, she felt more at peace with the situation. They would simply have to find a balance between his life and the way she wanted to live hers while she was in Paris. While she didn't understand Evan Michaels, the billionaire, she did understand Evan Murray, the inventor.

Perhaps during her final days in Paris, she would finally come to understand both of the men who'd captured her soul.

CHAPTER 2

When Evan returned home, he felt as if he were walking in a daydream. Telling Margie he loved her and hearing her return that profession had changed everything, particularly now that there were no big secrets between them.

Her concern about his money had carried through in the way she'd warned him not to go overboard. Somehow he was going to find a way to honor that, even though he wanted to give her everything she could ever want in the world. Like she'd given him.

He pulled out his computer to research the most romantic things to do in Paris. While romance shimmered on every block in Paris if one knew where to look for it, Evan wanted to give Margie the home run, the Halley's—a once-in-a-lifetime trip. After reading over fifteen different articles, he finally found a suggestion that struck him as perfect for her last night in town: tango in Trocadero Square above the fountains facing the Eiffel Tower.

He needed to brush up on his tango. As part of his makeover, he'd taken ballroom lessons so he'd be prepared for any party or club. When he picked up the phone to call his former instructor, he realized it was nearing five o'clock in the morning. Way too early to call, even for the billionaire who wasn't used to waiting for what he wanted. This was the kind of thing Margie didn't like. How he could snap his fingers and get what he wanted instantly.

As the golden and pink lights of sunrise filtered through the windows of the penthouse—he'd forgotten to close the curtains—he made a schedule of other romantic outings. He cross-referenced the weather forecast and made some adjustments to the timeline. Maybe he could slowly introduce her to grander activities during her time here. That way she could see how much she meant to him.

He would court her like she deserved to be courted.

And then what?

She would still leave. She'd made sure to remind him of that.

But he didn't want to think about that now. He *couldn't* think about it now.

Since he couldn't sleep, he read more blogs about the romantic things to do in Paris. Until today, he'd had no idea how many articles there were on the subject.

He revised their schedule again and decided to take her to the Rodin Museum, one of his favorite places in Paris, tomorrow for a picnic. Nothing lavish there, but it was romantic. Many locals went there to enjoy the gardens and the fountains behind the sculptor's house. Personally, Evan loved to walk along the windy dirt paths and study the various sculptures on display. Few people had ever captured the soul and the body in bronze like the master, and the museum showing his drawings and clay models was incredible. Margie would love it.

Satisfied with his plan, he decided it was time to paint. His sitting room had become a crazy kaleidoscope of color. Still, he didn't feel any closer to finding answers. He stirred the yellow paint he'd chosen because it reminded him of a dress Margie had worn once, and of the kitchen he'd painted for her in Hot Cross Buns.

The mixture turned into a tidal pool the faster he stirred, and his mind emptied. Then an image appeared in his mind, but it wasn't of an invention. He saw Margie in her yellow dress. The wind rushed around her, and her skirt twirled around her body. She laughed loudly, her green eyes sparkling.

Something oozed on his hand, and he shook himself. When he looked down, he saw a huge spot of wet paint on his skin. He couldn't see his skin, and for some reason, he was puzzled by that.

Paint was designed to add color, wasn't it? But it covered things up too. He stared at his hand so long his skin started to itch. Then he realized the paint had dried like a mud mask. He dabbed the end of his shirt in the glass of Perrier he had beside him. As he started to scrub the paint off, he realized Hugo Boss probably hadn't expected his designs to be used to clean up a paint spill. Oh well. Then he froze. The paint was changing the color of the shirt, the pigment staining what had been white to a muted yellow.

Again, he could feel there was something *there*. It was like a word on the tip of his tongue. The agony of that feeling was so frustrating he kicked at the paint can without thought. Paint pooled over the hardwood floor, and he could almost hear Chase say: *Evan, you're having one of your inventor tantrums*. He didn't care. What in the hell was the paint trying to tell him?

The sunny-colored paint pooled across the floor. He couldn't see the wood now. Only the paint. He ran his fingers in it. It covered up his skin again.

It covered up the floor.

It covered up his hand.

"What am I supposed to do with you?" he finally said out loud. "Tell me, dammit! No more horsing around!"

But all he could see was how the paint covered things up. Covered up everything in sight.

"Dammit, I know that already. Tell me something new."

He talked to himself more than most people did, so he didn't question it. He picked up the roller and stuck it in the pooling paint on the floor and swiped it across the floor in a long streak. It covered every square inch. Sure, there were spots that would require a second coat for uniformity, but it covered the surface. A patch of his cherry wood floor was now a sunny yellow.

Was he supposed to make a paint that covered up military installations? No, they already had paint to do that. He extended his foot back to kick the overturned can again, but then stopped himself. Destroying his home wasn't exactly helping matters.

He decided to let it go. His creative block was still there, but at least he was chipping away at it, like a lumberjack chipping away at a tree that stubbornly refused to fall down on its own.

"I'm going to figure this out," he said, raising his fist at the paint. "We can do this the easy way or the hard way. Your choice."

He cleaned up the paint as best as he could. If he used turpentine, he'd ruin the varnish on his floors, but then again, they'd have to be redone anyway. As he cleaned them, he marveled at how easily the paint came off.

Without quite knowing why, he painted more on the floor and then removed it with the cloth.

On again. Off again.

What in the hell was he supposed to do with this?

Frustrated beyond belief, he stood. It was time to let it all go and simply paint.

Since he liked seeing the different colors on the wall, he painted and repainted over the same section in that lush yellow. When he finished, he sat down on the floor and looked up at the wall, feeling like he was wrapped up in Margie's embrace.

She was all around him now, like the sunshine she emitted with her smile, like the sound of her voice when she said she loved him. He lowered himself onto his ruined floors in his ruined Hugo boss clothes and went to sleep with the paint roller still tucked in his hand.

When he awoke, the sun streaming in through the windows was blinding. His back felt like a mass of tangled wire as he stretched from his place on the floor. Maybe he should paint the windows. It would make everything outside invisible to him.

Invisible.

Then he straightened. His heartbeat paused as time seemed to lengthen around him.

That was it! He wasn't supposed to cover things up so much as make them invisible. Holy shit! He was supposed to make invisible paint.

He had to call Chase. Crawling across the floor, he finally tried to stand and stumbled from excitement. As soon as he found his phone, he dialed Chase. He only realized after he'd dialed the number that it would be the middle of the night for his friend.

"This had better be good, Evan," Chase said in a groggy voice.

"I'm going to invent invisible paint," he said, and then had to sit down on a nearby chair in the sitting room from the rush of energy those words sent through him.

This revelation had come to him because he'd told Margie the truth. He knew it in his gut.

"What did you say?" Chase asked.

"I'm inventing invisible paint." This time his voice was clearer and his head didn't spin. "Paint that can—"

"Make stuff invisible," Chase said. "I heard you. Holy shit, Evan. This is huge! When can you send me the prototype or the design or whatever the hell it is you've invented?"

He lovingly rubbed the paint clinging to his clothes. "I haven't invented the formula yet, but I will. I just needed to hear what I was supposed to invent next."

Chase groaned. "Hearing what you'll invent? Jesus, Evan, who told you? The Paint Prep Mistress?"

"If you're going to be nasty, I'm hanging up. I have to study the chemical composition of paint more." And he would. Somehow the formula to make an invisible paint would come to him.

Each of his inventions had begun with an idea. The rest was just details. Right now, everything was possible. Margie loved him, and she knew his secret and hadn't turned away like he'd feared.

"Hmmm…okay, when you have the *actual* invisible paint, give me a call. I'm going back to sleep."

"Chase, this new formula is going to change everything. Battleships will be invisible. Army bases will be undetectable. Maybe I can even design a human-friendly paint for soldiers. Just think of the possible applications."

"I am, Evan. I'm just not popping a bottle of champagne until I know you can do it."

Now that smarted. "Have I ever not delivered on a design?" Then he thought of the last two years. "Don't answer that. This is real, Chase. I told you there was something about the paint."

"At least you won't be creating a retail division of Quid-Atch Incorporated."

"I still might," he said, rubbing his chin. "Painters all over the world are going to want to kiss me on the mouth when they use the Paint Prep Mistress."

"That, my friend, sounds like a man who needs to get laid."

Evan clutched the phone tighter in his hand. "You promised you'd be nice about Margie."

"I know I did," Chase said. "I didn't say you weren't getting laid. And now I'll shut up. Go research paint, Evan."

"I'll need a new team, Chase." His brain was turning cartwheels, it was spinning so fast. "People from the paint industry. Maybe someone from Dow Chemical? And everyone who worked on the INV-333. I'll send you something."

"I'll have someone come up with a new R&D budget," Chase said, but his voice held more cheer than doom and gloom now.

"This is going to be epic, Chase," he told his friend.

"I know," he said. "Happy inventing, Evan. And welcome back."

Welcome back is right, he thought. When Chase ended the call, Evan realized he hadn't told his friend about the developments with Margie. Well, he would tell him later.

Now was the time to celebrate his new idea, the one that was going to change the world. He immediately began a text to Margie, but then forced himself to stop. She was at work. He checked the time. If she left on schedule today, she would be off in a few hours.

In the meantime, he could celebrate alone. He hobbled over to his Meneghini La Cambusa refrigerator, which cost as much as a luxury sedan, and located the bottle of Dom Perignon he had on hand. He popped the cork across the room and drank straight from the bottle. With champagne dripping down his chin, he hearkened back to Margie's toast in Dare Valley.

"To me and all my painting awesomeness," he said, lifting the bottle and doing a little jig, exactly like the woman he loved did when she was happy.

He couldn't wait to tell her his news.

***

Margie was glad for the hectic pace of the bakery. Even in the middle of the night, there was action. In the basement of Boulangerie Ma Belle, they were all like perennials in winter, their roots active underground as they waited for the light to bring new life to the surface. Margie's calves ached from all the trips she'd made upstairs, carrying the bread to arrange on the shelves for the customers who would soon flow through the door.

She'd worried Andre by showing up late. So much so, he'd ushered her to a private place upstairs to talk. After listening to a minute of apologies, he'd taken her by the shoulders and looked into her eyes. "Ma petite, if you need help, do not hesitate to ask Belle and me. We are your family here, no?"

She'd teared up and nodded at hearing him refer to her as family. He'd kissed her on both cheeks and then led her back downstairs, immediately handing her some dough from the mixers to set into the bowls to rise. Andre didn't like large quantities of dough trying to rise together. He said it was too much weight for the bread to reach its full height.

She focused on the bread and tried to be present to it. It was harder to make a proper baguette today. So she quieted her mind. Let her hands lovingly caress the dough until it softened under her touch, rather like she had caressed Evan's body. Love seemed to fill her until she was brimming over with it. And as she gave the bread her gentleness and attention, she felt it give her the same.

Her baguettes weren't works of art like the ones Andre, Fabian, and Ronan made, but they were much better now.

When Belle arrived, she popped down to the basement to give Andre a lingering morning kiss. Immediately afterward, she pulled Margie into a hug and led her to the side of the room.

"You are all right, ma petite?" she asked. "Andre and I were so concerned for you."

"I'm better. I was late to my shift because Evan chased me down as I was walking to the bakery." Even now, warmth filled her at the thought of it. "He said he loved me and then told me the truth. It was...one of the most beautiful moments of my life."

Belle gazed at her with a soft smile. "How romantic! I take back all of the nasty names I called him to Andre after we put the children to bed. And now Andre will not have to beat him...how do you say? To a pulp?"

She laughed. "I didn't tell Andre anything. He's a guy, and I arrived late."

"And he just wanted to make sure you were all right and then start baking bread. Ah, that man."

"Andre is as focused on making bread as Evan is with his inventions." Perhaps that was another reason she adored the baker.

"You will make a good wife someday," Belle said. "Our men need someone to tell their deepest secrets to. Like your man, Evan, Andre once feared sharing his secrets with me." Her smile was mysterious as she glanced over at her husband. "But he has no more secrets from me, and I have none from him."

"Is that the key to your relationship?" she asked.

Belle tilted her head to the side like she was thinking. "For us, happiness is always growing together. One of us will want something new, so we share it. It's exciting. There must be space to grow and remain curious about life."

She had grown up feeling skeptical about marriage. Her own parents' relationship had given her so little inspiration, but in the past few years, she'd met couples who'd made her consider the beauty of a life shared. Couples like Jill and Brian, and now Belle and Andre. "Thank you for sharing your wisdom with me, Belle."

"You're welcome, Margie," she said, heading back

toward the stairs. "Now, I'd better get upstairs and open the shop. Our customers need their bread."

The rest of her shift went fast, and soon she was washing the baking pans beside Fabian and hanging them to dry. Her cheeks were flushed, and her skin was damp from the steam of the water. The smell of baked bread hung in the air all around her. When she set her last pan aside to dry, she took a deep breath and savored the moment.

"Time for you to head home, ma petite," Andre called out as he came down the stairs.

He and Ronan must have finished making the croissant dough. She had yet to make croissants with Andre, but he said she would soon. Unlike bread, the croissant dough took days to properly set before it could finally be fashioned and baked. The more layers, the longer the process, he said.

"I can stay longer," she said, even though she was anxious to meet up with Evan. "Since I arrived a little late."

"Posh," he said, waving a massive hand. "You weren't that late. Fabian, tell her. We won't send you to the guillotine for that," he added in French since she was trying to speak more—and listen better.

"Your head is safe today, Margie," Fabian said with a deadpan face.

Andre laughed so hard, he clutched his belly. "But only today. Now, as for tomorrow..."

Fabian finally laughed too, and she joined in, from the humor as much from the joy she took from understanding their language enough to follow their jokes. Being around male bakers was more fun than she'd imagined. At her own bakery, all the employees she'd brought on to help her bake had previously worked with Grandma Kemstead, and all were women. She hoped that might change at some point now. It would be nice to have a balance.

"All right, I'll go," she said, taking out the clip she used to keep the hair out of her eyes while she was baking. She wanted to spend every minute she could with Evan.

Andre kissed her on both cheeks after she picked up her purse. "Take some bread with you, and don't hesitate to call if you need anything."

"Thank you, Andre." She grabbed the bread bag he thrust at her, smiling at the sight of the two almost-perfect baguettes.

"I mean it, Margie." His mouth had turned into a rare scowl. "Belle told me your man confessed who he was to you. I'm happy for you, ma petite, but if he hurts you again..."

He wouldn't, she knew. The only thing that would hurt her—hurt both of them—was when she left Paris. "I promise to call if I need anything."

There were customers in the shop when she came upstairs. Belle gave her a saucy wink, so she blew her a kiss. Then her friend laughed at something a young mother and child were saying in animated French about the baguettes they were buying.

Margie shook out her hair when she stood on the street. The sun was warm, and a breeze danced across her skin. She immediately thought of Evan and how his hands had felt on her. She wanted to hear him say he loved her when he was buried deep inside her, gazing into her eyes. Lust bloomed inside her, and she dug into her purse for her phone.

I'm finished for the day. Let me know when you want to meet up. I miss you.

Her phone immediately buzzed.

I've been missing you like crazy too. How about I pick you up? I have somewhere special planned.

Her diaphragm suddenly felt like a crusty slice of bread had gotten stuck there. Was it going to be something totally over-the-top?

Give me about twenty minutes to change, and I'll be ready.

His reply was immediate. *Can't wait.*

And then he added a red heart at the end of the message. So far they hadn't texted anything like that, and her heart melted. *Oh Evan, I love you. Please don't go all billionaire on me.*

Twenty minutes later, Evan buzzed the apartment, and she rang him up. Since the weather was warm, she'd chosen a simple purple cotton dress that looked great with her dark hair. Part of her had wanted to fuss over her wardrobe now that she knew Evan hung out with models wearing designer clothes, but since he had never once tried to change her, she let it go. He was with her because he wanted to be, not for what she was wearing. And this way, she could keep anchoring herself in the life she wanted to lead, the one where she could wear simple cotton and be herself.

When he knocked on the door, she swung it open. There was a shy smile on his face, and he was holding a huge bouquet of pink roses, not a wilted one among the bunch this time. She tried not to panic at the sight of the flowers. *They're only flowers, Margie.* Nothing super lavish about that. She stopped herself from thinking about how he'd wanted to ferret her out of this simple flat.

"Hi," he simply said, letting his eyes sweep over her.

"Hi." She'd noticed his clothes here seemed different from the ones he'd worn in Dare Valley, but now she realized why. Even though he was wearing jeans, a white T-shirt, and a charcoal jacket, each garment fit him to perfection. They had to be tailored and designer, the kind she used to have in her closet growing up. The memory was not a welcome one.

"You look beautiful," he said and then stepped toward her like he was going to kiss her. But he stopped and searched her face. "I promise we'll still leave...but I just have to kiss you now."

She couldn't help but smile. "You better kiss me. I've been thinking about it all day."

He nodded quickly, his ears tipped red now. "Good. Me too."

She took the flowers from him and set them on the counter. Then she came back to him and planted her hand on his chest. His lakewater blue eyes were filled with so much love she suddenly felt warm all over.

They both seemed to understand their talk on the quiet street had changed things between them. And that this kiss was another beginning for them both.

She laid her hand on his jaw. The spicy aroma of his cologne reached her nose, and her belly contracted with lust. "Come here," she whispered.

With aching pressure, she slid her hand around his nape and pulled his mouth to hers. He was gentle at first, only rubbing his lips over hers in a way that was both frustratingly sweet and arousing. But she wanted more, had daydreamed about more all day, and when she bit his bottom lip, she felt the quiver run through his body. She opened her mouth to him, and he did the same, matching her with deep strokes of his tongue.

Someone moaned, and she realized it was her. Then his arms came around her, and he pulled her flush against the hard line of his body. They took the kiss deeper, and soon she worked a hand between them, undid the button on his jacket, and lifted the edges of his T-shirt. She had to feel his skin. Right now. Her fingers traced the hard planes of his chest, but he grabbed them to stop her.

"I promised you we'd leave," he said.

She stepped back and let her lips curve. "Oh, we're going to leave," she said. "But first you have an appointment with me and the hobbit door."

His lips twitched. "Oh, I do, do I?"

She waggled her brows. "Do you think you're man

enough to handle me and the hobbit door all in one afternoon?" Before he could answer, she ducked through the door to her bedroom and began to take off the dress she'd just thrown on.

"We don't have enough room in here," he mused in a disapproving voice after he followed her in.

Swinging around, she pressed a hand to her breasts. She was not going to read any billionaire judgment into his tone. She wasn't. "Maybe you could design something to make the room *seem* bigger," she decided to tease. "You could call it the Lovemaking Mistress."

"Are you making fun of me?"

Since she could hear the humor in his voice, she knew she hadn't hurt his feelings. "Not at all. But that's not the right name. How about the Expandable Love Room?"

This time he tapped his foot. "Remind me not to ask you to help name any of my inventions. I had a huge breakthrough today, by the way. With the invention that's been bugging me since I started painting your bakery in Dare Valley."

Since he seemed talkative all of the sudden, she sat on the edge of the bed and pulled a sheet over her body. Another invention that would add to the billions he already had, a dark part of her whispered. But she ignored it. Hearing him talk about his inventions usually gave her joy. She wasn't planning on changing that.

"Tell me about it."

"Later," he said, taking off his clothes. "I thought I was going to blurt it out right away. I've been so excited to share it with you. But then I saw you, and all I wanted to do was tell you how much I love you all over again."

She had to swallow the lump in her throat. "I love you too."

Her hand extended to him, and he took it and sat next to her on the bed. They stayed that way for a moment, staring into each other, neither of them needing to move. In his eyes, perhaps because she loved him so much, she saw all the mysteries of life: fire, starlight, water, magic, and even freshly baking bread. She wondered what he saw in hers, but in some ways she knew it didn't matter. He saw what he needed to see.

Then they both leaned into each other. Their mouths met, slowly this time. The sheet she'd wrapped around her unwound as his hands freed her for his touch, for his gaze. And when she lowered herself to the bed, he settled his body against hers, igniting a whole host of new sensations.

"Evan," she said as his hands caressed her breasts, and she moaned deep and long in her throat as she welcomed his touch again.

He looked up and then ran one of his hands from the middle of her torso to her cheek. His mouth curved into a half smile. "I know."

And he really did. He knew what she needed. He knew where she needed his touch. He knew when she was close to the edge and how to take her over it. When she finally came back to herself, she opened her eyes. His head was resting on an elbow, and he was watching her, his blue eyes as dark as the sky before a storm. She reached for him, and when his body arched to her touch like the bread that rose to her every morning, she reveled in the joy of it.

When they could no longer wait another moment to be joined, he dug into his pants for a condom. She fitted it over him, and then he laid back and extended his hands to her. She straddled him and took his hands in hers as he sunk deep inside her.

Meeting his gaze, she whispered, "I love you."

"I love you too," he said softly.

Love flooded into her even more as she began to move, slowly at first. But soon it wasn't enough. He rolled her onto her back and thrust into her hard.

He stilled when she cried out, but she shook her head and said, "Don't stop."

And he surged into her with renewed force until she could no longer hold back the tides rushing through her. She surrendered to the flow, calling out to him, and felt him follow her to the other side, to the place where all time stopped and began again.

Like before, they didn't speak. They only held each other. Her head listened to the slowing beat of his frantic heart until it thudded in his chest like an easy melody. His hands stroked her back in a soothing motion, and she allowed herself to nod off for a while.

When she awoke, she realized he'd fallen asleep too. She took in every detail she could. He had a smattering of faint freckles on his nose she hadn't noticed before. His hair seemed to be held in place by a stronger hair product than he'd used Dare Valley, and she wondered if that was why his hair didn't curl as much here. Even his earlobes were adorable to her, round and heavy whereas her own were short and narrow like fairy ears.

Then his eyes opened, and her heart seemed to grow even larger in her chest, almost as if the sun had expanded to fit the whole horizon.

He leaned up to kiss her softly on the lips. She pressed her forehead to his, and right then, right when she was the happiest she could remember being, a desperate ache rose up inside her. She would have to leave him. Leave Paris. She took a deep breath, pressed back, and made herself smile. They had right now. That was what mattered.

"I believe you have a date with the hobbit door," she said finally.

He groaned again, but this time for a different reason. She tensed, fearing he was going to complain about the inferiority of her shower.

But then he scooped her up in his arms and

stumbled to his feet. Her anxiety faded, and instead the humor of the situation struck her. The door did seem smaller as he carried her to it, and she bit her lip to keep from laughing.

"If I knock myself out trying to get through this thing," he said good-naturedly, "at least make sure you land on top of me so you don't get hurt."

"I'll do my best."

He ended up leaning back to get them both through the tiny enclosure, which caused her to squeal.

"It's like limbo," he said as he set her down. His eyebrows rose dramatically when he opened the door to the narrow shower and turned on the water. "We're not going to fit in here."

She gave him a playful pinch to keep things easy between them. "I promise to make it worth your while."

"I can't wait to see how you plan on doing that," he said with an equally playful leer.

The space was beyond tiny, but it didn't matter. What mattered was the laughter between them as they both tried to wash each other in the confined space. Evan bumped his head a few times on the low ceiling and made a disparaging comment about hobbit showers. But it was what Evan the geeky inventor would say, not Evan the billionaire, who probably had a bathroom the size of her entire apartment.

After she finished dressing in the bedroom, she walked over to the hobbit door and settled back against it like she was in a silent movie to keep the ease between them going.

"Be honest with me," she said, trailing her hand seductively along the wood. "You want one of these now, don't you?"

He rolled his eyes. "We should go," he said, pulling on his shirt. "I probably have a parking ticket."

"Why didn't you tell me that?" she asked, rushing over to grab her shoes. Then she remembered how her parents would park in handicap spots because they could afford to rack up tickets. Her hands went lax from the memories, and the shoes clattered to the floor.

He took them from her, then led her to the bed so he could put each one on her like Prince Charming himself. "It's not what you're thinking. I forgot because being with you eclipses everything."

She felt her lips tremble, and then she clutched her hands together when they trembled too. "I know what you mean," she whispered. "I feel that way too." The rest of the memory slid from her mind.

He exhaled sharply, like he'd felt the darkness of the past rising in her. When he rose to his feet and held out his hand, she took it. Gathering it against his heart, they stood staring at each other, the rumpled sheets like mounds of whipped cream behind them.

"You can trust me, Margie," he told her.

"I do," she said and then gave a shaky laugh. "Just...be patient with me. About the money stuff."

He tipped up her chin to look at him. "How about we agree to be patient with each other, okay?"

She nodded.

"I'd like to show you where I live," he said. "When you're ready."

His wince sent pain shooting through her. This...this is what she feared for them both, what she hoped to prevent.

"I'm glad you want to show me where you live," she said with a slow smile to reassure him.

It was brave of him to ask, and she traced a heart on his chest to normalize them both.

"Good," he said cautiously. "It's kind of a wreck right now. I've been...painting."

She was able to laugh, wondering why a billionaire would paint his own apartment. "If I'd known you would miss it so much..."

He didn't join in with her like he normally did. "Just

tell me when you're ready to see it. I'll clean things up for you."

Delaying would only hurt him, and she couldn't bear that. "How about you show me where you live tonight?"

A smile filtered over his face before it fell away. "All right. After we go on our romantic outing."

She wanted to soothe him, but part of her wished someone would soothe her as well. Knowing the truth about his billions was like walking a tightrope without a net. Much harder than she'd thought it would be.

"Deal."

CHAPTER 3

The Rodin Museum was as compelling as the artist himself. Evan couldn't be happier to be here with Margie, holding her hand and talking with her about the art.

"What do you think...haha...he's trying to figure out?" she asked him after they stood in front of the famous sculpture The Thinker for a long moment.

He lifted a shoulder. "Every time I see this one, I feel like he's trying to figure out how to unlock a person from the medium he's working on."

"Oh, I like that." She swung their hands, and it felt childlike and charming—just like her. "I'd like to think he's contemplating the meaning of life."

"No wonder he looks so depressed," he joked and then swung her hand back, like he was giving her swing a push at the park.

Her smile made him feel like he owned the entire universe.

"I love this place," she said. "Some museums can be so formal and boring. The ushers hush you if you so much as laugh."

"That's one of the reasons I like this place too," he

told her as they walked down the path leading through the shrubs. The roses were old canes, and their yellow, red, and pink blooms were as large as small dinner plates.

"You also like it because he took things apart and made them new," she said, squeezing his hand. She might as well have squeezed his heart with that statement.

"Yes. I like seeing how he built his models. Did you know he first conceived of the figure that would become The Thinker in 1880, but the first bronze castings didn't appear until 1904? That's twenty-four years!"

"I can add and subtract, Evan," she said dryly, pushing back a lock of sable hair the wind had blown into her eyes.

"I wasn't trying to imply—"

"I know you weren't," she said, smiling at him.

He loved the way she seemed to just *get* him, even when he feared he sounded crazy, especially now that his billionaire status was out in the open. Now, if she still smiled at him like that when she saw the paint-speckled wall in his luxurious apartment, he might simply lay a white rose at her feet and offer to worship her for the rest of his life.

Okay, maybe he needed to get a grip.

"You feel a camaraderie with him," she said. "He might be a sculptor, but he was kind of an inventor too. Like you. He had to see possibility where no one did."

Jesus, a rose was such an inadequate gesture. He would lay diamonds or gold or the rarest metal on the planet at her feet instead. Which she would hate since such gifts would definitely be on the too-lavish list. "Why is it you understand me better than most people? Even Chase..." He broke off, unable to complete the statement.

She half hugged him, like she was trying to infuse him with her courage. "Even Chase..."

"Thinks I'm crazy sometimes," he admitted.

"You don't really paint much," she said, stopping in front of another sculpture. "Do you? That must have been part of your Evan Murray persona."

He felt the lie he'd told her creep back between them. "I wouldn't have taken the job as your painter if I didn't think I could do an incredible job."

"I know that." Her mouth looked tense at the corners. "I'm still embarrassed that I only paid you fifteen dollars an hour."

His belly twisted, and he turned to face her. "I'm only worth fifteen dollars as a painter," he said. "I don't want you to be embarrassed about that. I felt bad taking money from you in the first place. Can I give it—"

"No," she interrupted, looking down at the ground. "I hired you for a job, which you did. You deserved to be paid."

He could feel her withdrawing from their earlier ease together. "With practice, I could probably become a master painter," he said, hoping to make her laugh. Considering all the testing he would have to do to achieve his invisible paint, he would probably get to that status.

"I somehow don't see that happening," she said, meeting his gaze. The slight twinkle in her eyes made him want to kiss her, right then and there, smack on the lips. "You're probably right. I could never be a master painter like you're a master baker."

"I'm not a master baker yet. There are plenty of imperfections in my baguettes, and I haven't even started croissants."

"There are no imperfections in your baguettes! Anyone who says otherwise needs to see someone professionally."

"Thank you for your faith in me," she said in a voice so low he had to strain to hear it.

"I have more faith in you than I do in anyone."

Then she rose on her tippy toes to give him a kiss. "I have faith in you too."

"It humbles me to hear you say it," he said, kissing her on the cheek. "I promise to do my best to live up to your faith in me."

Her emerald eyes stared at him, and in them, he could see her love and all the questions she still had. He would have to court her harder to win her complete faith.

They wound their way to the back of the house. The fountains surged and gurgled, and the sculptures around them seemed to be expounding the power of the water. People sat on wooden benches in the waning sunlight. Some were couples. Some were families. Some were tourists.

And some were like he'd been—a single person sitting in the presence of the master, hoping for inspiration. During his dry spell, he'd come here a lot, hoping to feel a spark, to know what he was supposed to invent next. He'd felt nothing.

"He had a beautiful house," Margie commented. "It's too ostentatious for me, but it's so French with all the mullioned windows and sandstone."

"What kind of house did you grow up in?" he asked, wondering what his penthouse would look like through her eyes.

"A big one," she said with a frown. "Filled with famous art by the hottest painters, and marble, and lots of silence. I never felt like I could make a mess. My mother and my nanny always scolded me."

His house boasted a lot of art and silence too, but maybe she would appreciate the mess in his apartment, after all...

They continued along the gravel path. Other statues beckoned them to stop and linger. The armless figure of a woman looking at the ground, her leg raised on a rock, seemed to say, I may have been desecrated, but I am still a woman. I still matter. I still have things to speak. To share.

"He had such a brilliant way of capturing the human body," Margie said. "Every one of these figures feels alive to me."

The bronze sculptures were hot to the touch, as if they too believed they were alive, and they were scattered throughout the grounds. Evan led Margie through the narrow enclosures where the trees and shrubs had been cut back to perfection. They listened to the faint whispers of more of Rodin's figures before settling onto the blanket he'd packed in the picnic basket.

"Good thing I brought my baguettes," Margie said, nudging him with one of the loaves.

Memories flooded him from the mere touch, and he grew rock hard, thinking about how they'd fed and caressed each other with the bread before making love.

"I'll never see a baguette the same way ever again," he admitted.

Her eyes fired with heat, and he suddenly felt like he was standing amidst the flames of a forest fire.

"Neither will I." Her hand rested on his thigh briefly before trailing away. "What else did you bring for our picnic?"

His subzero picnic basket had kept the cheese and saucisson cold. And of course, the pink champagne they'd enjoyed at dinner after their first kiss in Paris. He drew out two champagne glasses that fit perfectly in their special holder. He popped the cork to the champagne, and she held out the glasses for him to fill. The sound of her joyful laughter before she took her first sip made people turn to look for the source of the magical sound.

"Why am I not surprised you have a basket that keeps champagne cold? Did you invent it?"

He wished he had, just to see her smile like that.

"No, but I have some ideas for improvements."

She laughed, and he waited for it to subside so he could feed her bites of brie. She, in turn, fed him bites of baguette, which made him very uncomfortable.

"So the baguette wasn't the best idea," she said, her lips pursing together like she was suppressing laughter. "Maybe you should put yourself in your subzero basket."

"Venus wouldn't apologize for raising my ardor," he said, feeling the pull of the past around him.

"I love it when you call me that," she said, running a hand up his thigh.

"If you keep doing that, I'm going to go Parisian on you and kiss you senseless right here on this blanket."

She propped herself up on her elbows and tilted her head to the side, studying him. "What's stopping you?"

He set down his champagne glass and was on top of her in a minute. The feel of her mouth was lush. The shape of her body under him was as curvy and welcoming as the goddess who'd given Margie her nickname. He could have devoured her, but there was enough American in him to pull away. He was breathing hard, but then again, so was she.

"How far is your place from here, Evan?" she asked.

Too far and not far enough, he realized. "We're having a picnic, Margie. Or we're supposed to. I made a schedule."

"Evan—"

"Stop torturing me," he pleaded. "I really want to court you. I promised I would."

She bit her lip as she poured him another glass of champagne.

He leaned in to kiss her. "I'm sorry for being cross. I've just never wanted to do something for someone this much. Margie, I want to give you all the romance Paris has to offer."

Her smile told him all was forgiven, and they supped on bread and wine and cheese and meats.

Simple, but flavorful, fare. The fountains babbled like little toddlers. The bronze figures bathed in glowing brilliance in the waning sun.

And all seemed well. For a while.

But the sun was going back to her bed, and Evan felt the change in the earth, and in the unnameable and unstoppable connection between them. They only had six days left, it seemed to say. And that was never going to be enough.

"I think it's time we went to your house," she said, reading his mind.

She was still lying on her back on the blue picnic blanket, drowsy with sleep.

He felt guilty suddenly. He wanted to spend every waking moment with her, and she had to be at work at two o'clock in the morning. "You need to sleep."

Her smile was as lush as the gardens around him. "I can sleep at your house, and then you can drive me to work." He liked that idea since she'd turned down his offer to have someone drive her to work.

They packed up the picnic and took off for the car, stopping only to marvel at the final sculpture on the pathway on the way out. It was perhaps the most impressive of Rodin's works, but it was deeply depressing to Evan's eyes. The Gates of Hell were two massive doors sculpted in bronze and about twenty feet tall.

"It's said there's something like two hundred figures in the piece," he told Margie as she studied it somberly. "Every one of them seems to delight in expressing their agony."

Some of the people looked like they were clawing back the bronze door in an attempt to set themselves free.

"He knew a lot about agony," Margie said. "It makes me sad. He had all this, but he still wasn't happy."

Evan gripped her hand. "I felt like that—before Dare Valley. Before you."

"I'm glad you don't feel that way anymore." She looked at him with her emerald eyes. There was some emotion there to which he couldn't put a name.

"You changed that," he told her, cupping her face. "You've changed everything."

"And now we really need to go back to your place. Evan..."

He waited for her to continue.

"You've changed things for me, too," she said softly.

He swallowed the lump in his throat, and then he kissed her sweetly on the lips. Who cared if tourists were milling around them?

When they separated, she gave a final look at the statue. He couldn't seem to look at anyone but her.

"Shall we go?" she asked.

He nodded and then walked quietly to the car.

His gut tightened. What would she see? The madness of the inventor? The lushness of the billionaire? Or the man who had no photos of himself or anyone else, because other than Chase, who hated pictures, there was really no one else in his life with whom he wanted to capture any memories. At least not until Margie.

***

Margie could sense Evan's nervousness as he parked the Fiat in an underground garage. Honestly, he wasn't the only one who was nervous.

She wondered what he usually drove because this car couldn't possibly be his normal ride. Not considering all the Internet gossip about his love for racing fast cars. But if he'd bought it to perpetuate his lie, why was he still using it now that she knew he was a billionaire?

Then it clicked.

He didn't think she would be comfortable in one of his luxury cars, and he was right. For the moment, she'd simply accept the Fiat as the prop that it was. Seeing his apartment would be jarring enough.

So while he jangled his keys in his hand as they walked to a side door, she took deep breaths to calm her nerves. But then he put his eye close to a red scanner on the wall by the door all super-spy-like. There was a click, and he opened it.

"A retinal scan?" she asked before she could stop herself.

"I...ah...have extra security...because of my inventions," he said, his brow furrowing.

"Right," she said as they walked down a narrow hall to another door. There was a keypad next to it, and he needed to enter a code before opening it. His security alone probably cost more than her Victorian in Dare Valley. "Are you sure I'm cleared for all this?"

"You're with me, so you're cleared." He held the door and let her precede him. "It's five flights up. Is that okay? You're small, but I don't think you'd fit in the dumbwaiter."

"I'm good," she said with a choked laugh, tackling the stairs. Their footsteps echoed in the narrow space. "I know you're looking at my butt."

"Of course I am," he said, touching the back of her hair gently. "It's the best view in Paris."

His compliment didn't ease the tightness in her chest. At the end of the stairs on the fifth floor, there was another industrial gray door. He reached around her and punched in a second code.

"Another one? And seven digits at that," she commented, breathing a little hard from the climb, or so she told herself.

"My company," he said, frowning now, "requires the highest security clearances. Since I work at home..."

He broke off, holding her elbow as they entered a hallway that felt like it belonged to another era. *This* was the billionaire's lair.

Soft light glowed from frosted cut glass sconces. A thick tapestry on one wall depicted a Roman scene of women lounging by a pool of water. Another wall held an arresting portrait of a woman gazing out a window while clutching a bouquet of flowers. Through the windows, the city of Paris was spread before her like a banquet, the Eiffel Tower captivating in the background. On the floor, there was a rich maroon and navy carpet with yellow fleur de lis on the dark cherry floors.

"It's beautiful, Evan," she said, because it was. Unfortunately the luxury of it all was wreaking havoc with her ability to breathe. "Just how I imagined Maxim's looked back in its prime." The bistro had become a famous dining establishment starting around the late nineteenth century, known for its lush decoration that seemed to drip with plush velvet and European sophistication. Growing up, Margie had loved watching the classic movie *Gigi*, which had filmed some famous musical scenes in the cultural icon.

"I wish I could have taken you to dinner there years ago," he said, leading her to a pair of large French doors that she assumed led to his apartment. "They recreate it for tourists now, but I don't think it's the same."

There was a black and gold gilded staircase to the left, which wound round to the lower floors, and she stopped for a moment to admire it in spite of herself. She had to give Evan credit. He'd made the most of his billions. "I take it that's where most guests come up."

He dropped his hand from her elbow, but not before she felt the perspiration on his palm. She tried to remember what a big step this was for him.

"Or I use those stairs when I go by foot," he said. "We have a...security guy in the building. I only use the back stairs when I drive."

Her mind veered again to his other cars, and she had to reel it back in.

At the front door, he paused. "Promise me you won't freak out when you see the paint...stuff. Or everything else. Margie, I'm afraid you're going to run down those stairs the minute you go inside."

She put her hand on his chest and felt his heartbeat knocking underneath. "I promise I won't run. Come here."

They both needed to touch each other. Right now. Rising on her toes, she pressed a kiss to his chin before he lowered his head. Their mouths met. His sigh gusted out, filled with anxiety, and she breathed out her own. She traced another heart on his chest and felt his arms come around her. This was what mattered, she told herself. Their love. Not his money.

"I love you," she whispered.

"I love you too," he whispered back. "You are the most amazing woman I have ever met."

"Thank you," she said, feeling a touch more settled. "Show me the rest, Evan."

He depressed a hidden panel in the doorframe and keyed in another code. The double doors clicked, and he pushed one open for her. The round entryway had a large gold mirror and a discreet crystal chandelier that looked antique. The walls were a rich emerald. The floor was a beautiful parquet with a sun in the center. Landscape paintings of seasides and country venues hung on the walls.

"It's beautiful," she said.

It *really* was, she was forced to admit.

She reached for his hand as he guided her down another hallway.

He jerked away from her. "Ah...I'm sweaty."

And he was, poor guy. He might be more nervous than she was. There was a spattering of droplets at his temple. She grabbed his hand anyway and made herself laugh. "Like we haven't been sweaty before."

He stopped and looked at her. She could almost feel him unwind like a fresh sail catching a gentle breeze.

"Good point," he said, his thumb caressing her skin.

His shoulders seemed to settle down more too. Before they'd been up by his ears. Realizing her posture wasn't any better, she dropped her shoulders down as well, then let him lead her further down the hall and into a large sitting room.

The furniture looked both comfortable and lush. The walls had to be twenty feet high, and the windows at least fifteen, giving a breathtaking view of curved rooftops and graceful archways below a larimar-colored sky. Painted a deep plum, the room was covered with more artwork: a peacock, a sailor in a small boat at night, and three cherub-like children reaching for croissants with a warm fire in the background. Oh, how she adored that last one. It made her wonder if Belle and Andre's children looked like that.

It was nothing like she'd expected. His tastes cemented him as a romantic, but it was the picture of the children that told her he'd tried to make this place his home—a haven where any child would feel safe and warm and loved.

Knowing how unhappy and lonely he'd been before Dare Valley, her heart broke for him. This was a man who was starving for a family. Just like her.

"It's beautiful, Evan," she said, ignoring the part of her brain starting to calculate the expense of her surroundings. "But I don't see the paint."

His mouth pressed into a tight line. "Turn around. I tried to keep it on one wall."

She slowly spun around, and since he was holding her hand, he followed her like they were those children in the painting. The patches of paint on the bare wall commanded her gaze. There was no pattern to the rolls. Some crossed each other like two roads meeting at an intersection, while others looked like an endless highway through the countryside. The colors he'd chosen were appealing. Periwinkle, teal, red, and yellow, and then she realized some of the colors were the same ones he'd used to paint her bakery.

Her heart felt like it turned over in her chest. "I notice some familiar paint colors."

His foot started tapping on the gold and green Aubusson rug. "I was...kind of missing you, I guess."

It took her a moment to speak. She turned to face him and traced the tense line of his jaw. "That's really sweet." And because she knew he needed to hear it, she said, "And I don't think you're crazy. Not one bit."

The rap-pa-tap-tap he was making with his shoe ceased. "You haven't seen what I did to the floor."

He led her behind the couch, and sure enough, there it was. Somehow he'd spilled yellow paint on the hardwood and hadn't mopped it all up. Paint cans lined a plastic sheet near the wall alongside a host of rollers and brushes.

"You forgot to put down enough plastic on the floors," she said with a tsking sound.

"I get impatient sometimes when I'm thinking about...things," he said.

"I seem to remember that," she said with a laugh. "Show me the rest, Evan."

He seemed eager to lead her away from his Pollack-like paint montage. His kitchen made her sigh. God's honest truth, money could buy a person a fabulous kitchen. And she had major kitchen envy here. Van Gogh might have painted it on a happy day. It was a rich gold fitted with cherry cabinets. Copper pots hung above a massive stove. There was a café scene on the wall of a man and woman drinking espresso. And there was one brick wall by the massive Viking range, which conveyed the building's age. Oh, the number of cinnamon rolls she could bake in an oven that size.

He led her to the wall when he noticed her gazing at it. "When I bought the place, I had the kitchen remodeled. There had been some water damage from the roof. My contractors uncovered this wall, and if you look very closely, you can see the date of 1777 carved into one of the bricks."

She leaned closer. "Oh, I see it! How marvelous!"

"I thought so. This apartment was owned by the Goulous family for two hundred years, but they fell on hard times after the Second World War. Since then, it's changed hands twice."

"And now it's yours. How lucky for you." She was grateful to realize she *was* happy for him. There was nothing wrong with him being wealthy, and the last thing she wanted to do was become some horrible judgmental person. Especially with him.

He led her through the rest of the house, pointing out two guest bedrooms and a smaller sitting room.

"Do you work on your inventions here?" she asked him.

"Most of the time," he said. "I...can communicate with my colleagues when the need arises. Mostly I like to work alone. Especially when I'm in my crazy inventor mode."

Thinking about him as the president of a billion-dollar corporation was a challenge, but then again, she knew Chase was the man who ran things.

When he would have continued with his tour, she stopped him with one hand. "I wish you'd stop calling yourself a mad inventor, Evan. How can everyone else start seeing you for you until you do?"

He buttoned his jacket. Then unbuttoned it. And then buttoned it again. "Why is it you see me so clearly?"

"Because I used to feel lost and eccentric in my own way," she admitted, feeling the common ground between them unfold, right in the center of his luxurious home. "I wasn't like anyone else I grew up around." And because she needed to say it, and he needed to hear it, she continued. "I was the only person around who seemed to realize having money didn't make us happy. It didn't give us value. It didn't make us more special than anyone else. It was simple economics."

He shook his head slowly, like her words were dripping slowly into his brain, like water droplets off a drainpipe. "Simple economics. I like that."

"My cinnamon rolls and other baked goods cost a certain amount," she said, "and that's what I will earn as a baker. Your inventions cost quite a bit because they're top-secret, which makes you a billionaire." If only her mind and heart could agree on it being that simple. "But I'll be honest. I don't know what to think of the paint. Are you redecorating?"

He stopped suddenly and grabbed her hand, and there he was again, the man who had gotten so excited while inventing the Paint Prep Mistress.

"That's the big breakthrough I wanted to tell you about. Earlier. Before you ah...distracted me with the hobbit door."

Her mouth twitched.

"It's the invention that started in Dare Valley."

When he took off down the hall in the opposite direction, she had no choice but to follow him. She needed to run to keep up, so she plowed into him when he skidded to a halt in front of what looked like a closet door. But he pressed an invisible panel in the wood and out popped another security box.

He keyed in another code, mumbling, "Chase is going to kill me," and then dragged her inside.

The door made this strange locking sound behind them, and she must have looked puzzled because he said, "Hermetically sealed. Sound proofed. The whole shebang."

When she finally absorbed her surroundings, she

gasped. "Wow!"

Everything was modern and sleek and almost overwhelming with its gadgetry. Four computers rendering three-dimensional images were arranged on a long metal table, and a clear touch screen like the ones she'd only seen in sci-fi movies was flashing a series of equations.

"This is my lab," he said. "I never bring anyone in here except for Chase."

Her heart started to pound a ragged rhythm in her chest.

"You have to swear to me you won't share what I'm about to tell you with anyone," he said, unbuttoning his jacket again and putting his hands on his hips.

"I won't," she told him.

He looked away, like he was still fighting with himself, and then returned his gaze to her. She would have sworn there was fire dancing in his lakewater blue eyes.

"I'm going to create invisible paint."

She heard his words, but they didn't compute for a moment. "What?"

He sprang into motion again, crossing to the touch screen flashing different equations. "Invisible paint! Just think of the applications. It's going to change everything. I'm still not sure what to do about the sounds made by tanks and submarines, but think of it, Margie. Imagine what might be possible with this invention."

She pressed her hand to her temple to sweep away a flash of pain. This was what he did. This was how he'd become rich. Genius and excitement. It was a potent mix.

"This is a lot to take in. Invisible paint. Invisible paint." He was making invisible paint. Considering his intensity right now, the creative fire that seemed to have consumed him, she almost believed it was possible.

But seriously? Invisible paint?

"Chase doesn't completely believe I can do it yet." Evan touched the screen, making another equation flash across it. "It's something in the binder," he mumbled. "I just know it is. I just have to change the matrix that holds the pigment in place."

His eyes were glassy, and he seemed to be somewhere else. She'd seen him like this before. Sitting on the floor of her unpainted bakery with a machine in his hands.

"Evan," she called to bring him back.

He shook himself and returned his focus to her. "Right. I was saying Chase knows that when I get an idea, that's it. I pour everything I am into my invention until it works. That's how I invented..."

When he trailed off, she pressed a hand to her belly. Boy, he wasn't holding back anything. The significance of him sharing top-secret information with her made her a bit weak in the knees. It was a good thing she was sitting down.

He walked over and gripped the top of a black office chair so hard his knuckles turned white. "I can't tell you what I've invented, dammit. But I want to, Margie. I can tell you about the invisible paint because there's no security clearance protocol preventing me from telling you. No one has bought it because it doesn't exist yet."

"It's okay, Evan," she said, walking over and taking a seat in front of one of his computers because she needed to sit down. "I'm honored you would tell me this much."

"All of this has happened because I came to Dare Valley after losing a poker game," he said, striding across the room to her and pulling her chair out so he could turn her to face him. "It happened because I met you."

Her head was buzzing like the machine rendering his three-dimensional images. "And because you painted my bakery."

"Now that I have my creative fire back," he said, gripping the arms of her chair as he leaned over her, "I feel like I can do anything. *Everything* is possible again."

Then he kissed her, and his mouth was hot and hungry and demanding. He pressed her back into the chair, opening her lips with his tongue and going deep. She met him stroke for stroke, but soon kissing wasn't enough for either of them.

He lifted her body to him. "I really want to make love to you here."

She was burning up from his heat and her own. "Fine by me."

Clearing the notepads and papers off the metal table with a wide sweep of his hand, he sat her on the edge. Then he was tugging up her dress. Even though they'd had each other only hours ago, they devoured each other again, right in his lab.

She was naked and sweaty by the time he folded over her, panting in her ear.

"I don't know how I'm ever going to get any work done in here now," he said between breaths.

"Maybe you should paint it," she joked and started to laugh.

He kissed the side of her neck and started laughing too. "Maybe I will. I went with a high-tech lab look, but who's to say I can't paint it teal?"

"A teal lab? Chase will really think you've lost it."

His laughter died, and she was sorry for being the cause.

"Probably. He means well. I mean, he has the hard job of running everything. I just invent."

Because she wanted to soothe him, she ran a hand down his back and hugged him. "Inventing invisible paint doesn't sound like a walk in the park, Evan."

"No, but I think I can do it. I'm studying all the

available paint formulas, going all the way back to lead paint. Things are already coming together."

"Maybe you need to include turpentine and other chemicals that remove paint in your research," she said and then closed her mouth. "Forget what I just said. I'm not an inventor. I never even liked science much."

"That's not true. You adore chemistry. Otherwise, you wouldn't love making bread so much." He leaned back, his blue eyes like the clearest ocean waters now. "And you're right. I need to look into everything that gets rid of paint."

"I don't think my suggestion is going to help you much," she answered as he lifted her off the table. She tightened her legs around him. "It's silly."

"I always want you to share your ideas with me, Margie," he said softly. "I...like it."

She kissed his cheek since her throat had closed with emotion. Sharing her bread with him had made her happy, so she could understand the feeling.

As he carried her across the lab, he said, "How about we research why turpentine removes paint after we take a shower? I don't have a hobbit door, so I can't knock myself unconscious."

He was all over the place from his excitement. She laughed softly as he left the lab and walked them down the hall.

"I don't see how I could possibly say no," she said. "You're adorable when you're like this."

"Adorable?" he asked with enough disbelief that she leaned up and kissed him.

"Yes, adorable. People who don't like inventors are crazy."

"I might need you to write that one down," he said, meeting her gaze and stopping before a large set of double doors.

She wished he would stop doubting himself, but he had to be the one to do it. All she could do was encourage him. "I can even make you a T-shirt, if you think it will help."

"I would rather like one of those."

There was a portrait on the wall depicting a grandmother figure picking roses in the hallway going to his bedroom. "Does that woman remind you of someone in your family?" she asked.

The shake of his head was perfunctory. "No."

Oh, how his voice had changed with that one word. "Evan, you never talk about your family."

"There's not much to say," he said, studying the picture. "You wanted to know if I have a grandma like this. I don't, but I always wished I did. Some sweet lady who would make me cookies and give me ice cream and let me stay up past my bedtime."

"What about your mother?"

"She still lives outside Chicago and cleans houses for a living," he said, not meeting her eyes when she touched his face. "I tried to give her...an easier life, but she didn't want it. She said she didn't know what else to do with herself. And I'm...not someone she understands. We talk at Christmas, but not much more."

Her heart broke for him. "What about your father?"

"He went to Texas for a job when I was a kid and said we'd join him when he had everything in place." He blew out a harsh breath. "I still haven't forgiven him. He sent my mom divorce papers in the mail like she was nothing to him, and he never tried to see me again. Not even when I made the cover of *Time*. I thought he might hit me up for money or something, but I didn't mean enough to him even for that."

He thought he was nothing, she realized, when he was capable of so much. "Do you remember what you said to me about my parents?"

Finally, he allowed her to see the pain in his eyes. "You'll have to remind me."

"They didn't deserve you," she said, tracing the tense muscles of his brow. "*I* see how special you are, Evan. And I love you."

His face bunched up, but then he pressed his forehead to hers. His heart was pounding faster, and she could feel him gathering together all of the messy emotions inside him. His loneliness made sense to her now, and it hurt to think about how alone he must have felt. No one had been there to guide him. Until Chase. She felt more gratitude for his friend than ever before.

"You're a miracle. Do you know that?"

The only answer she could give him was to wrap her arms around him as he hugged her.

Evan took a few more deep breaths and then he edged back to gaze into her eyes. "Well. How about I resume the tour? I guess the master bedroom and bathroom are the only rooms you haven't seen."

Since she knew he needed some time to settle, she nodded. "Please."

When he opened the door and stepped inside, he stopped at the foot of his bed. "What do you think?" he asked.

Like the rest of the house, the ceilings were easily twenty feet high with large double windows. A small balcony with a table and a single chair was visible through frosted glass French doors. It looked isolating, especially after what he'd told her. She scanned the rest of the room. The color he'd chosen for the walls was a rich cobalt, and more landscapes lined the wall. Over his bed was a single painting of an older man who was putting a machine together over a workspace covered with widgets and other parts. A soft glow lit the dark room in which he was working. She couldn't have imagined a better choice of art for Evan's room. She continued her perusal. The curtains were a welcoming but elegant white with gold stitching, and his bed linens were a matching gold.

"I like it," she said. "Your bed looks so soft I want to jump on it." Maybe it would help his sadness pass. And hers for him.

"Jump on my bed, huh?" His brow rose, and some of the tension left his face. "I don't know why I'm surprised. That's what I love about you." Before she could reply, he dropped her on the bed and stood over her grinning. "Jump to your heart's content. The windows have a special tint on them so no one can see inside. I'll start the shower."

She rather wished he would join her, but perhaps talking about his family had been too much for him. Even she was feeling off balance. She stood on the bed, her feet sinking into the mattress, and gave a test bounce. Then she put her hands on her breasts and jumped for all she was worth. Her laughter continued as she jumped higher and higher, and pretty soon she couldn't stop giggling. If there was one thing she'd learned in life, it was that she didn't have to stay sad or tense. She could always choose to be happy. Right now, jumping on the bed was just what the doctor ordered.

The bed dipped as Evan leaped onto it and grabbed her to him. "I don't think anything has ever looked so sexy."

"Jump with me," she said, taking his hands.

He looked unsure, but then she gave a few big bounces and started to laugh when he wove to the right.

"Jump or fall," she told him, and he finally met her gaze with a smile.

And jumped.

They turned into little kids, bouncing until they finally dropped onto the bed and lay there side by side, as close together as possible. Both of them were breathing hard.

"Do you feel better now?" she asked, turning onto her side and tracing a heart on his chest.

"Yes," he said with a grin. "Thanks."

Planting a kiss smack dab on his lips, she caressed the muscles of his chest. "There's steam coming out of the bathroom door."

"That's what happens when hot water meets cool air," he told her.

She playfully swatted him. "Then let's shower. What time is it anyway?" she asked, searching for an alarm clock.

He turned away and pointed to the side table behind him. "It's a little after nine o'clock."

Groaning, she closed her eyes. She'd resigned herself to not getting much sleep while she was in Paris, but she was averaging about three to four hours a night with a random nap here and there. At some point, she was going to have to play catch-up. By five o'clock in the morning, she'd be plying herself with espresso to stay awake.

Evan leaned over her and gave her a lush kiss. "Shower. Then sleep. I feel guilty about keeping you up when you have to work in a few hours."

Neither one of them wanted to spend any more time apart than they had to.

Wrapping her arms around his neck, she kissed him again. "I don't want to be anywhere else."

He rose from the bed. "Come. I promise all we'll do is shower."

She ran her gaze down his body. "Someone else disagrees."

"Most inventors have an alter ego."

But they did keep their shower mostly chaste. She could barely see him through the thick steam, but she felt him behind her as she washed. The jets pulsed on her body where his hands had been, where she wanted his hands again. But when she touched him, he took them and brought them to his mouth for a soft kiss.

"I promised you some sleep," he said and turned her away from him gently.

They dried off and then settled in the center of his massive bed, her head pillowed by his shoulder.

"You don't have to stay with me," she said, starting to feel heavy in her body.

"Try and stop me," he answered.

His heartbeat lulled her to sleep.

CHAPTER 4

Making croissants was hard.

There were no two ways about it. Even though Andre was sharing all his secrets with her in the ground floor of the bakery, she still hadn't changed her mind about that one essential fact.

Her night with Evan must have imparted a special magic to her because Andre had finally deemed her ready to tackle the challenge of the enchanting bread.

The time she'd spent with Evan had only strengthened her resolve to continue to open herself to him. He loved her, and she loved him. While she was in Paris, she was going to do her best to overlook all the obstacles that stood between them and simply enjoy their connection.

The croissants and Andre's instruction required her complete attention, so her mind had little time to wander. He'd already shown her how to make the dough that would be layered with the butter, which didn't seem too hard. The challenging part would be folding the butter into the dough in the process called laminating.

She asked Andre to write down his tips for her on a piece of paper she'd borrowed from the office.

"The major key, ma petite," he said as he wrote, "is

to make sure the dough and the butter are the same temperature when you combine the two ingredients together. If anyone ends up with butter stains on their hands from eating a croissant, it was because the dough was likely room temperature while the butter was cold from the fridge."

His handwriting was a precise print she would easily be able to read later. When he finished, he set the paper on a clean space on the metal table and turned to face her.

"I'm worried for you, ma petite," he said with a frown. "The butter I use is not one you can buy in the United States. Our butter has less water than yours, and it makes a huge difference. You will have to see what other bakers use in your country."

"I'm going to use the brand Grandma Kemstead favored," she told him. "It works well with all kinds of baked goods. Not just cinnamon rolls."

"Excellent! Now for the first step," Andre said. "Take the whole square of butter and set it on top of the larger square of dough I rolled out."

She unwrapped the professional-grade chunk of Montaigu butter sitting on the table and placed it on top of the soft dough.

"Now, you wrap the two up like a birthday present," he said, pulling the dough at the edges until he had indeed wrapped it around the butter. "Then you chill them. I like to do mine overnight."

She watched as he walked to the cooler with the "present" he'd just made and returned with another of the same type. "Tricky."

He laughed. "I always have croissant dough around. It's no wonder my children adore me."

It was hard to imagine anyone not adoring Andre. He was joy itself, wrapped up in a big, muscular body.

"Now, you take your rolling pin." His was a white plastic one, not the wooden one she favored. "And you slap the dough like you're being frisky with it. This lengthens the dough and the butter, which is now the same temperature. Remember how I said that was the key?"

"Yes," she said, wishing it was easier. "I'm just not sure that's going to help me."

"Of course it will. I am teaching you, am I not? How do you say smart mule in English?" he asked.
She thought about it for a minute. "I think you mean smart ass."

"Oh, I did," he said, chortling. "Smart ass. Smart mule. It is all the same, no?"

If she hadn't been so nervous, she might have laughed with him.

He slapped the dough strategically with his rolling pin, and it lengthened another few inches. "Now that you have removed the big bump in the road, so to speak, you use all the strength you have in your body to roll the dough out into the longest rectangle imaginable." He handed her the plastic pin. "We get to see how strong you truly are, ma petite."

So, this was a test, was it? She pressed her lat muscles down and squeezed her shoulder blades together, the way Grandma Kemstead had showed her. And then she pushed as hard as she could to roll the cold dough. It was next to impossible at first.

"Keep rolling. Put your body into it. Do not use just your arms."

Before long, she was sweating profusely. But he was right, the more she rolled, the more it gave. The process was slow.

"The more you roll, the more the temperature changes," Andre said. "It becomes easier as the butter and dough merge into one."

If he cracked another lovemaking joke, she might swat him with the rolling pin. Sex was the furthest thing from her mind right now.

"You need the dough to be about a quarter inch thick, ma petite."

Which meant she had a long ways to go. So, she huffed and puffed and rolled.

When she was finished—breathing hard, of course—Andre put his hand on her shoulder. "Now, that is how you make the layers, ma petite."

She was exhausted, but happy she'd finally transformed the dough to a rectangle of the right thickness.

"Now, you wrap it up all over again." He demonstrated. "Take the one side three-fourths of the way to the other, and then let the other side kiss its length like a lover. Now you fold the long end to the other edge. Voila. You have another present, but different."

Another wrapping? She groaned. "Again?"

"Again," he said with a pat on the back. "And here's another secret. Press two fingers into the top of the dough so you'll know which way is up once you finish chilling it again."

"You have to chill it again too?" she asked, rubbing the ache between her shoulder blades from all the rolling.

Many of the recipes she'd looked up didn't require all this work. But then again, most of the cookbook authors didn't compete in croissant competitions like Andre did.

After seeing what making them entailed, she was no longer sure she wanted to offer them at Hot Cross Buns. Cinnamon rolls would be enough for Dare Valley, wouldn't they? And she could return the croissant roller she'd bought, couldn't she? It was like a lawn mower, but bigger. She'd been naïve to think she could pull this off. She'd have to tell Brian since she was supposed to supply his restaurant. Okay, she was having a croissant freak-out here.

"Maybe I'm not cut out to make croissants," she said. "I don't think I can make them like you do."

"You don't make them like I do, ma petite," he said, taking her shoulders in his hands. "How many times do I have to tell you? You make them like Margie."

After all the time she'd spent trying to get her cinnamon rolls to taste just like Grandma Kemstead's, it felt good to have someone tell her that she should pour something of herself into each of the things she baked. "I think the jet lag and my general lack of sleep are talking," she said. "I'm sorry for having a moment."

"Few masterpieces are made in a day, Margie," Andre said, walking to the cooler again and swapping out the dough they'd just made with a chilled one. "And I had to practice too. We are all beginners when we try something new. Look inside yourself. You have courage. You are starting your own bakery."

"You're right. I can do this. Thanks for helping me remember." She straightened so she could prepare herself for the next round.

He arranged the dough in a quarter turn away from his body. "See the two fingerprints on top like I taught you? When you have gathered your strength, you can begin again."

Gripping the rolling pin in her hands, she took a deep breath and faced the dough. The first run was difficult. "It feels like skating over bumpy ice."

"No, no, no. You're trying too hard. Close your eyes," Andre said, close to her ear. "Don't fight it so much. Let your strength flow. You're the water, and the dough is the sand. It smoothes out beneath your touch."

She went by feel, fighting the urge to open her eyes to see if the dough was uniform. But then it clicked, and she felt the incredible power of her force meeting the dough. Everything seemed to roll out before her. She knew she'd gotten it right before she even opened her eyes.

Her mouth formed a grin, and she did a little jig.

"Very good," Andre said, patting her on the back. "We make more magic when we let go. Now, you fold it again. One end to the middle and the opposite side to the other end."

"Not another fold?" she asked. She'd thought they were done.

"Ah, don't complain, ma petite. When you master this, you can use the machine to roll it out."

She gave a longing look to the machine in the corner.

He lifted his brows playfully. "I only allow my bakers to use technology when they have mastered the technique. It's like letting a child use a calculator. You must still know how to add and subtract before you let something think for you. Besides, the bakers of old never had anything to make their lives easier. Goodness, even Marie Antoinette's personal baker didn't have a machine to make his life easier."

"He probably was getting paid better than we are," she mumbled, watching as he took yet another "present" to the cooler and brought back a chilled one.

"You do know the story of how croissants came to this country, right?" Andre asked.

She touched the chilled dough he'd set on the counter and picked up the rolling pin, ready to tackle the next step. "I only know what you just said."

"So, you don't know why they are shaped like a crescent?" he asked.

Shaking her head, she started to roll out the dough.

"Well, it's not very politically correct, but when has Europe ever been?" He sighed. "The crescents are the symbols of Islam. In 1683, the Ottoman Turks had surrounded Vienna and were starving the town. One night, bakers—the only ones up in the middle of the night—heard strange sounds and discovered soldiers trying to tunnel under the walls so they could sack the city. They alerted the authorities and saved the town. To celebrate, they made pastries into crescent shapes."

She wondered if Evan knew that story. She'd have to tell him when she saw him again.

"Now, close your eyes again," Andre said, adjusting her rolling pin slightly. "You do better that way. We might need to get you a blindfold."

"Har-de-har-har," she said, doing as he asked. He was right though. Everything did seem to roll out better when she wasn't looking. Was this like that old adage about a watched pot never boiling?

"Good," he said.

She opened her eyes and beheld the long rectangle she'd rolled across the metal table.

Andre took the pin from her and gave it a few more strokes, lengthening it by another several inches. He made it look so easy.

"Now, we are ready to cut them into triangles." He cut the edges of the dough so they were straight and then started slashing the dough with a knife, cutting perfect shapes she knew it would take her years to master. She'd seen some people on YouTube actually measure with a ruler.

Andre stopped and handed her the knife. "Your turn, ma petite."

She was slower than he was, but when wasn't she? Not all of her shapes were uniform, but at least they resembled triangles.

"Good," he declared, pulling one of the shapes toward him. "Now, you take the end and roll it over until it kisses the other side."

Like a snowball gathering mass, the croissant slowly appeared as he rolled it up. "Then you dab them with an egg wash, and you let Mother Nature take it the rest of the way."

"How long does it take to rise?" she asked.

He shrugged. "I let mine proof for three hours. We

have to keep the dough up here so the butter does not separate from the bread from the heat of the ovens. When they're ready, we bake them at one hundred and sixty degrees Celsius—not sure what that is in Fahrenheit—for twenty minutes."

Only twenty minutes to bake after all that work. "And what about chocolate croissants?" she asked. "They're a different shape."

"Correct," he said, nodding. He walked to the cooler and took out another "present" and rolled it out into another long triangle. After trimming the edges to make them straight, he cut the dough into short rectangles. "Now, all you do is add a chocolate baking stick. Behind you, ma petite."

She glanced over her shoulder and spotted a box on the shelf that said, "Cacao Barry, making chocolate since 1842."

"Take the stick," he said, reaching into the box for one. "Lay it about a quarter inch from the top and then roll it up. Voila. Pain au chocolat. Now, you practice for a while. I must go kiss Belle. My lips are all parched from missing her. She tastes like cherries, you know?"

Laughing, she grabbed the knife and started cutting the shapes for the chocolate croissants as precisely as she could. "I think that comes under the heading of too much information."

He made a very French noise. "Not in Paris." Then he disappeared through the door to the bakery.

As she made her cuts and rolled her croissants, she wondered what Evan thought she tasted like. Was it cinnamon rolls? Or baguette? She fell into a dreamy state as she worked with the dough.

"You are far away, ma petite," Andre said, startling her. "But the bread is satisfied. You have done well for the day. Put your croissants in the baking racks so they can finish rising. Fabian and Ronan will help you bake them when they are ready for the fire."

She smiled at her work. If the bread was satisfied, she was satisfied.

"I will show you how to use the machine to roll out the croissant dough," Andre said, pointing to the corner. "But not today. You might cry when you realize how easy technology makes things. And I think you have cried enough while you are in Paris."

She looked down at the spread of croissants to center herself. "Things are better," she said. "With Evan."

"I am glad." He tipped up her chin and studied her. "But I will not be the cause of more tears. When you bake your first croissants, you must take a few of them with you. And I think you might give one to the Lady. She will comfort you if you have need of her."

As he left the room again, she pressed her hand to her forehead, only then realizing it was dotted with butter and flour and dough.

Was she in need of comfort? Maybe not now, but she knew she would be. She loved Evan so much already. How was she supposed to leave here without him? But their lives were in two different places. He loved Paris as much as she loved Dare Valley.

They would make the most of their time together.

She was lying to herself if she said that would be enough.

***

Evan was trying to find out how he could share more about his inventions with Margie without breaching his security clearance. He'd contacted the head of legal at Quid-Atch to find out if there was any wiggle room. She wasn't an employee, so he wasn't sure how to make it happen. And a lengthy process of forms and background checks was involved. But that's what they paid their legal department to figure out.

Her openness to hearing about his new invention and seeing his lab had buoyed his faith in their connection. She hadn't even freaked out about the paint samples marring the sitting room wall. She'd kept her cool. How might she react when she saw the invisibility cloak and some of his other inventions?

Maybe he would have a work-around soon. Right now, he couldn't wait to take her on the next outing in what he'd dubbed his Courtship Schedule.

He was working in his lab when an alarm sounded. Glancing over at the pop-up screen in the corner of his computer, he saw Chase coming up the back stairs. A few years ago, Chase had insisted on having the codes to access Evan's apartment in case he went all Mad Inventor. Now, he wondered if there was more to the request. Sighing, he closed down what he was doing and made his way to the entryway to greet him.

Chase was letting himself into the apartment when Evan emerged from the hallway.

"How did you get here so quickly?" he asked, crossing his arms. "Last I recall, the Concorde is no longer flying."

His friend closed the door and studied him seriously. "I was in Berlin meeting with our key partners. Something you'd know if you'd agree to keep a copy of my schedule."

They walked side by side into the sitting room, and Evan rather hoped Chase wouldn't notice the wall behind them. Maybe he could coax him into the kitchen. "I don't feel the need to micromanage you," he said, giving Chase a look. "Apparently you feel differently. Can I make you some coffee?"

"After hearing you want to divulge key company secrets to Margie? Make it a bourbon. A double."

He wasn't surprised his friend knew. Most times, he asked Chase to implement the things he wanted. This time he hadn't. Chase would understand why. "You're being dramatic."

"You're being stupid," Chase said, following him to the antique bar caddy by the window.

"Watch it," he warned, splashing amber liquid into the glass. "I told you to mind how you talk about her."

Chase took the glass and downed it. "I'm not talking bad about her. I'm talking bad about you. What in the hell are you thinking, Evan?"

He faced him down. "That I can trust her. I want her to know about the things that are important to me. Just like she tells me about the things that are important to her."

"Our work isn't bread making, Evan. It's national security!"

"Dammit, I know that!"

For a moment the only sound was Chase tapping his finger against the rim of his crystal glass; then he downed the remainder of the contents. "Has she told you she loves you?"

"Yes," he said. "And I told her I loved her too. She also knows who I am."

"And she's still here, huh?" he asked, setting the glass down on the bar with a crack. "Well, well."

"You sound surprised." Now, he needed a drink. He poured himself a single shot of bourbon and downed it. "I wasn't sure how she'd take the news," he said, "given her upbringing. Are you still sure she doesn't want you for your money?"

Evan had the urge to pour another shot of bourbon and throw it in Chase's face. "I'm still driving the Fiat because I know my other cars would only make her uncomfortable." But the way she'd acclimated to his apartment made him hope she was softening her stance.

"I don't know how to take that," Chase said and then suddenly cursed. Fluently. In French. English. And German. Evan looked over to see him shaking his head at the multi-colored wall.

"Are you crazy? Splattering paint on your walls like this? Anyone could infer what you're working on. Wait. Did you tell her about the invisible paint?"

"I thought you didn't believe in my ability to make that happen," he said dryly, turning his back on his friend. If he didn't calm down, he would be at Chase's throat, and they'd been friends way too long for that.

"If anyone can do it, it's you," Chase said, mollifying him. "But we don't need a loose end knowing about this new idea. If our competitors got wind of what you're trying to do—"

"They won't, Chase," Evan said, turning back around. "You need to trust me on this."

"Evan, I am staring at a wall in your sitting room, not in your lab. Don't ask me to just let that go! I'm here to protect you from *being* too trusting. You don't know women like I do."

"Margie is not your ex-wife," Evan said in a hard tone. "Stop this."

"I can't," Chase said. "I can't let you do this. We could lose everything if she so much as peeps. I don't believe Margie would do that maliciously, but she doesn't know what a big key she's holding."

"She wouldn't use it like that."

"Evan, I have never interfered in your personal life, but I have to draw the line here. If you tell her what you've invented at Quid-Atch without having her sign a non-disclosure or a pre-nup, I'm walking, Evan."

Chase might as well have slapped him in the face with a white glove like an old French dueler.

"Don't give me that kind of ultimatum, Chase," he said, feeling sick.

Chase's eyes were hard. This was the man who played hardball in the boardroom. Evan had never faced off with him this way.

"I'm asking you to put the wellbeing of the company before her, something you've never had a problem doing before. I'm reminding you of your responsibility as the owner—to me, to our stockholders, to the board, and to our employees. Being with her has hurt your judgment. You know not to take risks like this. Evan, you've agreed to observe the protocols for the highest security clearances we have, the ones our company has. You're breaking your word here."

He walked over to the window again. Chase was right. No one unauthorized was allowed into any highly secure Quid-Atch facilities. And that meant Evan's lab.

"Okay, I made one mistake... I let her into my lab," he admitted.

"You definitely breached security there." Chase stormed across the room until they were on opposite sides of the couch. "What did she see?"

"Quit it with the interrogation, Chase," Evan said, feeling tired now. Fighting with Chase was depressing and exhausting. "She didn't see anything she understood, and none of it was secret. I'm running paint formulas. She even gave me some ideas on researching chemicals that remove paint."

"You did more than share your new idea, Evan," Chase ground out. "You brainstormed with her, and she's not even an employee! If you're going to do that, we'll definitely need to get her to sign a non-disclosure. We might even need to hire her."

"You're being ridiculous, Chase," Evan said even though his heart was rapping hard against his chest.

"Trust me, Evan," Chase said, rubbing the back of his neck like he had a crick in it. "The men I just met in Berlin wouldn't think so. Neither would our other defense clients."

All of them were a paranoid lot, and for good reason. So were inventors. He used to be that way. "I'll talk to Margie again and make sure she understands she needs to keep this quiet."

"I don't want you to have any more discussions with

her about your ideas," Chase said, striding across the room to the bar and pouring himself a Perrier. "And please don't let her back into the lab."

"I talked to legal about this because I knew it would make you more comfortable," Evan admitted. "You're my closest friend and the best business partner a man could have. Don't ruin this, Chase. Margie isn't the enemy, and I'll...be better about observing protocols in the future."

"You've never let any other woman in the lab, Evan," Chase said. "What are you going to do when she leaves? You're being irresponsible for a fling."

"This isn't a fling," he said in a hard tone.

"Then what is it? You live here. She has a bakery to open in Dare Valley." Chase poured him a glass of sparkling water and extended it.

Evan took it for the olive branch it was. "I'm trying not to think of her leaving, okay? Dammit! Why are you pushing me? I've...never felt like this about a woman." Chase shoved his hand in his pants pocket. "I know you haven't. You're in the big leagues now. I just want to make sure you understand that and act accordingly."

"That means you want me to lead with mistrust," Evan replied. "I'm not that jaded."

"You were before," Chase said, walking to the window. "She's changing you. Be sure you want to be changed."

His legs went weak, so he leaned back against the sofa. He *was* changing, but was it only because of her? No, he'd made that choice before meeting Margie, even before that fateful side bet with Jane and Rhett. It dated back to his trip to Greece—to seeing that statue of Artemis in that tiny Greek village and then shouting his wishes out across the sea.

Margie had only helped him remember what he already knew.

"I'm the one who's choosing to change, Chase. And

I like who I'm becoming." Evan walked over and pushed the curtain farther back so he could look out the window next to his friend.

Chase's hand rested on his shoulder for a minute like a father's might, but then it fell away. "Good. That's all I wanted to hear. And now that I know you'll be more careful, I'm heading back to Berlin."

Their duel felt like a draw. Chase hadn't walked, and Evan felt more grounded now. Like the two parts of him, the geeky inventor and the billionaire, had just merged.

"Have a good trip," Evan said as Chase walked in the direction of the entryway. "And don't worry so much. I won't let you down."

His friend paused at the door to the hallway and looked over his shoulder. There was a mysterious smile on his face, one Evan didn't completely understand.

"You never have. Give Margie my regards. It's too bad your time together will end when she leaves Paris. I might have wanted to meet her otherwise."

If pouring him a glass of water had been an olive branch, those words might as well have been a complete surrender.

He followed Chase to the front door. "Have a good trip, old man."

His friend had the audacity to laugh. "Next time cut the security feeds in the lab before you have a tete-a-tete," he called over his shoulder.

"Shit!" He let the door slam and ran back to the lab. He'd forgotten about that. No wonder his friend had made an unscheduled stop in Paris. Seeing Margie in his lab must have freaked him out completely.

Two minutes later, he'd deleted the very racy scene of him and Margie making love.

Then he texted Chase. *You better not have watched us.*

His phone beeped immediately with a response. *I*

have much more effective uses for my time.

Sitting down in an office chair, Evan leaned back and thought about their confrontation.

Chase was right. He had to be completely over the moon about Margie if he was breaking security protocols and acting irresponsibly. Now, he knew what he had to do. He didn't want their time together to end. He was going to court her harder. Show her more of the kind of life he could offer her—within reason. She wasn't ready to be swept away on a private helicopter to his yacht in the Med. But there were other things he could arrange—ones he knew she would like. Not all of them had to cost money.

He hoped to show her what Chase had only confirmed for him. This thing they shared was unique and special. And worth breaking the rules for.

And then he remembered his buddy's mysterious smile. Maybe that's why Chase had flown in from Berlin.

Apparently his mentor wasn't finished guiding him—even when it came to love.

CHAPTER 5

"I have croissants," she told Evan when he arrived at her apartment to pick her up. "They're not perfect, but they taste good."

He leaned down to kiss her. "Not as tasty as you, I expect."

She narrowed her eyes at him when he drew back. "Don't diss my croissants. My arms are already sore from all the rolling it took to make these babies."

"Okay, I take that back," he said, hands raised in defeat. "They may be tastier than you. Kiss me again so I can compare."

"How many kisses will you need to make a scientific determination?" she asked in her best serious professor voice.

He made a show of thinking about it. "As a serious scientist, a great many, I have to tell you. We might need to have a bona fide Croissant and Kissing Taste Testing. It could take years to gather enough statistically significant data."

Then he paused and gazed at her, and she could almost imagine them being together for years. Lines would appear around his eyes, and she would trace them and call them laugh lines because she'd brought laughter into his life. And he'd kiss her belly, still a little round after the birth of their kids.

"Margie," he said softly.

His voice jarred her out of the reverie, and something sour rose up in its place. Their time together wasn't going to last, she reminded herself. It couldn't.

"Shall we go?" she asked, speaking a little too fast. "Or do you want to try my croissants now?"

"We need a better place to savor your first croissants," he said, "and I know just where to take you."

They left her flat, and she was happy to walk. People sat in cafés as picture perfect as a Parisian postcard. Some were sipping a coffee while others were drinking champagne. God, she loved this town.

Evan led her down the stairs to the hidden inlet where they'd first kissed. When he'd arrived at her flat, he'd kissed her sweetly and said, "This seems like the perfect place to sample your first croissants."

He drew her under the willow trees like he had that first night. A tourist waved at her from a passing boat, and she waved back smiling.

"Would you like a ride down the Seine? I never thought to ask you."

"It probably isn't something a local does," she said, looking back at him. "But yes, I would love that."

"Hmm," he murmured. "I have an idea. Okay, but not now. Let's eat your croissants."

Crouching down, she sat on the stones under the willows and let her feet dangle over the side. The Seine flowed beneath her soles as she took the box from her purse and set it on her lap.

"I hope you enjoy my first croissants," she said, taking one out and handing it to him when he sat down beside her.

"They're beautiful," he said, kissing her cheek. "Like you. Curvy. Tasty."

She laughed. "Are you taste testing already?"

"Absolutely. I'm a serious scientist." He bit into the bread and closed his eyes. "Margie, these are unforgettable. Like you."

How was she supposed to leave him when he said things like that? Biting her lip to contain the well of emotion bubbling up inside her, she reached for her own croissant. Maybe the bread would comfort her. She needed that now.

"I love you," Evan said in that deep, sure voice. "With all my heart."

She looked over at him. "I love you too." For right now, it had to be enough.

They ate her first croissants in silence with their legs dangling over the rushing river as the sun broke through a cloud and cast its warm rays on them.

That night he took her to a restaurant called Chez Dumonet. According to Evan, it was one of the hottest restaurants in the city with a jovial atmosphere few places could top. The prices made her blink, but he playfully grabbed her menu.

"Don't make me take the menu away from you," he said sternly, but there was real fear in his eyes.

"You're right," she heard herself say. "I fed you my croissants earlier, so we're even."

His shoulders seemed to relax after that. He talked her into trying the pigeon with him, and by the time they finished their meal, they'd also enjoyed a bottle of very expensive pink champagne.

That night, they made love in her place, and she felt like they had a good balance going.

He confirmed it the next day when he took her to the famous cemetery off the Avenue de la Chapelle where Oscar Wilde, Jim Morrison, Chopin, Edith Piaf, and others were buried. They strolled through the rows of faded tombstone markers hand in hand in the quiet.

Afterwards, they drove to Luxembourg Gardens in his Fiat. She still hadn't asked him about his other cars.

It seemed the safer route. After he pulled into a parking space, he opened the trunk and brought out his picnic basket and took her hand. Along the way, he stilled suddenly and stopped. She halted with him and looked in the direction that held his attention. In the center of the small courtyard, there was a sculpture of a beautiful woman with a deer by her side.

"Do you mind if we go closer?" he asked.

"Not at all," she answered.

They crossed under an arbor of red roses. Dust from the gravel path rose in small clouds as they walked to the sculpture. The woman was over six feet tall, made of a white stone Margie didn't recognize. In her hand was a bow, like she was hunting. Except the deer wasn't her target.

"I don't understand," she told Evan. "She has a bow, but she's not shooting the deer."

"No," he said, "the deer is her companion. That's the Greek goddess Artemis. Or Diana in Roman mythology."

"You're pretty up on your mythology for a scientist," she said.

"We've...ah... this is going to sound crazy." He made a face. "Okay, we've pretty much established I can be a little crazy. I've been seeing her everywhere since I was in Greece a few months ago. I kinda asked for her to help me get my creative fire back."

She took his hand. "And you took it as a sign. Don't be embarrassed. I believe in them too even though it's a little woo-woo."

He laughed. "Woo-woo. Chase would call it that. I definitely have not told him about my Artemis encounters or my belief in the hand of fate, but I know it's helped bring back my creative fire. And I know it brought me to you."

She turned away from her study of the statue. "Then I want to leave her something to thank her." She took the picnic basket from his hands and reached inside for one of the croissants she'd baked earlier.

Setting it at the base of the statue, she patted the woman's feet. "Thank you," she whispered.

His arms came around her then, and he gripped her hard for a moment. She knew he was fighting strong emotion. So was she.

When they found a patch of grass to settle on off the gravel path where pedestrians walked, they feasted on more of her fresh croissants, some marvelous brie, saucisson, and foie gras. They drank the whole bottle of pink champagne he'd brought, and when he asked if she wanted to come back to his place, she was a little tipsy. And it was so easy to smile and accept the invitation without overthinking it.

They made love that night in his bed, and as she fell asleep with his arms around her, she realized she was becoming used to living in some of the places in his world.

***

As each day passed, Evan became more aware of the clock ticking, and it created a rabid urgency in him to make the most of each moment. He revised his Courtship Schedule to express all the love he had for her, all the gifts he wanted to lavish on her now that she was more accustomed to the idea of his wealth.

Chase's contact at the French Ministry of Defense was able to arrange an after-hours private evening at the Louvre. Margie was tense when she realized they were the only people in the museum other than the few docents available for their questions.

"Evan," she said in that measured voice she always used when talking about his money. "A private tour like this must have cost a fortune. I told you I didn't want you to do that. I would have been happy to come during regular hours."

But he was prepared for her objection, so he was able to smile. "This tour was free, so there's no way you can get upset over it."

Her raised brow told him she was dubious.

"I'm serious," he said. "We work with the French government, so this is like you giving me your bread in exchange for me taking you to dinner somewhere special. It's an even trade."

She was silent for so long, standing in the museum floodlights, his heart hurt.

"We can go if you want," he made himself say.

"No," she said and seemed to shake it off. "You arranged this, so let's enjoy it."

When she raced down the halls all the way to the Mona Lisa, her eyes alight with joy, he knew it was going to be okay. He was easing her into the life he could offer her. She would come to see that any lavishness on his part was simply because he loved her so much and wanted to make her happy.

Breathless from chasing her, he finally managed to convince her to take a selfie with him in front of da Vinci's most famous painting. He knew he would always treasure that picture, but he had a better one in mind. He led her to the Venus de Milo and made her pose for a picture, saying he now had two Venuses to admire. This picture was the one he was going to frame and put in his lab.

Since she'd ultimately embraced their evening at the Louvre, the next night he took her on the next adventure on the Courtship Schedule: a private cruise along the Seine. His ship, The Spell Caster, was too large for the river, so he'd had one of his assistants at Quid-Atch find him another boat to rent for the evening.

"I'm taking you on the boat ride you wanted," he said as they walked down the worn stone steps leading down to the pedestrian walkway along the Seine where the boats were moored.

"You are?" she asked, bouncing up and down like she had on the bed nights ago. She was radiant in a red dress.

"I am," he said, leaning down to kiss her on the top of her head.

The boat seemed to sparkle white as they stepped aboard. The brass work had been polished bright, and Margie looked around as if taking everything in. He followed the first mate of the boat to the white-covered table near the edge of the railing overlooking the river. Paris' golden lights illuminated the bridges ahead of them, and the city exuded the warm glow for which it was so famous. He pulled out Margie's seat for her and then took his own. She seemed to tense as soon as she realized they were alone.

"Are we eating early or something?" she asked, gesturing to the empty deck.

The skin between his shoulder blades tightened, but he gripped her hand and smiled. "I thought we might enjoy something more private," he said as the boat pulled away from its docking.

"This is your boat, isn't it?" she asked, biting her lip. Suddenly his jacket was too constricting, so he shrugged out of it. "No, I only rented it for the evening. We're going to have so much fun."

When she glanced away, he could tell she was struggling, but he squeezed her hand and didn't let go until her tension seemed to pass. When she turned back to him, she gave a tentative smile. He was finally able to breathe again.

The chef and wait staff he'd hired did a phenomenal job. She'd oohed and ahed over the appetizer of foie gras with fresh plums, and by the time the dessert of a chocolate bombe arrived, the tightness he'd experienced in his throat earlier in the evening was completely gone. They watched the sights of Paris go by, and when her hand rose to caress his chest, he turned her to him and fitted his mouth to hers. That night, he went back to her place and made love to her until they were too weak to move, and after sleeping for a few hours, he walked her to the bakery and left her with a sweet kiss on the street.

Suddenly their time together was coming to a close, and he found himself fine-tuning his plans for her last evening in Paris. Everything seemed fraught with new possibilities, and he made a decision that would surely change his life forever. He was ready to see it through like a man. Chase would be proud of him, he hoped.

He bided his time while Margie said goodbye to Belle and Andre. The couple had been kind enough to include him in a small farewell to Margie at their apartment. And even though everyone had eyed him curiously—okay, Andre had given him some seriously pointed looks—he'd managed to relax. The couple's three children had played in the small terrace of the building while they'd eaten a simple fare of baguette, cheese, and saucisson. Then Andre had brought out a special bread—three loaves braided into what looked like a crown—and presented it grandly to Margie.

"Now you are a queen baker," he told her. "It's time to take your place among the masters, ma petite, and make the magic in your own town."

She brushed aside a tear. "Thank you, Andre. Learning from you has been an incredible blessing. I will never forget it."

He coughed as if to clear his throat and kissed both her cheeks. "I will miss you, ma petite."

"We all will," Belle said, standing and kissing her as well.

Then the other two bakers, Fabian and Ronan, kissed her on the cheeks and gave her their best wishes in French.

By the time everyone was finished, she was crying. "Thank you. All of you."

Evan found his own throat thickening as he watched the scene. She'd been summoning confidence for her new venture for as long as he'd known her. Now, it seemed, a new mantle was around her shoulders.

And he felt a slight pinch of concern for what he planned to do. Was he right to do it? When she was about to begin something new? He set aside his questions, unable to second-guess himself at this point because he loved her so much, and soon they were off.

He led her to the car he'd chosen for the night. He hadn't wanted to deal with the insane traffic of their destination, so he'd told her he wanted to use the Rolls as another way of testing the waters. She'd only nodded, and he'd felt a moment of unease.

When the chauffeur dropped them off, he took her hand and looked up at one of the most marvelous inventions in the world. The Eiffel Tower pierced the sky as the sun cast its pink and golden rays down on them. He let her enjoy the view and then led her up the layers of stairs leading to Trocadero Square. The fountains on the hill cascading up to the Palais de Chaillot were bubbling, and a throng of people were out, most of them tourists snapping pictures or resting their legs.

As they reached the top of the steps, Evan heard the rasp of tango music from the record player. Couples were already dancing in a sensual embrace, locked together from passion and the agony of potential separation.

Evan understood that feeling as he gazed at Margie. The green silk dress she'd worn her first night in town made her eyes more dark and mysterious, but she was smiling as she looked upon the scene.

"Tango! How fun!" she exclaimed, her body already moving to the music.

"Margie," he said, extending his hand to her. "Will you dance with me?"

She turned back to him, and her mouth parted in amazement. "You know how to dance tango?"

He lifted a shoulder. "Chase thought some knowledge of ballroom dancing would be helpful when we did my makeover."

Her hand clasped his in a strong grip. "Please thank him for me. I don't know anyone else who likes to tango. Well, except for Jill, but it isn't quite the same."

Leading her to the edge of the dancers, he met her gaze. "How do you know it?"

She rolled her eyes. "My mother thought it compulsory for rich girls. She said men considered it sexy."

Since he could feel the storm rising inside her from those memories, he decided not to ask more questions. Instead, he clasped her to him in a perfect ballroom hold as she did the same. Her shoulders were back, and when she looked into his eyes, he saw the siren in her, the one who could love a man passionately and walk away without a backward glance.

But then she smiled.

Their embrace felt as natural as the powerful love he felt for her, and he took the first step. She flowed with him, completing the basic series with a lockstep. He kept it simple until her look turned molten, and then he knew his Pocket Venus wanted more. He fell into the music with her and gave her what they both wanted. Passion. Struggle.

Stalking her like a matador, he walked her back three steps in a progressive rock-step series before pausing dramatically. She raised her leg and caressed his calf before stepping over him, flicking him a flirtatious glance. On it went between them. They completed a floor boleo step, and then he led her into the ochos, a series of figure eights to the right and left side.

He stared into her eyes like he would if they were

making love, and his heart and body seemed to burn for her. She wrapped her leg around his thigh, and he could feel his blood beat in his veins as he lifted her.

She was the lushest, most sensual woman he knew. And he would love her until the end of time.

They danced and danced until she finally laid her head on his chest when one of the songs ended.

"I want to go home with you," she whispered against his skin, and then she traced a heart there. And then he knew it. He was doing the right thing. She knew he was her home just as he knew she was his.

His heartbeat was ticking like a clock, counting off the seconds until she planned to leave. But he knew how to stop time now. Love was the magic that would stop it, and right now he was filled with its power.

He took her hand and drew her through the crowd, glancing down at his watch. Everything was going to be perfect. It was a few minutes shy of ten o'clock.

"Come on," he told her as they raced down the first flight of stairs. "There's something I want you to see."

As he led her to one of the overlooks above the fountains, he heard the crowd gasp. He turned her around. The lights on the Eiffel Tower were flickering a lush red and gold. He helped her climb up onto the wide stone ledge, and when she sat, he sank down to one knee in front of her, reaching inside his suit jacket for the ring he'd bought earlier that day.

Since she was gazing off at the lights, he paused to enjoy the way they danced in her eyes. There was a warm smile on her face, like everything in the world was beautiful. And he could wait no longer.

He touched her knee. She turned back to look at him, and her mouth dropped open.

Popping the box open, he held out the ring. He'd chosen the darkest ruby he could find—surrounded by a string of diamonds.

"Margie. I love you more than I imagined loving

anyone, and I want to spend the rest of my life with you. Will you marry me?"

Her eyes narrowed, and his heart skipped a beat. She was shaking her head before she got out any words.

"Oh, Evan," she said, putting her hands over the ones that held the ring. It was as if she was trying to hide it from view. "I love you, but I can't."

He staggered back, and the box holding the ring dropped to the floor. It bounced across the stone until it came to a stop. All he could do was stare at the ring he'd agonized over buying earlier that day—the one that encompassed everything he felt for her.

She hopped off the ledge and gathered up the box, putting the ring back inside it and snapping it closed. She might as well have given him back his heart.

"How could you say no?" he asked in complete shock. "You love me. You just said you did."

She came toward him. "I do. I just...can't marry you. Our lives are too different."

The hurt crashed through him. So, she didn't accept him for who he was after all. Suddenly, it was all too much. People were taking pictures of them, and he felt exposed, rejected.

"My chauffeur will see you home," he said, and then he raced off through the crowd.

He heard her calling his name, but he couldn't stop.

THE
BILLIONAIRE'S
RETURN

To my favorite people when I used to work corporate and for all I learned.

And to my divine entourage, who always manages to take everything I've learned and spin it into gold.

CHAPTER 1

Evan fell back onto the mattress he'd dragged into the lab and stared at the ceiling. He finally had a working formula for the invisible paint.

For the last month, he had done nothing but work on his new invention. Now that Margie had refused to marry him, it was all he could stand to do. Luckily, even though she'd taken his heart with her, she hadn't taken his creative fire. Since that horrible night in front of the Eiffel Tower, he'd lived almost solely in his mind. The rest of him felt like an empty shell.

A beep signaled that someone had entered the apartment and deactivated the alarm. So Chase had finally decided to come to his rescue. Evan groaned. Didn't his friend understand it was pointless? Nothing was going to rescue him from this loss. He'd thought his father leaving him when he was a kid was bad. But this? Oh, how the fates had decided to punish him. His hubris must have been horrendous if this was the lesson they'd dished out.

Margie had told him she loved him, but she clearly didn't.

The door to his lab clicked open, and he heard

powerful footsteps cross the floor. He didn't bother to sit up. There was nothing he could do to hide how bad things had become from Chase. The evidence was all around him. He couldn't sleep in his own bed anymore after making love to Margie in it, hence the mattress in his lab, and the lab was coated in an array of trash from the take-away food he barely ate enough of to keep his body going.

"*Evan*," Chase said in a voice he'd never heard.

A ball of sorrow lodged under his ribs, and he closed his eyes for a moment, hoping it would pass. It didn't. "I found a working formula for my invisible paint. We can start producing samples and testing it."

That's how he thought about it now. *His* paint. She was lush and mysterious. Maybe she would bring him back to life. If she couldn't, he wasn't sure what could.

The mattress dipped, and a comforting hand settled on his shoulder. When he turned to look at his friend, Chase's face was tense, his eyes almost compassionate.

"You'd get your butt kicked in the boardroom with that mushy look," Evan said, deciding it was finally time to sit up.

"I'm happy to hear about your progress with your paint," Chase said. "But when was the last time you took a shower?"

He barked out a laugh, a wild one, he realized. "I don't know. Do I look like Howard Hughes yet? At least I hid the milk bottles."

"Jesus," Chase said, hauling him up. "That's not funny. You're taking a shower, and then you're either shaving that beard off or trimming it. You're a double for a criminal on *America's Most Wanted*."

That wasn't true. No one wanted him. Least of all the woman he loved.

"And I won't ask why you have a portrait of a Roman goddess resting against your workstation. I'm afraid to hear the answer."

Evan turned to look at the portrait of Artemis. "She's Greek, not Roman, and I hoped..."

Better not to mention his slender hope that she might help him again—like she had done in that fateful game of poker. It had been a desperate move, asking his art dealer to find him a painting of the goddess. And which one had the esteemed man sent over to him? One of Artemis with her faithful deer and a loaf of *bread* on a stone table. He'd almost sent it back, the loaf reminding him too bitterly of the baker who had stolen his heart.

"I also won't ask why you're sleeping in here," Chase said as they left the lab. "Promise me you'll at least start sleeping in the guest room."

He cast a quick glance at his friend. "You must think I'm a wimp."

A strong arm came around his shoulders. Chase led him down the hall, and Evan almost leaned in for comfort.

"No," Chase said in a quiet voice. "I couldn't sleep in my bed for a couple of nights after Trisha left me. But then I decided I wasn't going to let her have that much power over me."

"But Trisha was a cold-hearted bitch," Evan said.

"She wasn't in the beginning. My success changed her. The seeds were there when I married her, but...well, it doesn't matter now."

"I really loved Margie." It was funny to say it in past tense. He still loved her. He didn't know how to stop.

"I know you did," Chase said, guiding him into the bathroom. "Please tell me I don't have to help you the rest of the way."

When he reached to pull off his shirt, he noticed it was stained. And that he couldn't remember when he'd last changed. "I can manage to undress myself, Chase. Even if I am a total fool."

Chase headed to the door. "You aren't a fool. You're only a human being. Now get in the shower and wash off that grime. I'm going to make you some coffee and breakfast."

Was it morning? Evan had lost track of time. When he looked at himself in the mirror, he immediately turned away. He looked like a hiker who'd gotten lost on the Appalachian Trail for weeks. But what did it matter? He didn't care how he looked. He didn't care about much of anything. Except his paint.

After showering, he decided to shave off his beard. He'd only grown it to help disguise his identity while in Dare Valley. Perhaps erasing it would help dull his memories of Margie.

Except he didn't want that. She was one of the best things to ever happen to him. But he couldn't bear the pain he felt, and he didn't know how to keep the good and leave the bad behind.

He donned fresh clothes, and by the time he entered the kitchen, his stomach was growling. Then he noticed the letter Margie had given to him through his chauffeur wasn't sitting where he'd left it—*dropped* it—on the counter.

"Give me the letter, Chase," he said in a hard tone, striding across the kitchen.

Chase only slid him a cup of coffee. "I wondered why she tried to call and text you after refusing to marry you. She even called you from Dare Valley, which is pretty expensive."

"Dammit! You had no right to keep tabs on me."

Chase walked to the stove, put a pan on the gas burner, and turned it on. "Evan, I pay your phone bill every month."

He crossed the room, only stopping when he was close enough to feel the low warmth emanating from the blue flame. "Bullshit. You have one of our accountants pay my phone bill."

Chase shrugged. "I checked because I was worried about you. You know, Louis had some very interesting news to share with me when I called him."

His chauffeur so deserved to get fired for that, but Evan wouldn't do it. He knew Louis cared about him. He was a nice elderly man of fifty with a wife and three kids.

"Margie was pretty desperate to talk to you. But let's forget about that for the moment. Why did you have Louis take her to the airport, Evan? She'd just broken your heart."

His mind swirled like the eggs Chase was whipping with a fork. "Because I told her I would."

"I see," Chase said, grabbing some butter from the fridge and putting a dollop in the pan. "The letter is pretty telling, don't you think?"

He wasn't surprised Chase had read it. Even if it did make him want to punch him in the face. "She felt guilty. That's all. She has a good heart." But not big enough to fully accept him for who he was.

"She didn't say she *didn't* love you," Chase continued, pouring the eggs into the pan. "Quite the contrary, in fact."

"I know what she said, dammit!" The words were hardwired into his brain.

Dear Evan,

I'm crying as I write this because I don't know what to do. You sent your chauffeur to take me to the airport, and so I'm writing a letter for him to give you since you won't pick up the phone or answer my texts. I went to your building, but your security guard wouldn't let me in. I waited outside for a few hours in the rain, but you never came out. Did you see me? It hurts to think you would ignore me like this, but I understand why.

I didn't mean to hurt you, Evan, but I know I did. Oh, God, I know I did. Even though we aren't together right now, I can feel your pain, like I could always feel your emotions when we were together. I don't know how to do this, to explain. I never imagined you would ask me to marry you, and I didn't know what to say but no. My life is in Dare Valley. My bakery is opening in two weeks.

And you...

Oh, Evan, you were right when you said you feared I couldn't accept you as a billionaire. But it's not you. It's the money and the life. It's the private tours at the Louvre and solo cruises down the Seine with a wait staff just for two.

I don't want that life again. I left it so long ago. And even though I know you aren't my parents—and that you love me enough to want me to marry you—I can't go back. You love Paris and all it offers you. You love penthouses and yachts and race cars.

And you love inventing.

That's the part of you I always loved most. The simple Evan. The one who didn't need all that stuff to make him happy.

I'm writing this in the hopes that it will reach you, that you'll read it, and that some part of you will understand. Please don't shut me out like this. I don't know where we go from here, but I don't want our time together to end like this.

I thought about changing my flight and staying for a few days, hoping to catch you coming out of your building. But I'm stubborn and I know how stubborn you can be too. I'm afraid you're never going to speak to me again, and that breaks my heart more than anything.

Because I really loved you too. More than I've ever loved anyone. And I thank you for showing me so much. Things I can't even describe because I'm crying too much right now and my head is too foggy from being awake all night.

Evan, please let me explain better than this letter.

I'll even fly back to Paris for a couple of days to say this in person. Just call me, okay? I don't know how to make this better unless you do.
All my love,
Margie

Someone was grabbing his hand and putting something in it. He looked down and realized it was a plate of scrambled eggs. He walked woodenly to the kitchen table and sat down, but he wasn't hungry now. Her words had stolen his appetite again—like they had the first time he'd read the letter after Louis gave it to him. She'd also given Louis the box that held the engagement ring Evan had chosen for her.

He'd thought about going to the airport to talk to her, but by then she'd already boarded. And what was he supposed to say? *Nice knowing you?* He didn't think he could squeeze those words out.

He didn't know how to do this either.

"Eat, Evan," Chase said, setting a cup of coffee in front of him before crossing the kitchen to pour himself a cup.

Then he sat across from him as Evan tried to eat the eggs. They didn't taste like eggs.

"It's weird," he told Chase. "Nothing tastes good anymore. I've been too busy with my paint to look up why that happens to the body. Must be something about trauma."

"Just eat, Evan," Chase repeated. "Knowing why isn't going to change the feeling."

"But it's weird, isn't it?" he asked. "If you ask me, the whole love thing is weird. I'm starting to believe more in that whole mind-body connection."

Chase settled back in his chair. "Let's change the subject before you go all New Age on me. Have you given your paint a name yet? Please tell me it's not from Harry Potter."

He shoved a forkful of eggs into his mouth so he wouldn't have to answer. No, the name wouldn't come to him. Okay, that was a lie. He kept wanting to name it after Margie somehow, but that simply could not be done.

"You're evading, Evan," Chase said. "You didn't call her Margie, did you?"

He must be the most obvious idiot on the planet. "I haven't named it yet."

"Evan..."

"Why don't you name it?" he asked in his single flash of non-paint brilliance for the day. "You know our clients and our market best. You've been making fun of my names for years. Time for you to give it a go."

Chase studied him. "I know you have a name, Evan. You get pretty intimate with your inventions. I want to know what you're calling her."

"And I told you. I *don't* have a name." He set his fork down. There was no way he could shove any more of those tasteless eggs into his mouth.

He reached for his coffee and took a sip while Chase studied him. There was a line between his friend's brows, and Evan knew he was debating telling him something. His belly tightened.

"Whatever it is, don't tell me," he said, setting his cup down.

That only made Chase's mouth twitch. "I think it's time. Seeing you like this...reading Margie's letter... She called me, Evan. Called the switchboard at headquarters and asked to speak to me. When the secretary put her off, since she didn't have a clue who she was, your girl said bold as brass that she had important information about one of your inventions and needed to speak to me right away. Suffice it to say, she was immediately put through."

That hollow part in his chest didn't feel so hollow anymore. Suddenly it felt like it was filled with a million knives, tearing him apart from the inside out. "Please don't say any more."

"She's worried about you, Evan," he said gently. "Sick with worry. I think she might have been crying, but she was pretty brave about it. She told me who she was and gave me a short version of what had happened. When she asked me if I knew how you were doing, I told her I hadn't seen or heard from you in a couple weeks."

He had to clear his throat to speak. "I could feel you watching me on the security cameras in the lab. I didn't like it, so I disabled them." If his paint had been ready, he might have painted himself invisible instead.

Chase rolled his eyes. "I *let* you disable them."

"I could have kept you out of there," Evan said with a snarl, "but it would have taken time away from my paint."

"I told Margie I would check on you, and so I am," Chase said, sipping his coffee. "You have to resolve this, Evan. Like a man."

He pushed back from his chair as anger spurted through him. "Don't bring my masculinity into question. I didn't do this. She did." Turning, he left the kitchen and went back to the lab.

Just as he expected, Chase followed him. "A man doesn't run away, Evan."

He fisted his hands at his sides and turned to face his friend. "What in the hell was I supposed to do after she turned me down? Say okay, thanks anyway, and take her to the airport? I'm not that big of a person, Chase. Did you ever talk to Trisha after she took those confidential papers from your office and left *you?*"

The grooves around Chase's mouth deepened for a moment. "You better believe I did. I gave her the riot act, which she deserved, and then I sicced the best corporate espionage and divorce attorneys I could hire on her."

Margie didn't deserve the riot act. She'd only told

him the truth. He just couldn't thank her for it. "And yet you ended up giving her a considerable part of your personal fortune."

"She got a good lawyer too. But you're evading the issue, Evan."

He turned his back and walked over to the computer screen displaying the paint formula. Like most great equations, it was perfect in its simplicity. He'd finally figured out how to change the matrix in the paint so it wouldn't bind the pigment. Instead, he was going to use the polymers to make both the pigment and the surface it covered invisible.

"I want to get back to work," he told Chase. "I'm sending Rajan the formula today so he can start creating the physical paint. I'll fly to DC in a few days so we can test it out."

"Margie's bakery seems to be a success," Chase continued like Evan hadn't been talking business. "Have you looked it up online? There are at least sixty five-star reviews on Yelp already. Her cinnamon rolls are as incredible as the former owner's, apparently, but people are also touting her baguettes. They taste just like loaves baked in Paris, many say. And then there are the croissants..."

Those knives were twitching inside Evan again, and he could feel his life force bleeding out. Other people were tasting her bread now. For a time, she'd fed him, and his life had been transformed by it. No more.

"I'm happy to hear about her success," he said, and even he could hear how hoarse his voice sounded. "I always knew she would do well. She's a great baker."

"And a fierce business owner," Chase said, coming forward until he stood next to him. "I was impressed with her, Evan. When she called. It took courage."

He could almost hear what his friend wasn't saying. "Courage you don't think I possess."

"That's for you to decide. But I've liked this new you

since you visited Dare Valley."

"You've changed your tune," he said bitterly. "Before, you didn't trust her one bit."

"I was impressed by the way she reached out to me," Chase said, meeting his gaze. "Besides, I know women. I could tell from talking to Margie that she doesn't have one calculating bone in her body."

Evan scoffed. "You married Trisha, and she's as calculating as they come."

"I married Trisha partly *because* she's calculating," Chase said in an aggrieved tone. "I thought she'd make a good corporate wife. My mistake was to believe she'd only use her cunning nature for our mutual well-being."

"This is still a pretty big change. You never change your opinion about anyone."

It was Chase's turn to scoff at him. "That's not true. Okay, it is a little true, but let's face it; I was more worried about your judgment than I was about Margie. Once you assured me you wouldn't let her in the lab again, I felt better about things. And now that I've read that letter..."

"She hates the billionaire part of me," he said, staring at the letters of the formula on the screen.

"She hates her past. Her parents are leeches, Evan. They could be best friends with Trisha."

He didn't like hearing that comparison, although he'd already concluded they were the lowest scum of the earth.

"Perhaps she just didn't like your billionaire *lifestyle*," Chase continued. "I didn't."

Glancing over, he couldn't help but frown. "You didn't leave me."

"Cut her a break, will you?" Chase said. "She was scared of getting sucked back into a life that hurt her. She'd barely known you six weeks, and in that time, she'd only known you were a billionaire for...what? About a week? Give her time. If she's worth it, you'll make allowances."

Hadn't he rationalized the same thing over and over again? But it didn't change the one equation he was afraid to compute. Would she *ever* be able to accept him?

"What if I talk to her...and give her another chance and she rejects me anyway?" It hurt to even utter the words.

"Then you move on with your life. Right now, you can't even sleep in your own bed, Evan."

He sighed. "I hate this."

"Everyone who has ever had their heart broken hates it. And yet we all manage to put ourselves out there again."

"You don't love anyone."

There was silence for a moment. "I love you. And now that you've made me say it, I'm leaving. When you come to DC, I want you to stay with me. My place is big enough for you to hole up in, but I insist you shower every day. I have an acute sense of smell."

This was the first he'd heard of that peculiarity, but he was still processing those first words Chase had said to him.

He turned around as his friend reached the lab door. "I love you too, Chase."

There was a small smile on Chase's mouth when he looked over his shoulder at him. "I know you do, Evan. See you soon."

He worked more after Chase left, but his stomach started roaring, and he suddenly realized he was hungry. When he walked into the kitchen, Margie's letter was back in the original place he'd left it. Along with the engagement ring he'd given Margie. Apparently Chase even knew the combination to his safe.

"You're an interfering son of bitch," he said even though his friend was gone.

He hadn't been able to get rid of the ring. He didn't

know what to do with it. Maybe he should throw it into the Seine. Maybe he should throw *both* the letter and the ring into the Seine. Like right now.

Rain was streaking the windows, so he grabbed his red umbrella from the closet and took off down the stairs. His feet seemed to know where they were going, and soon he was walking down the stairs off Pont Neuf Bridge to the little inlet where he and Margie had shared their first kiss and expressed their love.

A now-familiar darkness arose in him as he walked along the path to the willows. This was also where he'd told her he was a billionaire.

If only he'd kept that from her, everything would be the same.

But that wasn't true, and he knew it. She would still have returned to Dare Valley to open her bakery, and he would have stayed in Paris to complete his invention. They'd known all along there was an expiration date for their romance.

He sank to the ground, holding the umbrella to keep the rain out, and let his feet dangle over the edge like he and Margie had done while eating her first croissants. Then he dug out the letter and the ring from his pocket with his free hand and looked down at them. The ruby winked at him even though there wasn't a ray of sunshine in the sky. The gray skies seemed to bear down on him and the sky thundered and flashed lightning.

His hand extended to throw the ring and the letter into the Seine, but it wouldn't open as it came forward. A powerful gust of wind rose up, and suddenly the willows wrapped around him. One of the branches brushed his cheek, and for a moment he closed his eyes, feeling like it was Margie tracing his face with her soft hand.

His heart thundered in his chest, and he bit his lip, fighting the pain inside him. And then he bowed over in place, clutching the letter and the ring to his chest.

Something brushed his back, and while he knew it was only the willows again, it was a comfort. He released some of his sorrow, unable to hold it back anymore, and when he was spent, he let the umbrella fall to the side.

Rain soaked his head and streaked down his face as he tucked the letter and the ring back into his pocket. He couldn't throw them in the Seine today. He wasn't sure he ever could.

When he glanced down the river, the Eiffel Tower was visible in the distance. The sight of it only brought more pain.

He'd loved her so much. He'd never wanted anything more than to be with her, and he would have rearranged his whole life around her.

And then he remembered what Chase had said to him. The willows slapped him on the back this time, encouraging him to admit the truth to himself.

They both deserved a better ending to what they'd shared.

He pinched the bridge of his nose as the pain flared inside him again. But would it be an ending? Or a beginning?

His life in Paris wasn't going to be the same anymore—not after being with her. He didn't want to go to parties with loud, extravagant people he didn't respect, people who only pretended to like him. Before, he hadn't felt like he had much to offer except...well...Evan Michaels, the billionaire. Who else *could* he be to them? Not the geeky inventor.

But Margie had changed him.

Now he believed there might be other people who could like him as the inventor, the one who geeked out over creating anything from the Paint Prep Mistress to invisible paint. The makeover he'd received years ago had changed him physically for the better, but perhaps it was time for another one. This time his billionaire habits and lifestyle were what needed changing. A vision flashed in his mind, and he stared into the rushing river of the Seine as all the pieces unfolded in his mind. He suddenly knew exactly what to do.

And he knew just the man to help him.

He fished out his phone and called Chase. "I want to become an inventor philanthropist," he said when his friend answered the phone.

"Wonderful! I was hoping you would come to that conclusion."

"You were?" he asked, feeling the raindrops plop harder onto his already soaked clothes.

"You have a big heart, Evan."

"I want to endow a university that will help young inventors," he said as his mind spun with new ideas. "And create a seed fund for inventions. It can be hard to get the initial money until you have a proven concept—or a patent—and we both know that can take years. And I want to...oh, I'll have to do more research. I have a lot of ideas."

"Dare Valley has a wonderful liberal arts university, I recall," Chase said. "I'm sure they would love to be involved."

His stomach tightened. Margie lived in Dare Valley. Could he show her a new version of the wealthy lifestyle she'd experienced as a kid? He didn't know, but he realized he needed to try. If not, he would always regret it.

"I'm at the airport," Chase said. "We're grounded until this storm passes. If you want to go to the US with me, you have a ride. You can drop me off in DC and then take the plane the rest of the way to Denver. You know your way from there."

He stared at the Eiffel Tower. As always, it inspired him to reach for more—even when it seemed impossible he would succeed.

He had to go back to Dare Valley and talk to Margie. If he didn't, he'd go back to his lab and likely never leave. And that's not who he wanted to be.

"Hold the plane," he said, standing up and leaving his wet umbrella on the ground. "I'm going back to Dare Valley."

CHAPTER 2

Margie heard the knock on the front door and walked to the sink to clean the dough from her hands. She'd just put her newest creation in the oven to bake, and she couldn't wait to try it. She had a feeling the sunflower bread was going to be another hit.

One would think she got in enough baking at Hot Cross Buns, but she didn't have enough time to experiment with new recipes between making the bread on her current menu and filling her regular orders. Don't Soy with Me and Brasserie Dare's orders had kept her busy for the first couple of weeks after the grand opening of her bakery, but now that she was also supplying baguettes for Chef T, she didn't have a moment to sit down.

She already needed to hire a new baker, and wasn't that the most incredible mark of success? Thankfully, she'd posted an advertisement for the job in the appropriate places a few days ago. She was hoping to fill it soon.

When she reached the door, she opened it in time to see a man walking down the sidewalk away from the house. Her heart seemed to burst in her chest from joy and pain all at once.

"Evan!"

He stopped and slowly turned around. Seeing him clean-shaven was a shock. Pictures of him on the Internet floated up in her memory. He was wearing tan khakis and a navy T-shirt, and when he shoved his hands in his pockets, all she could think about was that he'd lost weight. And how he looked like he belonged in Paris. She wanted to take off his designer sunglasses so she could see his eyes.

"I thought you were out when you didn't answer the door," he said, his mouth twisting into a frown.

She understood what he was thinking, as easily as she had when they were together. She rushed down the stairs. "My hands were dirty. I was baking." *I wasn't blowing you off,* she wanted to say.

He stared at her as she halted in front of him in the sunshine. "I thought bakers only baked when it was dark outside."

Her throat closed, and she felt a trembling rise up in her body. "I was trying out a new recipe. Will you...will you come inside and taste it with me?"

She wanted to touch the unfamiliar, smooth skin of his jaw, to make him laugh again, and to lean her head against his chest and go to pieces, all at the same time.

"All right," he simply said, and together they walked side by side into her Victorian house.

He took off his sunglasses when they entered, but he still wouldn't meet her eyes—and it hurt to know he was purposefully concealing the feelings he had once shared so freely.

As she shut the door, he ran his hand over the banister of the staircase, as though memories of the time he'd lived here as her tenant were flooding back to him. She took a deep breath, trying to get herself under control. It wouldn't help either of them if she went to pieces right away. But he had come all this way to see her, to talk to her...

She was glad he hadn't simply texted or called. Having him return like this seemed monumental, and her mind blanked for a minute, wondering what she was supposed to say. How could she make this better?

They entered the kitchen, and she busied herself making his favorite coffee. When she slid it across the counter to him, he simply said, "Thanks," and then everything went quiet again.

She glanced at the timer. "Ah...the bread won't be ready for a while." And then she realized it needed to rest so it would cleanly cut. "How about I—"

"That's fine, Margie," he said, and even to her ears, her name sounded different coming from his lips, like it had been stripped of all the love and warmth with which he used to say it.

Her hands dropped to her sides, and she realized she was still wearing her apron. It was dirty, she had her hair up in a crappy ponytail, and there wasn't a speck of makeup on her face. "It's good to see you, Evan."

His mouth twisted like he was trying to form a smile but couldn't. "I drove by the bakery when I came into town. Your storefront is worthy of Paris. How is business?"

She thought of strolling the streets of Paris with him—how she'd dash off to one of the artistic storefronts that lined Boulevard Saint-Germain, giving him no choice but to follow her. "Business is terrific. So good, in fact, that I might be able to stop renting rooms out next semester."

"I'm happy for you. Not that I'm surprised. I knew your bakery was going to be a hit the first time I tasted your cinnamon rolls. Your success was inevitable."

There was a lull again.

"Chase told me you called him," he said, still not meeting her eyes.

While she didn't blame him for being distant, it only made her ache more. She turned to make herself an espresso because it was the only thing she could think to do to keep from crying outright. She had made a mess of everything, and her regret was just as bitter now as when she'd first returned to Dare Valley.

"Yes. It was probably a crazy thing to do. But I was worried about you. When you didn't respond..."

"You know why I didn't respond," he said in a voice so low she barely heard it. "Why I *couldn't* respond."

There was no way she could go through the motions of making herself coffee now. She turned to face him, and those lakewater blue eyes she'd missed so much were finally staring at her, staring into her like they always had. The pain there stole her breath.

"I know," she whispered, feeling the first tears trail down her cheeks. "And I'm sorry. I didn't want to cry in front of you, but I can't seem to help it. I hurt you, and that's the last thing I wanted after everything we shared. Evan..."

Tears seemed to be gathering in his eyes too, but he blocked her view by pinching the bridge of his nose.

She crossed the room to him, wanting so much to put her hand on his arm, to touch him and reestablish that connection she had missed so much these last weeks. But she didn't have the right. Not now.

"I wish..."

"I wish it too," he finished for her, reading her mind again.

And then their eyes met and everything fell away. His pain seemed to coil around hers like two ribbons being braided. The first tears slipped from her eyes and slid down her face, but she couldn't make herself brush them aside. She had to keep looking at him. She couldn't stop herself.

"I was wrong to run away that night," he said. "Wrong to draw this out and worry you."

Hearing him say that made her bite her lip. "Oh, Evan. I was the one who was wrong. And I know I have no right to ask you, but I really want you to forgive me." She sniffed and brushed away her tears. "You don't have to do it now. Or ever. But I want to ask for your forgiveness just the same."

The long breath he took seemed as though it crested over a large hill. "You forgave me when I didn't tell you the truth about who I was in the beginning. It would be cruel of me to deny you that same understanding." Until that moment, she'd never registered the fact that the word *gave* was in forgave. It seemed appropriate.

"Thank you. Thank you, Evan. You don't know what that means to me." Tears streamed down her face faster now.

He slid her the coffee she'd made him. "Actually I do. Why don't you take a sip?"

Her hand was trembling so much she had to use the other one to support the cup as she raised it to her lips. He walked over to the kitchen cabinet and pulled out two glasses and filled them with water. It felt so right for him to make himself at home like that, and it reminded her of the beautiful month they'd spent in this house together. It was like he belonged here, but then she reminded herself of the truth. His time in Dare Valley had only been a stopover then, rather like his visit to see her now.

"When are you heading back to Paris?" she asked with a hitch in her voice. God, she would have to say goodbye to him all over again. She wasn't sure she could bear it.

He drank half the water in the glass before answering. "I don't have any definite plans yet."

Her eyes opened a bit wider at that. "But what do you mean?"

His shoulder lifted, and he looked away from her again. "I'm staying at The Grand Mountain Hotel for a while. I have some meetings with the president of the university here."

Now she blinked. At least three times. "I don't understand."

He shrugged like he was releasing a bunch of pent-up nervous energy. "I'm creating a center at Emmits Merriam to help student inventors. I thought it might be fun to help other people like me."

No one was just like him. "I...umm...I don't understand. You're staying? Here? In Dare Valley?" Why would he do that? His home was in Paris. He *loved* Paris.

"It depends," he said, peering into her oven like he cared about the status of her bread.

"What does it depend on?" she asked, spanning the distance between them. *"Evan."*

He stood up, and his lakewater blue eyes met hers again. And then she saw it. The love hiding there, almost like the sun hiding behind the clouds.

"Well, you, I suppose."

She pressed her hand to her chest. "You can't mean..."

"Chase told me to cut you a break. You barely had time to get to know me as a billionaire, and honestly, that guy needed as much of a makeover as the geeky inventor I used to be. So, I'm making him over. I'm not going back to that lifestyle. It's time to start something new. Be something more."

It was hard to breathe all of a sudden. A billionaire makeover? What in the world was he saying? But she knew. She *knew*.

He was trying to make himself into someone she'd want to spend the rest of her life with.

"I don't know if I can do it," she whispered. Over the past several weeks, she'd been haunted by dreams about her parents and their shallow friends.

His jaw clenched, and he looked down. Without even touching him, she could feel the tension in his shoulders, and she wanted so much to soothe it.

"I don't know if you can either," he said softly. "But I need to do it for me most of all, and it would be crazy not to see if it would make a difference to you when I still love you so much."

She laid her head on his chest. She found she couldn't stop herself. "I still love you too."

Something lowered until it rested against her hair, and she realized it was his chin. But he didn't wrap his arms around her. So, she fisted her hands at her sides to keep from hugging him.

"Then that's a start," he whispered.

The front door slammed, and he stepped back. The interruption made her want to cry out in frustration.

"Hey, Margie," said Gary, her new tenant, as he came into the kitchen. "Something smells..." He trailed off, seeing them. "Sorry, I didn't know we had company."

"It's no problem," Evan said. "I was just leaving."

"Wait!" Gary slapped his hand to his forehead. "Are you Evan Michaels?"

Evan had a guarded look on his face. "It says so on my driver's license."

"Man, I was wondering whose ride that was outside. Holy shit! I mean...you're *the* Evan Michaels."

Margie pressed back against the counter, wondering how often this sort of thing happened to Evan. No one had seemed to recognize him before—back when they were together. Perhaps it wasn't simply the beard. Maybe approaching public figures was considered gauche in French culture.

"I am," Evan said, his shoulders looking tenser as each second passed.

"I'm a huge admirer," Gary said. "I'm doing a PhD in Electrical Engineering, and I tinker with some inventions. But obviously nothing like you. I mean, man. No one even *knows* what you invent. You're like a Top Secret Inventor and shit. Wow! I mean, wow!"

But *she* knew about one of his inventions, and he'd wanted to share more of them with her. She felt confident he would have if her lack of a security clearance hadn't been an issue. It awed her to think of how much faith he'd put in her, entrusting her with his new idea and showing her his lab.

Gary swung his gaze to her and gaped. "Margie. How in the world do you know this guy? I mean, he's like the shit."

If Gary called Evan that one more time, she might have to pull the bread out of the oven early so she could stuff a piece in his mouth.

"We kinda met through a few people here in Dare Valley," Evan said vaguely.

"Wow! You know people in Dare Valley? That's, like, crazy. And now I know you."

This was becoming more embarrassing by the minute. "Gary. I think Mr. Michaels might appreciate you toning it down a bit."

The guy smiled winningly, one of the reasons she'd agreed to rent to him in the first place. Oh, and because he liked to talk science with her. She'd rather missed that.

"I was overdoing it, wasn't I?" he asked.

Evan's mouth tipped up on one side. "A bit. But it's okay. You'll have to come to the speech I'm giving at the university next week. I'll be talking about the importance of inventing in shaping our world."

She swung her head to look at him. He was giving a speech?

"And there's some other stuff going on, but it's all hush-hush right now," Evan added. "I know you won't say anything."

His mouth gaped for a moment. "Not a word, man. You can trust me."

Gary held out his fist, and Evan gave him a serious look before fist-bumping him back.

"Okay, I'll get out of your way. Man, oh man, this has been awesome." Gary gave an awkward wave, stumbled, and then turned around and walked out of the kitchen.

"I guess the beard worked pretty well, huh?" Evan commented with a wry look.

She studied him, trying to take in everything that had changed and everything that had not. "I rather miss it."

His eyes darkened, and her belly tightened with a power-pack of lust and longing. The silence grew between them again, and she waited to see if he was going to kiss her. But he didn't make a move, so she decided to ask him. It wouldn't be the first time—she had done the same thing at the beginning of her time in Paris.

"Are you going to kiss me?"

He took a deep breath. "No...I...no. I can't touch you until I know for sure whether you can handle my new makeover."

Her heart squeezed.

His hand reached for her before dropping to the side. "I want to, but I just can't."

She nodded, her throat tight. "I understand. I do. It's probably better that way."

The laughter that escaped from his mouth was forced. "I'll paraphrase what you said to me in Paris when I told you we had to wait to kiss. Don't wait too long to decide if you...heck...want me...*us*. I'm willing to be patient. But when you know, I need you to tell me. Even if the answer is no. Will you promise me that?"

She knew what would happen if she sent him away. But what if she decided she could accept this new life he was creating for himself? What if she wanted to be a part of it?

"What happens if I *can* handle it?" she asked. "You still live in Paris."

He stared into her again, and she felt her bones dissolve.

"My inventions can happen anywhere, but your bakery is here. So, I'll move here. We can always keep the apartment in Paris. I'll miss the City of Lights, but she...doesn't mean even near as much to me as you do."

There it was again, that deep ache she'd felt for him ever since she had returned home brokenhearted. "I'm humbled, and now I feel like I'm not giving you enough." Her voice sounded small to her own ears.

He took her arms and looked deep into her eyes, already breaking his rule about not touching her.

"Stop that. Stop that right now. If you decide you can be with me, you'll be giving me *everything*. You'll be giving me you. And that's all I want."

"How am I supposed to let you leave after you say that to me?" she asked as the timer rang.

He released her and then reached into the drawer where she kept her potholders and placed them ever so sweetly on her hands. "Because you know that once you tell me not to leave, I won't. So you have to be sure. Margie, whatever is holding you in place...I hope you'll let it go. We won't be your parents. Or have their life. Or their friends. We'll create what we want. Together."

On some level she knew that, but he would need her to go to parties, wouldn't he? There would be elite events and retreats and heavens knew what else. He was the head of a billion-dollar company. "I have questions."

He shook his head. "I know you do, and you'll likely have more once you've had some time to mull it all over. But we don't want your bread to burn."

Nodding, she opened the oven door to check on her newest creation. The crust was golden brown, and the bread was firm. She took it out and set it on top of the stove to cool.

"Will you stay and have bread with me?"

"Not today," he said in a hoarse voice. "Not...now."

The tension she saw in his body was different now, and it sent fire running through her veins.

"I need to go process this a little," he said after a quiet lull. "But you can save a piece for me."

Taking off the potholders, she stood in front of him. "I will."

"Then I'll go," he said softly.

"I'll walk you out," she added, not wanting to separate from him just yet.

When they were outside, she spied the car Gary had gone gaga over. It was an unapologetically bold red Ferrari. "I didn't see your car before."

"This is just a rental, but it's the kind of car I'd buy if I lived here." He tensed as he put on his sunglasses. "You need to know that I still like fast cars. I'm not going to hide the things I like from you anymore. Hopefully we can compromise and find a way to make things work."

So the car had been a test as much as a declaration. "I'm glad you brought it. I want you to be honest with me, Evan."

His mouth curved. "Good. Because I also adore sailing. I'm keeping my yacht."

She swallowed thickly.

"I hope you'll let me take you on it someday," he said, shifting his feet. "But that's enough for today. You need to get some rest. You have to be up early in the morning."

"I still use your sound machine when I sleep," she said, daring a quick glance at his face. "With three other people in the house and my crazy hours, it's been a godsend."

"I'm happy to hear that," he said after a long moment. "I'll see you soon, Margie."

And then he was striding down the sidewalk to his car.

"Evan!" She ran to the curb. "I forgot to ask you

about your invention. The one you told me about."

For the first time since he'd arrived at her doorstep, he gave her a full smile, the one she'd gotten used to seeing, the one she'd missed so much.

"I figured it out." He put his index finger to his mouth like he was sharing a secret, which of course, he was.

"You did?"

"What can I say?" he said, opening the car door. "I have skills."

He did indeed, and she wanted to enjoy all of them again.

"We'll have to celebrate," she called out.

His smile seemed to widen. "We will. Between your bakery and my new idea, we have a whole lot to celebrate."

And then he closed the door, started the engine, and took off down the street.

When she could walk again, she went as far as the front steps and dropped down to sit on them. Evan was back in her life. Relief and fear seemed to be pulling her in two opposite directions right now.

Could she put the past to rest and embrace all he brought with him from his world?

Because she loved him, she was determined to try.

CHAPTER 3

"So agreeing to do the speech might not have been my smartest move," Evan told Chase on the phone.

The mountains outside his penthouse windows at The Grand Mountain Hotel were a far cry from his view in Paris, but they were beautiful in a more quiet way. Even though he was ensconced in pure luxury—from the sunken Jacuzzi bath and shower suite to the plush California king bed—he would so have preferred being back in his single room in Margie's house. Being here, like this. Well, it didn't feel right.

"That speech is the perfect start for your billionaire makeover," Chase said. "The university president delivered me the signed paperwork for the new inventor center this morning."

Emmits Merriam's president had moved fast. He knew it was rare for a small, liberal arts university to be endowed with such a gift.

"I'm glad to hear it. You're putting out the press release?"

"I just sent the final approval," Chase said. "Dare Valley is going to be seen in a new light after today. You're going to help draw some of the finest students in the country to that small town. But you need to come up with a name, Evan."

"Dammit, I know that," he said, frustrated because the idea wouldn't come. "I told you I refuse to name it after me." Hubris was what had gotten him into trouble in the first place.

"What do you want to do about the other center? For adult inventors? I can't release a statement about it until you tell me where you want it located."

It would be in Dare Valley if things went well with Margie. He hoped things would go well with Margie. After talking to her yesterday, he was encouraged.

"I need some more time to see how things play out here."

"Things went well with Margie, then," Chase said. "I thought as much. Your voice doesn't sound like you're chewing dust."

"Is that a Montana comment? Never mind. When can I expect your comments on my speech ideas?"

"You need to *write* the speech first, Evan," Chase said. "Then I'll comment. I've been speaking on your behalf since you founded Quid-Atch. I'm not helping you this time. This is your time to be heard."

But he still didn't know what to say. Part of him wondered if anyone would even come listen...besides Gary, of course.

"Any suggestions?"

"Talk about what you know. About what inspires you."

He immediately thought of the Eiffel Tower. Few people knew the true story, but it would be corny if he kicked off with a history lesson, right? Besides, Margie had turned him down in front of the famous monument.

He was an idiot for agreeing to this.

A knock sounded on the door. "I have to go. Chase, I need you to find me a secure high-tech lab here. I'm going bat-shit crazy."

"I talked to our head of legal until midnight last

night. Technically, you can work on the new invention anywhere since no one has bought it yet, but according to company procedures, you need to work in a highly secure building."

"Then stick two security guards outside my hotel room or something," Evan said, going to the door to answer it. "Work with Mac's team at the hotel. I'm sure he has incredible security here. I need this, Chase."

"I know you do. We'll figure something out."

"Okay, call me back." He hung up and opened the door.

Jill Hale stood on the other side. "Daddy Warbucks, I presume."

Without the twins to soften her, she was ferocious. "Hello to you too, Jill. Good to see you. Are you here because I did something wrong?" But he knew why she was here. She cared about Margie, and he couldn't fault her for that, so he settled in to take whatever she wanted to dish out.

"You didn't tell us the truth when you were here before," she said, putting her hands on her hips. "You'd better not be messing with Margie. She was devastated when she came back from Paris."

He went for the truth since he knew she had softness inside her. "And I was devastated when she left Paris. I love her. I want things to work out between us."

A quiet smile appeared on her lips. "Good. That's all I wanted to hear. But if you hurt her, I'm going to stick the twins outside your room when they're having a meltdown. You won't be able to get any work done."

He'd heard how loud their pipes were. "Consider me suitably warned."

She nodded. "Good. If you go to Don't Soy with Me, tell Rebecca I said your order was on the house. As my way of saying welcome back."

Margie's friends were important to her, so he wanted to be on good terms with them. It was obvious

Jill felt the same way.

"Thanks, Jill. That means a lot."

She turned around and took a few steps before looking back over her shoulder. "And if you'd like to give me a spin in your red Ferrari, I wouldn't say no."

He laughed. "Word got out quick, huh?"

"It's a small town, Evan. See you around."

"We'll find time for a drive," he said as she walked off.

She gave a happy skip and then disappeared down the hall. He was shaking his head as he shut the door.

There was another knock about half an hour later. This time his visitors were Jane and Rhett.

He put his hands to his face. "Don't hit me. I swear I come in peace."

Rhett barked out a laugh. "It took you long enough to tell Margie the dagnabbit truth, so I won't say I didn't think about it. But now that you're here, I suspect you've fallen pretty hard for her. I'm not going to deck you for that."

Stepping back, he let them inside. "Good. Hello, Jane."

Jane narrowed her eyes at him. "I thought about punching you too, but I agree with Rhett. You wouldn't be here if you didn't care for her."

"I love her," he said, which was still weird to confess to other people. But if it helped smooth the waters...

"Good," Rhett said. "As a peace offering, Jane and I decided to ask if you'd like to play a few rounds of poker with us in Mac's marvelous Ponderosa Suite."

Since he couldn't technically work until he had an approved makeshift lab, what in the hell else was he going to do? "Are you planning on fleecing me?" he asked them.

Jane smiled and flipped her Artemis coin in the air. He could have sworn the goddess winked at him before it landed in her palm. "Definitely."

He walked to the door with them. "No side bets," he said even though he was grateful for the side bet they'd made in Paris that had led him here, back to his creative fire, and to Margie.

Rhett put his arm around his shoulders. "Let's see if we can lure Mac away from running his hotel empire for a little while. He needs to see what you've got."

Three professional poker players? He was toast. "It's a good thing I'm a billionaire," he joked.

"You might recall I have a new baby on the way," Rhett said.

"And I'm planning a wedding," Jane added.

He was definitely toast.

Hours later, he was eating a sandwich alone in his room after losing a considerable amount of money to his erstwhile friends. He'd managed to win a few pots, which was a miracle, but it had been a struggle to concentrate on the game. He kept wondering whether Margie liked the gift he'd had delivered. He'd wanted to get her a belated grand opening gift, and since he'd been unable to find a yellow chef's outfit, he'd had one made for her. And since she liked purple too, he'd told them to add purple polka dots. She would like that, he thought.

He'd used a courier from the hotel to drop it off for her at the bakery because he hadn't wanted to intrude while she was working. Okay, and he also hadn't wanted to see her frown if she was upset about the gift. She would know it was handmade. She was either going to get used to him doing things like that for her every now and then or she wasn't.

And now he really needed to work on his speech.

He hunkered down to research famous inventors and see if there was a theme he could use. Thomas Edison was considered spacy, to use a modern term, and home-schooled. Henry Ford started as a machine apprentice. Orville and Wilbur Wright attended high school but didn't matriculate.

The longer he investigated, the clearer one thing became. There were no patterns.

A potential first line for his speech took shape. "Inventing is not something that can be taught." He stared at the legal pad and then scrawled out the next line. "But it can be fostered." Isn't that what he wanted to do with this new center? He wanted a high-tech facility for young minds to use, one with access to the materials they would need to bring their imaginations to life. If MIT hadn't had labs like that, he wasn't sure he would have been able to invent INV-333.

He wrote what he suspected was complete gibberish. Researched more famous inventors. And when he got stuck, he researched oratorical abilities. Martin Luther King, Jr. came up right away. Okay, that was intimidating. He couldn't deliver a speech like that guy.

Chase *really* needed to help him.

But he knew his friend wouldn't. He had to do this on his own. A real billionaire inventor and entrepreneur knew what to say and did so with confidence.

This is what he'd chosen to do. This was the man he wanted to be, the one he wanted Margie to see, the one he hoped she would want to spend her life with.

He could do this.

His head was spinning with too many words, and since he was having trouble massaging his sentences on the computer, he switched to paper. The Grand Mountain Hotel had fine stationery in its desk drawers.

When a knock sounded on his door, he looked up. He'd lost track of time. Had he ordered more room service and forgotten? The sun was waning in the sky now, signaling the onset of evening.

When he opened the door, his heart seemed to crack his ribs. Margie was standing in front of him wearing the yellow chef outfit with purple polka dots. In her hands was a large bakery box, and his nose twitched when he smelled her famous cinnamon rolls.

"Hi!" she said, brightly, spinning around in her outfit. "Oh, Evan. I love my chef outfit."

And he loved her. So much. Seeing her again, especially so happy and vibrant, was like stepping into sunshine after a month of non-stop rain. "I'm glad. I couldn't find one in yellow, and then I remembered how much you like purple too." He was babbling, but she was grinning back at him.

Fighting the urge to snatch her up in his arms and kiss her senseless was tough. Like flying that first airplane off a tough cliff. And if that comparison wasn't proof enough that he'd fried his brain with his inventor research, he didn't know what was.

"I do love these colors," she said, stepping inside. "The polka dots are so happy, and the skirt is fabulous. Simply fabulous."

"I know it's supposedly safer to wear pants," he said, and he knew because he'd researched that too, "but that's mainly for people making soups and sauces and frying stuff in hot oil. You don't do that."

"But you had them include yellow and purple pants anyway," she said, coming further into the penthouse. "And I love them too. I'll wear them in the wintertime when it's cold."

"Maybe I can have ones made with fleece or a high-tech weather repellant," he said, already thinking about the different kinds of seasonal fabric that would be available.

Her hand touching his arm brought him back, and it was so soft and fleeting, she might as well have been a yellow monarch butterfly. "I think I'm good for now. Thank you, Evan."

Since he couldn't touch her, he shoved his hands into the pockets of his cream pants. His matching jacket was lying over a chair, and he tugged on his blue shirt, hoping it wasn't wrinkled. Okay, he was nervous.

She seemed to sense it because she frowned. "You

didn't give me this gift yourself because you weren't sure I'd accept it."

It wasn't a question. "You're right. I wasn't sure."

"Well, I did, and I'm grateful. It was the most thoughtful gift ever."

Her gaze rested softly on his face, and he could feel it happening again. The love she felt for him was blunting some of the edges she had about his billions. Accepting this gift was a huge sign. But they still had more to explore before they were out of the rocky shoals and out on the open sea.

"You're welcome," he said softly in kind, matching the intimacy in her tone. He wanted to say *thank you for accepting it,* but he didn't need to point a high-beam flashlight at their issues. "You look beautiful in yellow and purple."

They stood there, staring at each other. He took in everything: the slow rise of her chest as she breathed, the emerald light of her eyes as she gazed back at him, the way her pulse beat in her neck like it always did when she was nervous—or aroused.

She finally thrust out the baker's box. "These are my gift to you. To welcome you back to Dare Valley."

He opened the white flaps and lifted the lid. Inside were four giant cinnamon rolls, and on the other side of a divider were two croissants, two pains au chocolat, and a thick slice of bread with sunflower seeds on top— the kind she was making when he arrived on her doorstep yesterday. It had been wise of her not to bring him one of her baguettes, and he expected the choice had been intentional.

"Everything looks delicious," he said. *Like you do.* "Would you share one with me?"

Her mouth paused only a fraction, but he saw it. His body tensed, and they both stood there in the quiet.

"Those are all for you," she said, tucking her hands behind her back.

"I couldn't possibly eat all of these," he said and then shut up. He wasn't helping either one of them handle the desire racing through them right now. "I'll share with some friends. The guy bringing me room service would love some, I imagine."

"Room service, huh?" she asked. "So that answers my question."

"Which was?" With reluctance, he closed the bakery box and set it down on a nearby end table.

"Whether you have plans for dinner," she said, bouncing a little in her adorable white shoes. "I wanted to take you to dinner. If that's okay."

He gave her a measured look. "I'd love that. Why do I have a feeling there's more to it?"

"I thought about cooking for you, but honestly, I'm kinda tired after today. I didn't get much sleep last night."

"Neither did I," he admitted.

"And since this is my town, and you hosted me in Paris, I want to take *you* out for dinner." She stopped bouncing and looked at him. "Will you let me?"

This was part of the balance they were trying to find. "All right. So long as you promise to hold my hand when we go to dinner." He just had to touch her somewhere, some way.

"Oh, Evan," she said, holding her hands in front of her this time. "I miss you. I missed you last night. Okay, and now I'm stopping. You told me what you needed, and I respect that."

His throat was so dry now he wished he had a bottle of water to wet it. "Just to be clear. I'm not back on my celibacy kick again."

Her mouth curved. "I know that."

"It's not as if I don't want you like crazy." He took a step toward her and then stopped.

"I know that too."

Then? he wanted to ask. He wanted to shove aside

every obstacle between them, everything that seemed to be holding them back.

"Can I run home and change?" she asked. "I…ah…got all excited when I got your gift, and there were things to wrap up at the bakery. I'm getting ready to do payroll for the first time."

"Let me know if you need any help with that," he said, rocking back on his heels, hearing how flustered she sounded. "I'm pretty good at automating things. I can tailor some small business tools for you if you tell me what you need."

"Thanks," she said with a twinkle in her eyes. "I might take you up on that."

Her willingness to let him continue to help her with her dream made him pause. "I'll always be here for you, Margie."

"I know that, Evan," she said, wringing her hands.

"Over dinner, I'll tell you about the ideas I have for my speech next week," he said, wanting to share something of his business side with her too.

"And about the new center," she said eagerly. "It's all Gary can talk about. What you're planning to do is going to mean a lot to a lot of people."

"I hope so. How about I pick you up for dinner in, say, thirty minutes?" He looked over at the clock. It was a little past six. "You need to be home in time to get some rest." It took steely control not fantasize about her in bed. Besides, thinking about her in bed without him was depressing. How was he supposed to survive dinner without touching her?

"I can be ready that fast."

They walked to the door, letting their hands brush against each other's in a tantalizing caress.

"You know this means you'll be riding in my Ferrari," he said, searching her gaze for any hints of resistance or discomfort.

"I know that too," she said. "Evan, I really want you

to kiss me now."

He pressed his hand to the door to keep himself from reaching for her. "If I kiss you, I won't be able to stop there, and we..."

"Need to be surer," she said softly. "If you stayed here...with me...where would you want to live?"

He'd thought about that question long and hard. "You love the Victorian, so we'd live there if you wanted. But I'd want to make some improvements. Your toilet in the bathroom sometimes leaks, and the showerhead sucks."

Her smile beamed so bright, it seemed to turn into every shade of gold at once. "Not in my bathroom."

He gave her what he hoped was a flinty look. "I haven't seen your bathroom."

"Or my bedroom," she added in a husky voice.

"Are you flirting with me, Margie Lancaster?"

"I am, Mr. Michaels," she said. When she leaned in and drew a heart on his chest with one finger, he could hardly breathe. It was one of the ways she'd always showed her affection—one he'd missed like a man in the desert misses water. "I'll see you in thirty."

She opened the door, and he stood in the frame watching her walk off. In her hands, she held his every wish and desire for his new life.

When she disappeared from view, he closed the door and headed to the bakery box she'd left. He took out one of her cinnamon rolls and brought it out onto the terrace. Then he sat in the waning light and feasted on the bread made from her hands once again.

***

Margie was humming in the kitchen of Hot Cross Buns the next afternoon as she made her weekly order for ingredients with her supplier. The bakery was closing in a few minutes, and finally all would be quiet.

They'd sold out of cinnamon rolls by eight o'clock, only an hour after opening, so she and her staff had worked hard to make two fresh batches, which had sold out by one o'clock. They were going to have to increase their supply, that was for sure. They were already outselling Kemstead's numbers three to one. The changes she'd made had been spot on. They were drawing in a wider crowd of people. She did a little jig in place to celebrate.

"Margie," her sales clerk, Lori, called from the swinging door.

She looked away from her laptop. "Is everything closed up?"

The bubbly woman she'd hired shook her head. "A guy's still out here. He's been here for a couple hours—reading the local paper, talking on his phone, and working on his laptop. When I told him we close at three, he said he wanted to talk to you. He's...not from around here. I mean, he's wearing a pretty fancy suit."

She frowned. Was he part of the press corps descending on Dare Valley to cover Evan's gift to the university? She knew from Lori's occasional updates that there had been a few out-of-town customers earlier.

She hoped they weren't speculating about her relationship with Evan, although everyone eating at Brasserie Dare last night had seen them together. Going to the restaurant with him had been both joyful and a bit nerve-racking. People had openly stared at the billionaire inventor in their midst. Some had even thanked him for his gift to the university.

The attention had made him tense too, and it was obvious he wasn't used to receiving so many accolades from strangers. But their eyes had met sometime during the main course, and together they'd fallen into that place where nothing else existed.

The cassoulet had saturated her tongue with its intensity, and when the dessert of berries, Chantilly cream, and a decadent rhubarb sauce had arrived, she'd let Evan feed her a few bites. It had been arousing and heart-opening, which had made it even harder to part ways without a good night kiss.

But he had texted her when she was getting ready for bed, and his sweet wish for her to have cinnamony dreams had made up for it—mostly.

"Go ahead and head out," she told Lori, wondering why the guy wanted to talk to her. He was likely from the press if he was wearing some city-slicker suit. Not even the university professors dressed that formally. "I'll kick him out if it comes to that."

Lori went out the back while Margie headed to the front.

There was no one else in the bakery except for a ruggedly handsome dark-haired man wearing a gray suit, a white dress shirt, and a pale blue silk tie. He was working on a sleek laptop, typing like he was possessed. Then he stopped suddenly and looked her way.

His eyes were the same pale gray as his suit, and even though he'd shaved, he was the kind of man who couldn't stay clean-shaven for more than a few hours.

"I'm Margie Lancaster," she said, not coming past the baking case.

"I know," he said, closing the screen of his computer and standing.

He was tall and well built, but she didn't feel intimidated.

"You're Chase, aren't you?" she asked. Something about his voice had tipped her off.

His smile was a winner. "I am, indeed. It's good to finally meet you in the flesh. Not only because you've captured Evan's heart, but because few people can cold-call the switchboard of a major Fortune 500 company and find a way to be put through to the CFO."

"Evan mentioned your concern over him talking to me about his inventions, so I decided to use that when they wouldn't listen to reason." Since she didn't want any customers to interrupt them, she crossed to the front door and locked it, then turned the Closed sign to face the street.

"Concerned, huh? Guilty." He held up his hands.

She noticed all he had on his small table was a half-full cup of their regular coffee. "Why don't you let me pour you another drink? We can talk in the back of the shop."

He gathered his computer into a leather satchel and carried his cup over to her, which surprised her. Clearly he wasn't a man who expected anyone to wait on him.

"Can I get you anything else to eat?" she asked.

They didn't have much left in the trays. She'd made arrangements for her leftovers to go to a local church. Andre had made his impact on her there as well. Bread would never be wasted in her shop.

"I had one of your incredible cinnamon rolls earlier. I can see why you're already such a success."

She poured him a fresh cup of coffee. "It's not my recipe, but I've learned how to make it well." The key was to make it *her* way—something she'd learned at her baking internship in Paris.

"I'd say that and more," Chase said, lifting his cup to her in a mini toast.

Together they went into what she called the heart of the bakery. Since she didn't sit down often—no one did—she gestured to the single chair she'd been using while doing the ordering. He declined.

"So...you're here in Dare Valley," she said, not knowing where to start.

"Yes. Evan needed me to find him a secure lab to work in while he's here, and there were some details to finalize with the university regarding the center."

"Ah, the center. It's a wonderful idea. Evan is really excited about it." His eyes sparkled whenever he talked about it, but that probably wasn't the kind of thing Chase wanted to hear.

"Yes, he is. And then there's the speech. Evan is really stepping into his own. I've pretty much been the mouthpiece for Quid-Atch since he started the company. It will be good for the world to finally hear from him. He's a unique man with a unique vision."

She heard the warning a mile away. "And you're worried I'll hurt that."

"If I thought that, I'd be dealing with you in a very different way, Margie," he said, and now she could hear the steely tones of the corporate executive. "Evan wants you in his life, and since he doesn't let many people in, I was hoping we could be friends. Assuming you're able to accept everything he is, billions and all."

Yeah, that part. "I'm doing my best. We still have a lot to work out." Like could he *really* live in her house and be happy with minor improvements like better showerheads? She'd seen his penthouse in Paris. He liked luxury—something her home wasn't.

And then she realized her error. She was talking about her home, not theirs.

"Marriage is a big step," Chase said with a wry smile. "I speak as someone who failed miserably at it. I'm glad you two are talking about the practicalities. That's what it boils down to in the end."

Was it? She wondered. When she couldn't sleep, all she could think about was how much she loved him. But that hadn't been enough before. Could it be now?

"I'm glad you approve," she said dryly.

Chase's brow rose. "I can see why Evan likes you. You don't mince words much, do you?"

She lifted a shoulder. "Why waste the time? You hope I can handle it, and judging from your thoroughness, I expect you know my background."

"I do, yes, although I don't have the misfortune of knowing your parents."

She laughed at his turn of phrase. "Are you telling Evan to make me sign a pre-nup if we decide to get married?"

"Of course," he said, "but I don't think he's listening to me on that one. Or about the non-disclosure agreement. He trusts you—completely. I hope you understand how rare that is for him."

She hadn't fully understood until this moment, but perhaps it bore further consideration. "I appreciate you telling me."

"I hope you'll come to hear his speech," Chase said. "Evan may not ask you. He's still not sure anyone will come, which is crazy, but he doesn't fully realize his appeal. He never has. I also hope you'll accompany him afterwards to the reception the university is throwing to commemorate his gift."

Evan hadn't asked her yet, and she wondered about that. Then she caught Chase studying her. His pointed gaze answered her question. "Evan doesn't want to scare me off."

"No," Chase said seriously. "And this is only the beginning. You know what he has cooking right now. When it hits, it's going to surpass anything he's done. There will be more events. Evan doesn't like them per se, but he understands now that he has to lead. I can't be the only one steering the ship for a wizard behind the curtains who's directing the navigation."

"I can't imagine you letting anyone steer your ship."

"Then you would be wrong." He crossed his arms as he regarded her. "When I met Evan, I saw a kid who had a vision bigger than anyone I'd ever met. But it was like he was wearing shoes three sizes too big for his feet. He needed time to grow into them. Now, he's ready. You helped him with that, and whatever you decide, I'm grateful for that."

His comment squeezed all the air from her lungs. "You're trying to intimidate me."

"No, I'm trying to help you visualize how his life will be so you can see if you can have a place in it. He loves you. More than I've seen him love anything. Even his inventions."

Tears popped into her eyes as she remembered all the hurt she'd left in her wake the night he proposed. "I know he does."

"I hope you'll make the best choice for yourself," Chase said, walking to the door. "And that it just happens to also be the best choice for Evan."

She followed him out to the front of the bakery and unlocked the door. "I'm a little surprised you're not trying to persuade me."

"It's like I told Evan. Why would anyone want to be with someone who doesn't really like and accept all of them? Evan's a great man. And you're obviously a great woman. The unknown is whether you'll be great together long-term. That's for you to decide. We both know what Evan wants."

Yes, he'd made that very clear.

"It was good to finally meet you, Margie. I hope we'll see you at the speech and the reception. But if not, good luck with everything."

He was a couple of steps down the sidewalk when she called out his name. "Chase! Thanks for being such a good friend to Evan. He's... It's nice to know he has someone like you in his corner."

His nod was perfunctory, and then he crossed the street to a black Lexus.

She closed the shop, her mind spinning. Going to the speech would be easy. But the reception? She didn't know if she should go, whether she could go.

CHAPTER 4

Dating Margie without any of the kissing and touching pretty much had Evan fit to be tied. He'd been short with Chase, who'd flown in for a few days to help out with the arrangements for the center. Of course, his friend had also persuaded the university to allocate one of their top labs for Evan's private use. Since he felt guilty about the other people who counted on the lab to support their work, he'd agreed to only use it at night while Margie was working at the bakery. Once again, he was trying to mirror her hours as much as possible.

His speech was finished, which was a good thing since he was poised to deliver it in less than a week. Chase told him to practice rehearsing it in front of the mirror, and they'd done a few dry-runs. Being the master of public speaking that he was, his friend had pointed out areas for improvement. Shoulders back. Don't look at the teleprompter the whole time. Look at the audience as well. Make a connection. And speak from his heart.

Evan's concern that people wouldn't attend had shifted. Arthur Hale had interviewed him for *The Western Independent,* touting the gift as the biggest endowment Dare Valley had received since oil baron Emmits Merriam founded the university in 1960.

More and more people were stopping to thank him when he was out with Margie. It still felt super weird, but it also made him feel good. He was doing something that mattered to the people of this town he'd grown to care about. And even though Margie didn't act as weird about the accolades now, he could still feel her mulling over whether it was something she could handle in the long-term.

"It won't always be this way," he told her one late afternoon as they wandered down the street to have a coffee at Don't Soy with Me.

Her response—"Don't be so sure about that, Evan"— had given him cause to think.

When Chase mentioned that *Time* and *Fortune* wanted to do an article about his new vision, he had to admit Margie might be right. National and international press would be attending his speech in droves. A gift like the one he'd given Emmits Merriam, coupled with his announcement about creating a high-tech lab cooperative for inventors, complete with seed money to fund their ideas, was major news. Already people were talking on CNN about the impact such an investment could have on the current and future inventors of the world. Everyone knew most of the major developments in the world had come through inventions and innovation.

He felt the new mandate he'd dreamed about anchor more deeply inside him.

And in the dark moments when he was in bed alone, he told himself not to screw it up.

When Margie finished work—usually well after the bakery closed—she would text him after taking a brief nap. So far, they were averaging only two to three hours a day together, but it was all he'd allowed since he insisted she keep to her schedule and go home to sleep at eight o'clock. He had a harder time falling asleep at that hour himself, but he knew it was mostly because he missed her.

He hadn't asked her to attend the speech or the reception—the speech because it was during the hours of the bakery, and the reception because he hadn't worked up the courage yet. But that was changing today, he decided, as he greeted another day in Dare Valley with an exquisite cappuccino made by Chef T's fine restaurant staff.

When she invited him to the Victorian later in the afternoon, he dropped everything he was doing and pretty much rushed over. She greeted him at the door with a beaming smile.

"You're wearing the yellow dress," he said, kissing her on the cheek.

Without explicitly talking about it, they'd agreed to allow that much contact between them. She'd initiated it as a way of saying goodnight to him, and he'd followed suit. And they were holding hands sometimes. It still wasn't near enough.

Leaning in, he caught the scents of cinnamon and fresh baked bread in her hair. His muscles tightened as lust poured through him. It was agony to kiss her on the cheek and do no more, but it was an instructive agony. It had taught him what Degas was trying to convey in his sculptures—sometimes a person willingly endured pain to be close to someone they loved.

"I love this dress," she said, putting a hand on his chest. "How was your day?"

She was always asking him that, and he found he liked it a little too much. Before, he hadn't spent his free time with the sort of people who would ask such simple but meaningful questions—or care to hear the answers. "Great! My team made some more progress on that which cannot be named."

He'd reverted to the Voldemort joke instead of calling it invisible paint, since Chase had been emphatic about him not talking about the invention in a nonsecure area. The only place he could *talk* about it was in his penthouse, which Chase had deemed more secure than the lab at Emmits Merriam due to the lack of foot traffic. Of course, he still couldn't share any real details with her due to the company's security protocols, but that was okay. So far, he hadn't sensed any concern on her part.

He needed to make a trip to DC to look at the real samples himself, but he couldn't bear to leave Margie now. Not when he felt like they were getting closer, like she was starting to become more comfortable with the parts of his lifestyle he wasn't willing to relinquish.

"I'm happy to hear that," she said, dropping her hand. Well, she didn't drop it so much as trail it down his chest, leaving a trail of fire.

He shot her a look to let her know he knew what she was doing. She grinned, the little minx.

"And how was your day, beautiful?" he asked her. He'd started calling her that, and she beamed every time he did.

"Wonderful!" she said, holding her arms up and twirling around. "We sold out of *every* piece of bread in the store today. By noon. It was epic."

"Wow!" He loved seeing her this way—so full of light and life.

"The reporters who've arrived in town to cover your speech are hungry," she said, pausing. "And curious about me."

His protective instincts immediately kicked in. "Is anyone bothering you? Just say the word, and I'll have..." He stopped when he realized he'd been about to say he'd have Chase handle it. "I'll deal with it. Just tell me who it was. If you know the name. If not, I can come to the bakery tomorrow and run interference. I don't want anyone to bother you."

He could feel himself start to sweat. Jesus, this could ruin everything. She was worried enough about his fortune. The last thing he needed was for reporters to start following her.

"Evan, it's okay. I just told them we're friends. I was firm. I know how to be firm."

Friends. He rolled the word around in his mind. He wasn't sure how he felt about that. "Okay. Perhaps that's better. Maybe they'll leave you alone." How was that for a positive spin?

"I can handle them, Evan. Before we go, come inside for a minute. I want you to try something."

"I thought you weren't baking anymore after you got home," he said, giving her a playful nudge in the ribs.

"I didn't," she said as she led him into the kitchen. "I saved this last one just for you and brought it home. I thought you might like it," she said, holding it out to him. "It's a—"

"Punition," he finished for her. He took the French cookie from her and bit into it. "Oh, I adore these." It tasted like Paris, and he kind of got choked up.

"You're missing your home, aren't you?" she asked, reading him in that special way they shared.

You're my home, he wanted to say, but he'd told her that already. Now it was time to give her space so she could decide if he could be her home too.

"I do miss Paris. It's only natural, Margie. It holds a special place in my heart. Like you do." Okay, so he'd said something. Sue him.

Her green eyes were watching him, and he saw the shadows in them. "Are you really sure you can give her up?"

He broke his rule and put his hands on her shoulders, the better to gaze deeply into her eyes. "Paris is just a place—one I love and can always visit—but it's no Margie Lancaster."

Her face fell, and she let him see the struggle she usually kept from him. "Oh, Evan."

He couldn't stand her fear, so he broke his rule and

pulled her to his chest. "Hey," he said, rocking her in his arms. "I thought you knew how much I loved you."

"But it's Paris, Evan," she said, wrapping her arms around him. "It's your home."

So he needed to say it after all. "You're my home, Margie. Paris in all her glory can't compete with you."

"Will you please, *please* kiss me?" she whispered, raising her face to look at him. "I can't stand to be apart from you anymore."

So, she was experiencing the agony as much as he was. "Only a kiss." He could handle that, couldn't he?

But as she rose up on her toes to settle her sweet mouth on his, he wasn't so sure. She was hot and moist and demanding, as if the separation of their bodies had only heightened her craving for him. He heard the message and answered with his own gentle ferocity, dueling with her tongue and sucking on it until she moaned.

He was fast losing control. He could hear the chains snapping. Pressing back, he stared into her eyes. She was breathing fast, but then so was he. Her cheeks were flushed, her eyes wild with desire. The roar inside him broke free, and he had to turn his back on her to stop from gathering her up right then and there and taking her against the nearest surface in a rush of heat.

"Give me a moment," he said. Distantly, over the sound of rushing blood in his ears, he heard her footsteps move into the kitchen and then the opening and closing of the refrigerator door.

A glass of water *with ice* appeared in his vision, and he took it and downed the whole thing in a few gulps. He pulled on the front of his pants after setting the glass aside. And took a few more deep breaths.

When he turned around, he caught her dabbing the back of her neck with a wet cloth.

"You aren't the only one suffering here, Evan," she said softly.

"I know that. But you understand, right?" He crossed the kitchen until he stood in front of her. "What happens between us when we make love—"

"I understand," she whispered. "It's the same way for me. I promise...I promise I won't press you again."

"Kissing you," he said, taking the wet cloth and running it down her neck to cool her, "is never a hardship. I don't want you to think that. It's a joy."

"It is for me too," she said and gestured to the cloth in his hand. "Do you need it too?"

A surprising chuckle escaped his mouth. "Probably. The ice water was a good idea." Of course, it hadn't quenched the heat inside him. Only one thing could.

"Shall we...go...or do you want to take a break after..." Oh, the awkwardness in her voice.

"I don't want a break from you. Unless you need one. It's okay if you do."

"I don't want a break either—even if I do want to jump you right now."

His mouth tipped up. "Jump me, huh?"

"Just because we can't be together yet doesn't mean we can't talk about it," she said, and there she was again, his Pocket Venus, the one who called to him in his sleep. "Evan, are you..."

She trailed off, and he took her hand because of the tension in her voice.

"Am I?" he encouraged.

"Are you ever going to ask me to attend your speech at the university or the reception they're holding for you?"

His eyes narrowed. "How did you know about the reception?"

When she glanced away, he tipped her chin up so he could look into her eyes.

"Chase mentioned it. And I know it's a big deal. A really big deal."

Both she and Chase had mentioned the conversation

they'd had at the bakery, but neither of them had said much else about it. He trusted them, but it still worried him a bit.

"I didn't ask you to attend the speech because it's during business hours. And I didn't ask you about the reception because I was still scared, okay? I didn't want to rock the boat. I was planning on working up the courage to ask you tonight after dinner, but I might have chickened out if you hadn't asked about it first." That he could admit.

"I'm scared to go to the reception too," she said, looking away for a moment, "but it's important to you, and I want to try. And as for your speech. Evan, I wouldn't miss hearing it for the whole world. I'm planning on slipping away from the bakery. I do have employees, you know."

The aching thud of his heart echoed in his ears. "Delegation is a wise business practice."

"*Evan.*"

"Okay, I'm glad you want to be there," he finally said, staring into her eyes. "Relieved, even. I want you to be there. Dammit, I want you to be sitting in the seat reserved for the woman I love." How was that for honesty?

Her hand lifted slowly, and when he didn't move away, she touched his cheek. "I'll be there. And I'll come to the reception with you too."

He swallowed thickly. "You do realize there will be other people with lots of money there, right? The university has been able to command quite a guest list with this announcement." Even a few politicians would be attending, not that he'd ever enjoyed meeting any of them. They loved to hit him up for campaign donations.

"Those are the people who attend these types of receptions," she said, and he heard shades of the girl she'd been in her voice, the one who'd attended them with her parents.

"Be sure," he said.

"I have to be there. To see. It's like a test run."

"You don't have to go to any of these things for me. I hope you know that. The speech is enough."

"Evan, if I'm going to be..."

When she paused, he took a breath and said, "My wife."

She nodded slowly, lowering her hand from his face. "If I'm going to be your wife, I'll need to go to receptions and parties with you. It's what a partner does. You'd do the same thing for me, right? I'm sure there will be events for bakers and small business leaders we can attend together. Jill wants me to join the local Chamber of Commerce."

"I'd go anywhere with you," he told her. "But if you need more time, we can take it slow. It doesn't have to be *this* reception."

"Evan, if we take this any slower, I may spontaneously combust."

Since he felt the same way, he decided a little humor was warranted. "That's an urban myth. The human body cannot spontaneously combust."

"I love it when you go all geeky inventor on me," she said with a smile.

He hoped she could one day say, *I love it when you go all bold billionaire on me.* He wondered if it would ever happen.

"Okay, since we're rocking the boat, how about we rock it a little more?" he asked.

Her eyes grew wary, and he had to force himself to continue.

"Can I...shit...this thing will require a dress, and I don't want you to have to use your hard-earned money to pay for it." He exhaled sharply when she stayed silent. "Please say something. I promise I won't shower you in jewelry, but I'll want to at some point, Margie. You'd look beautiful in rubies."

The pain in her eyes made him wish he could call back the words. They were both thinking of the engagement ring he'd given her. It had been a ruby as well.

"This is hard for me, Evan. It's so important for me to pay my own way."

"I know it is," he said softly. "But we have to start somewhere." And then he made himself say it. "If you become my wife, what's mine will be yours. I wouldn't ask you to sign a pre-nup—in case you were wondering."

Her gaze flickered to his before she looked away. "Chase doesn't like that."

Chase might have changed his mind about Margie, but his own lesson with Trisha had been too bitter to be forgotten. "Chase isn't the one who wants to marry you," he said. "I am. And I trust you. With everything I am and everything I possess."

"I'm glad we talked about this, Evan," she said quietly and stepped away to pour herself a glass of water. But she hadn't given him an answer about the dress.

The front door slammed, and he wanted to kick the kitchen island in frustration. This was the reason they usually didn't linger in her home. Margie's bedroom was off limits to them for obvious reasons, and with three tenants, there was always someone coming and going from the common rooms. The only one Evan hadn't met yet was Alice, a history major at Emmits Merriam.

"Hey, Margie," Martin said at the kitchen door. "Hey, Evan."

They both gave a weak *hey* back. He waved awkwardly and stepped out of the kitchen. Evan was relieved. Martin had been a little weird with him since learning the truth about him being a billionaire inventor.

"I'll have to go to Denver for the dress," she said in a quiet voice in case Martin was still downstairs. "I know what's required for this kind of event. And I'll need shoes too."

That was no indication she would let him buy the outfit for her. He could feel her slipping away, awash in the past. Grabbing her hand, he squeezed it gently as if to say, *I'm here and you're not in that life anymore.*

She shook herself.

"Would it be over-the-top if I went all *practical* on you and had a designer come to Dare Valley to make you a dress?" he made himself ask. "I don't want you to have to take time off from the bakery to shop."

Her free hand was trembling as she lifted the glass of water to her mouth. "Is that practical?" she asked with a hoarse laugh after taking a sip.

"In my world, it is," he said, forcing himself to meet her troubled gaze. "It would be a pleasure to arrange it for you."

She was quiet for so long, he locked every muscle in place to keep himself from reaching for her and rocking her through the storm rolling inside her.

"All right," she finally said. "You can do that for me. I don't want to embarrass you."

"You could never embarrass me, Margie. *Ever.*"

Her nod almost broke his heart.

"You're talking to a formerly geeky inventor here, remember? I couldn't make an outfit match to save my life. I still can't tie a tie properly. I can manage a bowtie with a tux better somehow. Weird, huh?"

"I guess I should be grateful the reception isn't black tie, or I'd need a gown," she said with a forced smile.

But there would be others, he could hear her thinking. And there would be.

The front door slammed again, and she jumped. The realization that she was nervous because of him, because of what he was asking her to do, broke his heart.

"We should go," she muttered.

He took her hand when they were outside, but even though they were connected by touch, he couldn't feel her heart.

And it scared him.

CHAPTER 5

Margie had thought being fitted for her cocktail dress was bad enough, but then Jill stopped by the bakery to tell her she'd made the news. A picture of Margie and Evan walking down the street holding hands had made the front of a major magazine with the caption, *The Billionaire and the Baker*. The media had been around, sure, but she'd thought they were focusing on Evan's philanthropy. Or that's what she'd told herself. Most of them were, and while a few of them had asked how she and Evan had met and if they were dating, no one had given her the paparazzi vibe.

Until now.

"At least it's a good picture of you two," Jill said, patting her hand as Margie drank from the water bottle she kept near her while she was baking.

"Thanks for running over here and showing it to me," she told her friend, who was now sampling a pain au chocolat. Margie had already sent her other two bakers home since it was nearing one o'clock.

"You don't *sound* grateful," Jill said, licking the crumbs off her fingers. "You want to talk about it?"

"Not really." She handed Jill another pastry to head off more questions.

Her friend took it, but then wagged it at her. "I know a diversion when I see one. Brian tries to pull that with me all the time when he doesn't want to talk. You've been quiet since you returned from Paris, and I've let you stay that way."

"Let me? I think you might be going a little overboard."

"Do you think I can't get it out of you?" Jill asked. "You're worried about all of the other women he's been with, right? I've seen the pictures."

It was so far from the truth, she couldn't help but laugh. "No, that's not...oh, yes. Yes, it is." If her friend believed that, maybe she wouldn't have to talk about what was really bothering her.

Jill narrowed her eyes. "Okay, so if it's not the women, it has to be the money."

"You know my background," she said, taking some baguette dough out of the cooler to keep her hands busy. "I like things the way they are. I don't want them to change. Money changes everything."

She was scattering flour on the counter when Jill stayed her hand. "I hate to state the obvious, but you're in love with him. Things have already changed."

And now she was on the cover of a major magazine and there were national and international press sitting in her bakery eating her pastries. "I don't like some of the changes. And I'm not sure I'll be able to put up with them long-term."

"As much as I really want a crystal ball, I can't tell you what your future is going to be like with Evan. But one thing I do know is that when you talk about him you light up from the inside in a way you never did when you were with Howie. You light up the same way you do when you're talking about bread."

That made her stomach tremble. She knew she lit up around him—hadn't she seen herself in the mirror?—but like she did about bread?

Jill put an arm around her shoulders when her flour-dusted hands fell to the counter. "That, my dear, is worth the changes. Look at all the changes I had to make in my life for Brian. I kinda freaked out in the beginning, and sometimes I still do when Mia or Violet is crying for hours in the middle of the night, and I don't know what's wrong. But I wouldn't change any of it."

"Evan said he'd live with me in my Victorian," she said, only then realizing she'd said it again. *Her* Victorian.

"He did? Man, that guy must really love you then." Jill took a bite of her second pain au chocolat and moaned.

"Yes, he does." She picked up the dough and used the heel of her hand to roll it into a circle. "And isn't that too much of a compromise? I mean *really.* His penthouse in Paris is ridiculous. What if he's not happy here in Dare Valley? And what if he wants a bigger house two years down the road?" Perhaps he didn't intend to live in the house long-term at all. Maybe he was just accepting the option as a part of a carefully designed plan to win her over.

Then she realized how much mistrust was in her thoughts, and she knew the roots of her childhood still burrowed deep inside her, poisoning her.

"What if *you* want a bigger house two years down the road?" Jill asked.

She blinked.

"That's what I'm talking about," her friend said, pointing at her. "Change. *Nothing* stays the same forever, Margie, and we'd all be bored to tears if it did."

The back door to the bakery suddenly flew open, and Evan stumbled inside holding a magazine. She recognized it immediately as the one featuring their relationship. His face was tense.

"Hello, Evan," Jill said, giving Margie a look—one that said *do you see how worried this poor guy is?*

"Hi, Jill," he said, tugging on a pewter suit jacket that matched his pants. "Margie."

His tone was oddly stilted when he said her name. Jill gave her a kiss on the cheek and grabbed her half-eaten pastry.

"I'll see you later," she said and left.

As soon as she was gone, Evan dropped the magazine on the end of the clean counter. "I promise not to intrude on your regular business hours, but this was important. I knew you'd be upset about the article, and seeing Jill here..." He crossed to her, his lakewater blue eyes troubled. "Talk to me."

There were so many messy emotions rolling inside her, she couldn't hold his gaze. Taking the baguette dough in hand, she made the folds like Andre had taught her.

"It was a surprise to see the article," she said, pinching the ends to keep the seams tight. "I won't deny it."

He took her by the shoulders. "Look at me. Have I lost you already? Over something like this?"

Had he? When he cupped her cheek, her heart grew achy. His arms came around her when she lowered her head to his chest. Yeah, he could tell she needed this right now.

"My hands are covered in flour," she protested.

"Like I care," he said, reaching for them and fitting them around his body.

She gave in, and he seemed to lean into her as much as she leaned into him. They stayed that way for minutes until he edged back and stared into her like he always did. She couldn't help but stare back.

"I love you," he said, his voice strong and true even though she caught the fear still lurking in his eyes.

"You haven't said that since your first day back in Dare Valley," she said softly, letting the beauty of those words fill her and calm her.

"I was trying to give you your space—to decide."

"I love you too." He needed to hear it as much as she needed to say it.

Pulling her to him again, he rested his chin on top of her head. "Good. Good. Now, tell me how you felt when you saw the article."

It took some effort to draw oxygen into her lungs. "Exposed. Violated. Scared."

"All that?" he asked in a teasing voice, but she heard the tension there. "Good thing I have just the invention for you."

He let go of her and reached into his pocket. The pink device he withdrew was about as large as a smartphone.

"What is it?" she asked, noticing metal teeth at the top, covered by a plastic screen.

"It's a hand-held shredder. I wanted to rig up something special for you, so Wayne helped me find the right parts at the hardware store. When you see something you don't like in the papers, you can simply put it through this baby."

He walked over to the magazine and ripped off the cover. When he held the ragged paper out to her, she took it from him.

"You just made this?" she asked, even though she shouldn't be surprised anymore.

"Sure," he said. "The biggest hurdle was choosing the right shade of pink to paint it. Do you have any idea how many shades of pink are available?"

Her eyes filled with tears as she looked down at the device. He'd chosen a hot pink. "It's the same color as my tool box," she realized.

"Yeah! That's where I got the idea. So, you turn the power button on here. I used AA batteries by the way. Then you fold the paper and feed it into the device like this."

She did as he suggested, her vision blurring now.

The machine hummed, but it ate up the paper. She watched in awe as the metal teeth ground it into pieces that resembled confetti.

"Then you throw the whole mess in the trash," he said, sweeping the strands into her waste basket. "I suppose you could stomp on it if you like. Maybe we should tango and dig our heels into the shreds."

She knew what he was doing, and it warmed her. He was trying to make the situation lighter, but it didn't erase the fact that the article had been published. And it wouldn't prevent others from being published in the future.

"Say something, *please,*" he finally said, setting the pink machine on the counter. "I'm dying here. I don't know how to make this better for you."

Her mouth lifted in a poor attempt at a smile. "You are making this better. One pink homemade invention at a time."

A smile flitted across his face, but he couldn't maintain it either. "I'm still working on what to do when we see ourselves on TV. It seems excessive to bash a flat-screen with a pink bat, but I'll think of something."

News? They were going to be on the news? She realized it might already have happened. "They're going to find out who I am."

His eyes narrowed because he knew she wasn't talking about being a small-town baker. "I'll protect you. I promise you, Margie. If I'd realized how much press this gift to the university would generate—"

"No. You did the right thing," she said, taking his hand. "I'll handle it."

Their touch sparked immediate electricity, and she felt her belly pool with lust. His eyes met hers, and this time he smiled for real.

"I'm sorry for this. For all of it."

"I know you are." Her chest might be tight with nerves, but her heart felt warm and cozy. She was enthralled by the sweetness of her love for him, even as the possible consequences terrified her. Maybe Jill was right; maybe love was change.

"I don't want to cause you one minute of hurt or anxiety," Evan said, raising her hand to his mouth and kissing the back of her palm—like he'd done so many times in Paris.

"I know you don't. I need to remember that no one can get to me unless I let them. I had a…slight tumble here, but I'll be okay."

She could all but hear him ask, *Will you be next time?,* but she didn't have an answer for that yet.

"I can't control the press," he said, "but we can stay out of their line of sight until after the speech. That way we won't feed them any more pictures of us holding hands in public. That was an error on my part."

"Evan, if all I can do right now is hold your hand, we're not going to stop." And hiding would be cowardly. That wasn't who she wanted to be. "Maybe you could invent something to make the press disappear."

His mouth parted, and then he laughed. Just a few chords at first, but then he was holding his stomach and heaving with full-out laughter. She couldn't help but join in. It's what she'd hoped her comment would do.

"I'll have to tell Chase that one," he said, wheezing now. "We've been missing a critical application for years. People would pay us millions for such an invention."

They probably would. And he would keep getting as rich as Midas because his inventions didn't just change lives, they changed worlds.

Suddenly, it hit her. She was off her axis, like a planet hit by a comet. It had happened the moment she'd danced with him in her house after the cinnamon roll tasting. The deeper their connection grew, the greater her axis tilted.

"I'm looking forward to your speech tomorrow," she

said.

"You don't have to come." He pressed her hand to his chest now, not bothering to disguise how his heartbeat was racing. "Or to the reception either. The press will be there."

Butterflies danced in her stomach. "I'm coming."

"If it makes you uncomfortable—"

"I can always use the beautiful invention you made to destroy any stories they publish about us."

When he squeezed his eyes shut for a moment, she felt the deep well of his emotions, which he'd been burying with talk of the hot-pink shredder.

"Evan," she said, using her free hand to trace a heart in the center of his chest, around their joined hands. "I wouldn't miss your speech or the reception honoring you for the world."

He leaned down until their cheeks brushed, and it was still a new sensation to feel his clean-shaven skin brush against her own. "I'm glad, but if you change your mind, it's okay. I would rather have you happy and not present. I mean it, Margie."

"I know you do, but I'll be there because I love you too."

When he raised his head to stare at her, she could see the twin lights of hope and fear in his gaze. She understood. She knew those same lights were shining in her own eyes.

"I'm about to break my rule again and kiss you," he said, lowering his head.

Because it was hard on both of them, she kept the kiss light, only the merest brush of lips against lips. The word heaven might have been used to describe a kiss like that.

"I need to let you get back to work," he said finally, releasing everything but her hand, which he raised to his lips one last time.

"And I need to let you get back to rehearsing your

speech. Evan, you're going to do great tomorrow."

"I hope so, but if not, maybe I can borrow your girly shredder to destroy all the bad things they'll print about me."

"Look in the mirror when you rehearse this afternoon and try and see what I see."

"What do you see?" he asked.

She cupped his jaw. "A beautiful, smart, incredibly generous man who sees the world like no one else I know. And he knows how to change it for the better by just being himself."

"Thanks, Margie," he whispered, and his eyes seemed to flash like they did when he was talking about his inventions. "I'm...humbled."

Her heart squeezed from all the love she had for him. "I'll see you later, okay? We're still going to the movie, aren't we?"

He'd said he wanted to veg out a little to rest his brain before the speech.

"If you still want to," he said.

"I do. I'll even bring the shredder along. In case we need it."

His laugh was perfunctory, but at least it was something. He kissed her on the cheek and walked to the back door. "See you later, beautiful."

She waved, and he left. Picking up the pink shredder, she held it to her chest, wishing she could shred the last fears of her past that lurked inside her.

***

Evan was a ball of nerves the day of the speech. Even though he knew he wouldn't forget the speech—he had an eidetic memory, after all—he was terrified he would develop a lisp or hyperhidrosis and gross the audience out with the sheets of sweat on his brow.

A knock sounded on the penthouse door, and he

took a couple deep breaths before opening it, hoping to calm himself. It didn't work. Seconds later, Chase stood in the open doorway, looking like a titan of business. Evan felt like an ant in his shadow.

"You're pale, Evan," Chase said, giving his shoulder a quick jostle as he walked past him.

"I'm nauseated," he admitted. So much so he hadn't been able to touch the sweet collection of baked goods Margie had delivered before Hot Cross Buns opened for the day. Seeing her had been treat enough.

He was still worried about her coming today, but he needed to trust her. That article featuring them had put him in a tailspin. The invention he'd created in a fit of panic had bought him some time, but he suspected they were going to find out today if she could step into his world with him, if they could make it their own. Perhaps it was the Parisian in him, but part of him kept waiting for the church bells in town to ring out his fate. Okay, he was so expecting doom and gloom.

"It's perfectly normal to feel nauseated before an important speech," Chase said, pulling out a carton of antacids from his pocket and extending it to him. "Which is why I bought these at the local pharmacy. Take one. It will settle your stomach."

"Did you ever get nauseated?" he asked.

"When I was competing in bull-riding competitions, I used to puke in the empty stalls. By the time I gave my first major speech out of college, all I had to do was remember how I'd sat atop a two thousand pound bull that wanted to kill me. My nerves disappeared."

Evan chewed the antacid. "I haven't ridden bulls."

"Maybe not," Chase said, slapping him on the back. "But you have raced cars up to two hundred miles an hour. That takes balls."

"But that was fun!" he said, plopping down on the couch in the suite.

"Sharing your vision and inspiring millions of

people around the world isn't fun?"

"I'm still mad at you for getting CNN to agree to cover some of the speech live," he said, crossing his arms.

"*Evan*," Chase said, coming over and sitting beside him. "If I didn't think you were going to hit a home run, I never would have suggested it. You need to trust me, but mostly you need to trust yourself."

He knew that. But when he looked in the mirror all he could see was the place where he'd knicked himself shaving and how his hair had decided to ignore his professional hair products and become a ball of curl. Not even the memory of Margie's pep talk could help him see something different.

"You're going to tie my tie, aren't you?" he asked in a low voice. Watching more YouTube videos hadn't made his hands any less clumsy.

"I think it's time for you to learn how to do it properly," Chase said, grabbing him up by the arm. "It's not like you can't remember the steps."

They walked to the entryway mirror after Evan grabbed his tie from the couch. He awkwardly attempted to make it look presentable while Chase stood by and watched.

"Keep trying," Chase said, giving him what Evan could only describe as tough love.

On the fifth attempt, he finally managed to get it on straight. "Any other pointers?"

"I've told you everything I know. Now, you need to give your speech *your* way."

He remembered his conversation with Margie about how she needed to learn to make bread *her* way, not Grandma Kemstead's way and not Andre's. Suddenly he felt like he was embarking on his own rite of passage.

When Margie entered the penthouse ninety minutes later wearing a dazzling blue dress—one he hadn't seen before—he tried to smile. It wasn't a cocktail dress.

"You look beautiful," he said, giving her a light kiss on the cheek. "But I thought the fashion designer made you a dress."

She shook her head. "Oh, Evan, how could you have hung out with so many models without realizing a cocktail dress would be too fancy for today's speech? I'll need to change before the reception."

How could he have forgotten about the need for a second dress? "I didn't want you to have to buy anything for today. Let me reimburse you. Please."

"I didn't buy one. Jane let me borrow one of hers after Jill... Well, let's just say that girls help each other out. It's designer."

So, she'd compromised with him about the reception, but she'd found her own dress for the speech. "I would have had the designer make you two dresses if I'd remembered. I'm an idiot."

"I needed to do it this way, Evan."

He fought the urge to argue. The cost of the designer making her a second dress would have been less than nothing for him, but gazing at her, he realized it would have cost her some of her pride. Going forward, he would need to remember how important that was to her.

"I'm glad it worked out," he said as a white flag.

"You look handsome," she said, running a finger down his blue suit, the one that had been specially tailored for the occasion. "And you wore a tie."

He remembered his confession about not being able to put on ties properly and almost groaned. "I learned how to do it today. It seemed fitting."

Chase rose from the couch. "Margie, you look lovely. It's good to see you again."

"It's good to see you too."

"We should go," Chase said. "Evan, I can take a separate car if you'd like to ride with Margie."

The woman who held Evan's heart walked over to

his best friend and extended her hand. Chase eyed it with a puzzled look before taking it.

"Please come with us," she said with a soft smile.

It was the first time she'd spoken for him. And it felt right. Like something a wife would do.

"Then, I'll ride with you," Chase said, releasing her hand.

On the way to the university in the limousine Chase had arranged, Evan could feel Margie's discomfort. He wondered when she'd last ridden in a car like this.

Since the trip was short, they arrived in no time at the private parking lot behind the university's basketball stadium. To accommodate the interest, the administration had changed venues from the campus theater to the larger space where they held graduation ceremonies. Everything had gone well at the dress rehearsal the day before, but he'd caught a couple of awkward pauses in his speech. Hopefully it would be even better today.

When they reached the stage from the back entrance, Evan introduced Margie to the university president and a few of the chancellors seated in the VIP area. Considering how many chairs were arranged behind the podium where he would deliver his speech, he might as well have been taking the presidential oath. He leaned over and kissed Margie on the cheek once they'd exchanged greetings with everyone. It felt so good to have her standing beside him.

"You're going to knock them dead with all your invention awesomeness," she whispered for his ears only.

Smiling, he stared into her emerald eyes, which were filled with so much love and pride he almost didn't know what to do with it.

Then he realized he *did* know what to do. It was so simple. "I love you, Margie, and I'm so glad you're here."

Her eyes filled immediately, and she had to blink back the tears. "I love you too, and Evan, I am so proud of you."

He had to clear his throat before he turned to face Chase. The man who'd been his father, brother, friend, and partner for all these years looked at him with that unwavering gaze of his, the one that saw everything.

"I wouldn't be here without you," he said humbly.

"Yes, you would," Chase said, putting his hand on his shoulder. "Genius like yours can't be silenced, Evan. I've been honored to watch you become the man you are. It's finally time to share with the world what you've shared with me and Quid-Atch. Enjoy it."

Evan took his seat and reached for Margie's hand as the university president walked to the podium to introduce him. The sight of the crowd stretched out around the stage almost made him gulp. He'd been trying to ignore it before, but the basketball stadium held ten thousand people. And it seemed like every seat was taken. The press was camped out in the front row, and the big screens around the stadium were broadcasting live footage so people in the back could see what was happening. The scene looked almost presidential. Especially with the university flags displayed. Those hadn't been there yesterday.

The blue one seemed to grab his attention, and his heart stopped when he realized Artemis, the Greek goddess who had been part of his journey to Dare Valley, was depicted on it. She was holding a book in her hand, and a deer—the animal most associated with her—stood by her side. Under her feet were the Latin words *sapientia et veritas:* wisdom and truth. He remembered then that she was the goddess of wisdom.

His heart started to race as all the small moments that had brought him here came together like a finished puzzle. It was like there had been a plan all along, what the Greeks called destiny or fate. The power of that revelation coursed through him like a cleansing fire, burning away what remained of his fear and hesitancy. He was a world-famous inventor, and he had a powerful vision to share.

When the president finished his introduction, Evan rose as if on new legs. A great sense of peace settled around him, and when he stood in front of the microphone, he didn't glance at the speech that was displayed on his high-tech TelePrompter. He knew every word. All he needed to do now was speak from *his* heart.

He went through the expected introductions and then launched into his speech.

"When I was asked to give a speech about inventing, I researched other famous inventors to see if there was a common thread. It may surprise you that there wasn't, and I learned something important. Invention can't be taught. It's something you possess. I've had an innate curiosity about what makes things tick since I was child. I took things apart, and sometimes I managed to put them back together."

Muffled laughter spread through the crowd. Evan caught sight of Gary, Margie's tenant, sitting in the reserved section behind the press. He was grinning, like he was soaking up every single word of the speech, and Martin was seated next to him, looking uncharacteristically animated.

"You may be wondering why I'm helping the university create a center for students dedicated to inventing after I just said it can't be taught. Well, one thing I do know about inventing is that it can be fostered. Inventors need a space to create, and they need tools. Some inventions are pretty simple and don't cost a fortune to create. Others...well, all you have to do is ask my CFO, and he'll tell you mine cost a mint."

There was more laughter, and he could feel a smile spread across his face in response. Chase had talked about the moment in the speech where you know you have an audience in the palm of your hand. This was it— he could *feel* it.

"Not all inventions need to cure cancer or eradicate poverty," he continued. "Just think about how much less organized we'd all be if Spencer Silver hadn't created Post-it notes after failing to invent the super strong adhesive he'd planned for the aerospace industry. This center isn't going to make judgments about the usability of inventions. Sometimes you know how an invention might be used at the outset, but history has shown us enough happy accidents for me to conclude we simply need to support the science of inventing."

Several people started to clap, and suddenly the whole audience was clapping. The power of the clapping pounded through his veins and made his heart feel too big for his chest.

When the sound finally died down, he continued. "This center won't stop at invention because, honestly, that's only the first step. If you've ever tried to complete a patent application for the U.S. government, you know what I'm talking about."

Someone whistled in the crowd, and more people laughed. Including Evan.

"We're going to help young minds here at the university learn the business side of things as well. Too many inventors have never made money off their inventions. Daisuke Inoue invented the karaoke machine but never patented the idea. Depending on how you feel about karaoke, you may or may not feel bad for him."

Again, laughter rang throughout the stadium, and he could feel a fizzy effervescence surging up inside him.

"But then there are inventors like Sir Tim Berners-Lee, who invented something we all use every day, something some of you may be using on your phones right now if my speech is boring you. He invented the

World Wide Web, and he didn't patent it because he wanted his invention to be available to everyone."

Many people were nodding their heads, and he paused to scan the crowd like Chase had taught him to do.

"Inventors have a mandate, first to the idea that comes to them, and second to the world. The invention may only serve a small number of people, but who knows? Laszlo Biro invented the ballpoint pen because he was fed up with fountain pens that never seemed to stop leaking. Where would we be if he'd only kept that pen for himself?"

Several cameras flashed, but he found he didn't mind so much this time. They were capturing the new Evan Michaels. Chase was right. It *had* been time for him to show himself to the world.

"One thing I do know about this new center is that it's going to change things. Here at Emmits Merriam, there will be students inventing in their dorm rooms late into the night by bad light but with a great fire in their bellies. And I want to meet those of you in the audience who are like that. Because that's how I started. And I've never forgotten. This university was founded by a maverick businessman, I understand, an oil baron named Emmits Merriam. I would like to think he'd be thrilled to host this new center if he were still with us."

All of a sudden he knew he was going to deviate from his speech, but it had to be done.

"I noticed the university's motto of wisdom and truth with the Greek goddess Artemis depicted on one of the flags on this stage. I saw a statue of Artemis in Greece a few weeks before I came to Dare Valley for the first time. It seems only right to name this invention center after the goddess of wisdom. So please join me in celebrating The Artemis Institute of Innovation."

He stepped back from the mike to clap, and the crowd joined him. When the applause subsided, he took his place behind the lectern once again.

"If you're sitting in the audience with an invention burning in your belly, all I can say to you is this: you have a home with people like you. Welcome."

This time, when he took a step back, his hand automatically went to his heart. The crowd began to clap once more and then people started to rise to their feet. He smiled as he let the vibration roll over him and looked over his shoulder to look at Margie. She was clapping for all she was worth, a beaming smile on her face. Their gazes met, and her clapping only surged, like the love shining in her eyes. Sharing this moment with her made it so much more complete.

Evan Michaels had finally shared his vision with the world...and received a standing ovation.

CHAPTER 6

Margie was bursting with pride when Evan led her into the reception a few hours later.

His hand was warm and comforting on the small of her back as he introduced her to some of the division heads from Quid-Atch, whom Chase had flown in as a surprise to commemorate Evan's first major speech. The head of R&D, Rajan, kept trying to convince Evan to fly to the company's main headquarters to give another speech to their employees—even though Chase had arranged for everyone to watch the one today at their offices. He was a funny, geeky guy who reminded her a bit of Evan.

"We'll see how things pan out," Evan only replied. "I'm needed around here for a while."

She could all but hear him thinking that he needed to stay with her to solidify things between them. All of a sudden, she knew she needed to help him feel comfortable taking the trips he needed to take, the ones she couldn't go on with him.

Chase was watching the group from the side of the room— a part of them, but also separate. Evan and his head of R&D spoke the same language—inventing— which made their interactions easier. But the others were all gazing carefully between him and Chase, sensing the shift that had happened in his speech.

Evan had taken up the reins of his company in a new way today. Things were going to be different from now on.

She walked over to where Chase was standing and pulled him aside. "It's good of you to let him step forward like this. It takes a big man to do it, and I just wanted to say I admire you for it."

His brow rose, but he didn't smile. Unlike Evan, this man was impossible for her to read.

"I know we don't know each other well," she continued, "but I just wanted to...oh, heck...will you stop glowering at me? I was only trying to say—"

"I know what you're trying to say," he said now with a smile so slight it would be missed by anyone but her. "People are wondering if there's going to be a power struggle between Evan and me, now that Evan's stepping forward. There won't be."

"You flew them in so they could see him like this," she said, and it wasn't a question.

He leaned close to her ear. "Don't tell him. He's still getting used to internal corporate politics. It's going to take him a while, and this junk...I don't want to spoil the moment with it."

But he was already leading the way again for Evan. "You're a good man, Chase."

"Definitely don't tell anyone that," he said softly. "I'm going to grab a bourbon at the bar. Can I get you anything? We're going to be sitting down at the head table pretty soon, and all they're serving is wine."

Evan was deep in discussion with the head of European operations now. The distinguished older man was obviously trying to court Evan's favor and get in good with him. She realized Evan would have a lot of traveling ahead of him. He'd need to meet with his employees all over the world and likely their clients too.

After the reception, she would encourage him to leave Dare Valley and go to DC for a while. It would be okay. They would learn to make compromises like they had about her two dresses today. He hadn't tried to argue with her about the one she'd borrowed from Jane. And he hadn't suggested the custom-made one was better, even though it hugged her frame perfectly. The bold red color she'd chosen suited her declaration, and the neckline bordered the edge of modest since she hadn't wanted to look anything less than professional as his date. No one was ever going to accuse her of being a trophy wife like her mother had been.

"Do you think they have champagne?" she asked Chase, who was waiting patiently for her answer.

"They have pink champagne. Evan insisted." He winked at her. "It was the only suggestion he had for the entire reception."

She refrained from expressing how sweet that was. Chase didn't strike her as a lovey dovey type. "Can you grab two glasses? I want to toast with Evan."

"I'd be happy to," Chase said.

Conversations were buzzing all around her now, and since she didn't want to interrupt Evan and his employees, she scanned the crowd for some of her friends. Evan had included everyone from the cinnamon roll tasting, although Arthur Hale had a standing invitation to receptions like this one since his name was on the Hale School of Journalism. Evan had also included the students living at her house, which made her heart swell.

"Margaret!" a voice cried out. She hadn't heard that voice in almost a decade, but she recognized it instantly.

Shock poured into her as a hand cupped her bare arm. It was a gentle touch, but it felt like a shackle. She turned and looked into the calculating eyes of her mother. They were the same color as hers, but that's where the resemblance ended. "Mother."

Oh, God, oh, God, oh, God, oh, God.

"And father," a man said on her other side.

He hadn't changed either, still puffing his chest out like the peacock who'd snared a beautiful, younger woman—although her mother didn't look quite so young anymore.

All the air seemed to have disappeared from her lungs.

"What are you doing here?" she rasped out, but she knew. Oh, how she knew.

Her mother smiled, but the rest of her face didn't move. Botox had stolen her ability to even make a fake expression. It was almost like staring at a statue.

"Well, darling girl," her mother continued as if they hadn't been estranged for years, "we just had to come to support you and your new beau once we read about you two in the news."

She felt lightheaded. "I know why you're here, mother. What I want to know is how you got in. They didn't sell tickets to the reception."

The look in her mother's eyes turned downright feral, and she felt a familiar sickness rise in her belly. Her mother was the type of woman who would do anything to get what she wanted, no matter who it destroyed. And what Cindy Lancaster wanted was all the glitter and glory money could buy.

"I simply called the university president and told him your father and I wanted to surprise you by coming to the reception." She leaned in and pinched Margie on the arm. "I told him we were vacationing in St. Barts, and you didn't want us to interrupt our trip, but we just had to be there for our darling girl."

Margie tried to step away, but her father grabbed her other arm. Their hold was designed to keep her in her place. With them calling the shots.

It was happening all over again.

They were going to enhance their power and

connections—through her.

And she couldn't allow it. She *couldn't*.

Shoving at them, she finally managed to break their hold. Her breaths were shallow now, and she knew she was going to have a panic attack, the kind that had plagued her while growing up. She had to get out of here fast.

Even though she seemed to be moving quickly, she felt like she was wading through water. Her unnatural heartbeat pounded in her ears. She spotted an Exit sign at the side of the large banquet hall and made it through the door. A few people were watching her with odd looks on their faces, but she didn't care. She couldn't. She felt like an elephant was sitting on her chest.

When she made it to the hallway, she kept right on going, pushing through the water, fighting to stay upright and not give in to the faint she could feel pressing down on her.

She had to get away.

She had to protect Evan.

***

Evan had enjoyed talking with his executives at the start of the reception. It had been thoughtful of Chase to arrange for them to attend. He would have to start thinking like that now. There were so many relationships he'd let Chase handle for him in the past. Stepping up to the plate would be part of his new mandate after today.

It would mean traveling away from Margie, which worried him. He'd read her so easily when Rajan suggested he come to corporate headquarters next week. She thought he should go, but it felt too soon to leave her. Their future wasn't secure, and nothing was more important to him right now, not even his new invention or the company he owned.

When he finally managed to politely extricate himself from his employees, he searched the room for her. There was no sign of her, so he decided to head to the main table to see if she'd sat down early with Chase.

A couple rose from their seats beside the university president as he approached them. They both had the predatory look of money, and he wondered why they were sitting at the head table if he didn't know them.

Then the older woman gave him a flirtatious smile, and he took a step back when he realized her eyes were the same shape and color as Margie's—and her long, lustrous hair was the same rich sable. He knew who they were before the older man beside her stuck out his hand for a shake.

"Evan—"

"Get out," he said in a low but commanding voice.

The man had the audacity to look shocked. "Now, see here—"

"*Evan,*" Margie's mother said, running her fingers in a coquettish gesture that made him sick. "We're here to meet the special man in Margaret's life. Your speech was—"

"I said, 'Get out,'" he repeated in the same hard tone.

They didn't even call her by the name she preferred. She wasn't Margaret. She never had been.

"If you don't want the press to photograph a scene of my security dragging you from this room," he said, "you will leave now. Quietly."

Her mother simply shook her head. "Now, Evan. That would only embarrass Margaret, and we wouldn't want that. Would we?"

He broke her vile gaze to scan the room again for Margie. She was nowhere to be found. All he could think about was how seeing her parents would have affected her. He needed to find her. Immediately.

"The best gift I could give Margie would be to expose

you for the vile people you are. If you don't leave right now, I can promise you that I will give interviews to every person with a press pass about how you disowned your only daughter without a thought."

The woman pressed a hand to her heart like the poor actress she was. "But it broke our hearts to do that to our little girl. We were trying to do what we thought was best for her. And we were clearly right. She hasn't made the best choices—God knows it's embarrassing to have a daughter who spends her days in front of an oven like the household help—but at least she ended up with a powerful and successful man like you."

His vision turned red for a moment. "Any character Margie possesses is in *spite* of you, not because of you, you horrible, blood-sucking woman."

She gasped, and her husband elbowed in. "Suddenly you're an angel in the press because you gave this no-name school an endowment," he snarled, "but that can end in a moment. I'm going to tell them how you treated us."

This time he scoffed. "Feel free. We can bandy things about in the papers if that's how you want to play it. That is, if that isn't embarrassing for you and your friends," he said. "Now get the hell out of here, or I'll look into every one of your assets and find a way to take everything from you. *Everything*. That's a promise."

The older man was turning purple from outrage.

"Do you understand me?" he asked as a strong hand cupped his shoulder.

He knew immediately it was Chase.

The woman's surgically enhanced lips were trembling now. "But...but I'm her mother."

"Get out," he said. "And if you ever contact her or me again, I will destroy you. You'll be begging to work at a fast-food place to make the rent once I'm finished with you."

The man finally stood tall and put his arm around

his wife, acting like Evan had just stolen their only daughter. He started to lead her away, but she paused.

"We're going to tell everyone we know you're a heartless son of a bitch," she said. "We know some of the same people you do."

He bowed mockingly. "You can have each other. Our security team will make sure you leave."

Signaling to one of the men in the back of the room, he inclined his chin toward the couple. The man nodded and came forward.

"There's no need for this," Margie's dad blustered when the security guard reached them.

People were talking all around him, and Evan realized he was making a scene. The university president was looking deeply concerned, as if he'd realized he'd made a colossal mistake inviting the Lancasters without clearing it with Evan and Margie. Right now, Evan couldn't care less.

"I need to find Margie," he said to Chase once the couple was gone. He scanned the room again, but as he feared, she was nowhere to be found.

"Go see if security saw her leave," Chase said. "I'll handle everything else."

"Please give my apologies—"

"I will, Evan," Chase said, giving him a slight nudge toward the door.

With the help of the security team, Evan quickly discovered Margie had made it to the limo. She'd claimed to be unwell, so the driver had taken her home.

He strode back into the reception hall and headed to the table where her boarders were seated. After he briefly explained the problem, Gary lent him a key to the house so he could go check on her.

Evan left the reception without a thought.

When he reached the Victorian and knocked, she didn't answer. But he knew where her bedroom was, and the light was on in the tower.

He needed to get in there. He hated to invade her privacy without her permission, but her phone was going straight to voicemail and this was an emergency. Using the key, he entered the quiet house.

He hadn't been on the second floor since returning to Dare Valley. Passing the room that had once been his, he continued down the hall. As he neared her bedroom door, he could hear the sobs coming from the other side.

Oh, baby.

He opened the door quietly. The lamp by her bed was on. She was curled up in a ball in the center of the mattress, crying her heart out. His heart broke, hearing her.

He almost didn't know what to do, but then he realized there was only one thing he *could* do. Love her through the storm. Comfort her until she didn't need it anymore. He planted his knee on the bed and lowered himself to the mattress. Fitting himself to her body, he wrapped his arm around her.

She jumped from his touch and then turned over to look at him. Her makeup was a disaster, her mascara running down her face. But it was the utter devastation in her tear-drenched eyes that killed him.

"Margie," he said softly.

Her ragged inhalation sounded painful, so he rubbed her back as she struggled to breathe. She squeezed her eyes shut, her features tensed to the point of breaking. "My parents..."

"I know," he whispered. "They're gone now, and they will never bother us again."

Her lips trembled, and then she dissolved right before his eyes, crying and keening with so much pain he feared for her. But he held her tight through it all.

He didn't know how much time had passed when the violence of her tears finally abated, but it seemed like hours. Tucking her closer to him, he made sure to give her room to inhale oxygen. Finally she slumped against him, and he kissed the top of her head.

"Oh, Margie," he whispered. "I'm so sorry."

She shook her head and then lifted her gaze to meet his. "It's not your fault. It's mine. I brought them to you."

He sat up because he could feel it already, the jagged and gaping crevice between them, the one that had cracked open tonight after her parents' surprise visit.

"You didn't bring them. They came. And now they're gone."

Covering her eyes with a hand like she was ashamed to be seen by him, she let out a tortured breath. "Oh Evan, I can't do this. I can't..."

His fear rose up like a dark tower, one he knew he couldn't scale without her. "We're doing it. Together. You did what you had to do with them, and so did I. They know better than to try again."

"No, no, no," she cried out.

"Margie, you're safe now," he said, feeling it was important to say that. "I'm here for you. I'll always be here for you."

When she lifted her head to look at him, he felt it. He couldn't climb the tower at all, he realized. It was about to fall on top of him, destroying everything in its wake.

"You asked me if I could do this, and I...I can't. I just can't." Tears spilled down her cheeks. "Please don't press me anymore. If you love me..."

The tower struck him, and its debris drove into every cell of his body. "Don't say that right now. You're in shock. It's going to be better."

"No, it won't," she said. "Please just go. Evan, I'm begging you."

Tears stung his eyes. "Don't let them do this. Don't give your parents this kind of victory."

"It's too late," she said and then started crying again in earnest.

He tried to put his arms around her again, but this time she pushed back.

"*No,*" she said through the tears. "You have to go. I mean it, Evan. I love you, but I can't do this anymore."

For a moment, he couldn't think. The brain waves guiding decision making ceased to work. He managed to rise from the bed.

"You're hurting now," he made himself say. "You're going to feel differently about this."

Even as he said the words, he didn't believe them. When was she going to feel differently? She'd been honest with him from the beginning. She didn't want the kind of life he led. He just hadn't wanted to listen.

He walked to the door, and all he wanted to do was lower his head against the frame and cry. "I won't..." Oh, Jesus, he couldn't say it. It hurt too much to say it. But he managed to pool all the remaining strength he possessed into his voice. "I won't bother you anymore."

As he left, he hoped she would jump off the bed and come after him, that she would assure him it was all a mistake and everything would be fine.

But she didn't, and so he walked out of her house for the last time.

CHAPTER 7

For the next few days, Margie walked around in a fog. She forced herself to get out of bed at two-thirty in the morning when her alarm went off and started to make bread at three. She managed to tell Jill the entire story without bawling, but she cried plenty the rest of the time.

She cried more than she had ever cried in her whole life.

Her heart was broken, and so was Evan's, she knew. All she wanted to do was wind back the clock to before her parents had ruined everything.

But she couldn't.

And now Evan was gone. According to Jill, he had checked out of the Grand Mountain Hotel with the rest of the Quid-Atch executives.

The press had asked her why Evan had left the reception for an unaccounted period of time before returning to deliver a few short remarks to the attendees. He'd excused himself early, which had only caused more speculation.

She'd lost her temper and said, "No comment," which had only prompted one of the papers to report she and Evan were on the outs.

Work no longer gave her the same sense of joy, and tears filled her eyes every time she took a baguette from the oven.

When she made it back to her house, she didn't test out new baking recipes. No, she headed straight to her bedroom, which had become her sanctuary from her renters' curious gazes. Of course, none of them had asked her about Evan—not even Gary. The pale face she saw whenever she looked in the mirror was enough of an explanation. Her sorrow was written all over it.

She was brewing a cup of tea in the kitchen of the Victorian when she heard a knock on the door. Since she'd only just returned from closing the bakery, she couldn't imagine who it was. But part of her wondered if it was Evan, if he had been courageous enough to come to her door one more time.

When she opened it, Jane was standing there.

She told herself she was relieved, but it wasn't true. Not if the tears filling her eyes were any indication.

"I wanted to stop by," Jane said, clenching her hands. "See if you needed anything."

"Not unless you have a cure for heartbreak. Things with Evan didn't work out."

Her gaze was soft, and she nodded. "Jill told me. She's worried about you. She thought...well...can I come in for a little while? I promise not to stay long."

If Jill had talked to Jane, she likely knew the full truth. When Jill spilled the beans, she usually spilled all of them. Most of the time Margie found it charming— except when it was about her.

"Please, come in," she reluctantly said. "I was making some tea. I'd be happy to offer you some."

"That sounds nice," Jane replied, following her into the kitchen.

The kettle whistled, and she took it off the burner and poured the water into her cheery red tea pot. The green tea leaves she'd spooned in earlier swirled in the bottom.

"My parents are really wealthy," Jane said in a quiet voice. "I don't usually share that. People see you differently when they learn you're from money."

A massive lump had taken up residence in Margie's throat, so she only slid Jane a pottery mug as a reply.

"My dad's a politician," Jane continued, "and my mom's his perfect politician's wife. That sounds bitter." Laughing harshly, she clutched the mug handle. "Growing up with them always wanting to control my life, my every move, was like being in prison. I had to get out. That's why I became Rhett's poker babe. I knew it would—"

"Embarrass them," Margie finished. "It was like giving them the middle finger."

"Yes, it was. They didn't have to disown me, you see. I was happy to disown myself."

She nodded. "I understand. Jill probably told you that I did the same thing. And that my parents showed up at Evan's reception."

She was still having nightmares about it. In some of them, they were reaching their grubby little hands into Evan's pockets, shouting, *Where's the money?* In others, she and Evan were sitting in his penthouse in Paris as her mother tugged down his beautiful curtains and declared she was going to redecorate.

"My parents won't ever want to be in my life again," Jane said. "Even if Matt ends up becoming the governor or senator of Colorado. They have too much pride."

Margie poured the tea and then led Jane over to the kitchen table.

"I've been trying to put myself in your shoes," Jane said. "After Jill begged me to talk with you."

"Begged, huh?" she asked.

"I told her I wouldn't at first, but then I got to thinking about Matt and me, and how I might not have let myself be with him if someone wise hadn't spoken some sense to me. I was afraid I would be a liability for him, you see. Because of my past."

Margie remembered. "It was major news when it came out that you'd been a poker babe."

"And right during his campaign for the mayoral primary," Jane said, taking a sip of the steaming tea. "You're worried your parents will do something to hurt you and Evan."

"Yes," she said, burning the roof of her mouth when she took a gulp of the hot tea to soothe her throat. "And I'm...oh, hell, I don't know...seeing my parents reminded me of how people like them always seem to try and leech onto other wealthy people. I saw it all the time growing up."

"Those kinds of people are parasites," Jane said, setting her mug down. "But you're not like that. And neither is Evan."

She made her brow rise. "You didn't think too much of him in Paris, or you wouldn't have thrown out such a crazy side bet."

"You're wrong. I did think a lot of him. When I looked at him, I saw a lonely man trapped in a wealthy lifestyle I used to inhabit, looking for a way out."

Sighing, Margie set her tea aside. "So you think I should go back to him then?"

"I would never tell you what to do," Jane said, reaching for her hand. "I only wanted you to know I understand why you would want to protect him and keep yourself out of his life. And I think maybe you should have a little more faith in him...and in yourself. Besides, it's not like he isn't wealthy enough to keep people like your parents away from anywhere you two want to go. And, Margie, he doesn't want to be around people like them or their friends anymore. I think you know that."

"But he has all this money—billions—and I just don't know what to do about it," she said, heaving out a sigh.

"Why don't you spend it?"

Her head darted back. "I beg your pardon."

"Make it fun," Jane said, squeezing her hand. "You could be his philanthropy partner. He has a vision for the world. What do *you* want to do to make the world a better place?"

Blinking, she drank more tea. Philanthropy?

"You're looking at me like I'm crazy, but let me explain. Melinda Gates is her own woman, but she works by her husband's side when it comes to their philanthropic activities. I mean, their biggest charity is called The Bill & Melinda Gates Foundation, isn't it?"

She finally saw where Jane was headed with this. "But what about how we live? He said he would be happy living in this house, but..."

"Warren Buffet lives in the same house he and his wife bought in 1958, and he's wealthier than Evan. Why can't Evan live here with you? It's a beautiful home." She gave Margie a sharp look. "Oh, you think he's only telling you that to keep you. Perhaps you need to ask him about it."

"I did, and he mentioned...," she said, realizing what she'd known all along. He *had* told her the truth. He would be happy living here with improvements.

Jane was nodding slowly, letting go of her hand. "What else?" She pulled a coin out of her pocket and started playing with it—something she often did when thinking.

"He said he liked fast cars and that he was going to keep his yacht."

Her friend laughed and rubbed the coin between her thumb and index finger, almost like someone would do with rosary beads. "Maybe you're the one who wasn't listening."

Maybe Jane was right...and maybe that needed to change.

"My parents coming here made me go off the

rocker," she admitted, rubbing her forehead. "It was like everything I'd escaped from was front and center again, but this time it wasn't just hurting me. It was hurting someone I love."

"Then tell Evan that," Jane said, setting the coin on the table and reaching for her tea. "And quickly. No offense, but if he looks anything like you, it's hard to watch."

Even in a couple of days, she'd lost weight.

When she looked down at the coin, all her breath whooshed out of her chest. "What is this?" she managed to say, pointing down at it.

"Oh," Jane said, pushing it her way. "It's an old Roman coin with the goddess Diana on it. Rhett gave it to me as a lucky chip protector."

Carefully, Margie picked it up and stared at the image. "She's called Artemis by the Greeks. Evan and I saw her in Paris once." Fate. Here it was again, entwining their lives, their stories. They were meant for each other. She knew it. Maybe the solution was simpler than she'd led herself to believe. Perhaps, like the Greek gods, she and Evan simply needed to throw her parents off of Mount Olympus.

"You're right about Evan. About everything." She needed to find Evan, but she knew just the person who could lead her to him. "But the bakery... I suppose my bakers can handle everything."

"If you want someone to pop in and check on things, I'm sure Brian and Terrance would be happy to pitch in."

Now that really made her cry. "That would be the best." And she slid the goddess coin back to her friend. Maybe she could ask Evan to buy her one as a wedding present. She would like her own lucky coin to carry for the rest of their lives together.

"Jill can arrange it," Jane said, and this time they both laughed.

"She's good at arranging," Margie said, and she decided she owed her friend a basket of pains au chocolat.

As soon as Jane left, Margie picked up the phone and dialed Quid-Atch headquarters. This time she was immediately put through to Chase after giving her name.

"I was hoping I'd hear from you," he said without so much as a hello.

"I lost it there for a while, but my head is back on straight. Where is Evan?"

"He's staying at my house," Chase said. "When can we expect to see you?"

She had to take a deep breath. His friend had known she would call. "How did you—"

"You're way too much of a fighter to let your parents have the final punch," Chase said.

Funny how she hadn't believed that until now. She knew then what she needed to do. "Can you send one of the company planes to pick me up and arrange for a driver to chauffeur me to your house?" she asked.

He was quiet on the line, and her belly tightened with nerves.

"I thought Evan would like that," she added.

"He would, Margie," Chase said, and she could almost hear the smile in his voice. "I'm happy to hear you've come to your senses. When would you like me to have you picked up at the house?"

Right, he could arrange door-to-door service. "I need to make some arrangements with my bakers and staff. How about sometime tomorrow morning? Whenever you can have a plane ready."

"How about I have someone pick you up at five a.m. your time? Being a baker and all, you'll probably be awake. That way you'll arrive around lunch. You can make Evan eat. Even I can't talk him into that one."

She rubbed a hand over her heart to help ease the

pain. "Make it a grand lunch, Chase. There will be lots to celebrate."

"I'll let you two lovebirds enjoy my house for a while," he said. "Don't worry about me interrupting anything."

"You don't have to—"

"Margie, please, he's one of my dearest friends."

"Thank you, then. I'll see you when I see you."

"Oh, and Margie," he said before she could hang up. "I'll figure out where Evan stashed your engagement ring and send it with the pilot."

He hung up, and she sat back in her chair. Right. The ring.

It was about time Evan put it on her finger where it belonged.

***

Chase was pissing Evan off. Here he was ensconced in Quid-Atch's high-tech lab, working on one of the new samples of the invisible paint with his growing staff, and his friend was insisting he run back to the house for lunch with a mysterious person.

"You need to tell me who it is, or I'm not going," he said, dipping his fingers into their newest paint sample.

His fingerprints shimmered before his eyes and disappeared for several seconds before a paint stain covered his fingers. "Dammit! We're so close."

"Your idea to include modified polymers has put us on the right path," Rajan said, "but we're still missing something."

"I know we are," he said, using a turpentine-soaked cloth to remove the paint from his fingers. "Talk to me, you little bitch, and tell me what we're missing."

"Evan," Chase said in a wry tone. "I think you might have broken the company's sexual harassment policy with that statement."

He looked up and gaped at the R&D staff around him, all of them staring at him in open shock. "I was talking to the *paint,* you idiots, not any of you."

Chase chuckled. "Now, that we've cleared that up. This lunch—"

"Tell me who it is," he demanded. "Sorry. I know my fuse has been a little short lately."

Since leaving Dare Valley, he'd barely slept, ate, or worked. When he took even a moment to himself—like the quiet of a shower—Margie found her way back into his mind, and his heart broke all over again.

How was he supposed to live the rest of his life without her?

The thought of going back to Paris only made him ill. She would be everywhere he went, and reminders of her would stretch from his breakfast croissant to his evening baguette. He'd given up bread in a poor attempt to forget her, but he knew it would take more than that. Perhaps his next invention should be a machine to erase memories. But no, she had made him a better person and he never wanted to forget her. He just wanted the pain of losing her to go away.

"You're having lunch with the person you most admire in the world," Chase said.

Well, that grabbed his attention. There were few people he admired. "Is it Richard Branson?" The man wasn't an inventor per se, but he had vision, and when he believed in something, he invested in it. Heavily. Evan deeply applauded the man's attempt to put non-astronauts in space. "Maybe I can give him some advice on his space ships."

Chase hid a smile behind his hand, but Evan caught it. "I'm not saying it's Richard Branson."

But it was. He could almost sense Chase's glee—if you could call how Chase was reacting gleeful. Of course, his friend would probably sock him for using that term. Corporate Chase Parker was an intimidating figure. Evan had realized yesterday that he could never be that intimidating.

"What time do I need to leave?" Evan asked. He had lost track of time, so he glanced at the lab's clock. It was close to noon. "Dammit, it's lunchtime already."

Chase steered him toward the exit. "That's why I came and found you. There's enough time for you to clean up and change before the driver takes you back to my residence."

Yeah, his residence. Chase lived in a huge, quiet house in Great Falls, Virginia. The six-bedroom house sat on thirty acres, and when an owl hooted in the middle of the night, it was more noise than the place had seen in hours. He and Chase might as well have been church mice for all the noise they made when they were back there.

"Fine," he said, nodding to his employees as they left the lab and made their way to the executive offices.

When he started toward a door on the right side of the hall, Chase blocked him. "Evan, you need to use *your* office, remember?"

Right. Chase had insisted he have one. A big one, complete with a private bathroom and wardrobe. He hadn't bothered to ask how his friend had arranged it. "Maybe I'll stay here instead of going back to Paris."

Chase only made a humming sound.

"Did you hear what I said?" he asked, feeling like another part of him had died. If he couldn't live in his beloved Paris or have Margie, what would he become? Perhaps he'd join the shriveled, lonely ranks of the Washington DC powerhouse crowd. He'd work too hard, have a heart attack at fifty, and marry at least twice. His future seemed depressing—except for his inventions.

"Get the rest of that paint off your hands and clean up," Chase said. "Oh, and you might want to give yourself a fresh shave. If it *is* Richard Branson—and I'm not confirming that—his knightship or whatever you call someone who's been knighted would appreciate it, I expect."

Evan ran his hand over his cheek. "Okay, but only to please his knightship."

Twenty minutes later, he walked out of his office a new man. Turning on his heels, he showed off his pewter suit, crisp blue shirt, and cream-colored silk tie. "Not too bad, huh?"

"You look presentable," Chase said, and then came forward to put a pink rose in his lapel.

"What's that for?"

"It gives the suit an extra flair, don't you think?" Chase said. "The driver is waiting for you."

"Why can't I drive myself?"

"Just go, Evan," Chase said with a sigh. "You want to make a good impression, don't you? And try and enjoy yourself. You've been absolutely the worst houseguest on the planet, moping around like you have. If people saw us, they'd think we were Oscar and Felix from *The Odd Couple*."

Wasn't that a depressing thought? "I assume you have lunch prepared?"

Chase flicked him a glance. "Are you trying to insult me?"

He walked to the door. "No, I was only trying to get you back for that crack about me being the worst houseguest on the planet. I thought you understood, Chase."

"I do, Evan. I just think it's time to stop moping and move on with your life."

He almost told his friend what he thought of his advice. "I'll call you when I'm finished having lunch with Sir Branson. Maybe you can join us for a drink."

"Have fun," Chase called out as Evan left.

Fun. He didn't even know what that word meant anymore. He and Margie had jumped on beds together and fed each other baguettes. He'd invented corny things like hot-pink paper shredders for her. Working at Quid-Atch headquarters wasn't fun. It was interesting and serious. Maybe he needed to change that. Create a new vision about corporate life for his employees.

The driver took him to Chase's house in record time while Evan was busy writing notes on his phone about how they could gauge—and improve—corporate morale. Chase wouldn't like it. They'd gone head-to-head about some of his new ideas, and he would have to add this one to the list.

When they arrived, he didn't wait for the driver to open his door. He hopped out and jogged to the front. Since no one was waiting there for him, he would probably have time to check on the lunch preparations Chase had made. He hoped his friend hadn't ordered bread. He'd told him he was giving it up.

The house was quiet when he unlocked the door. The alarm wasn't on, and Evan wondered if Chase had left it off for the wait staff. The house was huge, so Evan almost texted Chase to ask him where he'd set everything up. None of Chase's staff were present, which was weird. It was nearing one hundred degrees with nearly equal humidity, so he didn't think Chase would have arranged for a lunch on the terrace. The weather was so bad that his hair had looked like a briar patch this morning before he'd glopped it with a healthy dose of his hair gel.

When he entered the dining room, he saw the shape of an arm. It was pale white and feminine. He stilled immediately. That arm did *not* belong to Richard Branson.

And he knew...

Margie stood and turned to face him. Her cheeks were pale, and she was wearing the yellow dress he adored. But her eyes were what captivated him most. They were filled with tears and so green he was sure he would become lost in their earthy depths.

"This time I'm the one who's come to say I want a second chance," she said in a husky voice.

All the blood seemed to leave his body, and he took a few steps back before advancing on her. "You'd better be serious about that," he ground out.

He needed to hear her say it.

"I took your private plane here after seeing Artemis on Jane's lucky coin."

He was already shaking his head in wonder when she held something up.

"And Chase found this for me. I forgot to tell you that you couldn't have chosen a better ring. It's perfect for me."

His eyes zeroed in on the object in her hand, and this time his knees almost buckled. "You have the ring?"

"Yes," she said, clutching it in her trembling hand. "Are you willing to forgive me for losing all sense when I saw my parents?"

"*I* lost all sense when I saw your parents at the head table," he admitted. "I can't imagine what it did to you."

But he could. He'd been unable to stop himself from replaying the image of her curled up in a ball, crying her heart out.

"It knocked me back, but I'm on my feet again." She stepped directly in front of him. "You were right to tell me not to give them that kind of victory. So, I'm here to ask you one simple question."

He waited.

"Evan, do you still want to marry me?"

His throat closed along with his eyes, and for a moment, he simply stood there and let the relief wash over him, practically swaying from the force of it. Her hand on his arm brought him back, and his gaze locked with hers.

"I still want to marry you," he said, his voice hoarse now. "Oh, Margie, are you sure?"

Her head bobbed up and down. "I am. And I have a

compromise. About the house."

His brow rose. Were they compromising now? "Okay."

"I think we should buy some land and move it out to the country so we can expand it," she said, shifting her feet. "That way you can make your improvements. Plus, you'll need a lab."

This was a huge step for her, and he ran his finger down her cheek to tell her so. "And we'll need a bigger backyard for the kids."

Tears filled her eyes and spilled over, but he was there to brush them aside before they could trail down her cheeks.

"Oh, Evan. Please put this ring on my finger."

He finally slid it on, and then he kissed it. "It's official. No turning back now."

"I don't want to turn back. I want to move forward with you and our new life together. I want that more than anything."

And then he could no longer stand the two feet still separating them. He yanked her to him and took her mouth in a deep, lush kiss filled with promises. She gave him back her every wish and desire as she slanted her mouth over his, heating his blood and enlivening his body like she had lit up his life.

"Margie," he whispered as he kissed the soft skin of her neck. "Oh, Margie."

She smelled like cinnamon and freshly baked bread and all the possibilities in the known universe.

"Make love to me, Evan," she whispered, drawing a heart in the center of his chest. "Please."

He swept her into his arms and carried her to the west part of the house he'd taken over. Only now, as he set her down on the bed, did he realize his clothes were scattered across the floor.

"It's a mess," he said with a wince.

Turning his head back to hers with a mere finger,

she said, "Like I give a damn."

Then her mouth was moving over his again, and she pulled him onto the bed beside her. Every stroke of her hand helped bring him back to life. And when he touched her, she softened and surrendered to the unstoppable force of love between them, which had guided them to each other from the very first.

Her skin was delectable and fragrant as he helped her out of her clothes and kissed his way down her body. Her quiet moans brought him a new sense of peace while stirring the volcano that had gone dormant over the past few days.

She became a virtuoso of his body, and he, in turn, surrendered to her damp mouth and urgent caresses. But soon it wasn't enough. She pushed him onto his back and rose above him like a goddess. He handed her the condom, and she fitted it over him. Her sable hair fell around her face, and her emerald eyes glowed as they gazed down at him.

When he sank into her, she cried out, the long, lithe line of her body a masterpiece of beauty and feminine grace. And then he thrust into her deeply and groaned, finding a new level of bliss. They traveled with each other until their bodies dissolved, and all he saw was that loving green gaze. Then she tensed and cried out, and he journeyed after her into the peace, into the light, where only love existed.

She fell onto his chest, and he caressed her back, breathing hard. When they finally touched each other—almost as though to confirm they were still here—he rolled them onto their sides and traced her face.

"I love you," he whispered. "I'll always love you. Until the day I die."

Her smile was soft and so heartbreakingly beautiful, he felt his heart crack open even wider.

"And I'll love you too," she said in a strong voice. "Forever and ever and ever."

And they continued to gaze at each other as the afternoon light changed, renewing their promises again and again.

EPILOGUE

Evan walked into the house that was slowly becoming his as well as Margie's. The old Victorian now had some of his favorite paintings on the walls, including the grandmother picking roses and Artemis alongside her steadfast deer with the loaf of bread on the table.

After talking things through, they'd agreed he would find nice apartments for the renters she had so they could have the house to themselves. Everyone but Gary had been thrilled to see their new digs. The young man had hoped to live with them and invent "things." Evan had promised to help Gary with his ideas until the new Artemis Center was up and running. That had seemed to pacify him.

"Hey!" Evan called out as he closed the door behind him.

"In the kitchen," Margie answered.

When he arrived in the doorway, he spied an entire pan of cinnamon rolls. He sniffed the air. "Funny. I didn't smell any of your cinnamon awesomeness when I came inside."

"That's because I made these at the bakery and brought them home," she said, dashing over and kissing him on the cheek.

He turned her head and pointed to his mouth. "Your aim was off."

Her mouth curved into a smile as she rose on her tiptoes. "Why don't you help guide me then?"

"I'd be happy to," he said huskily and then took her mouth in a deep kiss that had them both breathing hard.

She moaned as she broke their connection. "Wait! I have some exciting news."

Even though he was loath to allow the interruption, he gave her some room. "Tell me."

"I think I found our land. I chatted with Arthur today when he came in for a cinnamon roll, and he mentioned some land up in the mountains that's still owned by the Merriam family. He suggested it might be right up our alley."

His brow rose. "How nice of Arthur. How many acres is it?"

"He's not completely sure, but he said it would be plenty for our purposes." And she bounced on her toes as she said it. "Isn't that wonderful?"

"It is! And I have my own exciting news."

"Chase agreed to let you work from home," she said with a smile.

He frowned. "No, he's still insisting we don't have enough security in the house to meet our internal corporate security guidelines, least of all government ones."

Now she was frowning too. "Then what is it?"

He pulled out the stamped copy of the special citation he'd received from the municipal authorities in Paris. "I managed to find us a wedding site. How would you like to be married on the little inlet where we first kissed?"

Her ear-spitting squeal conveyed her feelings perfectly. The arms she wrapped around his neck were a bonus. "You mean the one off Pont Neuf Bridge?"

"Yep," he said, pretty pleased with himself. It had taken him and a dozen French lawyers to make it happen in record time, but they'd managed it. "I thought it would be the perfect place for our wedding."

"Oh, Evan," she said in a lush tone, the one that told him he'd pleased her. He loved pleasing her—especially when he was able to use his money to do it.

"I also have another surprise," he said. "We completed the first successful test case of the new invention."

She gave another squeal, not needing to ask what he was talking about. They always referred to his invisible paint in vague terms.

"Oh my God," she said. "This is huge! We have to celebrate. Oh Evan, I'm so happy for you."

"And I finally managed to name her," he said, taking her hands into his until their fingers were threaded together. "I'm calling her MAL-713."

Her brow wrinkled, and he almost smiled. So, she didn't get it either. Chase had thought he was crazy until he explained it. "It's your initials. And the month and date that I first met you. It was the day my entire life changed."

Watching her mouth drop open pretty much burst his heart.

"That's so romantic."

"I had to look up your legal name for the wedding license," he said. "Margaret Anastasia Lancaster."

"I've always hated that name."

"Then why don't you change it to Margie Michaels," he suggested. "Unless you want to keep your name as a testament to your independence and—"

"Evan, I don't need to keep my name to remind me of my independence," she said, squeezing his hands with her own. "Margie Michaels has a nice ring to it, I think."

"So do I," he said, humbled she would agree to take on even more of him and his life than she already had.

"And there's one more thing I have for you," he said, deciding now was the time to show her his other surprise. "I'll be right back."

He had to run up the stairs to his old room—the one he was now using as his office for non-confidential business. Rushing back to the kitchen, he held the paper behind his back.

She tried to look behind him, but he danced out of her way. "Just wait a second, will you?"

Taking a breath, he handed her the piece of paper he'd drawn up. Inscribed at the top was one simple phrase: The Evan Michaels and Margie Lancaster Foundation.

Her hand immediately went to her mouth, and he saw tears pop into her eyes.

"On the day you came back to me, you told me you wanted us to change the world together. I want your name to be next to mine on everything we do."

"This is just..." Then she hugged him hard, the paper crushed between them.

He wrapped his arms around her and kissed the top of his head. "We're going to make our kids proud, Margie."

"And we're going to love them to pieces. And foster every interest they ever have."

Dreaming about their kids was his new fantasy when he was in the lab in the middle of the night and she was across town baking bread.

"But don't you think you'll need to change the name?" she asked with a laugh. "It needs to be the Evan and Margie Michaels Foundation now."

He gave her a squeeze. "That sounds even better."

"And now," she said, stepping away, "I have something else I want to try out."

She pulled two cinnamon rolls a part and put them

on a blue china plate. "I got to thinking about what we did with the baguette. How about cinnamon rolls?" she asked brightly.

Lust poured into his system. "Do you really think you need to ask?"

Grabbing the plate, she darted out of the kitchen. He gave chase immediately. She squealed the whole way to their bedroom in the tower. Evan ran past the picture of the goddess Artemis that had hung in his lab.

The goddess watched the door close and smiled from her place on the wall, happy that mortals had once again learned the power of love through feasting on bread.

Dear Magical Readers,

Thank you so much for embracing Margie and Evan in this beautiful mini-series. It truly was a joy to research and write their love story. Paris holds as much of a special place in my heart as Dare Valley, and it was a gift to bring these two together in both places.

Where are we going next? The next Dare River book comes out soon, and it's called THE PROMISE OF RAINBOWS. This is Susannah and Jake's story, and so many of you have written me and told me how eager you are to read it. We'll be journeying back to Dare Valley soon for Andy and Lucy's story called THE CALENDAR OF NEW BEGINNINGS. I'll also be releasing a new series called Once Upon a Dare with all of the football stars you met in THE BRIDGE TO A BETTER LIFE. Jordan and Grace are up first in THE GATE TO EVERYTHING. Stay tuned.

If you enjoyed this mini-series, I would love for you to post a review since it helps more readers want to read my story. You can write one at the retailer or on Goodreads. When you post one, kindly let me know at readavamiles@gmail.com so I can personally thank you. To keep up with all my new releases, please sign up for my newsletter and connect with me on Facebook. I continue to post about food and other fun stuff, so come and join our big Dare family.

And if you're looking to read about more powerful billionaires, you might check out Kathleen Brooks'

Women of Power series. Her books are about female billionaires—something we need more of in the world. I highly recommend it.

Lastly, since you guys love it when I give you a recipe, keep reading for instructions on how to make a simple Parisian baguette like Margie (and I) learned how to make in Paris on our baking apprenticeship.

As always, thanks so much for reading and bringing so much joy into my life.

Lots of light,

Ava

And now for the recipe...

Classical French Baguette

The key to this recipe is to mix the dough in a bread machine on the dough cycle or with a dough hook in a KitchenAid mixer. And you need fresh yeast; it makes a big difference.

Combine 1 cup water with 2 1/2 cups flour with 1 1/2 tsp. yeast and 1/2 tsp salt. You have the option of proofing your yeast by adding 1 tsp. warm water and 1/2 tsp. sugar or you can simply add the yeast by itself to the flour, water, and salt.

Mix in the bread machine until complete (most machines have two rising cycles). If you're doing it by hand in the mixer, let the dough rise once, punch it down, and then let it rise again.

When the dough is ready, divide the dough in half and roll them out into two circles.

Now tuck one side of the dough into the middle and pinch the seams. Then, do the same thing on the other side. Then take one side and connect it all the way to the other side. Finally, like Andre said to Margie: "You use both hands to roll it into the shape of the slender arm of a beautiful woman. A dancer's arm." Then use a baker's blade or a sharp knife and make three cuts on the diagonal on the bread. Slash, don't saw.

Let the two baguettes rise again for about 30 minutes or so and bake at 450 degrees for 15-20 minutes until the loaves are golden brown.

* This recipe makes two baguettes.

ABOUT THE AUTHOR

USA Today Bestselling Author Ava Miles burst onto the contemporary romance scene after receiving Nora Roberts' blessing for her use of Ms. Roberts' name in her debut novel, the #1 National Bestseller NORA ROBERTS LAND, which kicked off her small town series, Dare Valley. Ava's books have  reached the #1 spot at Barnes & Noble and ranked in Amazon and iBooks' Top 10. Both NORA ROBERTS LAND and COUNTRY HEAVEN have been chosen as Best Books of the Year. Ava has also released a connected series called Dare River about the power of love and family. She's fast becoming a favorite author in light contemporary romance (Tome Tender) and is known for funny, sweet, emotional stories, sometimes with a touch of mystery and magic. Ava's background is as diverse as her characters. She's a former chef, worked as a long-time conflict expert rebuilding warzones, and now writes full-time from her own small town community. Ava is a big believer in living happily ever after and writes about her own journey on The Happiness Corner blog every Friday on her website.

If you'd like to connect with Ava Miles or hear more about her upcoming books, visit www.avamiles.com or find Ava on Facebook, Twitter, or Pinterest.